Blood Mo

Clutching the expenses claim, Walker strolled
out of the office and down onto the broad,
open-plan floors of the paper's workrooms,
the dark-tinted windows shielding the
inmates from a summer sun that was still
months away. He had wings. He had
signatures, he had money, he had a blessing
of sorts – he had wings. No matter how many
times a fireman got sent abroad, the thrill was
never gone. Not, he thought, until life's thrill
bowed out, at any rate. He was away,
following a speck on another continent, a
bank statement, a letter, a suicide in strange
circumstances. Poor bloody Arnold Secker.
For Walker, it was Arnold Secker who had
convinced him of the value of the story – but
you had to have seen Arnold Secker to be able
to understand that.

The desk men never got to see a source any
longer. They hadn't for years. For years they
hadn't had the thrill of a real live contact, a
man shaking and sweating on a seat in a bar
in a foreign city who showed his terror in his
every gesture, who wore the seriousness of
what he had to say on his sleeve. You had to
get the smell of a story sometimes, and the
smell of a story was never contained in a
document, in the 'evidence'. It was there in
the sweating fear of a man who had broken
himself to tell it, to hold a light for someone
else to take up and run with. The smell of a
story was a conversation, an exchange, a
death. It was a human smell.

'Cuando se danza con diablo,
no se da un paso falso'
South American proverb

'When you dance with the devil,
be sure to make the right steps'

ONE

The Money Trail

The street door of the bar opened. An ice-cold wind that had started in the mountains, scooped a bellyful of spray from the lake and flung it into the narrow alleys of Geneva's old town, was finally checked in reception along with the hats and coats. The howl of the gale outside abruptly ceased as the door squeezed back into its hermetic rubber seal, and a miniature dust tornado shifted and settled into the mat.

Walker looked up without anticipation. He saw the dying billow of the curtain between the bar and the lobby and wondered, would it be Arnold Secker this time?

Four old men with coiffed white moustaches sat in the corner playing a dice game. The soft sound of the dice shaken in leather cups was followed reliably by the clatter as they spread across the wooden table. The men wore trousers which reached their chests, and one had a red and green paisley cravat tucked into his neck. Apart from the men the bar was quiet. Two girls sat on high stools treating the world and each other with monosyllabic indifference, a couple ate at a table without talking, like pets at their bowls, and a solitary man sat on the edge of his seat as if undecided whether to stay or go.

Secker was already an hour late for their rendezvous. Walker's mind was stationary after the wait, the solitary drinking, and he now retained only an academic interest in Secker's arrival. God knew – as his landlady, who had listened to the phone call, also did – he had never wanted to meet Secker in the first place. It was a waste of time.

The call had come that afternoon, when he had been at home. Since he didn't know any Secker, the office had

1

obviously given him his home number. That they should have done so was thoroughly irritating: he was more ex-directory than the tooth fairy, they knew that. But when he had launched a minor tirade at them for their lack of discretion, they had actually defended Secker. He was desperate, they said; it was a matter of life and death. Of life and death to whom? he had reasonably enquired.

But that, of course, was after the event. Impaled on the end of the phone by Secker, he had been unable to wriggle off. 'Call me at the office tomorrow,' his landlady had heard him pleading, 'I can't go off on some wild goose chase now.' At which point his landlady, wrestling with the significance of the geese, had lost the thread. But Secker had proved an efficient leech, and so here he was in this mock-seedy bar near Geneva's cathedral, and it was a measure of the descent of the once-great Harry Walker, he thought, that he was sitting in this bar, in this town with its stainless-steel charm, and waiting for a cold-caller who said he had a 'story' and then never even showed up.

One of the old men let out a cry of triumph. He had won the game by eliminating his last opponent. Greedy little eyes danced across the table from the winning throw to the small piles of change in front of the other players. A new round of beers was ordered, and delivered in stemmed glasses, the white froth combed off with a wooden spatula. The old glasses with the discoloured brown foam dried onto the sides were removed. An indistinct squeeze-box jig sputtered from speakers somewhere in the ceiling.

What, since the afternoon, had he managed to glean about the secretive Arnold Secker? Very little, was the answer: that he had an American accent and a job with Rausch, the Lyon-based multi-national whose tentacles stretched around the world like a British Airways commercial, and who had set up camp in Geneva this week for their annual conference jamboree. But Secker had said he had a 'story'. A story! In Walker's experience, everyone had a story – if a story meant something they were desperate to tell. In the past eighteen months, since his posting, or exile, to Geneva, he'd even considered telling his own 'story'. But he'd found that the wars and the famines and the disasters had all run together in his mind into an indistinct blur.

So what would Secker's story be? He could guess. The man would be a disgruntled employee who had been passed over for promotion and was getting his own back with a tell-tale confession. Rausch were illegally polluting some European river, or they were employing child labour in the Far East, or they were circumventing trade agreements with the Americans in breach of the law . . . Walker considered the kind of half-truth he could expect, and the column inch it would receive. More likely it would end up on the spike, along with all the other rubbish he'd been assigned since his fall from grace. Tonight, his career, his patience and his sobriety seemed more than ever on the skids. Why on earth had he kept the appointment? Arnold Secker slid out of his mind.

There were four men who entered. The first two carried equipment. A sound-recorder, wrapped against the sleet, hung by a strap from the shoulder of the first man; the second taller man held a television camera, gripped in one hand with a weight-trainer's suede glove. He also wore a black nylon bomber-jacket and jeans with razor creases. With that curt wave that looked as if he was snatching something out of the air, Walker recognised him immediately as Jay O'Connell, news cameraman and ex-acquaintance. The jaunty walk, the restless tossing of the head that flicked the shoulder-length hair now this way, now that, were unmistakable. All four of the men had the newly fresh look of people who had just taken their first bath in a month. It was impossible to tell from what war, what calamity in what corner of the world they were returning, but wherever it was, they didn't carry the tragedy with them. They had the eager, hungry faces of men who had spent too much time in each other's company and hadn't seen a woman in weeks. They were not your average Geneva night out. The dust shaken from their safari jackets,

3

and the rot washed from their feet, they were looking for action.

The constipated squeeze-box tune agonisingly closed, and another began to grind out. The two girls at the bar had angled their stools towards the new arrivals, and for O'Connell that was sufficient. Snatching the air again as if he owned it, he went to the bar, ordered drinks for them all, and walked to the back where Walker was sitting. The girls followed. Did he actually know them, Walker wondered, or was it a sort of Pied Piper skill developed over decades of dedicated practice?

'The Geneva Fixer!' O'Connell thrust out a hand and grinned. 'What's your potion?' With another grab at the air, he plucked a waitress for a drink.

It was more than two years since they had last met, Walker thought, but in this business, a chance meeting between two colleagues in a foreign city was as common as running into your wife in the bathroom.

'Just the man we need,' O'Connell enthused, and slapped Walker's shoulder as if to revive a wobbly television picture. The girls sat down on either side of O'Connell. 'So where's the action? Harry Walker, News at Ten, Geneva,' he mimicked.

'You don't look as if you need a fixer,' Walker said.

'Some people have it,' O'Connell said, looking at the girls, 'and some people don't.'

'And anyway,' Walker corrected him, 'I'm not a fixer.' He looked at O'Connell's companions. 'A fixer hires cars, makes appointments, checks timetables,' he explained.

He regretted the remark as soon as he had said it. It had the small operator's pettiness. Another tiny indication of his decline, which O'Connell didn't fail to notice.

'Not a fixer? Of course he's not a fixer! This is *the* Harry Walker. Geneva Bureau Chief!'

What his landlady never saw in all her snooping were these brief, painful encounters with old colleagues that Walker occasionally couldn't avoid. Gossiping with friends in the

4

harsh Swiss-German guttural which sounded like an anchor dropping, she concentrated on the loneliness of her Englishman – and on his eccentric ties. Walker's ties were irredeemably sixties in style, and colour co-ordinated to restore a bat's eyesight: he thought of them as his one shot at personal vanity, his nod to fashion. They were like kidney donor cards or identity bracelets on other people; if, on some foreign battleground, beside some exploded truck, you turned Walker's dead body face up, you wouldn't have to search his pockets or check the tag on his wrist. There would be something mauve, olive and saffron in Indian silk around his neck that rendered further identification unnecessary. And yet despite the extrovert ties, Frau Hauswirth said, her lodger was a recluse. He was polite – yes, polite, she would reluctantly agree – but monosyllabic. He paid the rent, but he never had a friend, let alone a girl, to visit. He sat for days in front of an old, high-standing 1950 Underwood typewriter, she said, but she rarely heard the keys hammering. He said he was a journalist, which exasperated her, because all Frau Hauswirth's ideas of journalism were predicated on the film *Front Page*, where the scribes rolled up their sleeves, clamped on their eyeshades and *worked*. He made her suspicious, she said resentfully – as if he did it deliberately.

The reason why she never saw Walker with anyone was because he deliberately kept the steady stream of old colleagues who inevitably passed through Geneva, away from his base. Mostly, in fact, he preferred to avoid them altogether, but sometimes there would be someone he wanted to see again, a photographer, perhaps, with whom he'd covered some long-forgotten war, or another journalist he'd worked in harness with. Then he would meet them in the old town, almost always at the café on Cathedral Street, a steep, narrow mediaeval lane that led down to a shopping mall and across the tramlines to the bridges where the Rhône meets Lake Geneva. Geneva isn't a big city and Walker went nearly everywhere on foot. Hunched in a thick climber's jacket when winter came at last, hands deep in his pockets

5

and eyes on the pavement in front, Frau Hauswirth would see him leave her house on the rue Maupassant and watch him till he was out of sight round a bend in the cobbled road. Walker hated Geneva. He hated its mock old-fashioned air, its civic neatness, its inward-looking citizens with their suspicious eyes. He hated the twee shops and the Hans-Christian-Andersen dwellings of the old town, and he hated the spa hotels on the banks of the Lake in the new town that the English had built at the end of the last century, when you could join the dots of Europe through similar establishments from Biarritz to Budapest. Sometimes he told himself that Geneva was the nastiest place he knew.

Of course, much of Walker's anger with the place stemmed from the fact that he didn't want to be there. He was a prisoner. But it wasn't only that. Geneva, in Walker's opinion, was a city that concealed its true identity. It was a fraud. Along the banks of the Lake, and lining the grand boulevards in the diplomatic district, were the much-advertised International Commission for Refugees, the Red Cross, the great halls where peace treaties were discussed decade after decade. But not far away from these boulevards of flags, other, more anonymous buildings concealed the secrets Geneva didn't want to tell, buildings with small bronze plaques chiselled with bland company names. They concealed organisations that made Switzerland the largest exporter of anti-personnel bombs in the world. They sheltered the companies that bought and sold the vast majority of South African gold. They smothered with discretion the banks that made the country the largest profiteer from interest on Third World loans of any Western nation. Sensible business ventures to some, but to Walker they suggested that caring, internationalist Geneva was actually founded on self-interest and greed.

And so Walker stumped the streets of Geneva head down, silent, uncommunicative, or sat in his flat in front of a silent typewriter. Frau Hauswirth began to suspect that he might not be a journalist at all. Might his press card not be a cover?

she asked her friends. Might he not be a spy? But the reason for her lodger's reclusive behaviour, indeed for his presence in Geneva at all, was less alarming – if hardly less sensational – and the clue to it lay in the framed photograph that stood on the desk behind the Underwood. It was a black-and-white shot – a newspaper stills print, in fact – of a Chinese girl. She stared straight out of the frame, defiantly, almost as if she expected – and was ready – to be hit. She was the cause of Harry Walker's downfall. After fifteen years of plaudits from younger correspondents in bars from San Salvador to Khartoum, he was on the Geneva scrapheap because of her. While former colleagues and competitors, stringers and snappers, burnt-out foreign correspondents and young men with a future like O'Connell, passed through Geneva from the world's wars, Walker filed the occasional story about a Swiss cheese *exposition* or the declining role of the St Bernard. Yet even in O'Connell's world, where self-regard allowed little room for heroes, the name of Harry Walker still carried weight. People sought him out, if only to gawp. But as far as work was concerned, the Chinese girl had made him a pariah.

In his heyday Walker had been a 'fireman', the kind of foreign correspondent who would leave his wife in the middle of a restaurant, cancel a family holiday, rise unwashed from the bath, in order to be at the scene of a crisis, wherever in the world it occurred. In his heyday, as he would tell the younger journalists, he hadn't kept a dinner date with his wife in eight years. And eventually he didn't have a wife to keep a date with. The Chinese girl had been both business and pleasure, you might say. Hers was an intelligent face, a face alive with enquiry, the face of a traveller, an explorer, or a scientist – which is what she was. She had been a key figure in the development of the People's Republic's space programme, a specialist in low temperature physics, educated both in the United States and the Soviet Union – a uniquely won achievement at the time. And she had trusted her qualifications to protect her if she chose to buck the system.

No one really knew how Walker had persuaded her to do that, or even if she had needed persuading at all. But the fact was that he had drawn from her, exclusively, the most outspoken and radical interview that had ever emerged from the Chinese military establishment. It had been an astonishing coup, the finest of his career to date. Awards were mentioned; even the newspaper's owner was pleased. A major Chinese figure on the inside who was prepared to identify herself in her campaign for greater openness and reciprocity with the West . . . Yes, he had identified her. Instead of calling her a 'leading Chinese dissident' or 'one of China's top scientists', he had done what she had demanded, named her, photographed her, exposed her views to scrutiny inside as well as outside her country. Later, his critics would say that she had never asked him to do this, that he had done it off his own bat, even against her wishes. And two days after publication she had been arrested. There was nothing abnormal in that, it was entirely to be expected. But what had frozen the mind with its crass brutality was the bullet they put through her head, and the bill they had sent to her parents to cover costs.

Even then, Walker's fall might not have been so hard had not the tabloids sniffed out his other relationship with her. When they found that his newspaper had put him on sabbatical, on full pay, they reported that he had cracked up because the girl he had 'betrayed' had also been his lover. It was a good story, and they made the most of it, fabricating what they couldn't discover. Harry Walker was a dangerous man. Harry Walker was an irresponsible journalist. They dug up an incident from a war in Sri Lanka in which, it was claimed, rushing to get a story through, Walker had run over a peasant in his car without stopping, and the man had died. Walker sued for that, and won, but it was too late to save him. The paper eased him out to Geneva and made him 'Bureau Chief', a hollow title reserved for has-beens. Blown up in Gaberone, beaten up in Tegucigalpa, a tiny sliver of a Lebanese bullet sitting in the back of his stomach, he was now a relic like the stories he had once covered, resting on laurels of experience that were slowly turning to dust beneath him. And if he ever tried to write his story, the only image that would fix for any length of time in his mind was the one staring at him from behind his typewriter. Her photograph – the official, pre-execution portrait – hung in the gallery of his mind alone.

The shake and clatter of the dice punctuated the game at the next table. The gobbling couple had paid their bill and left, and the solitary man sat on at his table puffing nervously at a small cigar as if it would last longer that way.

'Total bloody waste of time,' O'Connell was saying cheerfully. 'Four weeks waiting to have our arses shot off, and all for nothing.' He turned and snapped his fingers at another waitress. 'We'll have the most expensive thing on the menu. It's on the company, girls. You only have to whistle.'

While he'd been sitting in Geneva watching snow fall, Walker wondered, what had O'Connell's contribution been to the great dissemination of celluloid news? 'Africa?' he guessed.

O'Connell's head stopped bobbing about and an expression of disbelief crossed his face.

'Swissair.' Walker pointed at the camera's baggage tag. 'They go to all the funny places in Africa.'

'Mozambique, actually,' O'Connell said, impressed. 'Went in four weeks ago. Just got out this morning. Just.' He laughed, and waited to be prompted, but Walker decided he wouldn't assist him to his glory. O'Connell lit a cigarette and bounced about on the stool, tapping his knees like tom-toms. The two girls looked as if they were prepared to wait for the world's supply of tobacco to run out as long as O'Connell eventually told the story. Finally he could resist no longer.

'We went across the border illegally to meet up with the MNR,' he said. 'They'd been planning an attack on a government-controlled town for months. We got to hear about it.' He grinned, and paused for effect. 'They put it off for ten days so we could film it.' Walker watched the girls' reactions. Not much chance of his wooing them away with a good poisoned yoghurt story now.

'The whole thing was a complete cock-up,' O'Connell continued. 'They were all over the place. A chain of command like a bleeding kid's party, supply lines that never arrived. By the end they were even firing on their own side.'

Get behind the lines in some civil war, Walker remembered; it didn't matter where as long as it was a bit exotic. Rebels, revolutionaries, guerillas – they were the trigger-words for television. A foreign war, some marginalised conflict so small you could fit assault dates for the TV companies' convenience; as long as it made good pictures, that was all that mattered. Stories with pictures were the ones that interested the TV people.

'We got some great pictures,' O'Connell said.

'But no story,' Walker replied – and for the second time that evening regretted speaking.

'Oh, there'll be a feature,' O'Connell said breezily. 'Yeah, four, maybe five minutes.' He began to take a pile of stills from his jacket pocket. One knee bobbed up and down restlessly. He kept the photos in his hands and flipped through to find the best. What would they call the feature? Walker wondered. 'Nothing Happening in Mozambique'? There were pictures of O'Connell in an amphibious assault craft, O'Connell riding point on a rebel truck, O'Connell in a snake of heavily armed men as it wound through the bush.

'Great pictures, Jay,' Walker said solemnly.

Back in the Falklands War, he remembered, the squaddies nicknamed some of the cameramen the 'When I's'. You could be up to your neck in a bog under heavy mortar fire at four in the morning, and some cowboy with a camera would start to reminisce. 'When I was in . . .' Watching a dumb Scottish squaddie getting the glory was nearly too much for them. The 'When I's' knew the best restaurants at the end of a day's shooting in Sudan, they could con a car out of an Afghan village chief. They were operators.

'Take a look at this one,' O'Connell said, and pushed a picture across the table under Walker's nose. 'That,' he said, 'that was really wild.' Three guerillas were walking through the bush with O'Connell at the back. 'We're in the middle of this minefield, right? It was like Grandmother's Footsteps. Except any moment you expected to get your bollocks blown away.'

As a means of conveying that his bollocks were whole, intact and ready to go, Walker had to admit that this gambit of O'Connell's was technically perfect. O'Connell took the photo back and one of the girls held it with him for a look.

'So, where's the action?' O'Connell said. 'We're going to paint the town red.' He rubbed his hands, clasped them together, bent them back and extended the pumped-up muscles in his arms and neck.

'Action?' Walker said. 'In Geneva you're lucky if someone sneezes.'

The evening, as far as the bar was concerned, was coming to an undistinguished conclusion. The old men had cleared up their dice and left, O'Connell and the girls would disappear to a club, with the camera crew somewhere behind them. It was time to go. O'Connell was explaining another picture as he got out of his seat and called the waitress for the girls' coats. Walker felt weary. O'Connell had bored him. It was partly jealousy, he had to admit, but the man was more interested in his role in getting the news than in the news itself; whether O'Connell was pointing the camera at a heap of fly-blown corpses or down the barrel of a gun, it didn't matter as long as the pictures *looked* good. You couldn't deny he had courage, but he was a lightweight. News was a sideshow to him; it was the way he got his kicks.

The television crew waited by the door for O'Connell and the girls to reach them. 'See you, Chief.' O'Connell winked, grinned and squeezed Walker's arm. The door to the street opened, and another gust of wind blew in and pumped up the curtain. The cold passed as the door fitted back into its seal, and the bar was quiet again. Through the whorled-glass windows and framed by the chintz curtains, Walker could see the snow tumbling from the darkness. The fake candle-shaped lights of the bar flickered unconvincingly; the place had the feel of a seaside tearoom in January. He rose to go; there was nothing left of the evening to salvage. He was on his feet and starting to leave when he felt a faint brushing on his sleeve, as if he'd snagged it on a bramble.

'Mr Walker?'

There was a man standing at his shoulder. He smoked a small cigar and wore a grey raincoat and a black Homburg hat.

'Secker. Arnold Secker,' the man said.

He was a short man with a thick moustache that bowed over his upper lip. He was wrapped for the cold, a scarf joining his coat to his neck, and he had thick, dry hands that made a rustling sound as he obsessively ran them over each other. How old? Walker guessed he was in his fifties. His mannerisms suggested some kind of nervous disease. Apart from the business with his hands, his mouth kept opening and shutting like a fish, and he blinked a great deal. Walker had seen these symptoms before in shell-shock sufferers. Secker must have been sitting in the bar for over an hour without daring to introduce himself.

'I know you didn't want to see me,' he said. 'I understand.'

Walker wearily sat back on his seat and beckoned the man to do the same, but Secker still stood uncertainly, his twitching hands seeming to act out the turmoil in his mind. At last he perched on the edge of the chair, his legs pressed tightly together and over to one side like a woman. For a few moments he looked around the bar as if he expected to see someone he knew, but his attention was won back by the waitress who arrived at his side and startled him almost to his feet.

'*Bier bitte,*' Walker said.

Secker apparently couldn't decide. '*Zwei Bier,*' Walker said for him. 'No, no', Secker protested, and quickly stammered out an order for coffee. 'I never drink,' he nervously

12

explained when the waitress had gone. 'I can't bear the taste of alcohol. I don't disapprove, you understand,' he said in a panicky way, as if he had caused offence. 'It's not important,' he said.

Having dismissed Secker from his mind altogether, it was doubly irritating, Walker thought, to have him arrive at the last minute. He'd almost got away scot-free, but now this nervous little man would put the seal on a disastrous evening. He looked at Secker and wondered how he would tell whatever it was he wanted to tell. He had the tension of a person who had something he wanted to get off his chest at all costs – and yet there was also, if Walker was not mistaken, a sort of tormented reluctance to give anything away. Conflicting impulses that could make the whole interview tediously long-drawn-out. Well, he would wait for the waitress to bring the drinks before he tried to pump Secker's story out of him, Walker decided. Perhaps he'd have calmed down a bit by then.

'It's late,' he said at last, when he had sipped the beer and Secker was cradling his coffee cup in his hands as if to warm them. He still wore the coat but had eventually discarded the hat and put it close to him on the table. The temperature in the bar was hot, but Secker didn't seem to notice; he seemed oblivious to everything but his own preoccupation. 'I was about to go,' Walker said when Secker didn't reply. 'You'd better tell me what it is you have to tell me.'

Secker looked at him as if he were trying to make a decision.

'Why do you think I came to you?' he asked.

'I've no idea. Why?'

'I've read things you've written,' Secker replied quickly. 'You were the only person I could approach.'

'What are you asking for?' Walker said. 'Is it something you want to sell?' There was a trace of distaste in his voice. 'I don't have any authority to pay you.'

'No, no, no!' Secker burst out, and widened his eyes in shock. 'Don't misunderstand. It's not money I want.'

13

'Then why don't you tell me?' Walker suggested. The man was nervous, but there was something else in his manner that briefly interested him. A fear? A desperation? He'd noticed it on the phone earlier but now, face to face, it was unmistakable. He found it was difficult to take his eyes off Secker for long; he had a face which seemed to register every passing thought, and every passing thought was bad.

'I don't know . . .' Secker began. His mouth opened and shut, and the blinking became even more rapid. 'I don't want . . .' he tried again, and stopped.

'You said on the phone it was urgent,' Walker reminded him. 'A matter of life and death,' he repeated, without managing to keep an edge of sarcasm out of his voice.

'It's against the law!' Secker burst out, and for a moment it was hard to tell what he meant, whether what he had to say was a story of corruption, or whether it was a breach of the law for him to say it. 'I could be prosecuted,' he said. 'But it's worse than that,' Secker said suddenly. 'It's not the law that matters.'

There was a trace of bitterness in his voice. As he'd suspected, Walker thought, Secker was going to be one of those who spilled the beans because of some personal animosity. They were the nastiest kind of informer.

'If you tell me,' Walker said, 'if you get a newspaper behind you, you buy whatever protection it can give. It's one thing bringing an individual to court, but people think twice about challenging a newspaper that isn't even printed in the country. You'd be safer if you told me, even if it is against the law.'

'How can you help?' Secker said, but more in general desperation than in answer to this suggestion. 'What can you do for me? Suppose you're not interested? I would have broken the law for nothing?'

That, Walker thought, was the most likely outcome. 'Is the information you have verbal or written?' he asked.

'It's on paper,' Secker said quickly. 'It's no good otherwise, is it?' he said, as if he hoped to be relieved of the burden of telling, as if Walker had given him an escape route.

'You have it with you?' Walker asked.

Secker looked round in desperation. His hands slid over each other like dry snakes in a pit; he looked as if he would cry. 'How can I be sure. . . ?' he spluttered. 'How can I be sure that. . . ? That I can trust you?'

Walker shrugged. This was getting them nowhere. He had no intention of spending the night coaxing out of Secker what was probably useless and un-newsworthy information. If the man wanted to tell him something, let him tell him; otherwise, why didn't he just get lost? But he kept the irritation out of his voice.

'You don't have to trust me, necessarily,' he said. 'If the information is written, if it's in an envelope and sealed, you can just leave it on the table. You can . . . forget it, if you like. You can get up and walk out of here, and you need never see me again. They can't prosecute you for accidentally leaving confidential papers behind. If that's what they are,' he added.

'It isn't just the law,' Secker said again, with apocalyptic melodrama in his voice. It made Walker want to laugh. He was becoming more and more certain that Secker was about to hand him a laundry list or a page of office memos. He wondered if Secker might not be just a little peculiar; a small man who thought he could make himself important by pretending to have secrets to reveal to the press.

'You don't have to decide now,' Walker said dismissively. 'Why don't you go away and think about it a bit more?'

But Secker, it was clear, would be quite happy for Walker to spend the whole night drawing the information out of him: it would make him the focus of attention, fulfil a need. Walker had met others like Secker – desperate, lonely men who longed to be noticed. They wasted endless hours of his time and then didn't produce anything resembling a story.

'I have to . . .' Secker burst out. 'I have to tell someone!' There was an appeal in his voice. Walker exhaled a lungful of air to maintain a sort of calm. He would give Secker a chance, but he wasn't going to be treated like a confessor.

'Is it Rausch?' he asked.

Secker's reaction was wild. His hands grabbed each other, and the hat flew off the table; his mouth jacked open and pumped up and down as if he were gasping for air. 'It's all right, it's all right,' Walker said with exasperation. 'That's not a closely-guarded secret, is it? I always like to know something about the person I'm meeting, the office checks people out for me all the time. I don't know much about you, but I do know you work for Rausch. So is it Rausch?'

Secker's blinking slowed, but he didn't reply.

'Is it Rausch?' Walker repeated. 'Or is it something in your private life?'

Secker slowly mastered his body's erratic twitchings, and this seemed to help calm his mind, too. He still blinked, but Walker could see that he was willing himself to trust, despite his panic. Much as the man irritated him, Walker found this moving. Secker's hands slowed to a regular brushing of each other that presumably indicated a greater serenity; his hands were his worry-beads, his comfort-blanket. For a minute, Secker's eyes were fixed on Walker's face. He stared at it for an answer.

'I can just get up?' he said at last in a small voice. 'Just get up and go?'

'If that's what will make you happiest,' Walker replied. He dragged his eyes away from Secker. It surprised him, how much he was in Secker's curious, unthreatening thrall; he wanted to break the tension, to give him the privacy of not being watched and allow him to make up his mind. When he looked back again, there was a brown envelope on the table and Secker was rising tremulously out of his seat, as if he had to force every movement. Without a word, Secker turned from the table and walked unsteadily through the bar, opening the door with its suction sound, and moving out into the snow.

The manila envelope was creased where Secker must have clutched it inside his coat. Walker could imagine him pressing it to him, as if it might fall from his pocket or slip past his convulsively twining hands; he could see Secker's startled face as he shied from anyone who caught his eye in the street. And now that he had got rid of the envelope, his fear of being caught in possession of it would be replaced by a new fear, that he had given it to the wrong person. Considering how much the envelope had obviously cost him in terms of anxiety, Walker wondered why Secker had gone to the trouble. It made him suddenly curious about the contents. For the first time in months, he felt the rush of adrenalin that he normally associated with the first hint of a story, when there was as yet no concrete information and the imagination could run riot, unhindered by facts.

He reached across and plucked the envelope from the table where Secker had been sitting, and weighed it in his hand. It would contain only papers. There were two rubber bands around it, to wrap it like a parcel, and dried glue lay under the flap where Secker, in his obsessive concern that the contents should be inviolate, had added extra glue. He peeled off the rubber bands, and had to tear the top away from the envelope because it was too tightly sealed.

Walker rubbed his eyes as he strained to pick out some sense from the jumble of words and figures before him. He should take the envelope and its contents back to his apartment, but he was suddenly gripped by a conviction that Arnold Secker was not the mere attention-seeker he had first thought him to be. Years of typing without having the proper skills not to have to look at the keys had left Walker's eyes weak, and he had to angle the papers away from him to pick up the light from the electric fake candle at the next table. The first sheet was a letter addressed to the Brunner Bank, Charlottenstrasse, Zurich 248, beginning 'Dear Herr Brunner . . .' It was not a letter for a manager or a minion, it was for the king rat, the owner of the bank.

Eight sheets in all: bank transfers, from Rausch to another company. A sum of twenty-three million dollars. But then there was a gap. The last couple of sheets appeared to pick up

17

the earlier theme – twenty-three million dollars again – but this time the money wasn't going out of Brunner in Zurich, it was going into Brunner in Caracas, Venezuela. There was a gap between the transactions.

Walker gathered up the sheets into an untidy pile and stuffed them deep into his coat. He held them as tightly as Secker must have done before him. The little man had cause for his anxiety; he had, after all, a story to tell. Only it was a story with a break in it, and Walker would have to talk to him one more time.

TWO

The Stakes

The first thing Stratstone noticed about the corpse was that it didn't have a face. For a second time, as he looked, the nausea almost overcame him and he turned away shuddering. The thick tropical heat of the city streets was turned down to butcher's-shop cold here in the morgue, and the violent drop in temperature was almost as great a shock to the system as the sight of the naked, plump grey corpse lying obscenely on the slab. A corpse with a flayed face, like a clumsy scalping.

'Señora?' The mortician held up the sheet the way a bullfighter holds a cape, so that the woman could take a proper look. She hadn't turned her face from the corpse since he had first turned the sheet back. Unlike Stratstone. She was slightly pale, but the hands that held a cross clasped in front of her stomach were steady, and her eyes never wavered. She had a natural dignity, and her dark brown eyes registered the flat inevitability of suffering.

'Señora?' the mortician repeated, and Stratstone put a comforting arm round her shoulder and held her wrist with this other hand. 'She'll do it in her own time,' he drawled in bad Spanish. The mortician shrugged and continued to hold up the cloth, now like an auctioneer lifting the dustsheet from a valuable piece of furniture.

Stratstone looked round the room to keep his eyes away from what was on the slab. The washed white tiles of the walls and the stone slabs of the floor stretched away into the dimly-lit distance of the high, pillared room. It was half church, half fish-market – spotlessly clean before the morning catch arrives. The chilly whiteness of the place seemed only to intensify the cold. A broad passage, almost a room in itself, led away from the vaulted viewing hall, and it was lined along each side with banks of coffin-sized metal drawers that reached to the ceiling.

Stratstone looked back at the woman. Her lower lip trembled slightly as if she wanted to say something, but then she resumed her tense calm. He didn't have to be here, didn't want to be here, it just seemed the best thing to do in the circumstances. It was better to know what was going on, to keep abreast of events. And, of course, he would be able to look after the women, make sure she was all right for money, make sure the thing on the slab really was her husband. It was an unusual identification.

'Why couldn't we do it with prints?' he asked irritably. 'They left his fingers on, didn't they.'

The mortician pretended not to understand his Spanish. The third man present, a minor government official who stood in a creased grey suit with his hands behind his back, looked lazily in Stratstone's direction with dark, heavy-lidded eyes.

'What would be the point? We have no record of his prints,' he said, and shrugged. 'He was not a criminal. Not if it is Santos Calderon,' he added.

'You could have checked first,' Stratstone snapped. 'We might have gone through all of this for nothing.' Stratstone's Spanish improved when he was angry. He was arguing for the woman's sake, but it was he who was most unnerved by the place. And by the corpse.

When he thought of it, it was a miracle they'd found the corpse at all. Some Indians in the north of the country had come across it in a creek. Perhaps it had been dropped from a plane, or heaved over the side of a boat – it all depended on who had killed him. But however the corpse had got there, it couldn't have been in the water for more than a few hours before it was found. Apart from the face – the hole where the face had been – the plump, spongy flesh hadn't degenerated any more than it had done in life. For a moment Stratstone frowned at the unprofessionalism of the job the murderers had done. Surely, in a country which was largely covered in tropical rainforest, they should have managed to lose the body more effectively? And the whole business with the face: normally, they cut off the head of a victim they didn't want identified. Someone was trying to be clever.

Stratstone was a man who was interested in method. Economy and appropriateness of method was the standard by which he judged any action, and when he forced himself to look back at the corpse, it was the absence of proper method that bothered him most. Only the blood-black hole of the bullet in the side of the head approximated to any neatness. The hole where the face had been looked thoroughly unprofessional. A jagged slit had been carved across the forehead, tearing more than cutting. The throat had been cut, and the flesh from both ends of the face had been torn off, slashed off, with some sharp instrument. A knife, a machete? A bayonet, perhaps? The skin that joined the upper lip to the gums had been sliced through, and the nose had been simply cut off, the soft facial tissue tugged away. The man's teeth, black here and there – too much Coca-Cola – still showed stuck in their gums, but the rest was sliced off, just bone and scraps of tissue, no eyes, like a skull wearing a balaclava of flesh around it. There was an ear on either side, the windpipe sagged out of the slashed throat, but the rest was a blank: a messy, pointless hole.

Stratstone gagged, and held on to the woman more tightly. The government official looked at his watch and the mortician had the impatient look of a shopkeeper with an indecisive customer.

'Yes,' the woman said at last. 'Yes, it's him.'

'Can you be sure?' the government official said.

'It's him,' she repeated doggedly.

'But . . .' the man began, and his words faded.

'When you've been married to a man for twenty years, you recognise more than a face,' she said bluntly.

'You want me to turn it over?' the mortician suggested.

'Him,' the woman said sharply. 'No, it isn't necessary to turn him over.'

The man tried to catch the official's eye with a look that said you couldn't please everybody.

So it was Santos Calderon. Stratstone was glad, relieved it was all over. He had been powerless while the woman looked on at the corpse of her husband, but now a decision was made and he could start to act: offer condolences, hold her up if she stumbled, give her some cash, keep an eye on her. That was the main thing – she needed to be kept an eye on. Stratstone could make everything go smoothly now the waiting was over.

'I'll handle everything,' he said to her in English, his Boston accent particularly reassuring. Santos Calderon had been an educated man, and even his wife spoke good English; he had been educated at an American university before he entered politics, Stratstone remembered. And then he'd gone on to become the head of the country's Truckers' Union, the largest and most powerful workers' organisation in Venezuela. Stratstone looked back one last time at the corpse. Always the same, he thought. You could educate them in America, you could teach them English, you could give them culture so they could pass off as the real thing – but it was still scratching the surface. His blackened teeth huge in the lipless hole, Santos Calderon was witness to the national obsession with sweet things, and a corresponding failure to attend to even the most elementary points of healthcare. Stratstone tutted silently. Tall and fit for fifty, he relished his rude health. He worked out at the gym, he ran, he swam. He was wearing now a sports shirt, a pair of tracksuit pants that looked like real trousers, and some deck shoes, without socks. Thick black hair crawled out at the ankle and re-appeared at the back of his muscular neck.

'All right, cover him up,' he ordered the mortician.

The sheet was laid down over the corpse in front of the woman, and her eyes never shifted from the dead man. She stood immobile, with no show of emotion. For a moment she was beyond awareness of anything but her dead husband. When she came to, she didn't push Stratstone away, but she plainly didn't feel she needed his help. The American had befriended her husband in the past few months, that was all; if she thought it strange for such a short-term friendship to result in this unnecessary display of concern, she didn't show it. If the American wanted to take her arm, open her car door, it was accepted, neither welcomed nor rebuffed.

'We want the body iced,' Stratstone said.

The mortician shook his head regretfully. 'There's no room,' he said. 'We're too full as it is.' The government official folded his arms and turned towards the entrance of the morgue. Stratstone dug a thick leather wallet out of his jacket, tugged two bills from it and threw them contemptuously on the sheet. The mortician made no move to take them. Stratstone removed another bill and added it to the first two.

'That's all there is,' he said bluntly.

The mortician picked up the notes and bundled them into a pocket under his white coat. He slid the body onto a trolley and wheeled it away into the broad passage. The woman went first and Stratstone followed, his hands clasped together in front of him. The mortician stopped in front of a drawer and hauled it out with some effort. He pulled a naked, ice-cold stiff out of the drawer and dropped it so that it slapped onto the tiles like a wet fish. The trolley tipped and the body of Santos Calderon slid into the other man's drawer. Without a second look, the woman turned and walked out of the morgue into the hot, bright sunlight.

Stratstone pulled out into the one-way flow of the Avenida Urdaneta, his fingers tapping on the wheel as he hummed to the strains of a sentimental ballad on the car radio. '*Corazon*,' the singer wailed in every line. The Latins couldn't write a pop-song without including the word 'heart' at every available opportunity. It constantly amazed him, the way every song sounded the same and they were all chock-full of the same mawkish sentimentality. But even the intrusive song couldn't prevent him thinking about the death of Santos

23

Calderon. How the death – the murder – of Santos Calderon had made matters more urgent. Things would have to be hastened along from now on. The union leader had disappeared a week before, and since then the union had been thrown into confusion; now a new leader would be appointed, and the country would slide one step further towards uncontrolled violence. Uncontrolled, that is, by all but those who had set it in motion. Stratstone knew the value of anarchy.

Down the opposite carriageway a personnel carrier drove at reckless speed with its complement of fourteen-year-old conscripts, trigger-happy, itching for a chance to fire.

He drove down the long, broad freeways that cut Caracas into pieces, past the Parque Los Caobos, under the huge blue neon sign for 'Polar', the national beer, and on by the Hilton Hotel, a grey monolithic box the guidebooks described as 'interesting architecturally'. Caracas was a completely modern, American city, and the look and feel of it pleased Stratstone. All through the four centuries since Santander de Leon had founded it – naming it Caracas after the local Carib chief he killed in battle – the colonial heart of the city had been preserved; until the nineteen seventies when, after the oil boom, it had been ripped out, like a stone from an unripe fruit. Caracas was built in valleys and on hills; at night, with hill after hill covered with the twinkling lights of the barrios, it looked like a dozen huge Christmas trees. In the daylight this flattering sparkle of light turned into a city of sprawling corrugated-iron shacks and the barrios of the poor built with red mud. It was a city where a vast tide seemed to have gone out. Up on the hills remained the dirty flotsam of the shanty towns, while the valleys still prosperously seethed with banks and hotels and fast-food chains.

'*Corazon, corazon* . . .' the singer wailed as Stratstone glided the large Buick across the traffic and turned left, up a slight incline to the Country Club, an area of the city where the rich lived and which received the cool breezes from the slopes of the Avila mountain. '*Corazon!*' The song finished in a breathless moan, with a crash of cymbals suggesting the usual destruction of hopes and dreams. Again, Stratstone marvelled at the way the Latins revelled in tales of misery and broken hearts. People spoke of the nation's resilience, but Stratstone believed they actually relished misfortune. How could a people endure such poverty, corruption, ill-health and general suffering unless they actually enjoyed it? And if they didn't, why didn't they get off their butts and do something about it? Their dreadful sentimentality, their devotion to hopelessness and failure, were reflected in the country's dismally mawkish music. Stratstone himself believed that anything, everything, was possible.

So what would be the effect of the death of Santos Calderon? And – a question of almost equal importance – what would the woman, his widow, do now? She was an educated woman, she wasn't the type to massage her stricken sensibilities by sitting in front of the radio singing, *Corazon, corazon* all day. No, he would have to keep an eye on her, there was no doubt about that.

The car turned into a steep gravel drive with twenty-foot walls topped with spikes wrapped in razor-wire. Automatic steel gates swung open and shut behind it, and a large house with mock battlements loomed through palm trees and patches of bougainvillea. Like all the houses in the Country Club, this was a fortress; whatever Stratstone's private beliefs about the dull capacity for suffering of the average Venezuelan, it didn't stretch to letting him get within half a mile of his house. No buses were allowed to pass through the Country Club, apart from those that brought the servants up in the morning and took them down at night, and if anyone did trespass onto the sacred ground, there were enough armed guards and fortifications to hold up an army. The houses here possessed art collections and swimming pools and satellite dishes, but outside the golf club – the nearest golf course to a city centre Stratstone had ever seen – sat a guard with a sawn-off shotgun on his lap and a pistol on each hip. Behind the glorious façade of the Country Club, there was fear; fear of the suppurating discontent in the barrios, and fear of Venezuela's rag-bag army if its guns ever came to be turned against its own citizens.

There were two other cars in the curved drive apart from the Buick. Both were four-wheel-drive Chevrolet two-seaters with an open-topped storage space behind – the kind of car that looked good in a city street but climbed mountains too. Stratstone stepped out of the Buick and walked towards his front door, which a uniformed maid had already opened. He walked down the wide corridor towards a closed wooden door, the right-hand side of which was studded with metal locks. Unlocking these, he entered a room that was almost bare; there were no pictures on the walls, the absolute minimum of furniture, no plants, no personal effects. It was how Stratstone liked it; an office to work, to plan, to make deals in, not to photograph for the pages of an interior decoration magazine. Beyond this bare room was another, and another door, this time made of metal. He locked it behind him and picked up an internal phone from an otherwise empty desk.

'Johnny?' he demanded. 'Come down here. The ball starts now.' He replaced the receiver.

Apart from the desk, this room held only one other item of furniture, a vast, solid-looking safe with peeling metallic-blue paint. It had a wheel the size of a car's, and it stood in the middle of the room, in the middle of the house, like a fat Buddha in a temple. Stratstone pressed the buzzer on the desk twice, to mark Johnny's progress through the two doors, and then he appeared in this inner sanctum carrying two large cardboard suitcases. The suitcases were extremely battered. Where the colour had cracked off from their being crammed too full, too often, the pale brown cardboard showed through like wounds.

Johnny was a smoothly handsome, tanned West Coast American male, with black, shoulder-length hair. He was a surfing poster, a jeans advertisement. When he smiled, as he put the cases down in front of the desk, the expression came

26

as mechanically as putting one leg in front of the other. But Stratstone already had his back to him and was unlocking the safe.

'It's all set,' he said, without turning around. The door of the six-foot safe swung lazily open. 'You're to go out tonight. Start stirring the porridge. Caracas, Maracaibo, San Fernando, Cuidad Bolivar . . . you've the whole country to cover in less than a week.'

Johnny grinned. As Stratstone handed him the wrapped bundles of dollar bills, he stacked them neatly into the broken-down suitcases. They came in batches of ten thousand dollars, the denominations ten- and five-dollar bills only. By the time the two of them had finished there was over three-quarters of a million dollars in each suitcase. It always surprised Stratstone how much money could fit into a suitcase. You might never have enough changes of socks, but you could always cram in a million bucks. Johnny picked up the two cases – bulging, the locks bent away from the cardboard – and walked back down the corridor, with Stratstone opening the doors in front of him.

No soldier, no cop was inquisitive enough to look at a couple of cardboard suitcases, but just in case, the windows of the Chevrolet were bullet-proof and the cabin was built of a single piece of reinforced steel that kept the driver and the money cocooned from any explosion. Johnny got in with the suitcases and pulled the vehicle out of the drive. The gates swung open in front of him and shut behind him.

Stratstone stood alone on the drive for a few moments, then, turning, went back inside to another bare room, picked up a pair of arm-weights and began, reflectively at first, then with total absorption, to pump each arm up and down, his face furious with effort.

THREE

Quince

A party of elderly American tourists walked through the foyer, looking around them like owls, as if they'd never seen a Hilton lobby before. They carried small pieces of hand-luggage, cameras, binoculars, and had spectacles slung round their necks so they wouldn't be lost. They huddled together under a sign which said 'Tropitour', and waited anxiously. Finally, a young man in a sharp suit bounced up to welcome them and they relaxed into low, leather armchairs.

Quince looked up from across the lobby at the sea of white golf caps and see-through yellow cotton trousers. He pulled hard at a large rum and tonic, until the liquid eventually made its way through the sheet-ice they smothered it with here. Irritably, he clicked his fingers at a waiter and waved the glass to demand another.

'No ice,' he snapped. '*Sin hielo. Comprende?*'

He picked half a lime from the bowl in front of him and squeezed it into his mouth. Across the lobby the young tour leader was also licking his team into shape. 'The afternoon is free,' he was saying. 'But there'll be organised trips to the art gallery to see the famous Venezuelan artist, Reveron, no extra charge, as well as to the house of Simon Bolivar. Tomorrow, you get a six a.m. call and have a full inclusive hotel breakfast. The flight to Angel Falls is one hour. Coffee and snacks will be served on board. A three-course lunch is provided by the company at the tropical village, and then you fly back, arriving at five fifteen. Dinner is at seven. Any questions?'

Quince withdrew his gaze from the tour party and looked back at the two Americans who sat in armchairs next to his.

He picked a large green olive from the bowl on the table between them and sucked the flesh away from the stone until it was completely clean.

'To some people,' he said carefully to the two Americans, 'a billion dollars is a lot of money.'

Quince distrusted meetings anywhere other than in hotel foyers. Rooms were too risky, he believed; there was danger from surveillance, a listening device was easy to conceal. But out here, in the broad, open expanse of the Hilton's marble and mahogany lobby where waterfalls tumbled into ponds and trees grew to the ceiling, it was like being under the sky. Far, far safer to discuss a tricky problem in a public place like this than in the most heavily guarded room. Quince knew; he'd had the most intimate talks in hotel lobbies everywhere from Tokyo to Johannesburg, and he'd never got it wrong. That was why the Americans had asked for him in the first place.

'That's why we've come to you,' Nethercott, the younger of the two, replied, apparently failing to detect any irony in Quince's observation. 'We understand you have special contacts who can raise that kind of money.' He leaned forward like a deaf man for Quince's reply.

'Let's not beat around the bush,' Hughes cut in. 'Okay, so we don't know much about this kind of thing, but you've done it before, right?'

Hughes sat in a crouched position across from Quince, his elbows on his knees and his thick hands clasped together to show he meant business. 'We didn't get you out of a hat, for Christ's sakes,' he said. His irritation was clearly with Nethercott, the junior partner on the American side, rather than Quince. 'I mean you've come highly recommended,' Hughes continued, to mollify Quince. 'You've done this kind of thing in Malaya, right?'

'Mauritius,' Quince corrected him.

'Mauritius, sure, Mauritius,' Hughes said roughly. 'The point is, it's possible. You can do it.'

Quince leaned back in his chair to get away from the

American's breath. For half an hour he'd remained equivocal about the proposition they'd made to him – so much so that Hughes now felt he had to have it confirmed that the thing was possible at all. He knew he'd wrong-footed them at the start. Whatever they'd expected him to be, it wasn't a fat, red-faced, middle-aged Englishman in a three-piece cream linen suit and a bow tie. Their business, company business – in particular the company business of a conglomerate like Continental USA – was traditionally pursued in the board-room, not in hotel lobbies with people like Quince. And so much the better, thought Quince. He plucked another carefully chosen olive from the bowl as the waiter brought him the chilled rum and tonic, and the Americans two multicoloured fruit punches with an array of cocktail sticks and umbrellas but no alcohol. He sat squarely in the chair, his arms on the chair arms like a fat ornament, and considered their story again.

The approach had come through a middleman, a German named Heinrich Schütz who said that clients of his wanted to raise a large sum of money. The amount had not been mentioned, but these clients, Schütz had told him, were to be state-of-the-art confidential: there was nothing illegal about the deal, he'd insisted, but it was necessary for their identities to remain secret. When Quince had finally met the two representatives of Continental USA half an hour ago, he'd understood why. They wanted to raise a billion dollars, they said. But this was not a spectacular sum of money for an organisation like Continental to raise, Quince had suggested, so why didn't they go through the banks, sell equity, make a share issue? They were big enough to do any or all three of these; they were vast, a household name. Why the secrecy? Hughes had explained it. 'We want to raise this money,' he said, 'but we want to raise it on behalf of another party.'

Quince wondered at their naivety. Did they think they were going to get away without telling him who the 'other party' was? Did they think they could ask someone to raise a billion dollars for them in a hotel lobby in Caracas and not tell them who it was to be raised for? Certainly Quince had useful contacts, but they would need to be properly informed. His contacts would be very angry indeed, for example, if they found they had taken the risk of evading their own banking laws only to lend money to a national enemy. The contacts Quince had with that kind of money to lend were not high street banks.

'Some people might ask to know who they were raising a billion dollars for,' Quince had said with a touch of frost.

'That's why we've come to you,' Nethercott had replied eagerly, leaning forward in his irritating way.

'I'm one of them,' Quince cut him off. And knowing that it disconcerted Nethercott in particular, he ordered himself a third rum and tonic.

From the start Quince had known it was Hughes he was really dealing with. Nethercott was no doubt there because he was some kind of financial bigwig, and also because a company like Continental didn't send one-man teams out to run an operation like this. Indeed, the fact that there were only two of them here hinted that the business in hand might be known to only a very few at the top of the Continental pyramid. But having Nethercott around was at least mildly entertaining. So far he hadn't caught a single nuance of Quince's ironic interrogation, and the ongoing annoyance he clearly caused Hughes was a bonus.

'I have to know who you're acting for,' Quince said. 'Not why, necessarily, but who. Without that, I can't help you.'

Hughes anticipated the question – as he'd anticipated other questions before, Quince had noticed. He showed no reluctance to give the information, he had known that he would have to.

'Continental has major interests in Venezuela,' he explained in a monotone that suggested he'd made the speech a hundred times before. 'We have a general interest in the welfare of the country and we have many specific investments, of course. Over the years we've formed close ties with the government. A good relationship.' He paused to

31

frown, a pause that was as much a part of the speech as the words themselves. 'But now,' he continued, 'now things aren't so good. Prices have slumped – all over the world, not just here. We still have our good relationship with the government, but we see a country caught in a spiral of foreign debt. Okay, no great problem. We're talking about a comparatively rich country, a country with collateral of its own. But the banks . . .' Hughes frowned again, as if he could scarcely believe such short-sightedness. 'The banks won't play ball. The government – the President himself – they want a reduction and a rescheduling of debt, but the banks aren't going to give it to them.' Hughes shook his head. 'Of course, things aren't easy anywhere. But here, here in Caracas and the big industrial cities, hard commercial values are skin-deep. The people don't understand hardship, and hardship's what they're going to get. There's unrest already, but what you see here in the city now – the odd riot here and there – that's nothing. Just beneath the surface there's a head of steam building up that's going to blow us all away – the President, Continental, who knows? Maybe democracy itself.' Hughes shrugged and bunched his lips and frowned again in a glib and formulaic way. 'The President can't afford to ignore that, so he has to have popular policies. And popular policies,' Hughes wagged his finger, 'popular policies cost money. If he doesn't pay the banks on time, the banks are going to hang him out to dry. If he pays them, he's got to squeeze the country further. It's heads I lose, tails you win. That's when the danger starts. That's when the place blows up.' Thoughtfully, Hughes bent his head to the multi-coloured straw and sucked his fruit punch through the cornucopia of fresh fruit and hardware deposited on top.

Nethercott leaned over further while Hughes sustained his look of pained sincerity; the truth was the truth and would have to be told. 'Let me give you the plain vanilla on this one,' he continued. 'We want to bail out the government. We want it to have the chance it deserves. That's why we're involved with you. It's like . . .' He paused for a second. 'Like

Mauritius,' he said. 'You did it for them, now we want you to do it for us. For the Venezuelans. Help them over a hump.'

'What about the normal channels?' Quince asked.

'As I say, the banks are holding the government over a barrel. The IMF's no good, nor is the World Bank. They won't advance anything more unless the President changes policy. They're holding him to ransom! As you know,' Hughes said piously, 'this is a democratically elected government.'

It was possible. That had been Quince's first thought. And it could all be done without treading on any toes. Whatever meetings he had in Europe to raise the money would have to be attended by a Venezuelan government representative, that was all. That would satisfy his contacts; they didn't care much about Venezuela either way, it certainly wasn't going to cause them any problems. And, as he knew, they had money to lend. Plenty of money to lend. A billion wasn't going to stretch them to any great extent.

Nethercott was leaning over eagerly again, waiting for Quince's reaction. On the other side of the lobby, the tour leader was winding up his instructions. 'Lunch is in one hour,' he stated. 'Right now, you swim in the hotel pool.'

'Time,' Hughes was saying, 'time is vital. If there's going to be any unrest on the streets, the President needs to be able to act. He needs the money soon.'

Nethercott leaned in even further. He looked as if he was going to fall off his chair. 'These contacts of yours,' he said. 'You're sure they can do it? At least we should have some idea who it is we're dealing with.'

Quince looked at the eager face craning over the table beside him. Why should Nethercott have some idea who he was dealing with? What bit of difference did it make to Nethercott as long as he got the money for Continental's little support operation? But Quince didn't like to be made to hide by a small man like Nethercott. Whoever was the Venezuelan representative at the meetings in Europe would be able to relay at least some information to Hughes and Nethercott anyway, even if he didn't know actual names.

'Islamic banks, that's all you need to know,' he said.

After that Quince sat back in his chair and began to knock out a timetable with Hughes, while Hughes obligingly expanded on the precarious position of the government and exactly what kind of assistance to its political life the money would bring. Quince was perspiring slightly in the air-conditioned lobby; the rums were starting to work their way out wherever they could. A slow stain spread under the arms of the linen jacket and an occasional drip fell from his forehead to the floor. But he was still perfectly lucid. He sat fatly in the leather wing armchair and watched irritably as Nethercott listened and nodded and smiled. He was the nodding dog, Quince thought. He was the man that companies like Continental always sent along because they never quite trusted the Hugheses to do a solo deal. In the face of Quince's obvious antipathy, Nethercott was all charm and polite interest. It was Hughes who asked the searching questions, but when they parted it was Nethercott who gratefully shook Quince's hand and patted his arm in the encouraging American way. Hughes just gave a short, curt shake of the hand.

Back in his room, Nethercott took off his jacket and folded it neatly over a chair. From the fourteenth floor he could see over the whole of Caracas' central district. Below him, half a mile away, was the bus station where the riots had erupted last month. The government had been able to put the lid on that quite efficiently, and judging by the hotel lobby, the effect on tourism had been negligible. But if only people knew, Nethercott thought, how fragile the situation really was – how much more fragile it was now than it had been even a month ago. The rich, always a sure gauge of a country's temperature, were registering distress: capital flight had increased fourfold in the past four weeks. There was little cause for confidence in the current policies. The government was on a knife-edge.

Nethercott took off his tie and loosened the top two buttons of his shirt. He carefully unscrewed a small wire at the back of his collar button and eased the button away completely. He untucked the shirt and reached his hand down the front of his trousers to pull out a small machine, disentangling it and the wire from his clothes. He hit a button that wound back a tape then set it to replay. *'To some people,'* came the crackled but audible voice of the fat Englishman, *'a billion dollars is a lot of money.'*

The smug, supercilious tone of the man infuriated Nethercott, but Quince was the one who had been the fool. Nethercott liked to think that Quince considered him naive, he positively wanted Quince to think him a bore, a dull time-server: when the blow fell, it would make it that much harder to bear.

Nethercott stopped the tape, and in the sudden silence he heard, fourteen floors below, the wail of a siren and the first thump of a tear-gas shell.

FOUR

The Company You Keep

RAUSCH – THE PROVIDER read the banner that floated above Walker and above the stage in Geneva's Holst Conference Centre. Beneath it, the now deserted table that sat the Rausch board was cluttered with half-empty jugs of water and haphazard piles of documents. The first of the morning breaks had democratically joined the board with their thousand delegates from all over the world, who milled about on the conference floor, drinking coffee and talking Rausch business.

Behind the table, which stretched the whole length of the stage, a vast world map – the world that Rausch, in its genuine if overblown statement did, in fact, provide for – was coloured in to show the length and breadth of the Rausch achievement. The colour used was red, like the colour on old maps of the British Empire. Across its countries, modernistic symbols indicated the products and provisions, the industry and agriculture Rausch embraced in its worldwide community. Tinted gold sheaves of corn bunched across the American mid-west, roasted coffee beans fell into piles beneath emerald trees down the isthmus of Central America and into Columbia, coconut palms, pineapples, banana trees, tea plantations, cattle ranches, maize, cotton, rice and sugar decorated the map from north to south and from east to west. Here painted factories puffed pretty smoke, there neat piles of gold bars indicated a mine; childish drawings of conveyor-belts and wheels and production lines showed where coal and soda were extracted, where diamonds, platinum, copper and zinc were dug from the world's great mines.

And all around the walls of the conference hall, which rose

36

for sixty feet up to a glass dome, were displayed statistics, data, graphs and diagrams that showed off to Rausch its own year's achievements. The Rausch delegates, in their suits and perspex identity badges, needed only to look up to see the picture of their organisation's success. They were men and women from all over the world who had gathered to be told the Rausch message, to hear of the advances in Rausch product and profit. To feel good. And at the end of three days of glitz, of trumpets and of self-congratulation, they would return to their own small niches in the organisation, take up again their own small roles and ensure that the message was as good next year as it had been this.

Walker looked around him, and listened to the subdued roar of a thousand eager, talking people. He had an identity badge, too, and a Rausch annual report, with the chairman's letter wrapped in a thick-card folder that also contained the usual late announcements, the details of hotel arrangements and parking facilities, and a list of restaurants and tourist sights that a delegate might enjoy in the few free hours that were available to him. The conference was a carefully structured, intensive affair which would reach a grand finale this afternoon with the chairman's speech and his rousing call to the faithful to go home and multiply. This year Geneva, the next Monte Carlo, perhaps, or Palm Springs or Singapore.

Walker watched a master of ceremonies ascend the stage in his red-tailed coat and gold buttons, to bang the table with a mallet and make a noise the hall had no chance of hearing. The microphone on the podium at centre-stage was switched back on, its head was tapped and the MC pleaded with the throng to take their seats again for the last-but-one session before lunch. At last they drifted slowly back; the board took their places on the stage and surveyed the swirling mass as it began to filter into the lines of seats, as people sat down, crossed their legs, took their folders in their hands and looked eagerly to the stage for further stimulus and inspiration.

In his unplanned seat, procured in spite of strict conference

37

security, Walker opened his own folder to look at the synopsis of the next session. The name of the next speaker, who was manager of one whole section of the Rausch organisation and would in a moment stand and report on his department's achievements, was Arnold Secker. Walker hadn't managed to find Secker in the crowd. He thought, perhaps, it was for the best. If Secker could be terrified by what he had done when he was alone with Walker in a bar, how would he react if he saw Walker actually in the heart of the organisation against which he had committed a serious crime? The crimes that Rausch had committed might be far greater than his, but company laws were strict, and whatever the outcome of an investigation into the documents he had stolen, Secker would almost certainly be convicted and gaoled for their theft. He could get as much as five years, Walker reckoned.

RAUSCH – THE PROVIDER. The banner was flaunted across the stage as if this were the start of a tickertape welcome for homecoming, victorious troops. Rausch fed the world; it fed the world not with basic foods and food products that sold in Asia, Africa, America and Europe, but also with mined raw materials that supplied the world's industries. For three days Walker had listened to the story of Rausch success, imbibed Rausch doctrine. The Rausch operation, he had to admit, was something approaching a miracle.

He hadn't really intended to stay for Secker's address, but curiosity had overcome him. He wanted to see how a man who three days ago could barely control his nervous mannerisms in a one-to-one conversation could today command the attention of a thousand people. He wanted to learn how it was that Secker had risen to such an important position in the Rausch empire; he wanted to watch the man again, and try to understand what it was that had made him pass on documents which could wreck his career and, in his own view, his life. Secker the corporate man, Secker the scared employee, Secker the thief who stole his master's secrets – Walker wasn't sure that he'd come across another Arnold Secker in his entire career. But this little man with the eastern European moustache and the Harvard accent – this little man who would soon be coming onto the stage, shaking hands with the chairman, then edging diffidently across to the speaker's podium – this little man had given Walker a story. A story! Not a story that the television companies would touch; not a story that O'Connell could possibly get his mind around. A story that was as yet buried in a string of shell companies from France to Switzerland to Panama to Venezuela. A story whose origins lay in the anstaldts of Liechtenstein, where the lawyers' and accountants' records slept under lock and key in a hundred miles of filing cabinets stacked in offices along the main street of the capital, Vaduz. It was a story that had only just begun. For the great question now was, what further plans did Rausch have? Secker had delivered, to him exclusively, a thread of evidence that could build to a story of unknown, perhaps limitless, proportions. A story that would give the lie to the puff and glory unfolding on the conference stage in front of him.

And now Secker, yet to appear, was being introduced by a cheery, red-faced man who spoke his introduction as if Secker had won the school prize. Arnold Secker, chairman of this committee, director of the company, head of Rausch CA – which seemed to mean Rausch Central America. There followed a list of all the Rausch subsidiaries in those countries, including a list of Spanish-named subsidiaries which allowed Rausch to be more subtly present in a region where the big gringo companies were not always welcome. For twenty minutes the red-faced man spoke. He talked of market share and sixty-three per cent increases. He talked of new factories and irrigation schemes, of triumph over competitors, of markets and monopolies controlled. He talked of employment, cost-cutting, and boosting production, he spoke of plant, human resources and the future. There was prolonged applause, as the speaker declared yet another triumph for Rausch's Central American operation, and the board led this clapping as if they were the Politburo at a May

Day parade in Moscow. Walker sat in a daze. Could this be the same company that Secker had talked about, little, scared Secker with a set of documents that spoke of subterfuge, conspiracy and crime? Here on stage was a story of greatnss, of bounty and benevolence – of corporate morality, nobility of soul, no less . . . Walker looked along the line of board members behind the speaker. He recognised three chairmen of major Swiss banks, two leading politicians, a judge, a famous lawyer, the heads of two leading Swiss multi-nationals, and the chief of Geneva's police department. No wonder Rausch employees stood and glorified their company. To them it must seem the very embodiment of both power and justice. Rausch wasn't just a company or an organisation, it was territory, sovereignty and power. It was an indestructible, self-perpetuating organism. Rausch wasn't above the law. Rausch *was* the law.

There was a small disturbance on the stage, a flutter of interest along the table as if a message was being passed. The MC came back onto the stage and spoke quietly to the red-faced man, who frowned. There was a hitch, the smooth course of the Rausch conference had been upset. The red-faced man bent down to ask a question of the seated board members behind him. When he turned back, the cheeriness had gone. This wasn't in the programme at all. Behind him, men were getting out of their seats and consulting, one or two leaving the stage altogether. Walker watched as the red-faced man stroked the microphone briefly, looked round the great hall to gather the attention of the delegates.

'Ladies and gentlemen. Arnold Secker is indisposed,' he said.

Arnold Secker. Walker looked at the lapel badges around him. They all had the christian names of the delegates; it was the intimacy of a family. The red-faced man consulted a sheet of paper. 'In which case,' he said haltingly, 'we will now adjourn for lunch.'

Walker slipped out of his seat and threaded his way towards the doors. There was bewilderment and confusion in the hall. It seemed a small thing, a speaker unavailable to speak, but set against the smooth efficiency of the rest of the conference, the last-minute nature of Secker's indisposition didn't ring true. Certainly it didn't ring true to Walker. What had happened to Arnold Secker? Had he been found out? Walker could imagine his superiors' disbelief; it would be inconceivable for a company man to betray Rausch as Secker had done. As he pushed his way through the heavy glass doors of the hall and away from the pandemonium, Walker recalled something he'd once heard a senior Coca-Cola executive say. 'I would rather lose my country,' the man had declared, 'than lose my company.'

The conference centre was near the airport, and the taxi pulled out onto the motorway that led back to the city. Snow was falling heavily, but it hadn't settled much in the valley yet. The steady stream of cars either carried skis or empty ski racks – they were heading for the mountains, obscured in the distance by snow and cloud, or for the passes to Italy. Walker's taxi glided past a snow-plough and turned left onto the sliproad into town. There was little traffic about once you left the motorways, people stayed at home like squirrels until the snow stopped. Once the taxi had reached the Lake, however, tourists filled the pavements and fur coats swished in and out of hotel lobbies all along the lakeside. They dipped into the warmth of the jeweller's shops and criss-crossed the pedestrian bridges that led to the smart, intimate restaurants of the old town. Walker saw the grim neo-Gothic railway station pass the taxi windows, and the ornate stone balustrading of the smart apartments and hotels that flanked the Lake. Out on the water, thinly iced for the afternoon, the huge central fountain opposite the river's entrance was frozen hard into an ice sculpture, and would stay like that for the remainder of the winter. Walker leaned close to the window so that his breath misted the glass and tiny ice-patterns formed on the other side. The taxi crawled down the street of banks, its tyres following the snow tracks in front.

Walker was looking for one bank in particular, a building without flags or banners, a place where clients' business was treated with extreme tact, if not actually with secrecy.

The bay-windowed frontage of the Brunner Bank, when he saw it at last, was discreetly set into a row of old houses, now businesses, along the waterfront. A modern bronze plaque with flat, black letters was all that distinguished it from a Victorian coffee shop. *Brunner. Geneva. Zurich.* And also, Walker now knew, though his information was not written on the plaque, Caracas. Though the Rausch documents that Secker had given him were incomplete, Secker's guess was that the twenty-three million dollars that had left Brunner in Zurich was the same twenty-three million that subsequently surfaced in Brunner's Caracas branch, but the middle part of the transaction was obscure. Had there been shell companies to hold the money, their names lost in a maze of accounting detail and only to be unearthed in some Liechtenstein organisation that specialised in this kind of clandestine operation? Walker needed Secker one more time – but Secker had gone, and all that was left were the papers and the inscrutable façade of a Geneva bank. Walker ordered the driver to move on. Either he must get the missing information from Secker, or he must connect Brunner's deal in Zurich with the corresponding one in Caracas without Secker's help. The taxi wound up through the narrow cobbled streets and deposited him at the familiar house in the rue Maupassant with its over-hanging gable and leaded windows.

In his sitting-room at Frau Hauswirth's, Walker sat at his desk and thought. Secker had given him no contact number. He certainly hadn't wanted Walker, or anyone else who knew about the documents, to telephone him at work. So what could Walker expect if he phoned the company and asked for Secker? Not to speak to the man himself, certainly. But he might, at the very least, get confirmation that Secker's absence was a fact, that he hadn't imagined the curious, apparently unimportant, scene at the conference. What he really wanted was to hear someone from Rausch say, 'Secker has disappeared, Secker is ill, Secker is dead.' He wanted to listen to the tone of voice as much as to the words themselves, to hear how Secker's secretary would cope with the question, how the public relations machine at Rausch had geared itself into action. What would it be? 'Secker has resigned from the company.'? 'Secker is under arrest.'? 'Tragically, Arnold Secker was run over in the snow this morning on his way to the company's annual conference.'? 'We have no information at this time about Arnold Secker.'?

Walker waited while the telephone rang at Rausch.

'I'd like to speak to Arnold Secker.'

'One moment, please.' A pause.

A minute, perhaps more, the seconds ticking unnaturally loudly from his wrist watch. Then another voice, another girl, slightly breathless. 'You're holding for. . .?'

'I want to speak to Arnold Secker.'

'I'm putting you through to our personnel department. Will you hold?'

Walker held, through another wait, another ringing tone. The phone was picked up – but then the answerer was suddenly intercepted, and all Walker heard was silence. But he knew what was being said. You don't put someone through to the personnel department cold, not when they're looking for Arnold Secker. You warn whoever answers the phone, you follow the procedure that has been laid down. Why? What was it that had to be said about Arnold Secker that was so difficult to say? And then a man's voice. 'Who's calling please?'

Walker gave his name and his paper and enquired just as sweetly if there was a problem. Another wait. And then the same man again. 'There's to be an announcement about Mr Secker this afternoon.'

'This is the afternoon.'

Another pause. 'That's really all I can say.'

'Arnold Secker came to see me. I thought it might be important.'

'Just one moment, sir.'

43

A new man's voice, older, less cocky and more assured. 'You're ringing about Arnold Secker?'

'That's right.' Walker gave his name, the name of his paper.

'There's no reason I can't tell you now. It's already in the afternoon editions. Arnold Secker was found dead in his hotel room this morning. The police are treating it as suicide.'

'Thank you. Thank you so much.'

Walker sat at his desk for a long time. Then he got up, slowly. In the bedroom he packed a small bag, then he returned to his desk and pulled some sheets of photocopy paper from a packet and stuck one into the typewriter. Downstairs, Frau Hauswirth heard the first sound of typing in the months since he'd moved in. It made her stop and frown; however much she had disapproved of her lodger's idleness, even that was preferable to inconsistency. She had reached a comfortable understanding about him and now he was upsetting it.

He typed letters. The first was to a stringer he knew in Liechtenstein, a man whose work mostly involved financial magazines. The letter, which he would fax from the office on the way to the airport, asked him to check, if possible, the ultimate owner of a company called Imronal. Rausch would have their connection buried very deep: Imronal, if it still existed, would be owned by another holding company, and that company would be owned by another and so on. The second letter Walker addressed to his landlady. He would leave it for her on the Somme-grey carpet in the hall. The letter told her he would be away indefinitely, and it would tell her after he had gone, when no objections or inquiries could be made.

FIVE

The Paris Account

Quince looked like a man about to start a poetry reading. The cream linen suit had been discarded in favour of something more European, more formal. But it was an antique formality. The suit was still three-piece, but it was dark green. A fob watch was slung from one waistcoat pocket to the other around Quince's bulging stomach, and a handkerchief blossomed in a flourish from the top pocket of his jacket. The bow tie was in place, emerging somewhere between his third and fourth chins. Around him, in the high-ceilinged fin-de-siècle lounge – as large as a ballroom – five men sat in a circle. The rain was beating on the windows almost silently, and the waiters in Paris's Raphael Hotel were equally discreet. They slipped soundlessly across the deep purple carpet to refill a coffee cup, replace a bottle of mineral water or whisk away Quince's empty glasses with the same straight-backed, po-faced disapproval they would have employed to smother a rat in the dining-room. In his drinking, as in his dress, Quince was making no concession whatsoever to the importance of the occasion or to the suave, elegantly-shoed Islamic bankers who sat in stylised positions on the Raphael's ample sofas. If they were here to break their great Islamic laws against usury, Quince malevolently decided, they could put up with the sight of a few vodkas as well.

This kind of effrontery was the secret of his success. It was invariably Americans who hired him, and Americans were always enthralled by his self-importance and lack of ceremony, by his assumption of command. They thought he behaved like an aristocrat, like the scion of a family with a thousand years of history, and they loved it. Quince, knowing that they loved it, had the part down to a fine art. But in fact there was no more behind Quince than a few acres of green flannel. No titled family, no stately home, no heirlooms from the Field of the Cloth of Gold. Quince was Irish. Few English people hired Quince's services. They could see 'fake' writ large across the braggadocio.

But if Quince was a fake in his speech and in the way he dressed, he knew how to deliver the goods. The Americans may have liked him for his outward show, but they were astute enough to know an operator when they saw one. He might speak in the short, stabbing sentences of the habitual drinker, his face might be mottling nicely down to the neck and he might appear to be as discreet as a talking macaw, but behind it all there was an agile and incisive mind. The average Englishman, introduced to Quince at the Paris opera or on the rails at Ascot, would put him down as a faker, a chancer, and hurry on, but Americans did not miss the steel beneath the surface. They could see that Quince believed in himself, totally and utterly, and they knew the value of such unshakable self-confidence.

And yet, however much you trust a man, you don't just ask him to go out into the big wide world and find you a billion dollars, and leave it at that. Even Americans – and Hughes and Nethercott in particular – didn't pay Quince's hotel bills and his air fares, and set him up with an account in an international bank to the tune of half a million dollars, and then wave goodbye and hope for the best. They knew that men like Quince, for all their effectiveness, could disappear without trace if things went wrong. Even with a commission on a billion dollars – and any commission was fantastic on a billion dollars – a man like Quince might take the short view. He might take the paltry half a million and run up a few bills here and there, and then cut loose. And so they didn't let him off the lead entirely. One of the five men who sat in Quince's magic circle, the one who looked the least at ease, was their insurance against Quince's good behaviour. He wasn't a banker, he wasn't the Venezuelan ambassador. He was there to guard Quince from himself – from his own temptations – and from anyone else with an idea that they could get their hands on him.

The fifth man was a short, thick-set Israeli, ex-army, ex-Mossad, ex-civilised human being, who wore a cheap, tight grey suit and was constantly shifting about in his seat – one foot under his leg, then the other foot, his head resting in one hand, then the other – and scowling. He did not speak, and was clearly not enjoying the company of the man whose bodyguard he was. Quince lost no opportunity to torment him; often in the course of the conversation, he would ask Soren – that was his name – for his opinion, knowing that it was impossible for the Israeli to make any contribution to the discussion. Instead, Soren would rub his hands together as if they wanted to strangle each other. Soren's job was to be as suspicious of Quince as possible, and he therefore lived in a state of permanent discomfort.

The other four men sitting round Quince in the deserted corner of one of the Raphael's lounges were three bankers who controlled three different Islamic banks, and the Venezuelan ambassador to the Fourth Republic.

Six days before, Quince had accepted the job from Continental. He had flown straight from Caracas to Lisbon, and then taken a flight to Nice. The south was unexpectedly cold even for mid-winter, and Quince had spent thirty-six hours shivering in an unheated holiday apartment that belonged to Continental USA before decamping to a small hotel in the mountains behind St Tropez where he had waited, fuming, for the arrival of the Venezuelan ambassador. He'd chosen to come here first because he wanted time to set the terms with the Venezuelans before moving on to Paris, where the real work would begin – but now he regretted not going to Paris immediately. On the second evening after his arrival, the ambassador had flown by helicopter straight from Nice airport to the Carlton Hotel in Cannes, where Quince was waiting for him. The south was empty of foreigners, now that the cold weather had come; it was a good place to meet. Their negotiations had gone well. All sides were nervous now, to the point of snapping. The ambassador, Continental, and the bankers themselves, all wanted the talks in Paris to last as short a time as possible.

While the ambassador returned separately to Paris, Quince and Soren had taken a private plane to Paris's second airport, steering clear of showing passports in the capital, keeping to the hedgerows so to speak. The night they drove into Paris from the airport was warmer than it had been in the south, but it had been raining then and it had rained ever since. They checked into the Raphael, one of several hotels Quince used when he came to Paris. The Arabs were staying elsewhere. Quince set up base and waited. He dragged Soren – his minder, Continental's watchdog – with him across the city; he drank raspberry champagne at the Taillevent while Soren chewed his knuckles, and travelled with him through the wet streets around the Arc de Triomphe and watched the blur of neon through the rain-streaked taxi windows up towards the Pigalle. Quince visited his old haunts like a dog marking its territory. He went to a prostitute on the Left Bank who wore a flower in her buttonhole to show that she was free, and forced Soren to wait for him, shivering in the entrance to her apartment block. He drank in bars and ate hugely in restaurants where he had eaten for thirty years. But he didn't make contact with old friends; he behaved like a man alone on an indulgent holiday – except that the unforgiving shadow of Soren was always there. He didn't go to the Venezuelan embassy on Faubourg, or to the ambassador's residence. He didn't even contact the Arabs, as far as Soren could tell, although he must have been in touch for them to be at the Raphael on the day appointed, when the ambassador had had clearance to proceed from Caracas and when the bankers were ready to deal. Once they had made their decision, the bankers were in a hurry. They had arrived at the Raphael in a limousine, shuttered from the world by darkened windows in the winter gloom, transported from one hotel lobby to another, hardly setting foot in the cold, wet, alien streets.

And while they waited for the Arabs to arrive, Soren, padding after Quince round the Raphael's most expensive suite, had bombarded him with questions. Why Islamic banks? he'd asked. He was doing his best, suspicious job. And in spite of his long-tried professionalism, he still couldn't conceal the deep prejudices that motivated him. Why are we borrowing from *Islamic* banks?

'Islamic banks,' Quince had explained by way of an answer, 'are not allowed to indulge in usury.'

And when Soren had not replied, presumably pole-axed by this apparent lack of logic, he reinforced the Israeli's confusion. 'They are not allowed to lend money,' he said. 'By Islamic law.'

'Then why . . .' Soren's hired suspicion was now fully activated.

'Oh, they invest, naturally,' Quince had continued. 'They pour their money into property and stock. They throw it away in casinos, they buy yachts and palaces in Marbella. But it's money-lending where Mohammed really throws the book at them. Don't ask me why, it's their bloody law.'

'So why are we wasting their time?' Soren burst out.

'That is exactly their weakness,' Quince said matter-of-factly. 'They *can't* lend money, but they've got so much of the stuff sloshing around doing nothing that they *want* to lend it. Which is where I – and you, in your nasty little way – come in.' He waved his hand expansively around the room. 'They have billions. And just a few of them are willing to take the risk to lend it. But we have to finesse it out of them, cleverly. We don't go at it in a great, oafish, ham-fisted rush.' He looked at the Israeli as if he were a manager inspecting a new waiter, and was rewarded with a scowl. 'They're even keener than we are to keep this out of the public domain. If this fouls up, you'll lose your job,' Quince flickered his small eyes unpleasantly at Soren, 'but they'll lose bits and pieces of themselves.' He smiled wanly at the thought.

'How can they be trusted?' Soren asked. Quince sighed and stared into his minder's burning-coal eyes. The expression on Soren's face said it all. How can *you* be trusted? the Israeli was saying. Remember that I'm watching you all the time, he was saying. Remember that for every veiled insult, every open humiliation you subject me to in front of the Arabs, I shall look forward with extra relish to the day when I catch you cheating on us. Then I'll tear your fat, jowled head from your shoulders with my bare hands.

'And because they are so keen to lend,' Quince continued, ignoring the question and turning away from the discomforting stare, 'their rates are good. If this money were being borrowed through normal channels, the rate might be thirteen of fourteen per cent. Our friends from Islam will charge perhaps as little as half of that.'

Then Soren had pressed Quince for the identity of the three bankers – which Quince, of course, had not supplied. More than likely, he thought, Soren wasn't just working for Continental; once in the service, he'd heard, you never lost touch with Mossad. And who knew, either, whether Soren's other employers might not plan to use him in some capacity other than that of simple guard-dog? The man's tendency almost to snap the wrist every time he shook hands was not reassuring. 'You're not a bodyguard, you're a bloody assassin,' Quince had joked without humour.

And now the meeting with the Arabs had reached a crucial stage. Quince looked up from the papers on his lap and round at the Venezuelan ambassador and the three bankers. It was a look to draw in their attention after a pause for a waiter to set down tea on a silver tray. The gloom of the winter afternoon beyond the windows seemed to make this corner of the Raphael's lounge smaller and brighter. 'The decision is that you will all act together if you agree to the loan in the first place?' he asked.

'We act as a consortium,' one of the Arabs replied. 'With such a sum of money, that is the only way. Any decision must be agreed by all three banks.'

'The problem will be in the underwriting. What guarantees can we have?' The second man had a large gold ring on the index finger of his right hand which he loosened every so often, to play with between thumb and forefinger.

'But that is a common problem,' the first man said. 'If we choose to lend at all, it is on the basis that it will be outside the international banking system. None of the usual international agreements can apply. A normal consortium can be underwritten by the IMF.' He paused. 'They'll always bail out their creditors,' he added scornfully, and the man with the ring laughed. 'We do not have such guarantees,' the first man continued. 'That is why there must be some agreement involving the assets of the country. Or, at least, its future potential,' he added.

The ambassador had remained silent until now, but this was clearly the cue he had been told to watch for. 'It is not possible to mortgage assets,' he cut in. 'This is a sovereign loan. When you lend to a nation, you have the guarantee that its government is in a position to raise taxes if necessary, in order to pay the money back.'

'If the government which borrows the money is still in power,' the man with the ring said. 'If your government falls . . .?' And he shrugged.

'The loan is being sought precisely for that reason,' the ambassador insisted. 'Without it, who knows, the government may fall. It is our belief, and you have the President's categoric assurance, that his government can survive with this loan. *Will* survive.'

The third Arab, who wore a white silk cap, made a heavy, sceptical face. 'The chicken and the egg,' he said. 'Our loan first, or the proof that your government can survive?'

'Let's look at it another way,' Quince said, and spread some sheets of paper from a file across the table. Now was the time when good chairmanship could tip the balance. 'Venezuela is a rich country. Oil, minerals, agriculture – you've read it all in here. It has potential. And you've seen the list of government projects: investment in railways, hospitals, roads, infrastructure – money that has been lent in the past has been put to good use. We aren't talking about a banana republic here, with a new military government every nine days; Venezuela is a country with a history of economic responsibility. But admittedly, providing guarantees is difficult. We are in a special situation here – a situation which *will* resolve itelf, with the help of this loan. Chicken or egg, it doesn't matter. What matters is that the loan comes first.'

'You mention investments,' the man with the ring said. 'Economic responsibility. They've spent thirty years investing in railways and built less than a hundred miles.'

Quince leaned back and looked around the circle. He had four men wanting to make a deal, really wanting to lend the money – but what they needed was something concrete to lend it *for*. Nobody walked in to South America and made a sovereign loan these days, not even if they were doing it on the sly. Nobody had done that since the banks had seen all their money ending up in private Swiss bank accounts in the seventies and eighties. The way people lent money in South America nowadays was by tying it to a specific project; a bridge, a hospital, a new port; the money guaranteed to enhance the country's economic prospects and make a return. The Arabs sitting round him on the Raphael's sofas really wanted a deal, but the trouble was that Continental weren't offering them a project, but talking vaguely in terms of 'shoring up the government'. It wasn't good enough, it wasn't definite enough, Quince could see. Willing as the Arabs were, he wasn't going to get anywhere with them unless he could offer them either a concrete project, or proper collateral.

Quince rose from his chair. 'I wonder if you'd excuse me for a moment, gentlemen?' he said. 'And please help yourselves to tea.' Soren rose too, and followed him heavily out of the lounge.

Back in his room, Quince loosened the buttons of his waistcoat and Soren sat on the window seat, chewing his knuckles. The meeting had made him nervous, and the casual way Quince had left the Arabs to talk on their own to the Venezuelan ambassador had worried him even more.

'It's all right, you can go to your kennel. I'm not going to jump out of the window,' Quince said. He picked up the phone and dialled, but when he looked round again Soren was still there in the window, looking coldly at Quince. He had a flat, bald head with tufts of black hair on either side, and the smooth, oiled skin of a Levantine. The brand of aftershave he wore disgusted Quince afresh every morning, when he found the Israeli waiting for him outside the door of his suite like a stocky pit bull terrier that might tear your throat out but never wagged its tail.

Hughes answered almost at once.

'Your trained animal won't get out of my room,' Quince said, still looking at Soren. 'He may be able to jump through hoops and walk on fire, but he couldn't take a hint if you flew it past his window tied to the back of a jumbo jet.'

Soren, listening, thought Hughes must have ignored his remark. The next thing he heard was Quince's description of the meeting. 'It's there. The money's all there,' Quince concluded. 'But we have to give them something to hold on to. Throw out the lifebelts.'

Soren watched Quince listening to Hughes' instructions. Quince's face had no expression. 'It's not enough,' he said. 'You have to tie it to a project, tell them what the money's to be used for. I can't get a bloody clue from their ambassador, he's not saying anything.'

'There can be no mention of a particular project.' Quince heard the steel in Hughes' voice. 'The money can't be tied down to any one thing. Who knows what the President might want to use it for in a month's time? He's living from day to day.'

'Then if you can't give them a project, you'll have to give them some form of collateral,' Quince said, exasperated. 'They're not going to pour their money out for nothing. You asked me to find a loan, not a gift.'

'Try someone else,' the voice said.

'There is no one else. It'll be the same, whoever we ask. It's these people or nobody.'

Hughes paused at the other end of the phone, and Quince heard him conferring with someone, though the words were muffled.

'Okay. Now. Listen to me.' The American was having difficulty starting; he didn't quite know how to say what it was he was going to say. Soren, watching Quince's expressionless face from the other side of the room, could have had no idea how Hughes' words were affecting him, but behind Quince's soft, fat features, his brain was seething. Hughes' instructions were quite extraordinary. This was no ad hoc response to the present difficulties – this had been planned. They must have had this up their sleeve from the start.

When Quince and Soren returned downstairs to the lounge, it was impossible to tell from Quince's manner that any problems which remained were effectively solved. He seemed neither elated nor triumphant, but plumped himself into his old seat and ordered himself another vodka – which could hardly be taken as a sign of unusual celebration. He also enquired what he could order for the Arabs and even, in a moment of lapsed contempt for Soren, tried to buy the Israeli a drink. Then, dropping the wad of Venezuelan investment details carelessly onto the table, he sat back, took a first sip of his vodka with the expression of someone listening to the opening bars of his favourite concerto, placed it carefully back on the table and clapped his hands lightly together for attention.

'You can have your collateral in part, gentlemen,' he said. 'There is someone who is prepared to underwrite your loan. With certain conditions, I think we can sort it all out in twenty-four hours.' He then laid out for them the proposal from Continental. But all the while he was doing it, Quince's mind was only half on the details of the deal. What he was asking himself, all the time, was why a company like Continental should depart from all past practice and underwrite such a large and dubious loan themselves. By any calculation, the risk must be enormous. Correspondingly, the stakes Continental were playing for must be very high indeed.

Quince looked across the table at the Israeli and, for the first time, felt a small doubt creep into his thoughts. He began to wonder how deep this whole business really went. For a moment, the Israeli seemed no longer a figure of fun; there was something essentially and finally cruel about him. He would have to get away from the Israeli later. It wasn't safe for certain things to be outside his knowledge any more; there were certain things he would have to find out – and he would have to ditch the Israeli in order to do it.

Quince stepped out of the Raphael's side entrance and onto the wet pavements, the shimmer of the city reflecting blackly from the stone. He had given Soren the slip. The Israeli was waiting for him now in the American Bar at the front of the hotel, where Quince had said he would join him. It would be some time before Soren realised he had gone, and by then Quince would have lost himself in the tangle of streets behind the hotel, in the dark anonymity of the Parisian night. There wasn't even any need for him to hurry. The deal had been struck four hours before, and he was glad of the breathing space to come down from the high a deal always gave him. He always had it; every time, he thought it wouldn't come, and every time it did. That was what had kept him in the game. He was addicted to the high the deals gave him – the secrecy, the deceit, the powerful intoxication of his own peformance.

Although he was not in a hurry, he moved fast for a large man. He was heading for the rue St. Denis, and a small café behind it in a street which had long ago been paved in coloured stone for the benefit of tourists – an anonymous venue, far from the night activities of the rich. The wet pavements were full of couples, hugging each other to fit under a single umbrella. A Victorian glow shone from the gloom in every apartment block, and through the misted windows of bars and restaurants Quince made out waiters in black and white carrying trays high over the heads of the crowds inside. Paris didn't lock itself away in bad weather. In dark doorways the prostitutes, male and female, hung back out of the rain in their ludicrously inadequate clothing, coaxing the passers-by from the shadows. Every doorway had its occupant, it seemed, like a pigeon in its box.

Mindful of possible pursuit, Quince crossed and recrossed the road several times. He felt different about Soren now, he would no longer gain the same amusement from taunting him. The lights were brighter here, he was away from the boulevards and into the intimacy of St. Denis. Here were the bars and restaurants for the cheap tourists, where every café had its accordion music and its artful posters of the Folies Bergères. The deal was struck, Quince told himself, but it could be sabotaged at any moment – at any time before pen touched paper. He, Quince, could sabotage it. And if he didn't get the right answers this evening, that was what he intended to do.

The rain drenched him. It fell from the sky and it ran in streams from the overhanging gutters of the older houses. The rue St. Denis was a street of cowboy shops, an American Western emporium that sold boots and hats and frilled suede jackets, shop after shop. But above the gaudy sixties conversions with their neon signs, the old buildings rose up out of sight into the darkness and the rain. Quince stepped across the street and into an alley. The rain ran down the inside of his sleeves and it got into his shoes. It trickled down the back of his neck where the collar of his coat stood out. The wet streets danced behind him with the lights of the cinemas showing soft porn movies, and the restaurants with their set menus of *bouillabaisse* and *croque monsieur* and *steak frit*. It amused Quince that this was where he'd asked the ambassador to meet him. In a café at the end of this alley, over a *pichet* of disgusting red wine, Quince would ask the ambassador why. Why his government, his President to be exact, wanted a billion dollars. He would ask what was the real relationship between a billion dollars and the possession of power. And if the President really wanted his precious loan that much, then his ambassador would have to come up with the answers. Then, and then only, Quince would close the deal for them.

He turned in out of the rain, and went down some steps to a shabby bar with fake wooden beams and doorposts set in grey, pebble-dash concrete. It could have been a French bar in Carnaby Street for all its authenticity. The red-tiled floor was mottled with spilled food and wine, the waiters had stains on their jackets, and most of them couldn't even speak French. Quince wanted to take the ambassador away from familiar territory, away from the world of helicopters and limousines and breakfasts at the Carlton; he wanted the ambassador to be uncomfortable. In this world it was he, Quince, who was comfortable – this world of china jugs of cheap wine. Quince felt most at home with the fake and the cheap. He sank now onto a wooden bench and summoned a waiter, and a wave of tiredness washed over him – it might have been the walk, or the tension of the deal, or the thought of Soren left seething behind him at the hotel. But ultimately, he knew, he was tired because he lived so much on his wits. In here, he could relax, but every time he stepped into another two-hundred-dollar-a-night lobby, he had to work at it. He was aware of this vulnerability, in fact he relished overcoming it time and time again. But he knew that it was wearing him down. He was a chancer and a chancer's life was sort. Already it had gone on too long for luck alone. He wondered if he could stop after this one, pull out for good. He would have enough money, far more than enough. This one, after this one, he promised himself, he would throw in the towel. He would give up the whole damn game for good.

Outside Quince's room, Soren sat on a Louis XVI loveseat like a fist planted in a face. In his hand he held a piece of paper which hours of screwing into a tight ball had rendered unrecognisable. Before he had destroyed it, it had read 'Beware of the Dog', one more simple insult from Quince that had stirred Soren to his very depths. There was a violent look in Soren's eyes, a look of lust and murder. Soren was barely in control.

SIX

Walker's Rehabilitation

The death of Arnold Secker had few reverberations in Lyons and fewer still in London. Unbelievable as it must have been to the Rausch faithful that one of their number should choose suicide, the company covered their awkwardness by giving the press, including Walker, stories about personal problems. Secker had been suffering from stress, he'd been on tranquillisers. His marriage, it was suggested, had not been happy for a long while. The same story was told in the bars and restaurants within striking distance of Rausch headquarters where Walker politely asked to be enlightened further, and a few more embellishments were proffered over drinks or lunch if he was lucky enough to persuade anyone from the company to invest so much time in his enquiry. But it was all the same story, a family tragedy. And the family were too distressed to talk.

Walker tried to trace Secker's wife, but, it transpired, she had left the country and returned to America. There was no question of talking to her, he was told on his fourth or fifth request to the man who had first given him the news of Secker's death on the telephone. She wanted to avoid press exposure, she wanted forget, to be allowed to live in peace. As Arnold Secker had been? Walker thought.

He did track her down, however. She was living in a large condominium at the expensive end of Coconut Grove in Florida, where her neighbours were television stars, the wealthy retired and the kind of businessmen who were prepared to pay a great deal for the proximity of Miami airport and the quick flight – in both senses – to Costa Rica. 'Millions', was the reply Walker received when he enquired the price of these condominiums over the phone. It was said with distaste by someone who could apparently tell from the other side of the Atlantic that Walker was not one of those people who have millions at their disposal. And he had been unable to contact the elusive Madame Secker, the dead man's Austrian wife, at all. Rausch had looked after her impeccably, it seemed. Her failed marriage had turned into successful widowhood.

By the time London got to hear about it, the story wasn't worth even a column inch. It was reported by Walker alone, to his sceptical editor, who sat occasionally looking at his watch, constantly twiddling a pencil round and round in his fingers until finally it fell out of his hand, and glancing repeatedly through the floor-to-ceiling windows of his office, which gave a fine view of the river – or would do, when the banks of cranes and construction equipment had finished their work. It was not a very good day, the editor had told him when he'd rung through to ask for a meeting. 'I thought we'd got rid of you,' he said. And, 'How did you get hold of those documents?' in a remonstrative tone of voice, as if Walker was about to bring yet more shame on the paper. 'Luck,' Walker answered.

The editor's office was in turmoil when he arrived. He was kept waiting in a secretary's office in a low leather chair, and watched a string of people without appointments go in ahead of him. Someone from another paper, it appeared, had got hold of a story that was worrying the editor deeply, and the office was now beleaguered by advisers, public relations people, and telephone calls from every newshound in the business hoping to blow the story up into a scandal.

What had happened was that on the previous evening, about seven o'clock, the editor had been sharing a bottle of wine or two in his office with a cabinet minister. Nothing out of the ordinary in that. A little bit of commons gossip might come up, better still, cabinet gossip that would do no harm to the government and make excellent copy – it happened all the time in such informal meetings. During the meeting the following day's leader article, written earlier by the editor, had been brought in by the copy boy for final approval before it went to press. It was a piece about the government's record in education. According to the story reported in rival papers that morning, the editor, benevolent with wine and conversation, had given the minister the copy for his approval. The minister had read it once, then started to put lines through it, changing this, sharpening that, cutting whole paragraphs – while the copy boy looked on aghast. Eventually the minister had written the whole thing afresh: the leader in a national newspaper had been written by a cabinet minister! As the copy boy reported it later, the minister had then given the new copy to the editor and he had given it his approval. It was returned to the boy, and despatched for immediate setting.

` Whether the copy boy had sold the details of this little scene himself, or whether someone he'd told had passed the story on, was uncertain. But the story was out, and the editor's office on the morning that Walker came to call was crammed with damage-limitation people, legal experts and those employed to conduct the witch-hunt into the leak. Walker sat in the leather chair from eleven in the morning, through lunchtime and into the afternoon, while another piece was concocted to scotch the story for good. By the time Walker was eventually summoned at four o'clock, the editor was not in the best or most attentive of moods.

'Suicide?' he said vaguely. 'People commit suicide all the time.'

'There's something fishy about it. Why did he do it?' Walker replied. 'Of course, I'm not suggesting that a company like Rausch assassinates its own employees . . .'

'What, then?' the editor asked, with the implication that nothing else would do. But before Walker could reply, he murmured something incomprehensible and pressed the buzzer on his desk to dictate his latest thoughts on his own crisis to his secretary next door. 'What is Rausch anyway?' he asked Walker when he'd finished this aside. 'Where's Peter? Shouldn't we get Peter in?' Peter Clive was the business editor. He had worked on at least three other rags since he'd left Oxford ten years before, and now had his photo at the head of a regular column.

'It isn't really necessary,' Walker demurred.

'I think we should have him in,' the editor decided, as if gathering a few more people around him was going to banish the day's bogeymen for good. He pressed the buzzer again and asked the secretary to hunt up Peter Clive and tell him to get his arse in here.

'I think it's going to be more a foreign story,' Walker said. 'The business side of it isn't that difficult.'

'It's a story all of a sudden, is it?' the editor said testily.

Dick 'Slick' Mather was thought by many to be sitting on his editorship for just as long as it took to get his gong. He would retire Sir Richard Mather, and in ten years time the slack, unimaginative hands that had once held the tiller of a once-respected paper would be forgotten. Even on less tiresome days than this, he exuded an air of boredom that was liable to depress the youngest, most ambitious reporter. Walker had got used to it – and he'd rarely needed to see Slick at all until his fall from grace and his despatch to Geneva. But when he'd contacted the foreign editor the day before – Reilly, his old boss, mentor and friend – Reilly had said he couldn't help him: if he wanted favours, he would have to go to the editor himself. No one wanted to touch Walker it seemed. The only advantage of the editor's mood on this particular day, apparently, was that he seemed to have forgotten all about Walker's fall from grace. The trauma of the previous night's private conversation turning into front-page news had left him with only one preoccupation – how was he going to escape the opprobrium of the minister and – if it went that far, who knew? – the Prime Minister? Slick Mather hadn't worked so hard for the government to see his reward slip from his hands now, because of some tittle-tattle traitor on the paper. A traitor who would be hunted out, no matter what the cost and how long it took.

'So. A man gives you what you say are company papers,

and then commits suicide. That's about it,' Slick said repressively.

'Secret company papers,' Walker answered.

'Not secret, please not secret!' Slick pleaded. 'Confidential, stick to confidential. Or private, or something – anything – but not secret. God!' He picked up a sheet from the desk. 'Why have I been sent this? Do I have to run everything from the accounts department to the company dining-room? Liechtenstein? Was it really necessary to go to Liechtenstein?'

Walker looked at the upside-down expenses claim in the editor's hand. One of his abiding enemies on the paper was the bastard who agreed expenses. Agree them before, Harry, before you undertake a trip, a small voice reminded him. Never, not ever, afterwards.

'It was pretty well on the way here,' Walker said. 'I don't think you'll find it cost very much.'

'Why. . .?' Slick began, exasperated, and waved the claim around on the desk as if it were a fly swat. But he couldn't formulate what the question was going to be.

Walker had a history of bust-ups with the accounts people, and they knew, better than anyone, that he should have been stuck in Geneva, costing them nothing. So why had he come to London, they would ask, and why had he come via, of all places, Liechtenstein? Barnaby was the man who really had it in for him. He'd had many angry exchanges about his expenses over the years with Barnaby, the last time two years before, when it had ended in a shouting match which had to be broken up before it escalated into physical violence. The month after that fight, Walker had been in Beirut. With a photographer, he'd been kidnapped, by no one more threatening, it turned out, than the family of a taxi driver they'd hired; the taxi driver had been blown up by an Israeli missile and his family were demanding compensation. Walker remembered sweating that one out for twenty-four hours, knowing that Barnaby was responsible for coughing up and getting them both out. 'I only did it for the other guy,' he told Walker when they did get home. 'Just wait until you get lost on your own.' That had cost the paper fifteen thousand pounds, and Barnaby had never forgiven him.

Slick sat behind the desk and looked distracted. 'I don't know what it is you want,' he said with a glazed expression on his face. 'Suicide, Liechtenstein, these Rausch people. Now Caracas. God!'

'The papers show a money transfer of a very dubious nature,' Walker began. 'The Rausch shell company in Zurich, called Centurion, was . . .'

'Stop, stop, stop. God!' Slick's eyes rose to the ceiling. 'What time is it?' he said. Then he looked back at Walker. 'Pity it isn't murder. No one likes suicide. People want to be either mindlessly happy or horrified. Suicide's too close to bloody home.' He said it with meaning, as if he had been seriously contemplating it himself for some time.

'It's not a suicide story, Dick. It's a story of company fraud, perhaps on a massive scale. Why should a company like Rausch transfer twenty-three million dollars through all kinds of shady accounts to keep it a secret? They're blue-chip, they shouldn't be doing this kind of thing. These companies, Centurion, Bantura, Imronal, were set up for the sole purpose of concealing this transfer. They . . .'

'Stop, please stop. God. Wait for Peter to get here. I don't want a lot of company names flying about the office. Wait for Peter.'

Slick pressed the buzzer on the desk again. 'For God's sake, Margaret, where's bloody Peter? What's going on?' The sound of an explanation could be heard from where Walker was sitting on the other side of the large desk. The office was modern, with metal-framed, bent-tube chairs for the visitors, but the editor still had his old monster desk, reproduction-Georgian with a green leather top, and a wing chair behind it on which he rocked and twisted with both hands on the arms.

'I don't know, I don't know,' Slick complained worriedly after he'd finished on the intercom, as if he were having an entirely different conversation than the one with Walker. 'Coffee?' he said suddenly, and his hand reached for the buzzer again.

'Yes. Thank you, Dick,' Walker answered, and looked out of the window behind Slick at the cold, grey water of the Thames and the colder office blocks that were shooting up alongside it. Five hours he'd had to wait for this interview. It wasn't uncommon, he supposed. The trouble was, the paper was trimming its foreign operation all the time. Perhaps he shouldn't have said it was a foreign story. He didn't have any reason to believe that the editor was wrong; perhaps it was in Peter Clive's department, a business story, pure and simple. But somehow, in his instinctive heart of hearts, he thought it was bigger than something for the business pages. Fraud was always awkward. Should it be in the business section, or news, or what? It tended to detract from the seriousness of the business pages, that was the trouble. People didn't like to see their company being reported next door to a fraud story.

'Margaret, coffee. Thank you.'

Slick released the buzzer again, reluctantly it seemed. 'Sure it wasn't murder?' he said.

'I wish it was,' Walker answered. Slick nodded disappointedly. 'The point is,' Walker continued. 'Why did he do it at all? When I saw him, he was scared, very sacred of being found out. Suppose he was found out? He might have killed himself out of fear of prosecution, shame for himself and his family, desperation . . . But who knows, if he'd thought about it, he might have decided to face the music. I don't think he would have simply killed himself. But then, what if Rausch decided to make things difficult for him? They could have made things very nasty indeed. Perhaps that's what pushed him. Perhaps he was pushed into suicide.'

'Very Roman,' Slick said. 'What do you think they did? Put him in a room and gave him a loaded gun?'

'He gassed himself.'

'All right, all right. So much for conjecture. What are the facts?'

'The papers themselves.'

'Where's bloody Peter?' Slick looked as if he was going to bang the buzzer again, but thought better of it. 'How is

Geneva anyway?' he asked. 'Went through it with the family before Christmas on the way to Verbier. Abortive bloody skiing holiday. Never, but never, take your kids on a skiing holiday when there's no snow. There's even less to do than there is at home. Luckily I managed to fly back early for a summit meeting. Otherwise I think I would have died of children's voices.'

Walker nodded. Thanks for saying hello, he thought.

'Got yourself a cushy little number, I should have thought,' Slick said. 'What on earth do you want to do, stirring it all up again?' So he does remember, Walker thought.

'How much are we paying you, anyway?'

There was a noise at the door and Peter Clive entered with a few files under one arm and a nod at Walker. They had never worked together, Walker had already gone to Geneva by the time Clive joined the paper, but Walker was sure that Clive would have all the background on him. He'd been front-page news, after all; just on the wrong side of the copy for once.

'Coffee, Peter?' Slick pressed the buzzer and ordered more. Clive took another low seat on a sofa at the far end of the room. 'The brains is here,' Slick said. 'Harry has something he thinks is interesting. What do you know about a company called Rausch, Peter?'

'Blue-chip. Swiss-based multi-national,' Clive sighed. 'Fingers in a lot of pies. One of the giants. They have interests all over the world. A nice spread, I'd say. Upright, powerful, good connections here and in the States.' He looked at Walker without interest. 'I suppose you'll find them up to everything these people are usually up to, but they won't be into anything out-of-the-ordinary shady. Sure of that,' he said aggressively. He paused and tipped his head to the ceiling as if to pluck a thought. 'There have been rumours. Recently,' he said, grappling with his memory. 'Rumours about the main competition. Another giant by the name of Continental USA. The two of them have always operated in South and Central America, but in the past twenty-odd years the world has got a lot smaller, and they've come up against

65

each other on a number of occasions. Take-over talk, so it's no doubt all nonsense. Rausch try not to attract too much attention, in fact. Keep a low profile.'

'Heard anything about one of their men killing himself?' Slick asked.

'No.' Clive looked wanly at Walker. 'Some people do commit suicide.'

'Harry has what are apparently stolen documents,' Slick said sceptically. 'Go on. Why don't you just explain.'

Walker placed copies of the papers on the desk in case either of them wanted to follow what he was saying, but they stayed, as he'd expected, where he put them. Clive watched Walker with the expression of someone who's about to be given one more conspiracy theory he doesn't believe.

'These are a series of money transfers,' Walker explained. 'All outside the normal run of their remit, I believe. I was given them by an employee of Rausch three days before he killed himself.'

'You're sure he killed himself,' Clive said with a trace of sarcasm. 'You don't want to pin a murder on them?'

'No. The documents speak for themselves, I think. There was a gap in the transactions I received, but since then I may have filled in the gap and it looks odd.'

'All right, all right, we've got twenty minutes,' Slick said. 'Can we just have what you've got.' He looked anxiously at his watch. 'Liechtenstein,' he said, savouring the word. 'Harry's been to Liechtenstein.' It could have been the moon, the way he said it.

'They're a record of bank transfers that start in Zurich and finish, apparently, in Caracas, Venezuela,' Walker said. 'Rausch have plenty of subsidiaries around the world.' He consulted some notes. 'About three hundred and seventy-five at the last count. But the money concerned didn't go through any of them.'

Clive shrugged.

'They set up an initial company in Zurich with the Brunner Bank. Know them?'

'No,' Clive said solidly.

Good, Walker thought. It suited him fine if he could start off with something the supercilious know-all didn't actually know.

'Pokey little organisation, are they?' Slick said.

'Not really. They have only three offices. One in Zurich, one in Geneva, the other in Caracas. Brunner himself is Venezuelan but he also has Swiss nationality. As far as I can make out, Rausch have never done business with them before. They may have done in Venezuela, I have to find that out. The Rausch subsidiaries in Central America all do business with different banks, so they may well have business there under subsidiary names. But Brunner aren't that small. The bank controls a lot of oil money in Venezuela. They've grown to a considerable size in the past decade.'

The telephone rang. Slick picked it up with a complaint. 'All right, put him through, put him through,' he said. He spoke for three minutes, then put the phone down without a comment. Why can't he just hold his calls for a few minutes? Walker thought. If he's only got twenty minutes, why can't he just concentrate on one thing at a time? Slick looked out of the window, apparently bored already. 'Go on,' he said, with some effort.

Walker picked up the first of the documents. 'The first of the documents in order of time is a letter of instruction,' he said. 'It's on Rausch letterhead from one of the top men in the finance department. Board member, very high up indeed. It instructs Brunner in Zurich to open an account in the name of Centurion SA.' He pushed the document closer to Slick but was rewarded with a wave of the hand.

'All right, all right, we believe you,' he said.

The door to the office opened and Margaret entered with a tray of coffee and biscuits. 'Over here, over here,' Slick said, and patted a pile of papers on his desk. He seemed to relax more when he had a cup of coffee cradled carefully in his hands.

'The letter instructs Brunner to open the Centurion

67

account,' Walker continued. 'Rausch then paid twenty-three million dollars into it.'

'You following, Peter?' Slick asked.

Clive nodded.

'Anything odd about it?'

'Nothing necessarily,' Clive said, blandly confident.

'Right,' Slick said, and looked at his watch again.

'Now,' Walker said. 'This account was a numbered account – the first mildly unusual thing about it, if you don't count setting up a mystery company by a blue-chip multi-national unusual,' he added. 'But even numbered accounts have to have a reference name in Switzerland. They have to have some form of indentification in order for the bank to have someone they can contact. This reference name is only known to the manager of the bank, in this case Brunner himself as it happens, and his deputy. Security demands this confidentiality. The chances are – and we don't know this because we don't know the reference name, of course – that the reference name is not the same as the name of the finance director who wrote the letter. That's the way these things work. That's the point of them.'

The telephone rang again, and there was another pause while Slick accepted the call and issued instructions about the story from the night before. He looked as if he was taking in very little of what Walker was saying.

'The letter from Rausch was addressed to Herr Brunner himself,' Walker said. 'Not just a minion, but the owner himself. Centurion SA has an accent over the O. It's the Spanish spelling.'

'Know your dago?' Slick asked Clive, but the business editor didn't reply.

'This is the bank statement recording the transfer of the twenty-three million,' Walker said, ignoring the interruption. 'The next letter from Arnold Secker's little batch is an instruction from the fledgling Centurion SA, with the signature of an untraceable party at the foot of it. Already Rausch are distancing themselves from the transaction; it's written on a letterhead of Centurion's own.' Walker waved his copy of the letter. There was a picture of a Roman centurion at the top right-hand corner, and an immodest, sweeping company heading right across the top of the page.

'This letter, written by the putative director of Centurion, is a further instruction to transfer the same amount, twenty-three million dollars, to an anstaldt in Liechtenstein.'

'An what?' Slick said.

'An anstaldt is a Liechtenstein company based in the capital, Vaduz. The idea is that the anstaldt controls the Swiss company, in this case Centurion, through a Liechtenstein attorney. The attorney controls the company in his name, so that a further distance is placed between the original transaction and the end transaction. The contact name that Brunner and his deputy have in Switzerland is the name of a Liechtenstein attorney.'

'So off it all goes to Liechtenstein, right. You following this, Peter?'

'The money doesn't actually leave the Brunner bank in Zurich,' Walker said. 'No actual money is kept in Liechtenstein at all. There are hardly any banks, in fact. What there are are miles of filing systems in offices down the main street of Vaduz. Filing systems that document similar transactions in order to hide the identities of the people who really control the money that is banked in Switzerland. Vaduz has the highest concentration of attorneys in the world,' he added, in order to try to put a spark into what Slick was obviously already considering a waste of time.

'So we disappear with Rausch's twenty-three million down this hole in Liechtenstein,' Slick summed up for his own benefit. 'Legal or illegal?'

'Perfectly legal,' Clive said. 'There are plenty of people who just don't want others to know what they're doing with their money. It doesn't mean they're doing something illegal, necessarily.'

'It's unusual, perhaps unprecedented, for a company like Rausch to act in this way,' Walker said.

'But legal,' Slick rammed home the point.

'Oh yes. Perfectly possible that there's nothing illegal. The point is, why?'

'Is that all?'

Walker pulled two more sheets from the bunch in his hand. 'There's a gap at this point,' he said. 'The point about the anstaldts is that they facilitate the transfer of money around the world while attracting no attention. They're a second line of defence, if you like, after the confidentiality of a numbered account. A lawyer's secret box, with the keys all but thrown away. You can stack one anstaldt inside another like a set of Russian dolls, each time removing the ownership of the money one step further from the enquiring eye. One anstaldt is put under control of another anstaldt with a different attorney's name. That one is owned by another, with another attorney, and so on. You can go a long way. Secker's papers at this point don't say what happened in Liechtenstein. The other papers concern a company by the name of Bantura. Panama-based, never heard of before or since this transaction.'

Walker considered the spectacular inanity of the titles people picked for shell companies. How did they do it? Did companies employ special people to come up with them? 'First, Rausch instructed Brunner to close the Centurion account completely. From now on, the money was travelling under a different name, Bantura. As far as Centurion was concerned, their trading effectiveness ceased forthwith. They disappear. The shelf life of Centurion was a matter of days.'

For one hectic moment, Walker imagined the piles of unused Centurion writing paper lying in some dusty filing cabinet for ever, never to be required, its soldier logo fading with the years. You didn't get a print-run of one sheet. The waste of paper was peripheral, however, to the thrust of Rausch's business.

'The trouble is,' he continued, 'we have no record of this new company Bantura until the money surfaces in Panama City. Twenty-three million dollars. There's a break in the chain. Secker handed me the other documents, clearly because it was his belief, or positive knowledge, that the twenty-three million appearing in Bantura's account in Panama City is the same twenty-three million that left Zurich.'

'Belief?' Slick said sceptically. Clive was fidgeting with something on the cuff of his jacket.

'So far, a belief. Until I went to Liechtenstein,' Walker said.

'Ah yes, Liechtenstein,' Slick said, picking up the expenses claim again. 'Seventy quid a night for a hotel's pretty steep, isn't it?'

'When did you last go to Liechtenstein?' Walker asked. Slick shrugged.

'They don't have any decent skiing, I suppose?' he said.

Walker felt the limited concentration in the room begin to slip again. 'Bantura transferred the twenty-three million again,' he said, trying to get back on the tracks. 'It went from Panama City to the Brunner Bank in Caracas under the name of Imronal, another faceless company that was set up just for the purpose of receiving the money. If Centurion's shelf life was butterfly-length, Bantura fared only slightly better. It was four days at most before it received another letter from an attorney in Liechtenstein instructing it to cease to exist.'

'All very dramatic,' Slick said. 'But there's no evidence, either, that the twenty-three million is the same twenty-three million, or that anything illegal is taking place. Perhaps the chairman of Rausch has a very expensive mistress in Caracas,' he said sarcastically. 'Perhaps he plays the horses. Perhaps he's building a palace in the Caribbean.' He paused for a moment, thinking that maybe there was a story after all. This was how people became editors, Walker thought. They talked themselves into a story and then tried to make it come true.

'The reason I went to Liechtenstein,' he said, 'was to make the connection. I agree, if we can't prove that the money in Caracas is the same money that left Zurich, then we don't have much of a case.'

'So what was there in Liechtenstein worth seventy quid a night?' Slick asked.

71

'I have a source there,' Walker said. 'Old journalist, does the occasional piece for financial journals, that sort of thing. Now he's semi-retired but he runs a couple of investment trusts out of Vaduz on the side. You don't see him anywhere except Vaduz and the Cayman Islands these days, but he's in very thick with the way things work out there. I gave him the name Bantura and asked him to run it around, see what he could find.' This was the moment when Walker needed to score. If Slick didn't go for this, he'd never get the go-ahead to follow the story. Clive was sprawled on the low sofa now, his legs splayed apart and one shoulder sunk sideways into a cushion. He yawned.

'Who's that?' Clive asked.

'The source? You wouldn't know him,' Walker said.

'That's right,' Slick grinned. 'We're a real family. Share everything.'

Walker ignored the interruption. 'He put Bantura through a computer, asked around, broke into a system, I don't know. But he came up with this.' He threw a sheaf of papers onto the desk, which was ignored like the previous set. 'They show a connection between Bantura and Centurion. Liechtenstein, Panama City, Caracas, all joined up. But the really interesting thing about it is how the connection is made. My source had to make a trace through sixty-five anstaldts before he could make the link. Sixty-five! What is a blue-chip company like Rausch doing hiding a transaction inside sixty-five shells? It has to be illegal. Has to be.'

Walker sat back in his chair and a silence descended on the room. Outside on the river, a slow grinding noise croaked across the grey water as a floating crane hauled tons of rusty-looking steel girders into the sky. Men in hard hats scurried along the quay and a police launch churned up the water as it headed for the centre of town. They were building a lot of offices, Walker thought. Who were they all for? A street of Victorian houses had been cut off at the end like half a French loaf, and a solitary pub, denuded of its neighbours by demolition, struggled on like the last survivor at Blood River. Inside the office the telephone rang.

'Put him through, put him through,' Slick demanded with a whine. 'Yes, sir,' he said, with a little more authority in his voice. 'We're doing everything we can. Whoever made this thing up is going to be rooted right out, I promise you. Yes, sir, yes indeed.' He put the phone down without getting the chance to say goodbye. 'Jesus God! Now the bloody boss is breathing down my neck as well.'

So he'd told the proprietor that the story in the rival rag was all an invention, Walker thought. He didn't really have much choice if he wanted to hang on. The trouble for old Slick was, the boss was probably on first name terms with the minister. No wonder he looked in a blind sweat.

'Right, right, where were we? God! Peter say something!'

'If they're genuine,' Clive stressed, 'Walker's got his hands on a set of papers stolen from a company, which constitutes a criminal offence,' he said.

Anyone would think he was the bloody law correspondent, Walker thought.

'Harry, what are you bloody doing?' Slick exploded with an ineffective bang.

'We don't know they're stolen,' Walker said disingenuously. 'In any case, though the theft of company documents is a criminal offence in Swiss law, over here we're fine.'

'As I say, if they're genuine,' Clive replied smoothly, and clutched his hands together like an old aunt.

That's right, have it both ways, Walker thought. If they're genuine, we're running too great a risk; if they're not genuine, then . . . well, no story.

'Well? How do we know they're genuine?' Slick demanded, and looked at his watch, another sweat breaking out on his forehead. Why doesn't he just smoke forty cigarettes a day? Walker thought. Calm him down, do him good.

'First of all we have the signature of the finance director of Rausch,' Walker said. 'The money has to start somewhere, and it starts with him. We know it's his signature, we can check.'

'Could be forged,' Slick said.

'Get a handwriting expert in, then. It's not that much of a problem. The second thing is – and we shouldn't underestimate this – I met Secker. I saw him and spoke to him. He was genuinely frightened – terrified. Three days later he was dead, gassed. A suicide. How many coincidences can we live with?'

It was the biggest weakness in the argument, this. When you dealt with the desk men, they didn't want to hear about your impressions of real people, real events, they wanted the facts and figures. The desk men could not deal with the concept of human frailty, psychological explanations were anathema.

'Yes, yes, yes,' Slick complained. 'Sure, the man was depressed. Who knows what he was depressed about? Eh? For all we know, his marriage was on the rocks. Come on, Harry, we have to do better than this. If Peter says there's a real possibility these papers aren't genuine, we have to have some proof. Come on, come on, you know all this, Harry.' Slick looked mournfully at Walker and, through Walker, at the world.

'All right. I think there's enough here to warrant further investigation, but if we want proof, fair enough,' Walker said.

At this Slick looked vaguely surprised. He didn't really want to follow the story, Walker thought, and he was looking for every reason not to. This wasn't just an editor being thorough, leaving no stone unturned, this was a genuine back-off. Slick was feeling himself enough on the ropes today as it was; he didn't want to agree to something else that would wake him up in the middle of the night.

'If we want proof,' said Walker, 'all we have to do is go to Caracas and find out if there's twenty-three million dollars in an account by the name of Imronal at the Brunner Bank there.'

'Caracas, God!' Slick said, and clung onto his mouth with the palm of his hand as if he was going to be sick. 'Stolen papers, Caracas, Liechtenstein, God!' He picked up the expenses claim again and looked at it gloomily. 'Why did you have to steal the bloody things, Harry? What on earth got into you? We're trying to run a bloody newspaper here, not a parole office.'

The editor's grasp of relative values, never secure in the best of circumstances, Walker thought, seemed to have slipped badly in the light of his own misdemeanours. It was never possible to feel sorry for Slick, he realised. Which was sad, because Slick always seemed like a man who desperately needed people to feel sorry for him. Too bloody camp to be a martyr, Walker thought, he just needs to hide in the shade of a large maternal pullover.

'Right, right, what are we to do?' Slick said, recovering slightly. 'Peter?'

Clive shrugged, and Slick seized the initiative before the business editor could speak. 'It isn't one for the business pages,' Slick announced with regained authority, and Clive looked up out of the depths of the sofa with a mixture of surprise and annoyance. 'No need for you here any longer, Peter,' Slick continued. 'We'll call if we need you. Back to the drudge, back to the drudge.'

Clive hauled himself out of the cavernous cushions, straightened himself out and left the room, with more than a little dagger in the look he gave Walker on the way out.

'Nor, in my opinion, is it a foreign story,' Slick was saying. Walker, thrilled at the sudden interest registered by the editor, was plunged back into doubt. What kind of a story was it, for God's sake? Bingo?

'We want a team on it,' Slick announced, eyes agleam. 'We want an investigative team on it. We want a front page. And if it's not going to be a front page, we want to find out as soon as possible so we can get out quick and cut our losses.' He looked up triumphantly at Walker as if he'd just scored the winning goal in the World Cup Final.

'A team?' Walker said finally. 'Our teams have hardly ever been out of Great Britain, Dick! They're great, but they've probably never been further than Gibraltar. They wouldn't know where to begin, for God's sake. I know the city. I've been there a dozen times. Know who to talk to, know where everything is, know how the place works. It's a completely different thing out there. Ask Tom.' Tom Reilly was the foreign editor. 'It's one thing getting an off-the-record quote from a copper in Macclesfield, it's completely different screwing down a bent army officer in South America to get at the dirt. Believe me. If you want the story, send me out alone. As soon as I've found something and can use the boys here, send them on after.' Slick rubbed his chin and looked suspicious. 'It's going to cost you twice, three times as much to send a team out now. And what if there's nothing there at all? A waste.'

Slick picked up the expenses claim again and squinted at it. 'God!' he said.

'Let me prepare he ground, find out a bit more. Then you can send the lot of them out there. You can send the bloody sports section for all I care.'

Slick paused and thought and wheezed slowly through the hand clenched over his mouth. 'How are you going to do it?' he barked suddenly.

'Do what?'

'How are you going to find out about this, this Imronal thing?'

'Come on, Dick.'

'You know what I'm saying. I don't want to receive a call from the Venezuelan ambassador saying I'm off the list for the garden party. You fouled up once, Harry. I'm going to give you a chance, and that's all. I want a front page story, not a bloody summons.'

'Okay, okay, Dick. I don't know how I'm going to do it right now.'

'You'll have to see Tom. Sort out the travel, money. God! Have you got your vaccinations?'

'I'll sort it out.'

'I'm going to call Tom, tell him to give you what you want.

Within reason. Get your vaccinations. There's an outbreak of dengue fever out there at the moment.'

Sometimes, Walker thought, Slick could really surprise you.

'Country's going to the dogs apparently. They've been having food riots or something; the President's on the ropes, the army's waiting on the sidelines. Could be just the place to send you, in fact. It could do with one more stir of the pot. Who's our man out there?'

'We have a stringer in Buenos Aires.'

'Need him?'

'Her. No, not yet.'

'Right, right. Now get out and don't come back. I'm going to tell Tom to put you on some other stuff while you're out there. You're not to have a minute's spare time, okay? You're doing stories on oil exploration, rainforests, Indians, you'll do a piece on the President's bloody bedroom habits if necessary. Justify your existence, that's all. God!'

Walker got up to go. 'Thanks, Dick.'

'Just go. Please just go before I change my mind.'

Walker picked up the expenses claim. 'Sign on the dotted line, will you, Dick?'

'Jesus God! God!' Slick signed on the dotted line.

Clutching the expenses claim, Walker strolled out of the office and down onto the broad, open-plan floors of the paper's workrooms, the dark-tinted windows shielding the inmates from a summer sun that was still months away. He had wings. He had signatures, he had money, he had a blessing of sorts – he had wings. No matter how many times a fireman got sent abroad, the thrill was never gone. Not, he thought, until life's thrill bowed out, at any rate. He was away, following a speck on another continent, a bank statement, a letter, a suicide in strange circumstances. Poor bloody Arnold Secker. For Walker, it was Arnold Secker who had convinced him of the value of the story – but you had to have seen Arnold Secker to be able to understand that.

The desk men never got to see a source any longer. They

hadn't for years. For years they hadn't had the thrill of a real live contact, a man shaking and sweating on a seat in a bar in a foreign city who showed his terror in his every gesture, who wore the seriousness of what he had to say on his sleeve. You had to get the smell of a story sometimes, and the smell of a story was never contained in a document, in the 'evidence'. It was there in the sweating fear of a man who had broken himself to tell it, to hold a light for someone else to take up and run with. The smell of a story was a conversation, an exchange, a death. It was a human smell.

Walker strolled on down the corridors between desks, offering the occasional nod to a secretary, a word to a colleague, and having a long chat with an old mate who was really excited to see him. There were a lot of new faces. It wasn't like the old days. You didn't work for a paper any longer, or an individual, you worked for a pay cheque, and the leisure time it would buy you; and worked to pay the mortgage. Not all of them were like that, of course, but there were more of them like that all the time. You only had to look around you.

He reached the door of Barnaby's office. The accounts people were shut away from the journalists: difficult to say who it was who didn't want to see whom. But it wasn't hard to hazard a guess at Barnaby's feelings when he said, 'Come in', and Walker saw the sour expression of deep unwelcome written in indelible writing across the hard-pinched face. He was crouched over the desk, expensive pen in hand, his right knee hammering up and down as if he was driven on a battery.

'What do you want?' Barnaby said rudely.

'Cash, cheque, Christmas bonus, life annuity, danger money, whatever's going,' Walker replied.

Barnaby looked back down at the pad on which the expensive pen was performing some task. He didn't reply. There was an apple on the desk; Walker remembered that Barnaby always brought an apple in for his tea. He picked it up and examined it. 'Put my fucking apple down,' Barnaby said gratingly, but didn't look up.

'Thought we might do a deal between the apple and three nights at the Palace Hotel, Liechtenstein,' Walker said, and continued to fondle the apple.

'Put the apple down,' Barnaby said, keeping himself barely under control.

Walker picked up a pin from the desk and impaled the signed expenses sheet to the apple, and placed it carefully in front of Barnaby. 'Good to be back,' he said. 'Tom'll be in for my tickets, money, company credit card, later.' Barnaby had flushed a deep red under his hair. Walker couldn't see his face because it was still bent to the desk.

'You'll get any tickets you need in Travel,' Barnaby said in a strangled voice. 'Goodbye.'

'They paying you enough?' Walker asked in mock sympathy. But Barnaby didn't reply, and he turned out of the office and left.

He found Tom Reilly by the Foreign Desk, worrying about a story that was supposed to have come in from Rumania. Reilly was a fattish man who wore a big suit which didn't seem to have a clear shape to it. His shoes were grubby and looked as though they hadn't seen a polish in years. Walker had always thought of him as the kind of man who forgot to wash. He was always in a rush, always fretting over something, but he was generous, as Walker had cause to know. If he'd been non-committal the day before, now, with the editor's approval, he was delighted that Walker was signed up again. Already he was talking in a steady stream about his visit to South America three months before, telling Walker what to look out for, showing him a copy of the piece he'd done in Venezuela last time out, giving him contacts, phone numbers. To Reilly, the paper meant a great deal. He'd worked on it for over twenty-five years.

'Glad you're back, Harry,' he said, and gave an honest handshake.

Armed with more signed letters from Reilly, Walker stepped into Travel on the floor below and asked for a ticket to Caracas. 'When?' they asked him, and he hadn't thought

79

when. What would he do in London? Ring the kids. Were they on holiday? He wasn't sure when their holidays began and ended. A night would sort it out. They were living in a house on the outskirts of London which he'd given his ex-wife, and which, as far as he could remember, had now been turned into a kind of commune that included her brother and sister and their children as well. It was somewhere out near Epping, he thought, but he'd never been to see it. Whenever he was due to see the kids, they'd always been delivered up to him in London as if he might contaminate the place. Hannah must be thirteen now, he thought with a pang of guilt. He couldn't accurately remember either of their birthdays.

'If you can get me on a flight tomorrow,' he said. 'Or as soon as you can after that.'

He walked out into the grey winter afternoon. In the old days, you would just go across the road if you had a few hours to kill in the afternoon, to the pub where the setters and printers and a few of the older journalists congregated for a drink and a flutter on the dogs until closing time. Walker had been out of the country for a year, and in that time the paper had moved its offices away from the Street and down here to Docklands. It wasn't possible to cross the road to a pub because there wasn't a pub and there wasn't a road. Perhaps there had been method in the newspapers' move: as soon as the licensing laws were relaxed, they had exiled themselves to a moonscape with no watering-hole. He gazed back at the building, a brand new edifice, not bad to look at really. Plenty of columns, plenty of high windows, it reminded him of an elegant Victorian waterworks. It stood in the midst of the building rubble of a hundred other office blocks, like some recently excavated artefact on a site in the desert. He should have ordered a taxi from inside, he suddenly realised. There were none going past the building, there was no traffic, no road, just the overground line that wound its way on concrete stilts through the rubble and across the river to Tower Hill.

At Tower Hill he picked up a taxi easily. After a year away,

London was alien. He'd never been away from it for anything like this length of time, not even when he'd been the Washington correspondent for eighteen months. Even then, he'd returned at least once every three months. He realized with a slight chill that there was no one he wanted to drop in on and see. How can you drop in on someone after a year when you're leaving again the following day? He'd have to come back and spend time in London, see the kids. He stopped the taxi at a newsagent and bought a card and some stamps, just in case his suspicion about Hannah's birthday was correct. Then he walked the mile and a half up the grey streets, and turned right towards Dalston and St. Peter's Street, where the hastily-bought and hastily-furnished flat he'd purchased temporarily eight years before but had never got around to selling or improving, was waiting for him.

The flat was damp, deserted three months before when the girl he'd rented it to, a friend of a friend, had terminated the agreement and gone to Cambodia to work for an aid agency, Walker couldn't remember which one. He wandered around the place and re-learned how to operate the heating. Outside a slow sleet had begun to fall and sting the window panes. The fridge door was open and the fridge was defrosted; the bed was bare, the sheets lying damply in an airing cupboard; and the cupboards contained a half-jar of decaffeinated coffee and an oxo cube. In the lounge he switched on the television without result only to discover half an hour later, from a letter buried in a knee deep pile, that he was being prosecuted for not having a licence; also, that the telephone had been cut off. A dead plant drooped over the television screen. There were a bowl of mouldy muts and a few half-empty bottles of Scotch which had lain around the house and been collected neatly together by the tenant but not drunk. The tufted fawn carpet, which still shed its fur, led him up the stairs to his study and bathroom. In the study, a word processor was buried under sheafs of paper that didn't seem to have anything written on them, and there were boxes overflowing with computer paper, whole filing systems he couldn't remember the purpose of, and a cardboard box of tax returns, invoices, blank company receipts for him to fill in, making up for all the invoices he'd forgotten to collect – and letters from his accountant. The knee-deep pile of letters he'd brought up from downstairs joined the boxful.

Walker picked up the phone and cursed the dead response. He put on his coat again, and walked out onto the street and tried to remember where the nearest phone-box was. He walked a few hundred yards and saw one down a street to the right. Inside, in the stifling cold of London which seemed colder than Geneva, he dialled the Epping number, but there was no reply. Quite often he went through her other sister. He rang her number in Hackney and got her voice immediately. He'd always got on well with her, and she seemed no less pleased than usual to hear him now.

'I'm trying to get hold of the kids,' he explained. 'I'm just here for a night. The phone's cut off and I haven't anywhere for anyone to leave a message. Can you act as our honest broker as usual? Sorry to ask you.'

She asked him round, but something told him that he didn't want an evening with Sam and her husband, not tonight. He thought it would be too quiet, it would just depress him.

'I wish I could help, Harry,' she said, 'but they're all away in Ireland.'

'Ireland! What on earth have they gone there for?' To Harry, Ireland meant nights staying at the Europa Hotel in Belfast, after an explosion or a riot or an asassination.

'They've all gone,' Sam was saying. 'All eight of them, including Hannah and Beth. They're staying in a small hotel on the west coast without a phone. You could say the two of you have never been further apart.'

He knew she could hear the disappointment in his voice, and she tried to encourage him round for dinner, saying she'd invite a couple who were acquaintances he vaguely remembered, but this only decided him definitely not to go.

'When's Hannah's birthday?' he asked.

'The next one or the last one?'

'Oh God, I'm that far out, am I?'

'Only three months,' she answered.

They exchanged their love, and he promised to call her when he got back.

'Where are you going?'

'Venezuela,' he said.

'So you've finally got off the hook,' she said, with a smile in her voice, and they hung up with a promise to say more 'anon', as she always put it.

Outside the roads dripped with melted sleet and glistened in the orange street-light. Walker retraced his steps to the main road and turned in the direction of the flat, but then stopped himself. It was seven o'clock. He had the choice of staying in a damp, warm flat on his own with a half-jar of coffee and an oxo cube, or of heading into the West End.

It took him twenty minutes to find a taxi, and he was sitting in a bar in Soho fifteen minutes after that. The soft rumble of bar talk filled the room, the hooded lights cast a warm glow across the chairs and tables. Already three old friends had joined him briefly, and one looked set for the duration of the evening: 'Whatever you want, it's yours, Harry.' Then another friend arrived.

Walker felt a purpose enter his life for the first time in a year. It wouldn't last, and the whole story might turn out to be moonshine, but he was happy nevertheless. Tonight, he decided, he would stay in a hotel. He was back on the road.

SEVEN

The Burning of Jimenez

It had taken Walker three days to get out to Caracas. Direct flights were fully booked – and flights out of the city were double-booked. Anyone who didn't like the whiff of trouble was quietly packing and leaving. Walker had to go via Lisbon and change planes, which had added a whole day, but now, on the morning of the twelfth day since he had left London, he sat in a hired fawn Chevette on the shady side of a street which quivered with the sounds of hopelessness coming from a dozen radios. '*Corazon, corazon!*' mourned an alto voice with ear-splitting tremulousness. It seemed to stamp tragedy on the day before it had started, and it was a bit much for seven in the morning, Walker thought. The metal shutters had come off the local shops and bars half an hour before, when the sun broke through the mountains to the east of Caracas, and the streets were already full of people travelling to work. At the far end of the street where he sat, Walker watched the crowds of secretaries and office staff pouring out of the Bellas Artes underground station on their way to the business district. The hundreds of unlicensed buses, spilling over with people from the roof and doors, crawled up the six-lane boulevard, coughing smoke and rending the air with a cacophony of horns and wailers. It was only if you listened to its doom-laden songs that Caracas seemed like a city on the slide.

Walker looked up once more at the fifteenth-floor window of the flat in the block across the street. From down here he could see very little, just the bullet-scored walls and broken windows two floors below where three days ago an armed gang had taken final refuge from the police – who had destroyed them all in a hail of bullets, along with two members of the family the gang had taken hostage. A chance occurrence, but one that would certainly have softened up Luis Jimenez and his family two floors above, Walker decided. He needed all the help he could get if he was going to persuade Luis Jimenez to talk.

He crunched the styrofoam coffee cup in his hand and threw it onto the floor of the car with half a dozen others. Jimenez would be emerging from the bottom of the block any time now. He had spent more than a week watching Jimenez and another bank clerk, until he had decided that Jimenez was the one. Twenty-five years old and living in a two-room flat on the fifteenth floor of the Gomez Tower with a wife and four children, Jimenez was the best Walker could do. He owned a bashed-up American car that must have been fifteen years old and didn't work any more, and he didn't have the money to have it mended. On Saturdays, instead of driving the family the twenty miles down the mountain to the beach, he took them by bus, an hour there, two hours coming back in the crawl of Caracas' weekenders. On beach day, he played with his kids in a piece of polluted surf with a couple of hundred thousand other Caraquenos. The other six days a week, he worked; at the bank from Monday to Friday, and on Sundays as a security guard at a set of expensive apartments in the Country Club. Luis Jimenez was a lucky man. He had four kids and a wife, and two weeks after the local currency had slid from four to forty to the dollar, he not only had his job still, he had also managed to find a second one. Soon, if he was even luckier, he'd be able to find a job to fill his Saturdays, and then maybe the family wouldn't have to move out of their pokey flat and in with his mother-in-law. Someone like Luis Jimenez could go on for quite a while without cracking, Walker thought, and it worried him. He needed Jimenez badly, but how much was the bank clerk going to need him?

There was one point in his favour, however – the one point, in fact, that had finally decided Walker that Jimenez was the right one to burn. His eldest son, aged six-and-a-half, had cerebral palsy which kept his legs in makeshift calipers. Walker had watched the previous Saturday as Jimenez unfastened his boy from the crude home-made supports down on the beach and carried him into the surf. Jimenez had played with the child for nearly two hours before he wanted to come out. How much did a father have to love his son, Walker wondered, before he was prepared to cheat for him? How much could Jimenez stand before he cracked? If he worked twenty-four hours a day for seven days a week, he could still never afford treatment for his son, not in a country where the currency had just devalued tenfold.

Walker looked down the street to where the underground entrance still seethed and the traffic fumes turned the blue sky to brown. The government had concealed the worst of the trouble so far. Petrol here was still the cheapest in the world, and public transport was massively subsidised. But the spark of discontent had exploded in the bus station a month ago, when they put an extra penny on fares, and had led to riots in which five people had been killed. How much further could the people be squeezed? When Walker looked back, he saw Luis Jimenez framed for a moment in the doorway of the tower block, before he stepped down into the street.

Jimenez was a slight, short man, very thin in a Latin way, his angular face sunk behind its cheekbones and a thin aquiline nose hooked over beneath two jet-black eyes. He probably weighed no more than eight stone, Walker reckoned. With his sallow skin and his black hair greying at the temples, he looked more like forty than twenty-five. As he stepped down onto the pavement, he walked past two street traders selling cheap Indian artefacts, bead necklaces and round polished coconuts with Indian scenes painted on them. There were few people to buy them, and no one stopped. Another man had a supermarket trolley filled with green oranges brought up that morning from the country and selling at a few pennies a dozen.

Walker watched Jimenez stop to exchange a few notes for a copy of *La Prensa*. Since the weekend, these small banknotes had flooded the capital, replacing the old coins which had become so worthless that they were being melted down for the nickel. It hadn't been possible to get change in Caracas for weeks, and shopkeepers had resorted to a system of barter, compensating for the lack of change by adding something to the shopping list. Jimenez folded the paper and walked the few paces to the corner, as he always did, and turned into a *fuente de soda*, a bar open to the street on all sides which sold thirty different types of juice and a cheap breakfast. Maybe, no matter how much Luis Jimenez loved his kids, Walker thought, he couldn't face getting up in the morning and eating with all of them in a room they'd all just slept in. He watched the bank clerk sit down in a swivel seat at the bar and order the usual juice – tamarind, Walker had discovered – and a cup of coffee, while he opened up the papers and looked at the day's news.

Walker stepped out of the car. The heat, even at seven in the morning, even in the shade, was savage. He locked the door and crossed the street, side-stepping the near-stationary vehicles until he reached the other side. He stopped at the same kiosk Jimenez had stopped at and brought himself a paper, the same paper, walked the few paces up the street into the *fuente de soda* and slid onto the small round seat at the stainless-steel counter next to the Venezuelan. He'd reached first base. Here was the man who could help him, a small cog, perhaps, in the big wheel that was Rausch and Brunner, but a man who had a disproportionate role to play. The papers that Arnold Secker had left behind on the bar-room table in Geneva sixteen days before had got him this far, and the small clerk beside him with a host of troubles of his own was about to be handed one more – the chance to betray his job and his employer, Brunner.

Walker had spent some time checking the background of Herr Brunner. Unlike sixty per cent of Venezuela's citizens, Brunner hadn't come from Europe in the years since the

Second World War, his ancestors had come from Hamburg to Venezuela at the beginning of the nineteenth century. The family member who had actually made the move had been a mercenary in Europe, fighting Napoleon until his final defeat in 1815. Suddenly, after years of profitable fighting, years of amassing the booty of war, he had been out of a job, looking for other wars and other opportunities. With a few thousand others, mainly British mercenaries, he had answered the appeal of Simon Bolivar for troops to fight the war of independence against the Spanish in South America. After Bolivar achieved independence, Brunner had settled. He had invested what he had brought from Europe, and added the spoils of the Spanish war, and by the turn of the century the Brunners had a bank. Thirty years later, they achieved Swiss as well as Venezuelan citizenship: the move back to Europe had begun. The Brunner family settled first in a small town near Geneva, then in Zurich. They built a school and a theatre, and the present Brunner was currently engaged in building a library. They knew how to make their money work, and how to behave themselves in their adoptive country. In the past two months, Walker noted, Brunner, along with many others, had contributed to the vast flight of capital from Venezuela. It was this that made the Rausch account odder still. Why, when everyone else was moving their money out of Venezuela, were Rausch moving theirs in?

For the umpteenth time Walker questioned his wisdom in cornering Jimenez in a public place. Different people reacted differently to an approach, and he had no idea how Jimenez would behave – how anyone might react when asked to betray a company confidence, break the law, in a café on the open street. But he'd been over it a dozen times and there was no other way. The problem with Jimenez was that he was never alone unless he was in public, so it had to be like this. He had no private office and his home swarmed with family; this was Jimenez' relaxation, his privacy, sitting in a packed public bar with a traffic jam outside and a cloud of exhaust fumes passing through one door and out of the other.

Every seat was filled at the counter. Walker waited until the seats on both sides of Jimenez were empty. He had to take some precaution, even here. He ordered a pineapple juice and watched while the raw pineapple was crammed into a liquidiser with nearly a quarter of a pound of sugar, and left to spin while the man served another customer. The man on the far side of Jimenez slurped back the frothed milk from the bottom of his coffee cup, belched loudly and walked out of the bar, leaving a pile of the new Monopoly money on the stainless-steel counter.

Walker opened his paper at the page Jimenez was reading and tapped the sheet with the back of his hand. It was a piece about loans, debt and the President's most recent appeal to the international banking community.

'It only gets worse,' he said in Spanish.

The Venezuelan just grunted, and carried on chewing the edges of a ham roll.

'What's going to happen?' Walker said ruefully. 'We're in a better position to know than most people, but for the life of me I don't know the answer.'

Jimenez strayed a quizzical look at Walker.

'We're in the same business,' Walker said, and smiled. Jimenez looked round fully now, unsure if Walker had addressed the remark to him. He still held the newspaper up in front of him.

'Banking,' said Walker.

Jimenez frowned. Walker could see he wasn't going to say anything, but he didn't take his eyes away either.

'You are with the Brunner Bank,' he said. Jimenez nodded slowly. By now, Walker could see that Jimenez was suspicious of him. He could hear the gringo accent and he was worried that a gringo had opened up a conversation in a pokey *fuente de soda* so far off the tourist's beaten track.

'You've no reason to know me,' Walker said, and extended his hand. Jimenez' hand was drawn by invisible force into the large, white, patient gringo hand held out in front of him. Apparently it didn't occur to him that he knew Walker no better after this meaningless gesture. No name, no introduction had been offered. Walker gave him a big smile, but still the Venezuelan didn't speak. 'I've known about you for a long time,' Walker said in a friendly way. He knew that at any moment he was going to have to take the leap into darkness that could result in Jimenez jumping to his feet, or flinging his coffee in his face, or shouting for a policeman. The man was already looking out the side of his eyes at the street. Walker would have to arrest his attention once and for all.

'Luis Walther Jimenez,' he said sharply. 'Aged twenty-five, married to a woman two years younger by the name of Raffaela. Four kids, the three youngest are girls, the youngest of them aged only three months. And one son, aged six and half and crippled. You live in flat 55a on the fifteenth floor of the Gomez block down the street. You work for Brunner in the week and for a firm of security guards called Jaguar on Sunday. You are paid four thousand dollars a year by Brunner and you collect another four hundred bolivars for a twelve-hour, all-night stint at the Country Club. Only the trouble is, Brunner doesn't pay you in dollars, does he? If he did, you wouldn't be behind on the payments on your flat and you might even be able to mend the car which is rusting away at your parents' home in Chacaito. If you were really lucky, you might even be able to find a doctor who could cure your son. He has a wasting disease, but it can be cured, you know that. But Brunner isn't like a high street bank, is it? Its customer relations are restricted to a few millionaire, billionaire gringos, who have taken most of their money out of the country in the past few weeks anyway. And Brunner doesn't need to keep its employees sweet with health plans and pensions and holiday pay, does he? Because there are plenty of people out there who can do your job if you ask too many questions, right? Right?'

Walker drew breath, but Jimenez didn't move.

'You aren't that much of a high-flyer, are you? This is about as far as you're going to go. But unfortunately, your expenses are going to go a lot further. Perhaps you will never be able to cure your son – unless you listen to me, now.'

Walker had Jimenez' forearm in a tight grip. The arm was so thin he could easily get all his fingers around it with room to spare. Jimenez was looking scared. He looks guilty already and he hasn't even done anything yet, Walker thought. But is he beaten? Or is he just temporarily off-balance?

'Luis Walther Jimenez,' Walker repeated. 'Walther from your grandfather on your mother's side, of German extraction. Your father works out in Altamira as a packer in a warehouse, your mother's a cleaner in the Country Club in a big, rich house owned by a diplomatic family. You have no brothers, two sisters, both married.' Walker paused. 'You see, you don't know me, but I know you.'

Jimenez flinched slightly, but he didn't look so scared. The initial shock had worn off. It wasn't difficult to grab people's attention, Walker thought, you could mesmerize them briefly with facts and figures – but how long could you hold them once the first shock was past?

'Brunner won't give you help where you need it,' Walker insisted. 'And no one else is going to do it for you. I can help. As I say, we're in the same business.'

'Who are you?' Jimenez said suddenly – and tried to tear his arm away from Walker and then smash Walker's hand against the counter. When he could do neither, he spat onto the floor in a gesture of macho aggression that misfired badly. 'Leave me alone!'

'I have five hundred dollars in my pocket,' Walker said quickly. 'That's who I am. And there's more than that if necessary. It's yours, you can earn it. I have two hundred and fifty for you now and another two-fifty if you help me.' He reached into the inside pocket of his jacket without releasing Jimenez, and pulled out a bill-fold in a clip. There were fifty ten-dollar bills, and it was a thick wad of cash. Dollars. Worth ten times more than a month ago, if you could only get your hands on them.

'Count them, if you like,' Walker said, and pushed the bill-fold along the counter at the same time as he released Jimenez' arm. Jimenez didn't move or try to count the money, but he didn't take his eyes off it either. Maybe he can tell five hundred dollars just by looking at it, Walker thought. He works in a bank, he has the eye.

'Your salary, worth four thousand dollars a month ago, is now worth four hundred,' Walker said. 'You're looking at more than your annual salary.' He reached an arm across and drew the bill-fold back down the counter. Jimenez didn't take his eyes off it.

'Two coffees. With milk,' Walker ordered, and kept the bill-fold in his hand, but resting on the counter in front of the Venezuelan. Neither of them spoke until the Venezuelan broke the silence.

'It's a lot of money to be carrying around a place like this, gringo,' he said with a faint threat in his voice.

Outside, a street cleaner was clearing the gutters of fruit and vegetable waste from the night before, and a scavenging dog was rooting around in the refuse. But it was the shout that had made Walker turn round and Jimenez finally drag his eyes away from the money to look as well. Tied to the dustcart with a piece of string was a young man – it was hard to tell how old – who shouted and mouthed obscenities at the cleaner, and sometimes tried to grab a passer-by. His shrieks shattered the eardrums. As he screamed and wailed, he crawled about on his hands and knees, occasionally approaching the cleaner with his hand raised as if to hit him. But every time he got too close, the cleaner would turn on him and make as if to hit him with an upraised shovel, when the screams of anguish would start again. The young man was filthy and wore hardly any clothes, what there were were torn and shredded like the rags on a cartoon Victorian chimney-sweep. Everyone in the street stopped to look, and the first-floor windows of accommodation blocks and shops opened to jeers and catcalls. One or two people threw things. The young man wasn't hurt, and he didn't look particularly hungry or even tired. He was mad. The sweeper never actually hit him with the shovel, merely cowed him with an angry shout and an aggressive gesture before he got back to his work. The young man was the sweeper's son.

Walker looked back at Jimenez, whose eyes were still focused on the young man. It wasn't an unusual sight: the streets of the capital were full of the demented, the crippled and deformed. Jimenez' son was lucky, just like the sweeper's son. Jimenez' son didn't have to drag his crippled legs around on a wooden board on wheels, begging for scraps while the other kids kicked him down the grand steps of the public monuments.

At last Jimenez took his eyes off the scene outside the bar and looked at Walker properly for the first time. 'Five hundred dollars is a lot of money, gringo,' he said. 'What could I do that was worth five hundred dollars?'

The coffees arrived and were tacked onto Walker's bill. There was a look almost of humility, or perhaps it was hope, in Jimenez' face. 'I want to offer you a job,' Walker said slowly. 'I need your help, if you like, just as you need mine. I want you to take a look at an account at the bank for me.' He could have been discussing a restaurant they were going to for lunch. 'Nothing major, nothing difficult. It's one of your big ones, I'm sure of that. Probably contains twenty-three million dollars, perhaps less. That's the amount that was paid into it four weeks ago, anyway, but naturally there may have been some withdrawals since then. The twenty-three million was paid into an account by the name of Imronal.' Walker wrote it on a dirty serviette. He leaned back. It had come out as smoothly as a natural conversation. There were no busybodies looking over Jimenez' shoulder, and his voice had been natural. 'That's all,' he said. 'Nothing more than that. One small account and then it's over.'

Walker looked down at the name he had written on the serviette. For the second time since he had first heard it, he wondered who on earth thought up these names. Imronal could be a noise in the throat, or a new contraceptive, but it was hardly a major shell company. Perhaps that was why they used words like that.

'The money was paid from an account in Panama City,' he continued conversationally. 'Imronal was invented solely for the purpose of this account. I want to know the details of this account; how it was paid, what form of transfer it was, cash, credit, bonds, whatever. I need to know everything about the account there is, but most of all I need a name. I need to know who in Caracas has authorisation to draw on the account. I need to know how much he or she draws, and in what form.'

It was out. Now Jimenez would either cut and run, or he would delay that fatal second. If he delayed, at least there was a chance. There was a pause, but Jimenez didn't move. And then he spoke.

'You think it's that easy,' he said calmly.

It wasn't the reply of a desperate and beaten man, and it wasn't the reply of a man stretched with debt and with a family to support. Perhaps Walker had made a mistake. Maybe this diminutive bank clerk with enough family worries for ten men wouldn't crack. But Walker had done his research, hadn't he? The man was on the ropes. He'd expected an agonising, internal struggle, perhaps, and then surrender, or an immediate positive response. But not this, not a calm rejection. Worse than a rejection, an objective criticism of the approach itself.

Jimenez laughed softly, scornfully. 'No problem bribing a spic,' he said in a harsh way. That's right, Walker thought nervously, no problem. Please, no problem. 'The spics have palms that are made for greasing. That right?' Jimenez said.

Walker felt any initiative he'd thought he had for one moment, for one glorious foolish moment, begin to slip away. The clerk was asking *him* questions. And the man was right: he hadn't expected this, he'd expected anything but this. He'd acknowledged that a bribe might be rejected or accepted in this country, but that the very ethics of corruption might be called into question, that he hadn't bargained for. He hadn't even considered the possibility of it – not here in a country whose recent leaders had finagled in excess of four billion dollars out of the economy with the aid of false invoices, and where it was generally accepted practice to bribe a policeman rather than go through the ponderous rigmarole of the law.

How in hell had he managed to pick an honest man in this country? Jimenez was living in two rooms in a high-rise slum. He was as stretched and as over-committed as you could get – the man was gasping for air, for Christ's sake. And he was turning down a sum of money that, thanks to a collapse in the economy, was worth more than his annual salary. Where had it gone wrong? Did Brunner have a safety net after all? Did they look after their employees better than he'd anticipated?

'It's your chance,' Walker said. 'You can be free of all your troubles, just by looking in a file and then making a phone call.'

Jimenez looked away as if to check that there was no one to overhear. When he looked back, there was a hard expression in his face. He was no longer amused by Walker or by the offer. 'If I want money, I can get my reward from the bank,' he said. 'They'll be interested to know there's someone enquiring into one of their accounts. They'll want to know who it is.'

Walker saw that the situation had slipped from his control. Maybe the man wanted more money, but he doubted it. He'd had a piece of bad luck; Jimenez, the honest family man, was unexpected. In a city rife with cholera and rabies and even leprosy, the chief fear of the aid agency doctors was high blood pressure, high blood pressure from the stress of poverty. Walker had banked on the stress of poverty tempting Jimenez, but the man didn't want to know. He was prouder than most would have been, Walker thought; you couldn't anticipate running into too many men like Jimenez in Caracas. But he, Walker – clever dog that he was, he thought, with a sick feeling in the pit of his stomach – he *had* anticipated it. He had allowed for the remote possibility that Jimenez might be an honest man, and had planned accordingly.

Walker reached inside his jacket and withdrew the photograph that he had hoped he wouldn't have to use. But the Rausch bank account at Brunner was more important than the sensibilities of a minor bank clerk, that's what he told himself, and once you made that decision, the rest, if not easy, was acceptable. He placed the photograph carefully on the counter in front of Jimenez, who didn't look at it at first. Only when he saw it out of the corner of his eye did he swing round, pick it up and hold it close to his face as if everyone in the café might be looking at it. Jimenez the family man; Jimenez the poor bank clerk with two rooms to fit a wife and four kids; Jimenez, the man who, as Walker could testify, played for hours with his crippled son and loved him too much to give him a father who would steal, even to cure him; this same Jimenez, in the photograph, was embracing another woman, just as he embraced her every weekday at ten minutes to seven in the evening on his way back to his family from the bank. Christ knew, Walker couldn't blame him. To want to get away, just once a day, from the relentless struggle; to want to get away even from your wife, whom you loved, but who was an inescapable part of that struggle – it wasn't much of a betrayal. It was a safety valve, that was all. But that would not be the way Jimenez' wife would see it. Who knows? Maybe Señora Jimenez was the kind of Latin wife who'd take a knife to her husband's throat, or maybe she would go without a word, silently taking the man's children out of his life forever. Maybe she would scream and rant and exhaust them both with grief. One thing Walker was certain of, Jimenez would not want his wife to see the photograph. Walker felt a close and sleazy sweat crawl across his face.

The collapse of Luis Jimenez came in three stages. First, he played the macho, flaring-eyed Latin. If he'd carried a stiletto he would have whipped it from his shoe and stuck it at Walker's neck. Instead, he snatched the photograph from Walker's hand and spat on it, then screwed it up and tore it into smaller and smaller pieces until the action turned into farce. But he soon began to realise the futility of this. Jimenez wasn't slow, he knew that Walker would hardly pass on the only copy of the photo if his intention was a bribe. And so the violence ebbed and Jimenez, still clutching the torn scraps, sagged at the shoulders and slumped a little against the bar, his hands shaking with repressed emotion and his eyes wide and fixed on the stainless-steel counter, frozen, caught by surprise in the middle of an everyday action, like one of the dead at Pompeii.

Then Jimenez became lost in his internal struggle. Walker watched him as he feverishly ran every possibility through his brain. He didn't speak, but occasionally his head would sway from side to side in despair like someone mourning the dead. His eyes darted backwards and forwards across the counter as new terrors filled his mind – his wife, his family, his job, his life. And then, when he saw that he really was caught, that the gringo sitting next to him really did hold all the cards, his old anger returned, his fists clenched and he ground his teeth in rage.

Finally, he brought himself under control. He didn't exactly look at Walker, but his head tilted slightly sideways to show that his self-absorption was over and that he was ready for whatever it was that Walker still had to say. He remained monosyllabic as Walker told him exactly what he had to do, when he had to find the information Walker needed, how he was to get it to him, the telephone numbers, the system of calling, the times when he would expect the calls. Walker had laid down the plan with more than military precision; he wanted the bank clerk to gain security from having a system, a discipline. Above all, it was necessary that Jimenez have confidence in Walker, for now Walker was his only lifeline. However much he hated him, Jimenez must know that in Walker alone lay his second-class salvation. He protested a good deal, threw up objections, practical difficulties. But it was bluster, and it revealed that he could, in fact, do what Walker asked.

'And what if the files are in special security?' he asked. 'What if access to them is impossible?'

Walker looked him in the eyes so that there was no doubt about the seriousness of what he had to say. 'Then find a way to get access,' he said. 'Remember, it's a small thing, a solitary file, just one account. But everything you have depends on it. Everything.'

Jimenez left the bar first, and seemed to slink away, his thin bones hunched beneath his jacket and an expression of near despair on his face. He was trapped and he knew it. Walker left the *fuente de soda* quite oblivious of everything around him. He left the car, he knew he wouldn't be calm enough to drive it, and ducked into another bar further along the street, where he bought a bottle of cheap brandy. He walked on, unaware of the street traders who held their wares out almost under his nose. He walked for nearly a mile, out onto the freeway that led past the Hilton Hotel to the mess of flyovers and bridges and underpasses. He ducked through a tunnel and walked on until he reached the botanical gardens, where he sat down opposite what the plaque claimed was a five-hundred-year-old tree. He tugged at the brandy from the bottle as if it were a mouthwash. Perhaps you could call it that, he thought. It was still only eight-thirty in the morning.

EIGHT

The Beast Stirs

Slick Mather's assessment of the situation in Venezuela was two weeks old – or thirteen days, to be exact – before the 'insurrection', as it was generally called, began to hit the headlines. To some, the disturbances were just riots; dangerous, certainly, but nothing more than mindless eruptions of violence. For others, they spelled a challenge to the government, to democracy, to life itself. There were people being killed as the disaffected in the barrios went on the rampage. The economic crisis was closing its teeth, and inevitably, as the politicians pointed out in order to calm fears at home and abroad, some people were going to be caught in them.

On the morning after he'd seen Luis Jimenez, Walker woke up without any clear plan for the day. He knew he had to wait now, wait to see if Jimenez behaved as he should. He had given the bank clerk two days, that was all. Any longer, he calculated, might induce a blunting of the threat; any less than that might result in a failure in the operation through haste. He sat in the restaurant at the Hilton and sipped a fourth coffee as he flipped through the pages of the local papers. There were three important Spanish rags, and one in English that an American had set up in the thirties, which had the lowest circulation of the four and contained the best foreign news. But Walker wasn't interested in foreign news, he was interested in what was happening three miles down the road, in the barrios, where the police were moving in in ever greater numbers. Two dead the day before, tear gas, riots, and another policeman killed. The President had made an announcement. If the 'troubles' escalated, he said, if there were more deaths in the security forces, he would have to bring the army in. That morning, at five-thirty, Walker had seen a column of conscripts rolling down the Avenida Urdaneta. Troops had already started to come in from the interior.

He signed the service chit and took the bunch of papers to the lobby. He looked out for signs that things were changing, but there didn't seem to be people taking flight just yet: a group of tourists were queueing under a sign for the bus that would take them to the airplane for Angel Falls. Admittedly, there were few Americans about, and the Americans were the first to desert at the whiff of a crisis. But if anything, the collapse of the currency had boosted tourism. The balance was a fine one. A certain degree of instability actually attracted foreign visitors, and could be tolerated by the locals; just how dangerous did things have to get before the scales tipped towards catastrophe?

Walker crossed the marble lobby to the bank of telephones and put through a call to London. It was lunchtime in London, Slick would be out of the office and he could check in with Reilly without getting trapped in explanations and updating.

When Reilly came on the line, he told him about the President's announcement and said that in his opinion there was a bigger crisis brewing than the President had admitted in any of his press conferences so far. He filed a short piece with one of the copy-takers about the imminence of martial law, the calm-before-the-storm atmosphere currently prevailing in the city, and then was put back to the foreign editor. 'I'm going down to the barrios,' he told Reilly. 'I want to get a first-hand account of the way the riots are being handled. In the local papers they're admitting a number of deaths, but it's sure to be an underestimate. I want to see for myself.' He paused for a moment while Reilly asked some questions and made a few notes. 'I also want to make contact with a woman who works with the poor down there,' he said. 'She's the wife – the widow – of a union leader who was assassinated. I think there may be a story. They found her husband six weeks ago with his face cut off.'

'Is that the story?' Reilly asked doubtfully.

'Nobody here will talk about it,' Walker said. 'None of the papers will touch it, I haven't been able to get a single comment. It's taboo even in high-up circles. Maybe the story is that no one will touch it, and why they won't. He was the head of the biggest union in the country, the Truckers'. He wasn't killed by a lone fanatic, he was killed professionally and dumped from a plane. At least, that's the way it looks. Have you read anything about it there?'

'No.'

'Well?'

Reilly didn't reply immediately. 'Look, Harry, we just want something on the crisis,' he said at last. 'You're the only person out there at the moment, but if it gets any worse, everyone'll be there.' Reilly sounded doubtful again. Eventually, he came out with what Walker knew he had wanted to say from the start. 'You may have to drop the Rausch stuff for a while,' he said gruffly. 'This is a news story, Harry. You're going to have to cover it, particularly if it develops any further. There's already interest brewing up in Europe, people coming out there. We want an interview with the President, first-hand news. You're there now so we'll get it first. Let's use our advantage.'

'That's fine,' Walker said. 'I go to see the widow, I see the crisis first-hand and I get whatever she has to say about her husband.'

'All right,' Reilly said sceptically. 'But just stick to what's happening now, okay? The other stuff can wait.'

It could wait just as long as he had to wait for Jimenez, Walker said to himself. Just as long as it took for Jimenez to come up with the goods on Imronal.

The taxi drivers were charging special fares to get to the riot areas; they said it was danger money, that drivers had been attacked and cars looted and burned. They were a true barometer of the crisis; they knew that journalists and the curious would pay over the odds to see the police in action, and Walker was the first of what they hoped would be a long line. It would be the same with the hoteliers, Walker knew. If things got much worse there would be a lot of money to be made; in a real disaster there would be three or four hundred visitors with unlimited dollar expense accounts. In the end, Walker hired a taxi for the whole day.

'You want to see the landslide?' the driver asked. 'There's been a landslide in Los Chorros, many people have been killed. Now they're going wild down there. Wild, man!'

Walker looked at the map in the back seat of the taxi and found Los Chorros. According to his information, that was where Francesca Santos Calderon operated her clinic. It was one of the larger barrios, near the centre of town. Caracas' hilly geography meant that it was actually cheek by jowl with the Country Club – the Country Club up on the hill, Los Chorros down in the valley, a slum and a rich enclave, one literally on top of the other. If serious violence was going to break out in the city, Los Chorros was as likely a place as any for it to start. 'The landslide, let's visit the landslide,' Walker said. But the driver had never heard of Santos Calderon.

Within half a mile of the shanty town it was clear to Walker that there was trouble. The streets were jammed with cars and buses, and every one of them seemed to be sounding its horn. The landslide had cut off the road; a great section of the hill on which the slum houses were built had caved in, and there were earth-movers trying to crush the fall back into the hillside and off the road. Around the earth-movers crowds from the shanties had gathered, and anti-government slogans were being chanted; and there were huge swathes of people coming to join them, milling along the streets, coming in from other parts of the city – and there were anti-riot vehicles and trucks full of troops flooding in to meet the supposed crisis, and stirring the situation up further. Walker told the driver to wait for him, all day if necessary, and got out. He was immediately swallowed up into the crowd.

He saw at once that the landslide was both the focus for the crowds, and their excuse. Police megaphones were sounding down the street, ordering people to return to their homes, but they were having no effect. Walker saw sharpened sticks and machetes in the hands of a gang who had started to rush up the street, driving the curious and the innocent in front of them. For a moment he was caught in the panic. A trio of Hippo riot vehicles ahead of the gang turned slowly to face the crowds and stop the charging mass, now several hundred strong, from approaching any closer to the landslide, but those in front were forced on by the terror behind. Suddenly, a tear-gas shell was fired. It was fired straight at the crowds where Walker was trapped, and exploded above their heads. Another shell fired, and this time the throat-tearing reek of the gas struck the crowd head-on. Walker, with his jacket off, and covering his mouth and nose, managed to run out of the side of the crowd and onto some waste ground.

Turning, choking, he looked back on a scene of mayhem. Despite the tear gas, the crowd pressed forward carried by its own momentum. Those at the front were being driven towards a three-deep line of riot police with gas-masks, who now immediately charged, separating out their victims with masterly precision and bludgeoning them to the ground. At the back of the crowd was the gang, and Walker could see that they were now fifty or sixty strong, all armed, and skirting around the sides of the crowd now, to get at the police. For a moment the air was filled with gas as shell after shell was fired from the trucks, and more police ran up from a street on the opposite side of the road to Walker and attacked whoever they could find. Walker turned and ran up the slight incline of the waste-tip away from the road, and stopped again to look round. They were students in the crowd mostly, he saw now, who had gathered to protest at the recent price-rises in everything from petrol to foodstuffs. He saw their placards waving helplessly, saw them felled, one by one, by the police.

He climbed further up the hill. He was above the front of

the crowd now, above and behind even the riot trucks and the police that confronted them and he had the perfect view of the battle below. Far away he could see his taxi reversing, slewing in its tracks as it tried to get away from the advancing police. He could see many bodies, some dead, some unconscious perhaps, others writhing helplessly on the ground – though this didn't save them: he watched as one of the trucks advanced and drove over a man's leg. Deliberately? It was impossible to see. He climbed higher, as the fumes of the gas began to climb higher too. The earth-movers below, on the other side of the hill from the battle, still ground away at their task. Walker climbed higher still, until he reached the first of the shacks. Seriously out of breath, he stopped and looked around him.

The barrio, he saw, was like a small town on a hill, surrounded by wasteland, enclosed by a rudimentary concrete wall, with the arteries of the city functioning below it and the great Avila mountain rising behind it to a further thousand feet. Now it seemed almost deserted; the people who lived here had switched their attention from the landslide to the battle a hundred feet below, and only a few children still stood perched on the edge of the newly-made cliff where the earth had fallen away. There were stretchers on the dirt paths between the shacks, and here and there people groaned as they waited for attention, but Walker could see few carers, and even fewer medical personnel. The road to the hospital, in any case, was closed; whatever medical attention they were going to get, it would be here, lying in the dirt by the open sewer. Some of them were covered in earth, and had clearly been dug out of the landslip by hand; others had injuries that suggested they had been excavated by the earth-movers. Perhaps they were the lucky ones, Walker thought. Perhaps there were others who would never get out of the earth. He walked along the line of victims in a daze. The shouting and banging of the tear-gas shells below seemed somewhere else. He saw people without limbs, and corpses whose faces had been covered hastily with plastic sheets from the shanty roofs or thick paper sacks. There had been a huge loss of life. Thirty, forty? It was a disaster.

Walker stumbled over some cans and bottles piled in the path and saw a woman ahead of him, obviously a figure with some authority for she was issuing instructions while a man on a stretcher was being carefully laid on the ground. He was bleeding heavily from a gash in the neck, Walker saw. He was an old man and didn't look as if he could survive. The woman immediately stopped and turned the man on his side. She wrapped a liniment-soaked bandage round and round his neck, but the blood was still seeping through, and then it started to pump out as it had before. Walker broke into a run, but stopped a few yards from the stretcher, fearing that the dust his feet stirred up would get in the man's eyes. The woman didn't look up as he approached, but he knew it would be Santos Calderon's widow. In spite of the taxi driver's ignorance, she was gaining a reputation in the barrios, the poor were beginning to turn to her for help. Walker laid his jacket down in the dirt and knelt by the stretcher. He could see immediately that the man wasn't going to live; only blood could save him, and he needed it now. A small crowd gathered, but there was no one to help her, no one who knew even the rudiments of first aid. She was on her own.

'He needs a hospital,' Walker said. 'He needs blood.' He held the bandage onto the side of the man's neck which Francesca Calderon had released to him while she cut another strip of gauze. Blood soaked through his fingers and dripped lazily onto the earth.

'We cannot get him to a hospital,' she said. 'Look out there. There is nothing we can do for him.'

The man blinked up at her, hearing everything she said. There was little in his eyes now, not even hope. He knew he was dying, and he wanted to die with her there. Walker was shocked at the simplicity of it all. She cut another wad of gauze but didn't put it against his neck, just under his head to take the hardness of the ground away.

'There are others we can help,' she said, and Walker looked into her face, searching for a callousness to match her words. What he saw was unfathomable; a calmness that he might have thought an indication of fanaticism, but for that small gesture of resting the dying man's head on the gauze.

The heat beat off the ramshackle collection of huts on the blazing hill. Below them was a modern city and a hospital. For the first time the woman looked at Walker, though with no particular curiosity. There were only a few reasons why a gringo might be in the barrios.

'You are a journalist,' she stated.

The dying man's breaths began to surge in spasms, and the blood pumped through the soaked bandage in ever decreasing gouts. There wasn't much blood left in him at the end. 'What will you write about this?' she asked, letting the man's head rest finally on the earth.

'I came to find you,' Walker said, and thought he saw her wince, but immediately she recovered her composure. She hung onto her calmness, her control, Walker noticed, with a terrible tenacity. 'I want to know why your husband was killed.'

'More people have died than just my husband,' she said. 'Write about them.'

She gathered her meagre medical supplies together, washing the scissors in a kidney-bowl of brown water before she emptied it away on the ground. She put the scissors, gauze, a syringe and a roll of bandages into the dish and stood up, brushing down her skirt as she did so. Walker stood up, clamping his jacket in a fist. She made a few meaningless movements, brushing dust and flecks of dead grass off her clothes, gestures that enabled her to ignore him.

'Everyone's writing about the riots,' he said. 'I am too. I came out here to speak to you about your husband. He was killed before all this started, but I can find no reports beyond the factual announcement of his death. Is no one curious? Don't you want to know why it happened?'

'You are from London?'

'Yes.'

'What interest is it to people in London?'

Walker thought of Slick Mather and Peter Clive. 'Why did no one here carry the story?' he said.

She looked him in the eyes with a steady gaze. When she spoke, he saw she could be as tough in talking about her dead husband as she could be with the dying. 'He was dropped from a plane,' she said. 'That sort of thing is rather out of reach of the average killer.'

'The army did it?'

'In this country you don't investigate the murder of someone who is dropped from a plane,' she said. 'It makes about as much sense as enquiring who killed a victim of the electric chair. They practically signed their names on him.'

'But surely someone. . . ?'

'And if they sign their names, it's a warning. You don't touch, or maybe you will be the next to drop.'

The sewer that ran along the edge of the path babbled pleasantly, but the filthy stench of it, borne to him on a sudden drift of air, almost made Walker choke. She saw his expression of disgust and, smiling, beckoned him to follow her to the shade of a tree by a wall. She sat down with her back against it, brushing the flies away with her hand, and Walker sat down next to her.

'In Venezuela people are interested to know why my husband was killed,' she said candidly. 'But they cannot afford to be. In London – they can afford to be interested, but they aren't. I am a lawyer. I was trained in the United States. I know how to press a case, but here there is a cover-up.'

'An official cover-up?' Walker said, and she turned to look at him.

'What is official?' she said. 'There are many centres of power in this country. It is not like the United States. How much support does the President have from the government? How much support does the government have from the army? You see, it is not that simple. There are factions. One faction – the army – wanted my husband dead.' She paused and gazed out over the scene of carnage in the streets below. 'But the army itself has different loyalties within it. So let us say, one faction in the army, they killed my husband.'

'Why? Why did they kill him?'

'I have tried to find the answer to that question. I have tried to take his case to the courts. I have raised it with the International Court of Human Rights. They either won't or can't find out. Now, I receive threats.'

Walker looked at the sharp profile of the woman next to him. She felt him watching her, and turned as if to block his look. Walker wondered if threats could scare her; whether she was really so brave, or if she had simply stopped caring.

'My children are in America,' she said. 'Yes, they've even taken the trouble to threaten them.'

'What is it they fear you'll discover?'

'They're staying with a cousin of my husband in Detroit. Going to school, making friends. Maybe they'll become American. The Americans have been good to me since my husband's murder. Yes, perhaps it's best they stay there, even when this is over.'

Walker leaned in closer to her. 'What is it they're afraid you'll discover? What was your husband doing? Why did they have to kill him?'

'He refused to take bribes. I don't why, or what the bribes were for.'

'I can help you,' Walker said, and really, suddenly, wanted to help her. Perhaps it was because of the bitter memory of his treatment of Jimenez, or perhaps it was just because she was alone, with her husband dead and no one else to help her. It was partly, he knew, because she wasn't asking for help.

'That's all I know,' she said. 'You think I'm hiding something? I risked my life to find out why. You think I wouldn't tell a journalist from London?'

She instantly regained her calm, and turned on him a shrewd look that stripped away deceit. In the maelstrom around them, she was curiously, religiously, serene again.

'I may have more chance of finding out than you,' Walker said. 'More access.'

She seemed to think for a moment, and make a decision. Her shoulders relaxed and she leaned forward and clasped her arms around her knees. 'There are things you must know,' she said to the distance, as if a bargain had been struck between them and only the details were left to be hammered out. 'He was an important man when he was alive, he was head of the Truckers' Union. You may not think so, but that's a big position in this country; the Truckers' is the biggest and most important union. The reason why it's so important is because the country has few railways to speak of, and everything must go by road. So in many ways the truck drivers hold the key to the economy, and their leader is a political figure. My husband was a friend of the President. That made him many friends and many enemies. Who are they, who are his enemies? The army? As I say, the army is not a beast with a single brain.' For the first time she laughed, and rocked back slightly. 'The army is a beast *without* a single brain,' she laughed. Then her seriousness returned and she stared into the distance, the moment of intimacy over. 'He wished to help the President with his reforms,' she said. 'And then he was killed.'

Down below, the riot police had gained the upper hand. They were mopping up the slow and the dim-witted, the people drawn into the riot by the gangs who'd fled long before.

'And the new Truckers' leader?' Walker said. 'Does he support the President's reforms?'

She looked at him through half-lidded eyes. 'No,' she said finally. 'He wants to make trouble. He wants to start strikes against the government. My husband was against the strike and they called him a communist. This man wants a strike, yet he has powerful friends in the army.' She shrugged. 'The army holds the key, whichever faction in the army gets the upper hand.'

She looked at him again as if to decide his worth. 'You write about my husband for the people in London, Mr Walker. Find out who killed him, and who wants to kill me. Maybe it is not just the death of some insignificant little official at stake.'

Walker stood and pulled her to her feet. In the havoc that had gripped the city, hers was the human face that told him the story of the nation's tragedy: the face of Francesca Santos Calderon. She needed help, and it never occurred to him to do anything but answer her need.

'What do you think you can do really to help me?' she said.

Small, neat puffs of smoke exploded in the air like clouds in a children's illustration. They were followed by short bangs as the sound travelled more slowly up from the shanties to the hillside. Stratstone sat in the car with Johnny and looked down at the scene. There was a good viewpoint from up here, it was almost like being at the theatre, and with a pair of field-glasses you could get close in to the violence.

The police were doing a job of sorts. But how long would they be able to hold the line before the army got involved? He watched the inhuman shape of another Hippo riot vehicle crawl up the road towards the barrio and loose two more tear-gas shells into the mess of huts and narrow earth streets. There were two more short bangs, and the rioters scurried away choking, clutching their American baseball shirts to their faces. It made Stratstone snort. Scampering in all directions, they looked like blind rats in an uncovered nest. But soon the air cleared and there was no one to be seen again. The grey froth of the open sewer bubbled on through the streets and sent a stink right up here, onto the hill; Stratstone's eyes were watering, too, as the edges of the gas wafted a quarter of a mile up the side of the mountain to the car. He watched tearfully as the riot vehicle turned sharply to the left and sliced through one of the shanties built of flattened-out kerosene cans. Then he lowered the glasses and sat back in the car with his legs out of the door.

'You sure she's down there?' he said.

'That's what all our reports say,' Johnny answered, raising his voice and shoulders on the word 'say', as if the more the reports concurred, the more unreliable they were likely to be. 'But you know she has these good works she does. It's probably no more than that.'

Stratstone picked at some hard skin on the edge of his thumb. 'She's always down in the shanties since her old man croaked,' Johnny added.

'We've given her money?' Stratstone checked.

'She wouldn't take any for herself, so we've made a handsome donation. The blind or the crippled or the god-dammed orphans, I forget.'

Stratstone nodded methodically. Ever since the death of her husband, he'd known she would have to be watched. She'd never stopped her 'good works', but now she was down in the barrios every day, and if she wasn't careful, she was going to get into trouble. The police didn't care if it was an automatic weapon you were on the end of, or a doctor's syringe; when the rioting started, they went after anything that moved. They'd done that yesterday, when there'd been rioting here after the landslide: a chunk of one of the hills in the centre of town slipped away and carried a hundred or so shanties with it. Through the glasses Stratstone could see the bulldozers down below to the left there, still trying to clear the road. Where the slip had occurred small children were balancing on the precarious wall high up on the precipice, and the mound of earth was dotted with the insides of the shanties that had fallen. A cooker was half-sticking out, a ramshackle cupboard had slewed wildly through the dirt, bits of clothes and toys and oil drums and wooden beams were scattered at angles across the desertscape of the earth. And underneath the earth, Stratstone thought, buried some-where in the tons of garbage, were the human victims. The government were always making a hullabaloo about increas-ing safety in the shanty towns, and no doubt there would be the usual hue and cry now, after the landslide. But it would soon be forgotten about – until the next one.

Stratstone picked up the field-glasses again and scanned the scene below like a general. The Santos Calderon woman hadn't taken her husband's death lying down, he'd been right about that. She'd raised hell down at the public prosecutor's – until she realised she'd get nowhere. The police had declared that there was nothing to investigate. Remembering, Stratstone's mouth twitched in anger. They were so crude in this damn country. Fine, so don't investigate the murder, but don't *don't*, for Christ sake, say there is nothing to investigate. The woman was a frigging lawyer; she, of all people, knew there should have been an investigation. Now, of course, she knew there was a cover-up. They might just as well have announced it in the papers. And that was another problem he'd had to take care of. When the woman had got nothing out of the police or the prosecutor, she'd turned to the papers. She knew all the tricks. So he'd had to sort *that* out. Only one of the national papers had given it any space, thanks to him. The others were silenced.

And now she was mixing down in the barrios every day. It wasn't safe. The shanties were swarming with subversives. You only had to look at the trouble in the Truckers' Union, practically a civil war, with some of them wanting to strike, some of them supporting the government. A strike could halt the country, bring down the government. Rausch knew that . . . If she stayed down there much longer, she'd hear something. She'd find out about the bribes. Then she *would* be dangerous, then she could get him into real trouble. Just keep things steady, that's all he had to do, and make sure she didn't find out. Things were going nicely so far, things were fine, but it was all coming to a head. Soon the rioting down below would be remembered as kid's stuff.

'She shouldn't be allowed to interfere,' Johnny said, echoing Stratstone's own thought. He looked at Stratstone for an answer. Johnny described himself as a boat-repairer if anyone asked him, it was a job which took him plausibly to different places around the world. He looked like a boat-repairer too, and you never knew, Stratstone thought, maybe he could even repair boats.

'What can we do?' he asked rhetorically. 'She's not going to respond to threats, she's not the type.'

'Maybe not just threats, then,' Johnny said.

'One step at a time, one step at a time,' Stratstone soothed him. Johnny was enthusiastic, and he liked that; but despite the soft brown tan and the engaging marble-gravestone grin, Johnny could also be hot-headed, violent. They didn't need that. Not yet.

'She's gonna find out something soon,' Johnny said. 'It's just a matter of time. Every day I take that money into the barrios where she works, there's a risk, and even if she doesn't see me handing it out, sooner or later she's gonna hear about it. She'll hear from someone who was told by someone else whose goddamn sister told him. You know what it's like in those places, you only have to look at it.' And he looked down with refined distaste onto the shanty roofs, their corrugated iron reflecting savagely in the sun. 'It's not a grapevine down there, it's a friggin' jungle. They're crawling over each other like ivy.'

Stratstone didn't like the thought either, but it was difficult to know what to do. Francesca Calderon was an intelligent woman, and she didn't look like giving up. Now she was even appealing to the international courts for justice for her late husband. 'I don't think we can stop her doing her good works,' he said. 'Just as long as they don't interfere with ours.' He turned to the younger man. 'What's the lowest level contact we can have with her?' he asked. 'Something we could build on. We don't want to give everything all at once.'

'A threat? "Remember what happened to your husband." "Your husband needn't be the only one." That kind of thing?'

'I've already said she won't respond to threats. She's not the kind. I'm talking about physical contact. Something small, something, God help us, that may make her stop and think.'

Johnny shrugged and looked into the distance, narrowing his eyes against the glare.

'You know the kind of thing. A broken arm. Rough her up a bit,' Stratstone added.

'A leg,' Johnny said thoughtfully. 'A leg's always better.

With a broken leg, she couldn't get down to the barrios for days, maybe weeks.'

'That's tough,' Stratstone said sympathetically. 'But we do have to get her out of those places.'

'Or maybe just rough her up,' Johnny agreed, turning over the problem out loud as he continued to gaze at the horizon. 'Give her a few bruises, bust up her face a bit. If she's covered in shit, they won't want her down there looking after the sick, it'd put them off too much. Split her lip, bruise her up, cut her here and there,' he mused.

'You won't intimidate her,' Stratstone said, shaking his head. 'Like I say, she's not the type.' Stratstone had a real admiration for Santos Calderon's widow. She wasn't just tough, she wasn't just intelligent, she was classy. He liked the way she held herself. For thirty-eight years old she was still very nicely made, he reckoned. She wasn't like these other Latin women who let themselves go as soon as they got married – they had too many kids, of course, that was what was wrong with most of them. She had just two children, a boy and a girl. They'd been sent to a cousin in the States after the murder of Santos Calderon, they were being looked after out of harm's way. Yes, Francesca Santos Calderon was a clever woman. She'd got them out of reach – in the States, ironically enough, Stratstone thought. It was a shame, really. If her kids were still around, he wouldn't be having to think about hurting her. She was a very smart girl.

'Rape,' Johnny said carefully. His brow knitted into a frown of concentration. 'There's always rape.' This was a real problem which deserved to be solved, his expression said.

Down below, the Hippo riot truck had turned abruptly to the right. There were some kids throwing stones at it from another part of the barrio. Stratstone watched, deep in thought. You put one lot down in one place and another lot sprang up in another. They were street-fighting streets, that was the trouble, and the Hippo was hopelessly over-qualified to be lurching around the kerosene-can huts, it was built to withstand mines, it had armour all around it and watchtowers down the centre. The police lurked inside; occasionally coming up for a pot-shot over the heads of the crowd. They were still fighting with tear gas and warning shots. But for how long? This was a common riot: when would the real action start?

The Hippo scudded over a pipe in the road and spun on its tail as the front wheels dragged across the dust. The rear end smashed a wall down into the small yard of a mud house, and a woman ran out of it screaming, carrying two babies in her arms. There was a shout and pointing from the truck's roof. Up the street, a man was standing yelling at the truck and waving what looked like a large stick, except that he pointed it like a rifle. Smoke burst out of its end, and the sound of the bang eventually reached the vantage point on the hillside, where Stratstone had taken up the field-glasses again and got out of the car. The truck's roof exploded, but it was the explosion of pistols and a small sawn-off gun. The man reeled and threw up his arms. The shot-gun flew out of his hands and he turned and fell to the ground, clutching his stomach and rolling onto his back, then slowly turning again, his hand holding his stomach in. On the truck there was consternation. One of the policeman who had been standing out when the man fired had been hit; he was lifted over the side of the truck and onto the ground. There was shouting, mayhem. No one did anything to help the policeman, and when Stratstone looked through the glasses he could see that he was dead.

Stratstone lowered the glasses briefly. The President had announced on state television three days ago that if another policeman died in the rioting, there would be a state of emergency. They all knew what a state of emergency meant, it meant martial law. The police couldn't control the situation with pistols, so the army would have to come in.

Stratstone put the glasses up to his face again. The truck roared forward as if to run the dying sniper into the ground, but it screeched to a halt in front of him with an angry sound. The police leapt down from the roof, suddenly emboldened by the sight of a dying man, and rushed through the streets chasing everyone who appeared and beating them with sticks. Two of them stopped long enough to kick the sniper's guts out into the dust and watch him die.

'No!' Stratstone said suddenly and vehemently to Johnny. 'We're not animals!' He thought of Francesca Santos Calderon again, her jet-black hair and eyes, her tall, graceful figure. 'Rape will achieve nothing with her.' He paused and tugged at the top of his trousers to hitch them up, a gesture to hide his irritation. He looked back down to the barrio and picked up the glasses again. Another mopping-up operation was beginning – but the trouble-makers would soon reappear when their fear at the man's death was forgotten. There it was down there, a little, bubbling pot of trouble. 'Simmering' was the word the papers used – a pressure-cooker. When, if, the whole thing exploded, it would be much more than a routine police action like this. Then the killing would really start, and the city would be filled with journalists from every corner of the world. That was when the Santos Calderon woman would be most dangerous – when there were journalists about who weren't under the thumb of the censor. That was when she could get her husband's death aired in the foreign papers.

'Maybe she'll catch it down there one of these days,' Johnny said. 'Save us a lot of trouble if she got a police bullet.' He looked at Stratstone meaningfully.

'A leg. I like just the leg,' Stratstone said. What he had to do now was keep the lid on this as long as he possibly could. They had to go carefully with Francesca Santos Calderon. You could get away with killing her husband, perhaps, but supposing things went too far and she was killed too? Then there'd have to be an investigation, even in this God-forsaken place.

'A leg it is,' Johnny said, content with a decision.

The Americans climbed back into the car and roared away above the hell below them. The cleaning-up operation would start now, Stratstone thought with a grim smile, and there was nothing the police liked better than cleaning up. But the soldiers, when they arrived, would enjoy themselves even more. He smiled again with the satisfaction of knowing that it would all go just as they had planned.

NINE

The Vultures Gather

'They say it's the Cubans,' Kenny, the young Australian photographer said, and concentrated on polishing one of several lenses that hung around his neck. 'Smuggling machine-guns into the shanty towns.' Jay O'Connell leaned on the bar next to his sound-recordist shadow, and smirked.

'Who says it's the Cubans?' an older voice rasped from behind him. 'The Almanac de Gotha? The Papal Nuncio?'

The sarcasm left the Australian unmoved. He didn't look up from his polishing and he didn't rise to the bait.

'Fidel Conquistador!' shouted someone from the card table. 'Riding through the continent like Simon bloody Bolivar, handing out guns like college sweatshirts.'

The card game resumed in a new deal, and the speaker leaned over the table and forgot the bar for another ten minutes.

'What time is it, someone?' an English voice asked, but there was no reply. The clock on the wall behind the bar was broken, and a general disinterest greeted the question. Grimes, the enquirer, a London Sunday stringer based in Bogota, ordered a round of drinks, and overhead the string-pull fan whirred and wobbled on the ceiling. Raucous cartoons screeched from a television on the wall and would continue to do so for the next six hours. It was ten minutes to six at the Foreign Correspondents' Club on Las Mercedes, and the occupants were settling in like sand.

'It's ten minutes to curfew,' the Guyanan barman said to Grimes, as he gave him the round of drinks.

'Blast!'

Outside the window, with a sound like a telex in some

117

distant room, the first disjointed rattle of machine-gun fire split the evening.

Walker looked down the mahogany bar at the groups of disparate individuals who had collected here in steadily-growing numbers in the past few days, and felt yet again how odd was the camaraderie that united them – a particular, peculiar bond that came from their only ever meeting in places like this, where the tension was high and danger not far away. They had come here first in dribs and drabs, then in greater numbers, and finally, during the past twenty-four hours, since the rumour had got out that the President was going to close the airport, in one great rush. Martial law was now four days old, and the country was erupting into violence. Walker looked up at the television screen above the bar, where a duck was being beaten into the earth with a large frying-pan. Every evening the government enforced a curfew with its conscript army, and then, when it had the population locked away at home, inflicted on them a solid diet of cartoons. The television supplied no shred of information – on the grounds that the rebels, as they were now called, must be denied the 'oxygen of publicity'. It was more likely, Walker thought as he watched the application of a baseball bat to the duck's head, that the government didn't want its troops confused by facts. Once again he felt the full frustration of the curfew; the shoot-on-sight policy applied to gringos as well as native Venezuelans – whether they waved their laminated press cards in the air or not. Above the bar was the ubiquitous portrait of Bolivar. It displayed the aquiline good-looks that were obligatory for all idols and saints in Venezuela, the same features that the images of Christ bore in the churches.

The recent discovery of secret caches of weapons in the barrios had been the main topic of conversation in the bar for the last hour. The Australian's explanation for them was just one of the many currently going the rounds, and though it was frowned upon by some of the older jounalists as perfect propaganda for the government, it had its supporters too. The discovery of automatic weapons was, as even Walker had to admit, a new and unexpected element in the situation, and set the crisis in even higher gear. Students railing against the paying of foreign debt, and parading with banners that read YANQUIS OUT, that was one thing; the same slogans were written on every piece of broken wall from Tijuana to Tierra del Fuego. But a full-scale armed insurrection, that was something quite different; and that was why the vultures of the world's press had gathered here, in the expectation – hope, even – of witnessing out-and-out revolution. The question of where the rioters had procured such weapons would have to be answered.

Walker had filed a short piece after the Los Chorros fighting, entitled 'Writing on the Wall'. It had gone down well with Reilly, and temporarily taken the heat off him in his new and now formally confirmed role of Our Correspondent in Venezuela. His piece had noted the irony implicit in the demonstrators' loudly-voiced anti-American sentiment: nearly all of them wore Miami Dolphins and Cleveland Oilers football shirts. The yanqui was hated and loved here, both at the same time; Caracas was an American city. If the revolution ever did come, if the rebels ever did storm the presidential palace, the rewards of victory, Walker had pointed out, would be a modern Metro and twenty-one Auto Mister Donuts.

'They're saying that two Cubans were arrested on the border,' Kenny, the Australian, persisted.

'Who's saying it?' rasped the same sarcastic voice as before.

'What do you mean, who's saying it?' Kenny answered crossly.

Walker saw the reddened face of Adrian Peters turn slowly towards the young photographer like a rattlesnake on amphetamines. 'Have you never heard of hype?' he suggested. 'Never heard of slant? A feed, an angle, bait?'

'Look, all I said was, two Cubans have been arrested. All right?'

Kenny had stopped polishing his lenses, and looked at Peters, with a challenge in his eyes.

'You said *they say* two Cubans have been arrested,' Peters muttered. 'Who are these bloody anonymous friends of yours? Right? Do you get my drift?'

'They were saying it at the barricades,' Kenny protested. 'The soldiers were saying it.'

'Ahhhh! Well. The *soldiers* were saying it,' Peters replied, and fixed the Australian with a withering look before he turned away to his drink.

Another, heavier burst of machine-gun fire shattered the dusk and momentarily silenced the chattering of the tree-frogs.

Adrian Peters was a veteran foreign reporter Walker had known since he first started touring the world's trouble spots ten years ago. He'd been trained on a local paper in Scotland in the early sixties by the Thompson organisation, and then, after a stint in Brazil and Peru, gone to work for Reuter's. He still dined out on the story that the man who ran the French Desk next to his at Reuter's had been Frederick Forsyth. A lot of dining-out later, the story had worn about as well as Peters had. He wore a crumpled white suit and had a heavy, jowly-red face. He didn't like Americans, he said, because of what they'd done to the southern half of the continent they shared. At other times, he said he was misinterpreted in this: he wasn't anti-American, he was anti-imperialist. He had recently done a mischievous piece for *Newsweek* that guilefully suggested it was not where America's backyard ended that mattered, it was where it began – and that, he had intimated, was at downtown Los Angeles. While Uncle Sam reached into South America, the people he really wanted to influence, Peters hinted, were sneaking round the back.

At the moment, Walker saw, Peters was sitting with the editor of the local paper *La Prensa*, a man by the name of Armando Higson – an editor, Walker had noticed, who had ignored the story of Santos Calderon's murder almost shamelessly. And what the editor of *La Prensa* was doing in the Foreign Correspondents' Club with Peters was anyone's guess. But Walker gave this only a passing thought. Nor was he really concentrating much on the argument about the Cubans, or the nearby card game, or on the distant rattle of machine-gun fire. Walker was worrying about the non-appearance of Luis Walther Jimenez. Four days since martial law had been declared was also four days since he had bearded Jimenez in the *fuente de soda* – twice the length of time he had given Jimenez to reach him with an answer. What had happened to the scrawny bank clerk with his plump, big-lipped mistress? He surely didn't expect Walker to forget all about him?

And what worried Walker most of all was that Jimenez seemed to have disappeared. He hadn't been able to find him at the Brunner Bank today or yesterday. Had something happened to him? Had he been discovered with his nose in the Imronal file and been hauled away to gaol, or worse? And now, with the curfew, it was impossible to find Jimenez anywhere except at his place of work; you didn't dare go out at night. Or did you? Even the police no longer appeared on the streets after curfew, it was said, because they were scared; scared not so much of the rioters, but of the raw fourteen- and fifteen-year-old conscripts who sat up on the high walls round the Country Club mansions and took potshots down onto the shanty roofs and anywhere else that took their fancy. It would be madness to go out at night.

'So what else have your friends the soldiers been telling you?' Peters was saying. The photographer was not going to get off lightly tonight. With so much restraint on their freedom, tension among the journalists was running high. 'Figures? Given you any figures, have they? Estimated the number of tragic but inevitable casualties?'

The Venezuelan, Higson, sat in the seat next to Peters and smiled thinly at the Australian's discomfort. Peters tipped back his head and intoned with the automated neutrality of a newsreader: 'The government is successfully controlling the situation. Twenty-six people have been killed, four seriously.' He winked without humour at Kenny. 'Any of that sort of thing at all?' he said. 'Any rock-hard, no-nonsense figures from your soldier friends, with the deep grief of civil war in their eyes?' He pointed two fingers at Kenny's head and pulled an imaginary trigger. 'This is going to hurt me more than it's going to hurt you! Bang!'

Kenny angrily waved away the hand and the indignity. 'You might be interested to know, arsehole, they're admitting two hundred and ninety-eight dead in the past three days. Admitting it! But you probably weren't down there when the announcement was made, were you. You were no doubt sitting in here with a fresh glass of whisky and a few old mates.'

'Two hundred and ninety-eight!' Peters whistled, falsely impressed and ignoring the Australian's jibe completely. 'Let's call it three hundred. Facts and figures from the soldiers. Right? Any advance on three hundred?' Peters looked around the bar and caught Walker's eye. 'Come on, Harry. Three hundred. Going . . . going . . . ?' Peters had got out of his chair and was walking down the bar now, eyebrows raised in mock enquiry. Outside, the heavier thud, thud, thud of an army machine-gun was answering the lighter rattle of the rebels' guns. Peters walked back, but got no answer, even from the few who found the Australian's discomfort and Peters' sarcasm mildly amusing. He stopped at last behind the chair where Armando Higson was sitting, and put his hands on the Venezuelan's shoulders, like a witch doctor picking out a victim. Higson smiled warmly. 'This man,' Peters said, 'this man will give me an advance on three hundred, won't you, Señor Higson?' He didn't wait for Higson's reply, but took his hands away from the man's shoulders and sat down again next to him. 'Tell them, Armando,' Peters said. 'Tell them it's worth a lot more than three hundred.'

Interest in the room had grown now. Even the card players had looked up from the table to see what it was that Higson had to say. This was a typical Peters' trick, Walker thought. He could never bring a subject up directly, it always had to be presented obliquely, tortuously, in a way designed to show off his own cleverness.

'Señor Higson is a local expert, as you know, gentlemen,' Peters said. 'He's not some ignorant bloody soldier following orders.' Higson shrugged and looked embarrassed. 'It's there for all to see, if you care to look,' Peters said. Higson looked again at Peters for support and received a courteous nod.

'I have a friend at the University,' Higson began. 'A doctor friend. He teaches the students there in the business of, amongst other things, chopping up the human cadaver. For the benefit of science and education, you understand,' he said. 'These are the future doctors of Caracas and all of Venezuela. They must know how to tell the difference between a liver and a kidney. This friend teaches, then, at the University hospital. He has taught there for ten years, he knows the place inside out and he knows how it works. In normal times, according to my friend, he can never get his students to have enough practice. There simply aren't the number of corpses around that are necessary to keep his classes up to scratch.'

By this time, everyone in the room was listening except the Guyanan barman, who stood and watched the silent cartoons on the television screen. Higson was starting to play to his audience. It was, Walker thought, oddly like a performance, like a prepared performance. But no one else in the room seemed inclined to question its authenticity.

'There aren't enough volunteers after death, apparently, who are happy to have their organs examined by our students,' Higson said. 'People aren't happy to end up as an educational aid in a laboratory. One or two a month only, according to the doctor. The University hospital is not an abattoir. Not, at any rate, in normal times,' he added. 'This month, however – this week, to be exact – our medical students have the chance to be the best-trained doctors in the world! Do you know how many corpses they've had delivered for experiments?'

'How many?' Peters said, joining the act.

'They have five hundred and fifty carcases to split and open and bottle in the labs. And those are just the ones they have

123

on ice!' Higson looked around the room, warming to his theme as he saw he had completely captured the interest of his audience.

'You don't exactly have to stick your nose to the ground, gentlemen,' Peters chipped in, 'to know there are plenty of bodies out there who never saw a cold flannel, let alone a refrigerated drawer. The stink of human flesh is hanging over the city. The buzzards are so fat they're sitting on the buildings and having to concentrate not to fall off! Three hundred!' He looked at the Australian with contempt. 'More like three bloody thousand. Three thousand and rising!' He lifted his glass to toast the figure, and drank.

When Walker looked around the bar, the others who had listened to Armando Higson didn't exactly have their pencils and notebooks out, but in every other respect they hung on his words – and on Peters' conclusion at the end. There were some who looked, if not exactly sceptical, then peeved that they'd had to be given this particular scoop by another journalist. The bodies at the hospital, Walker could see, were already being mentally written into articles for a hundred front pages right round the world. Nobody in all probability, Walker thought, knew Armando Higson from Rex Harrison, but they all knew Peters, and Peters had endorsed the Venezuelan. He was okay. Once again, Walker wondered why Higson had come to the Foreign Correspondents' Club, and how it was that his story of the hospital had come so perfectly on cue: it was the kind of story that everyone was getting desperate for.

But Walker didn't have a chance to dwell on the *La Prensa* editor's story, because Peters had already moved on again, determined, it appeared, to rub further salt into the Australian photographer's wound.

'Accuracy, sonny,' Peters was saying. 'Or, to be more accurate, exactness. Doesn't a figure like two hundred and ninety-eight strike you as odd at all? A bit over-precise, perhaps? In a city with no news,' he said, and nodded at the television screen, 'why should a common bloody soldier know such an exact figure? Did he get it from Donald Duck?'

People were returning to their own conversations now, and the card game had resumed. One or two had gone to make phone calls in the Club's lobby, and new rounds of drinks were being stood up right along the bar.

'Why – any more than you and me,' Peters persisted, 'should a soldier know any figure at all? Why did you hear this magic figure from a soldier and not from a pineapple-seller?'

Stevens, the *Washington Post* correspondent, was one of the few who had stayed glued to Peters' inquisition of the Australian. He was an old sparring partner of Peters'; they were about the same age, and they had been around for ten years longer than most of the other journalists in the bar. It was common knowledge that Stevens and Peters didn't like each other – Stevens objected to Peters' anti-American slant. Perhaps he had stayed with Peters and Higson at the bar in order to pick a quarrel as soon as Peters went too far, Walker thought.

'The soldiers are parrots!' Peters exclaimed now. 'They can repeat a figure! Great! Maybe they won't say it when they're told to say it, but if their mouths should drop open to catch a fly and something should drop out, then it's the army line, isn't it. They're bloody country bumpkins who can't even *count* up to two hundred and ninety-eight. Did you notice how these fourteen-year-olds talked?' Peters asked.

Kenny looked as if he could hit him. 'They sounded bloody Spanish to me,' he exploded. 'Or do you speak to you in Swahili?'

'They're from the provinces,' Peters said, in the knowledge that he was one of the very few people in the bar who knew the difference between a provincial accent and the capital's. 'The army isn't going to get under-age conscripts from the city to fire on their own people in the shanty towns, is it? So they wheel in the country boys. And they tell them the bloody Cubans are coming. How would a common soldier in Caracas know that two Cubans had been arrested at the border? Of course he wouldn't, would he? So what does that mean? I'll tell you what it means, it means there are no bloody Cubans, that's what it means. But these provincial half-wits have been told there's a full-blooded communist revolution and an invasion of Fidel's hit-men to boot! It helps them aim their guns straight, it greases their trigger fingers until they can't stop firing! They can never kill *enough* commies. The holy shit of terror runs through the average arse at ninety miles an hour at the mere mention of the commies! But' – and here Peters paused to bring Stevens closer into the conversation, and it was clear to Walker that most of what he had to say from now on would be aimed at him – 'but there *are* no communists out there, and that is where we plumb the depths of this conspiracy to the limit. If there are no commies, who has gone and invented them? The President? The generals?' He paused. 'What about just for a moment, just for a moment, considering the Americans? Someone out there has manufactured a situation. All we have to do is sit back and see who profits from the little story. Isn't that right?'

One or two people, like Walker, had stopped to watch the growing confrontation between Stevens and Peters, which Peters was now obviously playing for all it was worth. There was a certain déjà vu, a certain entertainment-value in the clash. It was better than the television screen, at any rate, where a singed cat was being pulled through a meat-mincer backwards.

'The Cubans have been running guns down here for years,' Stevens said huffily. 'Everyone knows that. You don't have to invent the Cubans.'

'Fidel at the gates of the bloody city, on a white charger to free the poor from the hateful yanqui yoke?' Peters taunted.

'Why not?' Stevens said. 'They were in Nicaragua, they were in Colombia, why not here?'

'They're a pretext,' Peters snapped, 'for every sideshow on the bloody continent. The Yanks have got a lot of old scores to settle down here, and with the commies on the run in every corner of the globe, that's what they're going to do. If they have to jack up a frenzy with the locals by saying the communists are coming, they do it. Come on, Stevens! Okay, there are communists, okay. There are probably still half a dozen journalists in this city paid and fronted and feather-bedded by the Russian embassy – they've probably just forgotten to cancel the standing order. But *they're* not the revolution; they couldn't win a bar-room argument, let alone a bloody country. But the Yanks,' and Peters paused again, 'the Yanks, they have to invent their enemies. It's paranoia. No bloody self-confidence, that's the trouble with the Yanks. If you make a man a criminal for burning your beautiful flag, how are you going to distinguish who are your real enemies? The Yanks can't tell the difference between a thorn in the side and a stake through the bloody heart, so they start to spread their favourite rumour. This President scares them, that's what it is, so they want to whip him into line by stirring up a bit of civil disobedience.'

'You're surely not going to write that!' Stevens said sniffily.

Peters put his reddened face up closer to the American's. 'They're not rioting because they're Cubans, they're rioting because they're starving, for Christ's sake! And they're starving because their lovely fertile country which has everything they could possibly want, is too stuck with foreign debt to give it to them.'

'Starving people don't fire on the army with automatic weapons,' Stevens said with disdain.

Walker got up from the stool, went across the room to the window, and looked down into the street with his back to the argument. The Club was on the first floor, and the windows were old-fashioned high sashes which came almost to the floor. On the far side of the road, two soldiers 'guarded' the intersection, though at night their presence was almost entirely superfluous: no one could penetrate so far into the cente of the city without being shot. At night, the fighting was outside the city, in the shanty towns and away from the eyes of journalists and other observers.

The centre of Caracas was built on a grid system, with occasional departures from the pattern, the main one being the huge plaza of the Parque Central which the government had stretched into a mile-long pedestrian garden walk, joining the business district where the Club and the Hilton were both situated, to the shopping malls of the Sabana Grande. It had been a grandiose project, full of good intentions, and was dotted with the statues of South American heroes – but it was unfinished. The grid system was easy to guard; the whole huge area could be made safe by placing just two soldiers at each intersection. But out in the mess of the new construction sites, which had been plundered in the past few days for bricks and other missiles, it was not so easy. There would be plenty of cover there, Walker thought. And once you reached the Sabana Grande? It was a short, dangerous, duck-and-dive away. That was where the middle-class housing blocks were, including the Gomez block, where Jimenez lived.

Behind him, Walker heard the argument rise and fall. Soon, no doubt, when drink increased the belligerence level, Peters would malign something American that was *too* close to Stevens' heart, and Stevens would call Peters a communist, and the argument would be back where it had started. Walker sipped from the tumbler of Scotch in his hand and lit a cigarette. The two soldiers, Peters was right, were no more than fifteen, and country boys. Some of them loved the gun, but some of them just wanted to be back home. If they saw you, they would all shoot on sight, there was no doubt about that. *If* they saw you . . . Walker looked further along the street to the next intersection in the grid. The orange street lights glowed over the empty city. The street was impossible. You might get a few yards, if you were lucky – no more than that, certainly. But a few yards was how far it was to the alley that connected the street to the rear of the Club, past the dustbins, over a wall and into the Parque Central.

Starving people don't fire on the army with automatic weapons. Stevens' phrase rang alarm bells in his head. In a way, Stevens and Peters were both right, but the telling remark, in Walker's mind, was that one. To blame the Cubans for the

128

uprising was all too easy, and consequently it was right to be suspicious of that explanation. But the real question, in Peters' admirably concise phrase, was, who would profit from it? Who was supplying the weapons? Walker's thoughts turned full circle and back to Jimenez. He had to see Jimenez before the Imronal account was finally wound up and its work completed. It wasn't really inconceivable, was it? That Rausch were putting up the money for the guns? The stakes would have to be higher than anything Walker had imagined, but wasn't it possible that in this case his imagination had been just too conservative?

As inconspicuously as he could, Walker slipped out of the bar, across the hall, and stood in the shadow of the Club's narrow doorway. The huge moon looked over the mountains and onto the city like a searchlight waiting to be turned on him. He watched as, only thirty yards away, one of the conscripts scuffed the tarmac with his boot while the other stood up and strolled to the centre of the intersection to stretch his legs. They didn't seem particularly observant. They smoked, they chatted, they idly watched the four streets that converged on their section of the grid, they even slumped on the pavement and looked as if they might sleep – though they never did this together. Like everyone else in Caracas shut in their houses from dusk till dawn, they were just trying to devise methods of getting through the night.

He stood in the doorway for twenty minutes or so, as the small trickle of sweat stopped inside his collar and itched as it dried. The silence was more eerie than the sight of the two conscripts, and the heat intensified the silence like a blanket. This empty city, built for the movement of millions, was now a huge, broken-down machine, with only the occasional distant rattle of automatic gunfire to suggest that somewhere, some part of it was in working order. Once a truck filled with troops rumbled past, but luckily for Walker, it was travelling fast to the east, along the road that was at right-angles to the one Walker was hiding in. They were regular troops, and the conscripts waved enthusiastically to them as they passed, but they didn't get any acknowledgement. The regulars came from the Regimiento di Guardia Honor, judging from their red epaulettes, the President's own guard who occupied the barracks opposite the President's Miraflores Palace. The barracks had been built by the dictator, Gomez, in the fifties, and the troops had guarded both him and his civilian successors. A cynic might have said that the army could be trusted no further than the twenty yards that divided one side of the Avenida Simon Bolivar from the other.

Walker watched as the soldier who had stretched his legs returned and urinated against a wall on the corner. He shouted something to his partner, who walked slowly over to join him. They exchanged a few words, then strolled round the corner, perhaps to look at something the first one had seen. Walker waited five seconds for them to come back, waited to see if it was a trick. Sometimes the conscripts played a game of Grandmother's Footsteps in the hope of catching someone dodging down the street behind them. It was fun, their only entertainment in the small hours, to shoot those who broke the President's curfew. The last two mornings Walker had seen the bodies of two people shot in just this fashion – tramps who had nowhere to go but the streets.

But they didn't immediately return, and Walker ducked out of the doorway and ran the ten yards to the alley's entrance in less than two seconds, and threw himself into the pitch black where the street lights couldn't penetrate. He stopped and held his breath and listened, but there was no shout and no tramp of running, booted feet. His heart raced from the tension, from the stillness of the past twenty minutes broken by the sudden dash, and he peered into the gloom at the end of the alley, where he could see the Club yard's single light dimly illuminating the wall behind, and the rusty barbed-wire that was coiled along the top. He could reach the yard easily through the darkness, and behind the wall and the wire was the Parque Central, the President's abortive attempt at turning Caracas into Paris. There, with luck, there was enough cover to take him all the way to the Sabana Grande and to Jimenez.

Starving people don't fire on the army with automatic weapons. The implication was clearer than ever to Walker. Peters was right about that. People were going hungry, they didn't have the money for fundamental needs – they certainly didn't have money to purchase guns.

The wall was ten feet high. Walker struggled to the top, using an old air-conditioning box the Club had thrown out to clamber up, and began the tortuous process of unravelling a length of the wire large enough to get through. It was old, and worn by the rains, so that some places where he tried to extricate another loop, it simply snapped. The rust stained his fingers, and brittle bits of wire fell away into the dark chasm on the other side of the wall. He hauled himself up at last, the corner of his jacket snagging briefly as it flapped to the side, and then he dropped to the concrete paving of the park. His eyes had adjusted to the darkness. There was a bench a few feet from where he had dropped, and an unemptied waste-bin next to it. The grass began at the edge of the path and, criss-crossed by other paths, stretched away to the broad boulevard on the far side of the park where the street lights still glistened, and where there was a truck-load of troops speeding towards the Miraflores Palace a mile away. To his right, a quarter of a mile away, Walker saw the Polar beer building with its huge blue neon sign, still flickering on in stages, then wiping itself out, then flickering on again. People still drank beer, even in times of crisis. But the building was a landmark for Walker, for beyond the Polar building was the Sabana Grande and Jimenez.

The eeriness of the streets was nothing compared to the mile of planned paths and gardens, half-finished, that Walker hurried through. The statues of great South American heroes loomed blackly every thirty yards, freedom fighters, liberators, presidents, revolutionaries – men from every country from Mexico to Argentina. Plaques too dark to decipher announced what role they had played in the great unravelling of history that spanned a continent. They loomed out of piles of builders' rubble, and beside discarded machinery. Bricks and sheets of metal, kerbstones, scaffolding and sacks of cement were strewn, abandoned, on the great pedestrian walkway that was still just sand because the different-coloured herringbone-pattern bricks that were to pave it had been looted even before they were laid down. The empty ghost of the Los Ingenieros Metro station, the only finished structure in this desert, stood ghost-like in the moon. There can never be a revolution in a city with a modern Metro – who was it at the Club tonight who had said that?

There were rows of army trucks parked along the boulevard near the Polar building, troops who could be rushed to a trouble-spot wherever it appeared. Walker watched a soldier light a cigarette and saw the brief flare blind him before it settled into a steady flame. Another stood, legs apart, away from the circle of street light, buttoning his fly. The rest were hunched half-asleep in the backs of the trucks. Walker looked back in the direction he had come from. The city's three biggest buildings stuck up into the moonlit sky. What could you say about a city whose three biggest memorials were a bank, a hotel and the barracks of the Regimiento di Guardia Honor? Walker asked himself. He took brief cover behind a pile of masonry, slipped past the trucks, and found himself in the tiny dark street with its shuttered bars and shops where he had met Jimenez four days before. If Jimenez heard knocking on his door in the middle of the night during curfew it would mean only one thing to him: soldiers, come to arrest him. He would be terrified before he even discovered that it was only Walker. And that, for the purpose of their little meeting, could only be a good thing.

Back at the Club, no one noticed at first that Walker had slipped away. The argument between Peters and Stevens washed sluggishly backwards and forwards like water in a boat's bilges, without ever reaching the crescendo Walker had anticipated. From the start, O'Connell had not been interested in the argument, only in the warring personalities, and he was the only one eventually to look up and down the room, idly at first, then like a fox, for Walker. O'Connell didn't care too much whether it was the Cubans or the Americans, the Venezuelans themselves or even the Martians who had inspired the revolt. What drove O'Connell was the prospect of a story, any story.

O'Connell walked out of the bar and looked in the hall, but Walker wasn't telephoning London. Upstairs, the bedrooms were unoccupied. He even poked his head into the toilets and the laundry room, and his curiosity was even further aroused: no one went out during curfew, yet Walker wasn't here. At last O'Connell strayed back to the bar and thoughtfully drank another beer. So the Geneva Bureau Chief had a story, a story that was important enough to risk a bullet for.

TEN

The Source Runs Dry

There was no lift, and the light bulbs had been removed or broken long ago, but moonlight was all Walker needed for the climb, and as he mounted the bare concrete staircase the steps were patterned with geometric bands of light. The flats in this block had two rooms to a family; the staircases were open to ground level, so that entry had been easy. But there was no breeze tonight, and the stairwell was littered with old scraps of newspaper and stank of urine. The one comfort was that the higher he climbed, the further he left the mosquitos behind – they never came above the third or fourth floors. When he got to the tenth floor he could make out a fire-fight – it must have been two miles away, in Santa Theresa – and heard the delayed rattle of the guns as they sang through the night. By the time he reached Jimenez' flat on the twelfth floor, he was exhausted, both by the climb and the choking heat.

Take the intitiative, he told himself now, standing breathless on the landing. Hammer on the door as if you wanted to break it down – that's what the soldiers do. Soldiers would have woken the entire block by now, and be making holes in the door with the butts of their guns. They didn't do it just to frighten whoever it was they'd come to take away; they were themselves afraid. The resistence they met with wasn't always passive. Walker regretted not bringing a heavy instrument, a stick or an iron bar, to hammer at the door. How would Jimenez react? A night-time disturbance, during curfew, ought to put the fear of God into him, but with Jimenez you couldn't be quite certain of anything. He still carried the photographs – there were several of them, not just the one he had shown Jimenez in the bar – in case Jimenez got nasty, or he hadn't done the right thing. Walker ran through a scenario in his head: Jimenez had come clean with his wife, told her about his mistress and begged her for forgiveness. He had promised her he would never stray again. Now he would meet Walker at the door and, seeing it was only the gringo journalist, he would set the whole block on him . . .

Walker paused to suck in what air there was in the still hot night, and to collect his thoughts. When he looked out over the city from this height, it relaxed him. It seemed so calm and normal – the neon advertising blazing out from the company blocks in the city centre, the lamp-lit streets and avenues like orange snail-trails. Only the absence of people and of cars was odd. This was a silent city, with soldiers waiting on every corner to kill anything that moved. In the morning normality would return, people would go about their business – until night fell again, locking them in their homes for six hours of cartoons. Ten floors below, as he surveyed the street, he saw a body slumped in a doorway, someone gunned down earlier in the night. A tramp? A woman taking water from a neighbour? Or a Cuban revolutionary? For a moment, the smell of it seemed to rise all the way up to him from the street; the stench of blood and defecation.

Walker picked up a piece of broken stick from the floor and gripped it in both hands to smash against the flimsy plywood of the door. The blow sounded hollow down the concrete stairwell. There was silence. He hammered again, for longer this time. He could hear the door of the flat below scrape open slightly and he saw a sliver of light creep out into the stairwell. He heard the urgent 'Sssshhh' – a woman's voice, he thought – and then the light faded out as a television set was switched off in the flat. But he could feel that the flat's occupant was still there, waiting, watching, and the last thing he wanted was to attract the attention of the rest of the block. Jimenez' flat was dead. Had Jimenez gone? To his family perhaps, or his wife's family? Conscious of other doors opening above and below him in the stairwell, Walker struck the door again and again, each blow leaving the round mark of the stick embedded in the wood. He saw himself surrounded by Jimenez' neighbours; he saw them emboldened by the realisation that it was not the soldiers who had come to call, but a lone gringo, an enemy, a victim for them in their fear; he saw himself being torn to pieces by them, thrown from high up to join the other corpse in the street below. And then Jimenez' door opened. He jammed the stick into the crack and heaved the full weight of his body against it, throwing the slight form of the bank clerk away from the entrance and back into the centre of a small, badly-lit room with a rank smell of stale cigarette smoke and a television set dancing with silent cartoons.

The room had hardly any furnishings. A low table sat in the centre, partly covered by a patterned cloth. Against the wall nearest the window was a cooker with two hobs, and a sink with pipes and bare, plasterless wall showing underneath. At the window, one curtain hung limply, half attached to a broken rail. On the other side of the room, as Walker took it all in with a single glance, was a square shower. A few cupboards lined the other walls. There were glasses and the remains of a meal on two plates on the floor. On one wall was a cheap print of the Liberator, Simon Bolivar, looking out incongruously with his hooked nose and his nineteenth-century military uniform. Jimenez stood in the centre of the room, off balance, confused, and behind him, framed in the further doorway, was his wife in a pale yellow nightdress, her face wide-eyed and scared, one hand gripping the doorframe and the other clutching the top of her nightdress to cover her neck. Walker slipped past the front door, slammed it behind him and locked it, without turning away from the bank clerk's gaze. From behind the open door where the woman stood came the low wail of a child's crying.

'You're a fool,' Walker said harshly, and the sudden break in the tension made the woman gasp. 'Two days, you had two days. Where is the information?'

Disbelief clouded Jimenez' face as it slowly dawned on him

that this was not the soldiers. It was replaced by a furious anger, inspired by fear – but he didn't speak. The wailing in the back room rose to a small scream. Jimenez half-turned, and a frantic babble of Spanish that Walker couldn't follow sent the woman scurrying back into the bedroom, but she didn't shut the door; Walker could see the glint in her eyes reflected in the television screen. Jimenez shouted at her again, and this time the door was shut firmly and Walker was left alone in the room with the bank clerk. Take the initiative, he thought, don't let him gain his confidence. Don't give him the time to consider his options. It crossed his mind that Jimenez might not act as rationally as he had done in the café; he might scream, or physically attack him. Through the smell of cigarette smoke there came the more pungent odour of fried peppers and oil.

'Did you want your wife to know?' Walker said, and prayed again that Jimenez had not already told her. He stepped across the room and took his elbow gently, and led him to one of the two hard wooden chairs that stood by the table. Jimenez looked scared again. Thank God, Walker thought, he hasn't told his wife. 'Why haven't you contacted me?' he said, and eased the clerk into a seat and stood over him, looking down into the scared face. 'We had a deal: the photographs or the information. Which do you want? Tomorrow you can forget everything – either way.'

'I don't know,' the man stammered, and Walker felt a pang of guilt. 'The time, it isn't easy for me,' he said. He was not the man he had been two days before, Walker saw. If it were possible for Luis Jimenez to shrink, he had done so.

'The bank . . .' he said. 'I do not have access to this account. There are difficulties, so many difficulties. What can I do?' He wrung his hands and looked everywhere in the room except at Walker.

'You're lying.'

'Please. Please not here.'

The tension in Walker began to ease as he saw the bank clerk's anxiety increase sharply. There wasn't going to be a

137

fight, the Venezuelan was ~~helpless~~ – and for a moment Walker felt sorry for the man, and for his wife's unreasoned fear, her face that had shown such blank terror when he first came in through the door. For her, Walker didn't have to wear a uniform to be a soldier; to her, anyone who could call at night in the middle of the curfew was a killer.

Walker pulled another chair across the room, the only other chair, and drew it up opposite to Jimenez. He wanted the man to talk, not to be frightened into silence – or worse, lying. 'I want to know what you have found,' he said.

Jimenez turned an agonized look towards the inner door and screwed up his face in indecision. 'Please,' he said. 'Not here. Not now.'

Walker lowered his voice so that it barely reached the slumped figure of Jimenez in the chair before him. 'Then you *have* found something,' he said.

'I can't help you,' Jimenez pleaded. 'I can't. Please, I can't.'

Walker leaned forwards, staring into the face of the terrified clerk. 'Don't lie to me. Just don't lie to me or I'll take the photographs here and now and show them to your wife. Is that what you want?'

'There's a man,' the clerk stammered in a half-whisper.

'Who? The signatory of the account?'

'Yes, yes!'

For a moment Jimenez was frozen in his seat and his lips were drawn back over his teeth in exasperation. He couldn't look at Walker. His fear of his wife was greater than Walker could possibly have hoped for. When he spoke again, he mumbled his words at the floor like a child confessing.

'He comes to the bank two, sometimes three times, a week. I have watched him before. He came first four weeks ago, maybe more, I can't remember. I never noticed him particularly. As far as I was concerned, he was just an ordinary customer.'

'What was he called?' Walker said.

'I can't say. I don't know!' Jimenez corrected himself, and a profound guilt overcame him. He risked a glance at Walker to

138

see if he'd been found out, then he looked away again immediately. Walker could see his mind desperately searching for a story that was plausible, for some version that would get the gringo off his back. 'I never see the account itself,' he assured Walker hurriedly. 'The president deals with the man on his own. He is a special customer, always with the president of the bank, in his office. Never in the front.'

First he's an ordinary customer, Walker noted, then he's a special customer. Jimenez was flailing in the dark, trying to avoid the truth.

'All right,' Walker said. 'The president always meets him. You see him two or three times a week and he makes a splash. He's noticeable, he's never dealt with by anyone else. So tell me some more about him. What is he, American? Six foot tall? How many heads has he got?'

Jimenez had fallen silent and was playing with his fingernails. He was wondering exactly how far he could go, Walker thought; how much the gringo would swallow. Either that, or he didn't have a clue what he was talking about.

'American,' Jimenez said painfully. 'Yes, I think he is a yanqui. I think so.'

'Why do you think so?' Walker pressed him closely. He was getting close to the man's breaking point. Jimenez would soon have nowhere left to run, and that's where the truth would be. He leaned towards the Venezuelan and caught the smell of fried oil on his breath.

'I don't know. I don't know, for Christ's sake!' Jimenez wailed. 'The man is with the president of the bank. How could I know?'

How could he know? Walker thought. But at the same moment he knew that Jimenez knew exactly.

'If you don't know if he is American,' Walker said, 'if you know nothing about the man at all, how is it you know he is the man who is the signatory of the Imronal account?'

For a moment Jimenez seemed to wrestle with himself in an agony of indecision. He fought to suppress what was on his lips, or maybe to invent something else, something even less plausible than before. His head began to sway and he wrung his hands. There was a sweat on his forehead that broke out in beads and ran down his face and over his eyes. He didn't look at Walker, but screwed his face up and struggled with the demons in his mind.

Walker stood up and walked across the small room in three steps. He stopped by a low table and picked up a half-empty flagon of rum, looking at the label as if that was really all he'd come for. Apparently satisfied, he sloshed some of it into one of the glasses on the table, picked it up and gave it to Jimenez. As an afterthought, it seemed, he poured a small measure into a second glass and, sipping it, turned away from Jimenez and walked slowly towards the front door of the flat. Then he stopped and looked back. Jimenez' eyes were fixed on him now, and there was a new fear in them, the fear that Walker would go, leave the flat, and he would see his chance of salvation disappear for ever with the photographs. Walker knew that Jimenez was wondering how on earth he came to be at the flat at all, after dark and during curfew. He took some malicious pleasure in the thought that the clerk would assume he had a special licence to be out, perhaps that he had influential friends in the military. . .

Suddenly Jimenez began to speak. It came in a halting rush at first, like someone who is scared that unless they speak fast they will forget what it is they have to say.

'He came in four days ago, Thursday, yes, it was Thursday, I knew it was him, so confident, he never comes to ask any of us in the front, he goes straight to the door at the back of the bank, to the president's office. The guards always salute him, they open doors. They know him. Sometimes he tips them money, they greet him as a special customer, no one else gets the same treatment, I know, I've worked there for six years, no one, not even the gringos who come from the big companies, the oil people, the people who have the contracts on the Metro. Not even them. He is unique. I know it is him. I know!' He said it with such determination that it made Walker look at him in alarm. He didn't want the clerk to drive himself into a corner from which he saw no escape. There must always be an escape for him – and that escape must be Walker.

'How?' Walker repeated. 'How do you know he is the signatory on the Imronal account?'

Jimenez was nearly in tears. Walker could hardly pick out the words he mumbled in his misery. He said them in a feathery whisper now, and all the time he glanced behind him at the door to the bedroom, as if his wife was going to leap out at him from the darkness.

'There is a woman,' he said. 'She is the president's secretary. The president's secretary,' he repeated as if he didn't quite believe it, and Walker knew that now he had his finger on the truth. Jimenez was having to drag the words out; this was no longer invention.

'It is she who told me,' Jimenez added.

But in spite of knowing that the man slumped in the chair in front of him was at last telling the truth, for a moment Walker missed the implication in Jimenez' hesitant words. There was a long silence, reinforced by the silent cartoons on the screen behind them, and Jimenez looked up at Walker with an appeal in his eyes. What was the understanding he was looking for after this apparently minor confession? For a moment it puzzled Walker. And then he realised that the slight, small man in front of him, who went in such fear of his wife's reappearance at the bedroom door, had just revealed a secret that was infinitely more important to him than the mere identity of the man who signed the Imronal account. He had just told Walker the identity of the woman he was seeing behind the back of his unforgiving wife. And of course, it was obvious. How would a man who worked five days a week in a bank and spent the sixth with his family, and then did a shift as a security guard on Sundays, ever get to meet a woman with whom to conduct an affair? There could be only one explanation: that she was there all the time, working in the bank with him. Jimenez' mistress was the bank president's secretary – and now he had implicated them both. This was the reason for his grotesque discomfort.

Walker sipped thoughtfully at the cheap, bitter drink. 'Just tell me,' he said. 'Tell me what happened last Thursday. Is it what always happens? Does the man vary his pattern? Take it slowly and don't miss anything. Talk me through this man's movements in the past four weeks. He *is* American, is he?' Jimenez nodded and looked at the floor. 'Do you know where he goes when he leaves the bank? Tell me everything, don't skip a single detail. Tomorrow it will all be over for you. The photographs will be yours.'

Behind them as Jimenez talked, Walker was just aware of the soporific flickering of the cartoons as they played out some macabre comedy.

'The Imronal account was opened on the fifth of December,' Jimenez began in a voice that was barely audible. He still didn't look at Walker, but he had stopped the desperate shaking of his head from side to side and seemed to be laying out the facts in his mind before he spoke. He was genuinely trying to remember, perhaps. He spoke falteringly, always picking up the thread of the story again after a hesitation, but always with some effort. 'He comes on Tuesdays and Thursdays, every Tuesday and Thursday since the account was opened. Always personally. No one else accompanies him unless they are outside. I don't know. I don't see that.' He shrugged. 'They are in a car maybe. He enters the bank at nine-thirty in the morning as soon as the doors are opened. He must wait across the street, he's never late. There is hardly anyone in the bank at that time, people don't start to arrive until nearer ten when he has gone. Of course, he has an arrangement with the president, otherwise it could never be so quick. But he never rings. He always picks up the amount of money at the same time, twice a week, without a break in the past four weeks. The money must be waiting for him. If he does not telephone first, then he must make arrangements for the money for the next time when he is in the office. That is the only communication. But the amounts are different. It started off slowly at first, a million dollars twice in the first week, cash. It is packed into a metal trunk which he brings with him whenever he comes. Then the amounts began to rise. In the second week, he removed nearly five million dollars. Five million! But it has remained steady since then. Now there is just under seven million dollars left of the original amount. The twenty-three million.'

'How is the money handed over?' Walker said.

Jimenez paused. 'How does he pick it up?' Walker pressed.

'Always dollars,' he said at last. 'Never bolivars, always dollars. The denominations are low. That is always the case. Just five- and ten-dollar bills each time. It is a huge quantity of money. The sheer size of it! That's why he needs the trunk. All used notes, nothing new. Fives and tens, fives and tens. He won't, he doesn't, take anything else. But that is the strange thing. Why those denominations? The bank doesn't carry that amount of cash in those denominations. It can always arrange for them, of course, but who wants that? Who wants five million dollars in half a million, a million, different notes?'

Walker crossed over to the cooker and saw an old cracked frying-pan with grey oil swimming in the bottom of it. There were the remnants of a stew beside it, just the tops of the vegetables, bits of green stalk and the seeds of the red peppers lying on the side. 'So how does the money enter the bank?' he asked. 'If you don't carry that amount of bills, how does he take that amount out?'

'When the account was opened,' Jimenez said, squeezing the words out like bitter pips, 'it was a straight transfer. All cash. All bills in the denominations I've described. Fives and tens, fives and tens. What does the man need them for?' he repeated in amazement. 'The cash, all used bills, was transferred wholesale in a security van four weeks ago. It came from an account in Panama, I don't know the name of the account, but that is where it came from, and it was deposited here. In Caracas.'

Walker leaned over Jimenez and could smell his breath, he was so close. The man's trembling lips revealed blackened teeth, and there was a reek of stale food and rum. Jimenez took a huge swig at his glass and pulled back in his chair as if he thought Walker was going to hit him.

'The name,' Walker breathed. 'What is the name of the gringo who comes twice a week for his trunk full of money? Your friend . . .' He paused. 'Your friend, the president's secretary. She must know the name of the gringo.'

'He calls himself Franks,' Jimenez blurted. 'That's how he signs the account. Señor Franks,' he said, and his thin lips pulled back over his teeth again in anguish.

The light of dawn in Caracas creeps slowly at first down its narrow valleys. Some parts of the city remain for some time in darkness, where they are wedged against the mountains or where a valley dog-legs and shuts the sun away, but these small key-holes of early light illuminate the top of a tower or the Hilton Hotel, and burn the tops of the mountains before other parts of the city receive the sun at all. The long, slow, grey tropical dawn goes on like this for an hour or more before the sun bursts out at last above the dark line of hills.

At six o'clock, when the curfew ended, Walker found himself still sitting in one of the two cramped wooden chairs in Luis Jimenez' flat. Outside the window, twelve floors below, there was as yet none of the usual daytime noise and confusion of hawkers and fruit-sellers, the hooting of horns and the rancid smell of petrol fumes; the lorries that brought the city's meat and vegetables up from the country would only just be starting off. The cafés were closed still, and the bored, tired conscripts who had stood and sweated the night away in the centre of town had no one to extort a cup of coffee from. No one, after curfew ended, wished to be the first to open his doors.

If, during the night, it had occurred to Luis Jimenez to wonder why Walker could not step out again into the darkness as easily as he had arrived from it, he had not said anything. He was exhausted by the burden of his confession and by the long night. He had sat slumped in his chair; sometimes falling into a light sleep, only to be woken by another question from Walker; sometimes looking up in alarm as Walker paced the room against a background of crying babies in the room next door. 'What was he like?' Walker kept insisting. 'Was he tall, or fat, dark-haired or fair? How did he dress? A suit, or casually? Did he dress like a gringo or a Venezuelan? And was there no first name? How can you be sure the name was Franks?'

But all the bank clerk could answer was that he didn't know anything about the man's appearance, and how could he tell whether or not he even had a first name, let alone what it was? The gringo signed his name Franks, that was all he knew, that was all the woman had been able to tell him. He'd already risked his job, and perhaps more, by telling Walker so much; on top of that, he'd risked the woman's job and his relationship with her. From his despair, Walker guessed that Luis Jimenez had had to sacrifice a great deal with the woman to get her to help him. What she had demanded of him, he couldn't guess, but now, undoubtedly, she had involved him in another coil of deceit which trapped him as effectively as the photographs in Walker's pocket. The photographs, which he hadn't yet handed over. Jimenez had been too exhausted and too beaten even to ask for them. Perhaps he knew that Walker would never have brought the negatives with him to such a dangerous meeting.

As the dull dawn light, reflected from the low, grey clouds above the city, began to spread across the silent streets, Walker rose to his feet again. His eyes were red from lack of sleep, his lips burned yellow from the tar of so many cigarettes. Empty cigarette packets lay screwed up across the low table, and butts overflowed from two dinner plates that had stuck to its dirty surface.

'Cash?' Walker kept asking. 'You're sure the money came to the bank in cash!'

'Yes, yes, yes,' Jimenez replied from his despair. 'I've told you, it cannot have come any other way. The bank doesn't keep twenty-three million dollars in small bills in its safes. It doesn't keep twenty-three million dollars in any denomination, not any more. No one wants their money in Venezuela any more, not in the Brunner Bank. Not any more,' he repeated. 'The Imronal account is the only account that has been opened in the last month.'

Jimenez' breath now stank of rum and rotting teeth and his speech was slurred from the drink. He kept repeating himself, as if that was the only way he could get through, as if those were the only words he knew how to speak. He couldn't have been a better victim of interrogation, Walker thought, if he'd been tied to the back of a steel chair with a five-hundred-watt bulb shining in his eyes . . .

But cash! That Rausch should want to transfer the money around the world at all was odd, and that it should be done in so clandestine a way certainly suggested illegality. But cash! Cash in bills of five and ten was astonishing. What could you do in Venezuela these days with twenty-three million dollars? Quite a lot, was the answer. Quite a lot, when just over a month before, twenty-three million dollars was worth two hundred and thirty million. It was money that would go a very long way indeed in Venezuela. But it was also money that could only be used for buying things inside the country. What did Rausch want so much?

Starving people don't fire on the army with automatic weapons. Stevens' utterance wouldn't leave him. Surely it couldn't be Rausch buying the weapons? Apart from anything else, you couldn't buy that amount of guns under the nose of the government. And they simply weren't available in this part of the world in that kind of quantity; this wasn't Cuba or Nicaragua, no one was dumping truck-loads of guns on the Venezuelans, there hadn't been a war round here for thirty years, not since the fifties. And Venezuela was an American dormitory, and the Americans didn't supply revolutionaries on their own patch.

Twice Jimenez' wife had tried to come out of the bedroom, and twice the clerk had bawled her back inside. Whatever his exhaustion and his state of physical collapse, he could still raise enough energy to shout at his wife. The second time bolder than her husband, she had sworn at Walker in vivid

Spanish. She'd threatened to tear his eyeballs out and feed them to the buzzards. Who was he? she had screamed. And whoever he was, why didn't he get out and go back to the sewer he had come from? And behind her, in the bedroom, the children had screamed too. But, obedient to the strange etiquette of her marriage, when Jimenez commanded it she had meekly returned to the bedroom, even when she was in mid-rant at Walker. And she didn't rant at the slumped, broken-down, black-toothed figure that was her husband, sitting with his head in his hands in front of a tableful of cigarette butts, with rum spilt down the front of his shirt. She wouldn't do that, Walker thought. Not unless she found her husband had been unfaithful. Then, maybe, she would tear out his eyeballs and feed them to the buzzards.

Seven hours after he had entered the building, Walker stepped out into the heat of dawn. He ached from sitting in the cramped chair, and his tongue stung with the cigarette smoke. There were a few people about now, and they looked at him warily. A gringo was a rarer sight in Caracas now, especially in this part of the city. The families of the company men had all packed up and gone home in case the President carried out his warning and shut the airport. The swimming pools in the Country Club were no longer cleaned, for the foreigners had locked everything up and sacked the servants – or put the lucky ones on half pay – then they themselves had gathered up their portable goods and left the country. The golf club was now a firing range for undisciplined conscripts, and the foreign clubs had shut their doors and battened the windows with solid metal shutters to wait for better times. There were no more Sunday barbecues, Walker thought, because there were no more families. Yesterday had been a Sunday, and on the next day, Tuesday, all being well, Señor Franks would make another call, at nine-thirty on the dot, at the Brunner Bank in the commercial district near the Parque Central. Señor Franks. What kind of a name was that? One thing he could be sure of, Walker thought as he stepped off the kerb and out into the dust of another overcast and humid day, was that it was not a real name. No one would use a real name to pick up cash that had such a fugitive and chequered history. Franks. At least it had about it something a little more plausible than Imronal, Bantura and Centurion.

By the time he entered the Hilton Hotel the sun was high in the sky. In spite of his night-long session with Luis Jimenez, he felt an elation that no exhaustion could dispel. He had a name, not a real one, perhaps, but a name that, tomorrow, he could put to a face. It was a name that would be made flesh. The story was moving again. He put a call through to London and spoke briefly to Slick Mather's secretary at midday, London time. The editor was at a lunch in Scotland, he was told, and had been expecting a call from Walker for several days. The tone of the secretary's voice was exactly what her boss's would have been, Walker thought; perhaps it was like dogs and their owners – though he couldn't remember which was supposed to take after which. He showered and ate breakfast in his room, and called the Foreign Correspondents' Club to ask for Grimes, the Bogota stringer, but Grimes was out already, no doubt impressing his London paper with his diligence.

When he had put the phone down, Walker stood in thought for some moments. Then he unlocked the safe in the bedroom wall, took out a small envelope and put it in the inside pocket of his jacket. He suddenly felt a residual pity for Jimenez, brought on by his elation, a shower and a clean set of clothes. The man deserved to have his photographs. There was nothing more that Luis Jimenez could do for him, and the photographs were all that remained between them. Walker descended to the ground floor and took one of the smart black American taxis the Hilton had in its own stable, and told the driver to take him downtown to the Gomez Tower. If Jimenez had already left for work – though it seemed reasonable to expect he might be late on this morning of all mornings – he decided he would go to the bank and simply hand the envelope and its contents over the counter. He felt a sudden need to put the little bank clerk, with his cascade of other worries, out of this particular misery at least.

What Walker saw as the gleaming car turned left into the street where Jimenez lived, and banked low over the pot-holed surface of the road on its Pontiac springs, didn't alarm him at first: a body being carried into the back of an ambulance, the blanket pulled right over its head. It would be the body in the street from the night before, the ambulance service was back on call again – even they were banned during curfew. It was the crowd that made him pay more attention; the crowd suggested a fresh death, not an old one. But it was the howling madness in a face, a face he recognised, the face of Señora Luis Jimenez as she screamed and clawed at the body under its blanket, that made him stop the taxi. The woman was bleeding tears. Walker turned cold in the stifling heat.

'What is it, what's happened?' he shouted at the driver.

The man shrugged.

'Ask someone! For Christ's sake, ask what's happened!' he shouted.

The driver was dragged from his torpor by the angry demands from the back of the car. He lowered his window and spoke to someone, too fast for Walker to follow. The body was disappearing into the back of the ambulance now. A police bike had pulled up and a policeman in dark glasses climbed off it to help the ambulancemen push away the crowd so that they could close the doors. Señora Jimenez still screamed, and battered the back of the van with her hands. She had her back to the taxi.

'He jumped,' the driver reported. 'You want to get out here? You want to go to the riots?'

'Take me back,' Walker said. 'Take me back to where I came from.'

ELEVEN

Armando Higson's Stratagem

Walker had only one day to kill before he could wait in front of the bank for the arrival of Señor Franks, but it was one day too many. When he returned to the hotel from the Gomez Tower, he burned the photographs and the negatives in a large green china ashtray shaped like a dragon, and then he stood by his ninth-floor window and looked out over the city. It was the same height, more or less, from which Luis Jimenez had jumped. The time was around nine o'clock now, and the city was running normally again. The soldiers' combat fatigues had faded away, replaced by the bright reds and yellows of the ordinary populace. There were teams of lottery-ticket sellers down below there on the plaza, two men in sombreros were playing guitars, and all along the Parque Central's pedestrian walkways there were stalls selling everything from coconut milk to copies of Dickens. Walker turned away.

A day to kill in Caracas. He was too restless to write, and anyway he didn't have anything that was worth filing. His mind cast about for something that would help him forget Luis Jimenez, and he thought of the woman, Santos Calderon's widow. He suddenly wanted to see her now, as if by helping her he would somehow be exculpated for Jimenez' death. He had promised to do what he could for her, anyway, and he wanted to help her. But he was too weary, he realized suddenly, to follow it up now. And what was Jimenez' death, after all, but just one more in a city of death. He lay down on the bed, and closed his eyes to rid himself of the headache that had been hammering on the inside of his forehead ever since he had first spotted the ambulance outside the Gomez Tower.

But he couldn't lie still for long. He got up and changed again, putting on a tennis shirt and jeans. With his jacket slung over his shoulder, he walked out of the Hilton foyer to the pick-up area. This time he didn't take a taxi, he wanted to walk. He dodged across the six-lane highway in front of the hotel and somehow reached the other side without being sworn at, let alone hit. He passed the new complex of concrete stairways and plazas that made up the entrances to the theatre and concert halls. A dance company from the USSR was apparently still playing. But how could it be, Walker thought, when nobody was allowed out after six p.m.? Maybe they were old posters. On the left was the art gallery where an exhibition by the Venezuelan artist, Reveron, was still attracting the crowds. Walker strode across the plaza and down more concrete steps into the Parque Los Caobos, where the mahogany trees shrouded the gardens from the harsh sun, and from the traffic noise of the freeways that ran all around it. Once the park had been well-ordered and clean, and you could still appreciate the boldness of the design. There were huge, ornate fountains with tumbling nymphs, and fishponds where the water reached to the very top of the surrounding walls so that they looked more like mirrors than pools. But since the crisis, the fountains had dried up and the ponds were clogged with weed; children had fished them out weeks before. The leaves that fell throughout the year were uncollected, and vandals had had a field-day: the army was busy elsewhere, and the police hardly showed their faces now. Walker walked the quarter of a mile across the park and came out under a flyover close to where he had been the night before when he was trying to reach Jimenez' flat. The authorities had intended to create a mile-long strip through the centre of the city, consisting entirely of parks and pedestrian walkways, but the project had never been completed, and the city centre was now a mess of ground-level and overhead highways, many of them still without pedestrian bridges, so that it was almost impossible to get from one side of the city to the other on foot.

Under the flyover, there were two Indians selling puppies in tiny palm cages. Each time a car went past, which was every two seconds, the puppies flinched as if it was the first they had ever seen.

Walker dodged across the traffic again, and followed a small path across unmown grass to another broad pedestrian street with planted trees and huge concrete tubs waiting to be filled with flowers. There was a roundabout with the big Polar beer building towering over it, and then a short walk past empty tourist gift shops to the Plaza Venezuela with its English chemist. He stopped in one of the many street cafés for a coffee with whipped milk frothing on its surface, and pondered again the oddness of all this normality. In a city where, three hours ago, the streets had been full of the night's dead, there was now no hint of violence. Now, as he looked around him, he was reminded of the main drag at a coastal resort in Europe, not of a city in the throes of violent civil war. It was as if there were two separate cities, the one a night-time horror, the other perfectly ordinary. Walker looked at his watch. He'd managed to kill an hour and a half on the walk, but it was a long time until lunch. It would be a much longer time before he could shake off the image of Luis Jimenez' screaming wife. How close he had been to her. If she'd turned, if she'd looked at the taxi . . . The body in the street. What had happened to the body in the street? Was it picked up in a van at the same time? Had Jimenez obligingly jumped when the van was doing its rounds?

Walker shivered in the heat, and thought of the *La Prensa* editor at the Foreign Correspondents' Club. Armando Higson. His story, which Peters had used to silence the young photographer, Kenny, had concerned the number of bodies the government was keeping on ice at the University. Five hundred and thirty, was it? Five-fifty? Keeping them out of sight to limit the damage done to its reputation. Walker gave himself a mental kick. He should have filed that piece, it was a good story. The others had all written it up somehow, it would be appearing everywhere in the next few days, except on the desk of Slick Mather. He'd become too obsessed with the Rausch account, that was the trouble. He'd landed himself in the middle of a proper foreign story and he'd been blinkered to it by his preoccupation with Rausch.

Rausch could wait if necessary. The mobs that were nightly descending on Caracas weren't going to.

Walker finished his coffee, paid a waiter who wore tight black trousers and a dirty white shirt, and walked away from the Plaza Venezuela to the south, towards the Botanical Gardens and the Cuidad Universitaria.

An imaginative design, the University had been built in the seventies, like a small town set deep in the botanical garden in the centre of the city. The seventies were the time when the country was awash with oil money, the time when all the grand public projects had been inaugurated. The University was one of the lucky ones that had been finished. Now, fifteen years later, though the quality of the design was still evident, the concrete-chunk building material had begun to rot and discolour in the tropical humidity. Stuck in the middle of its jungle garden, and not properly maintained, the University was beginning to look like a modernist Aztec ruin discovered in the rainforest.

There was a one-way drive that ran around the whole of the Cuidad Universitaria, and the hospital was at the far end. It was a teaching hospital, and all along the curved concrete walls that shut the road in from the foliage around it, Walker read the student graffiti, a mix of the usual revolutionary exhortations and more recent rallying cries against the 'deuda', the debt. For a moment, Walker wondered why the place wasn't crawling with soldiers. Then he remembered that the University had been shut down right at the start of the troubles, when the President declared martial law. That hadn't applied to the hospital, though. But if the hospital was filled with the secret corpses of those killed in the President's campaign against the rioters, they would hardly open the doors for a gringo reporter, make him coffee and take him on a tour of inspection. What had Kenny said? Two hundred and ninety-eight, that was the casualty figure the soldiers were quoting. But Walker tended to agree with Peters; that would almost certainly be a propaganda figure. Higson had said that in the University hospital alone there were five hundred and fifty.

Two ambulances were drawn up outside the hospital's front entrance, but neither seemed to be in haste; there were no lights swinging around on their roofs, and the driver's seat of one was unoccupied. Walker approached the front of the building and was not challenged. There was a soldier standing lazily against a wall, with one foot resting on it and the barrel of his automatic rifle nose-down in the dusty road – against all military maxims of cleanliness and safety, Walker thought. The soldier looked at him, first carelessly, then with the professional interest of a profiteer: the gringo would have to pay for whatever it was he wanted. But Walker stepped right past him, never meeting the eyes of the man behind their regulation dark glasses. Never meet the eyes, Walker thought; treat them with disdain and contempt, that's what they understand. If you look like a friend, they will treat you like an enemy.

He walked through the doors and emerged into a high hall dimly lit by electric light, where he was temporarily blind after the brightness of the sun outside. It was a circular area, he saw when sight returned, with a grey, institutional chipped-stone staircase that curved in a semi-circle up to the next landing. The floor was also of chipped-stone blocks in green and red, with black borders around the wall – and everything else was hospital-white. Still there were no soldiers, no challenges. What was there to hide if there was no one on guard? Walker stepped up the stone stairs and came out onto a landing with a reception desk and four corridors leading off it in a sunray pattern. There was the same brisk air of minimum waste here that you found in any hospital anywhere in the world; the nurses walked in short, fast steps and they spoke in short, fast sentences. He didn't see any sense in lying to them.

'I'm working for a paper in London,' he said, and showed the nurse at the desk his press card, and another local card he had obtained with the word 'Periodista' written on it, for the benefit of the occasional army captain who would arrest you and hold you for twenty-four hours on the pretext that he didn't know what 'journalist' meant. The desk nurse looked at the card with cursory indifference.

'You want to look around the hospital?' she said.

Walker was taken aback. She looked into his eyes with a direct, neutral gaze. She was young – and dark-haired, like ninety per cent of Venezuelan women. Her skin had the soft sheen that comes from working all the time under electric light, and as she talked she tapped a pencil up and down on the pad she had been writing on before Walker disturbed her.

'Well,' he said. 'There's a story going round. I wanted to talk to someone. Perhaps see for myself.' He stopped, and felt the pin-pricks of sweat break out under his shirt like an itch. At any moment he expected the shout, the hand on the shoulder that wheeled you around until you almost fell over, the shake-down and the threats. The desk nurse turned round, more relaxed now, and called to another uniformed woman, her senior, who was standing just inside a room to the left. She came out of the office, and with much pointing at Walker, and grinning, the young nurse explained who he was and asked what the procedure was for journalists seeking access inside the hospital. The older nurse nodded, but didn't respond to the younger one's good humour.

'What do you want to see?' she asked Walker severely.

'I want to visit the morgue,' Walker said.

The young nurse burst into fits of laughter. She gabbled something which sounded like, 'With everyone going to the morgue against their will, at last we have someone who really wants the trip.' And then she laughed loudly and looked at Walker under her eyelashes.

'Come with me,' her superior said calmly, and led Walker into the office from which she had been called. She sat him down, but herself remained standing, riffling through some papers on the desk. 'What have you heard?' she asked, without looking up.

'It's a story I want to deny,' Walker lied. 'That you have five hundred and fifty corpses from the riots hidden here, in the University hospital morgue, so no one can see them and no one can know about them. It's a story that damages the government. I want to know if it's true.'

'To deny it?' she said.

'To deny it,' he replied strenuously.

The nurse put the papers into a file and the file under her arm. 'Come with me,' she said again with the same peremptoriness.

She led him down the stairs and through a door at the far end of the circular hall. Then, after a number of twists and turns, she opened another door, in front of which a man sat at a desk, making notes in a large book. Walker felt the sudden chill of the lowered temperature. The floor here was paved with tiles; it reminded him of going to the public swimming baths, which he hated, when he was young; he half-expected to pick up a rubber tag and a basket for his clothes from the man behind the desk. The nurse addressed the man, who reluctantly put down his pen, shut his book and picked up a set of keys which he brought round to the front of the desk, then led Walker and the woman through another door and into a pristine, tiled enclosure with twenty drawers set into the walls.

'This is the morgue,' the nurse said. 'Room for twenty. All full up.'

The man obligingly opened up each drawer until Walker, after repeated attempts to stop him, finally succeeded.

'Your friend must have made a mistake,' the nurse said. 'We don't have room for that number of deceased.'

'It wasn't a friend,' Walker said.

'Whoever it was must have made a mistake, then,' she said snappily. 'They must mean another morgue. I don't know. The city is full of them. You'll have to find out upstairs.'

'But this is the only University?' Walker asked.

'Oh yes,' the woman said, and Walker followed her from the coldness of the morgue back into the stifling heat of the hall.

Higson had said the University, Walker thought, stunned for a moment. Of course he had. He'd had that stupid story which he'd told with such obvious relish, about his doctor friend who normally didn't have enough corpses for the poor students to experiment on. 'Cadavers' was the word Higson had used, or was it 'carcases', Walker wondered with distaste. The editor of *La Prensa* had lied. Lied to them all at the Foreign Correspondents' Club.

When they were outside, she turned to him. 'Have a look round the wards,' she said. 'They are full of the wounded. I can give you a pass. You can visit anywhere here you like.'

For an hour he walked round the wards with her. When he left she held out her hand. 'Be sure you write what you see,' she said. 'Not what you hear.' He shook her hand and left.

None of them had come down here. None of them who had heard Higson's story had bothered to come and see for themselves. Walker thought for a moment about Jay O'Connell. Five hundred and fifty corpses was a scene the cameraman would have loved to film.

He took a taxi this time, he was tired of walking. But it was more than that. He no longer wanted to kill time. The shock of Jimenez' death that morning had faded and he no longer felt aimless and sick. He had the driver drop him at the Foreign Correspondents' Club, but there was no one there he wanted to speak to. They were nearly all out, apart from the Guyanan barman who had an unpaid bill he wanted settled from the night before. And there was no sign of Higson. Perhaps there would be no sign of Higson until he was sure that none of the foreigners had checked his story. Walker returned to the hotel and, in his room, began a piece about the hospital and about the stories that were circulating concerning the dead and wounded. He mentioned Higson by name and accused him of deliberate disinformation in the Club the night before. He had been to the University hospital, he had seen the morgue there, the only morgue, and it was full, full to the brim with twenty corpses. It was a good piece, largely, he knew, because it would drive a stake through the competition. Slick would like that. The visit to the hospital that had started as a means of distracting himself from the responsibility he felt for Jimenez' death had resulted in a piece that would buy him time. But he still had to find an answer to the question why: why Higson had told that story. It had been a brilliant story because it had been aimed at the kid photographer. Everyone wanted to see his nose rubbed in it, and Higson had obliged. He'd obliged very neatly indeed. And they had all believed him.

TWELVE

The Imronal Stakeout

It was just after nine-fifteen in the morning, and the doors of the Brunner Bank across the street were still bolted with chains on the outside and God knew what other security devices concealed within. Walker sat in the hired fawn Chevette thirty yards away, in a line of other parked cars. He watched as two security guards with sawn-off shotguns paced up and down outside – the morning shift – and two soldiers lolled in the heat on the corner of the street like wilting fruit. Nine-thirty on the dot, Jimenez had said. For a second night running, Walker hadn't slept. The first was thanks to Jimenez alive, the second, thanks to his death. The night before, he'd choked up a room-service meal and drained half a bottle of Gold Medal, the local whisky, which had stayed down – though now he wished it hadn't. Maybe, all those months ago, his critics had been right. Maybe he shouldn't be doing this any more. How far should you try to push a story? How many other risks, to other people, did Jimenez' death justify?

The staff must come in through the back. That was the way banks did things, for security reasons. Twenty-four hours after Jimenez had died, his lover would be coming to work as usual, to sit at the bank president's desk and wonder what had caused him to kill himself. Walker tried to imagine what she was feeling – if she felt anything at all. She would know that whatever the reason for his suicide, it must be connected with the information he had persuaded her to give him. Perhaps she doubted that he had killed himself at all, perhaps she was afraid that Jimenez had been murdered by the person to whom he had passed the information, and that the same person would narrow down the possibilities until he worked out how Jimenez had procured it. Perhaps Jimenez' lover was scared for her own life. Walker worried about what she might do in those circumstances. Would she own up, in order to obtain some kind of protection? Or would she conceal her role in the hope that she would never be discovered? If Señor Franks failed to turn up at nine-thirty on the dot, did it mean that the breach in the bank's security had been discovered? He crunched another styrofoam coffee cup with his fist and prayed that whatever happened now, Franks would arrive on cue. Nothing, nothing could be worse, after what had happened, than for him to lose the trail now.

He looked anxiously at his watch, to discover that it had scarcely altered since the last time he looked at it. The big hand was edging towards the four: twenty past nine. Franks would be here in ten minutes, unless the death of a bank employee had alerted him. Unless whoever Franks was working for, whoever controlled the Rausch account from above, had instructed Brunner to close the account within hours of the news of Jimenez' death. Walker worried, and watched everything that moved in the street. Was the money now waiting elsewhere, safe in another Caracas bank for Señor Franks at nine-thirty? It seemed unlikely. The operation had taken Rausch a long time to set up, and it all depended on the goodwill of Herr Brunner. You couldn't alter months of arrangements overnight and suddenly secure the confidence of a different bank altogether. No, they would have to stick with Brunner. The only thing they might do would be to alter their normal pattern. Perhaps Franks would not come at his usual time. Perhaps he wouldn't come for days, or even weeks.

Walker looked slowly down the pavement on the bank's side of the street. Where the patrols of the security guards in their dark blue uniforms stopped, there was a pavement café with round tables encroaching as far as they dared towards the kerb. It was half-full. A few tail-enders from the morning rush to work still sat and slowly drank their coffee before dragging themselves away. For a moment Walker's eyes rested on a large red Buick parked on the kerb just outside the café. There was no one inside it, but two young, wealthy Caraquenos sat at the nearest table with two beers. They wore their wealth for all to see. Both had expensive-looking clothes, but it was the shoes that told Walker the clothes didn't just *look* expensive – you couldn't buy shoes like that in Caracas, only in Europe or America. The boys had hair-styles you only saw in magazines, and the car was obviously washed and polished by hands less clean and manicured than theirs. They were relaxed, laughing and joking, sipping their beer, and apparently untouched by the social disintegration that was taking place around them. They would be residents of some smart fortress in the Country Club, rich by any standards anywhere in the world, representative of that small element of the population that had kept its wealth and continued to flaunt it – dollar wealth, earning its interest far away from the troubles at home. In Miami, the boutique owners called people like them the 'Two of Its'; when they asked the price of some coveted item and were surprised at how little it cost, they invariably asked for two of it.

But what most riveted Walker's attention was the snake that was coiled around the neck of the darker, more handsome boy. It would slip up his arm and look at the other customers with total indifference, then slide down the other arm to dip its head into the beer glass the boy offered it. Sometimes he let it leave him altogether, and it wound its way across the table and climbed over the shoulders of his friend. They both laughed at it, and at the consternation of one of the waiters who refused to go near it. The few other customers on the pavement watched it with a mixture of disgust and fascination, but no one took his eyes away from it for long. It was the local playboy's ultimate toy, a status symbol that spoke of opulence and carelessness. Walker watched it as it coiled itself slowly into the boy's shirt, pulling its body behind it in a series of slow, extended thrusts.

When Walker dragged his eyes away and looked again at

his watch, it was nine-thirty-one. With a feeling of panic he looked up again at the bank's entrance, only twenty yards to the left of the café. A security guard was undoing the padlock on the door and clanking the chains away. Inside, unseen hands must have released the electric locks of the reinforced, tinted-glass doors, and they swung open to reveal a broad, polished-stone interior with the usual mess of plants in pots. Nine-thirty on the dot, Jimenez had said. There was no sign of anyone entering the bank. Perhaps Franks had chosen to enter through the rear, use the staff entrance as a precaution. Walker cursed himself for not having checked the road at the back. It was a simple precaution that Franks might easily have taken. If you let a man walk in and out of your bank with millions in cash in his hand, it was likely you would let him use the staff entrance if he asked for it. Where the hell was the gringo with the metal trunk who came every Tuesday at nine-thirty on the dot?

At nine-thirty-two and a few seconds, Walker saw a woman, elegantly dressed, carrying a handbag and wearing what are called in smart circles court shoes, step out of a large four-wheel-drive Chevrolet pick-up which drew up directly outside the bank. A security guard held the car door open for her and exchanged what looked like a familiar greeting. She was a regular, it seemed. She stepped up the three stone steps to the door of the bank, and the second guard, with his sawn-off shot-gun thrust into his belt, opened the dark-tinted glass door for her to step inside the bank. It was so unexpected that Walker was thrown for a second. Señor Franks was always the first to enter the bank, Jimenez had said. Had he taken that too literally, Walker wondered briefly? Was it simply a Latin exaggeration? Surely, when Jimenez said that Señor Franks arrived first, always first, on a Tuesday and a Thursday, it could just be a common generalisation. No one could always be first, not unless they were waiting as the guards undid the padlock and the doors opened for the first time. Someone with something to hide and a trunk full of money to follow would hardly draw attention to himself by waiting outside a bank door for it to open. This was a freak occasion, Walker told himself, and the sweat that had broken out on his forehead, no longer just from the heat, began to dry. He was too jumpy. Calm down. It couldn't always happen the way they wanted it to happen, not always. The woman wanted to get to the bank as early as Señor Franks normally liked to, that was all. Her business, if not as awesome as that of Señor Franks, was no less important to her. Besides, Señor Franks was not a woman, was he. Señor Franks was clearly a man. The bank president's secretary saw him twice a week, signing the withdrawal for however many millions he was removing and then carrying it back through the bank in a metal trunk, past the window where Jimenez had worked, through the door and . . . away. This was a woman who had entered the bank and she carried no trunk, just a handbag from Cartier or Vuitton or wherever rich women bought their handbags these days.

For the first time it crossed Walker's mind that Jimenez had lied to him. For the first time he thought, perhaps, just perhaps, Jimenez hadn't jumped from a twelfth-floor window because he had broken the bank's secrets and expected to be found out. The nasty thought that the bank clerk had jumped because he had told a lie to him hit Walker like lead. Suppose Jimenez had jumped because he knew, not that the bank would find him out, but that Walker would find him out in a lie and show the photographs, in consequence, to his wife? Walker broke into a full and free sweat. He found he was drenched with it. His heart was hammering with the thought that he really had killed the bank clerk, that the fear of the photographs had been too much for Jimenez to bear. He felt sick again. He wanted to retch but he knew that what he wanted to retch would never come up. What he wanted to be rid of was the responsibility for, and the horror of, Jimenez' death. Of course, he realised now, it had been impossible for Jimenez to do what he had asked him to do. The man had been trapped between two immovable forces – his first meeting with Jimenez should have told him that. The man was proud. Only when Walker had shown him the photographs had he caved in. For his wife's sake, he had agreed. And then, when he knew he couldn't betray the bank, he knew also that he couldn't face the shame with his wife. The shame of the photographs.

As his chest began to tighten in disgust at what had happened, and as he turned away from the front of the bank for the first time in over half an hour, it was only chance that prevented Walker missing a middle-aged man, dressed casually in slacks and a sports shirt, who walked slowly along the pavement to the front of the bank, ascended the steps and received the same courteous treatment the woman had before him. But this time, the man they tucked away their guns for, for whom they opened the door with as much grace as guards could muster, carried a metal trunk. He carried it as if it were heavy already, Walker noticed, as if the trunk were already full before he reached the bank. Walker could see no car that he could have emerged from. There was only the Chevrolet, still parked at the bank's entrance, the single parked car in either direction on that side of the road for a hundred yards. Señor Franks had materialised. He was three-and-a-half minutes late, but he was here. He had appeared out of nowhere and Jimenez had not lied.

Walker sat back in the car seat and tried to calm down. He was shaking, he realised. A completely novel thesis had passed in and out of his mind in the space of two minutes and had completely destroyed his equilibrium. He was too jumpy, too jumpy, he told himself. The woman was a freak incident, she had entered the bank on some entirely uncon-nected business and it had thrown him totally. For Christ's sake, he had to concentrate, to calm down!

Now there was just the wait. That was all he had to do, wait for Franks to leave the bank. How long would the transaction take? Jimenez had said that normally it was all over before anyone else entered the bank. Not this morning, though. But there had only been a minor departure from routine. You couldn't stop someone entering a bank before you.

He leaned back again and tried to tune down his nerves. He had to be ready. In a few minutes, forms signed, trunk packed, Franks would be emerging again, and he would have to have his wits about him in order to follow him. Of course they wouldn't leave an unarmed car waiting outside the bank for him to step back into. There would be a car, Franks' car, that would approach the bank when it was deemed correct to do so. It would be waiting somewhere further up the street.

It was now, for the first time, that Walker realised that Jimenez could only have told as much of the story as he and the bank's president's secretary, his lover, could see. Actually *see*. He waited, the race of his heart dulling again. But it bothered him. He didn't know quite why, but it bothered him that Jimenez' story could only be based on what Jimenez and the secretary actually saw themselves.

Walker had lost the exactness of the timing by the time Franks came out through the door again and placed a pair of sunglasses on his face to shield it from the light. There had been too much on his mind to notice how the time had gone. But when Franks did emerge, he was ready. He watched him casually put on the glasses and carry the trunk down the three steps to the pavement. But there was no car waiting for him to step into. He didn't pause. He didn't look up and down the street in indignation as Walker expected him to do, he simply opened the driver's door of the Chevrolet pick-up and slung the trunk into the back. None of the security guards stepped forward to help him as they had done earlier, and as they had done with the woman. He climbed into the driver's seat and gunned the engine into life. The Chevrolet began to move away from the kerb as Walker started the Chevette's engine and pulled out to follow him. But something was wrong, something had gone very badly wrong. As he pulled the car away from the opposite side of the road, the doubts he'd had before returned. It wasn't just that Franks – or whoever Franks was – had driven off in the woman's car; it was what had irked him before, seconds before, that Jimenez and his lover could only report what they actually *saw*. What could they see, according to the story that Jimenez had told? Nothing that took place outside the doors of the bank. They couldn't see the woman arriving in a car which Franks then drove away, that was for sure. Jimenez could see Franks enter, walk past his window, have the interior door to the president's office opened for him by the respectful guards inside – and then it was over to the secretary. She could see a man enter with a trunk, greet the president of the bank no doubt, sign the withdrawal forms, and leave with the trunk the same way he had come. There was no reason for either of them to notice the woman because she wasn't part of the transaction. It was Franks, Señor Franks, who showed himself acquainted with the Imronal account. The focus was on Franks. Why should anyone notice the woman since she had nothing to do with the Imronal account at all?

For Walker it was a sudden and immediate decision. He pulled the car to a halt and watched the Chevrolet accelerate up the hill straight ahead and lose itself in the traffic. Walker turned his car violently to the left and tore down the side-street next to the bank. He craned to the left to find the street that led to the rear of the bank. A car pulled out ahead of him, slowed, and began the slow, halting movement that meant the driver was trying to find a shop or particular house – looking for a piece of hardware, or a garden seat, or breakfast, God knew what, but it was slowing Walker down almost to a standstill. He jammed the palm of his hand onto the horn and left it there, but the man didn't take a shred of notice. Everyone in Caracas sounded their horn at the slightest opportunity. In London, Walker thought wildly, you could be arrested for excessive use of the horn.

He jammed his foot down on the accelerator and overtook. Now it was the other man's turn to hoot, but it was too late, Walker was past him. He flew down the street, desperately looking for an opening to the left, but there was none. Finally he reached the intersection at the bottom and slewed to the left, through red lights, and put his foot down for the next intersection where the lights were still green. The road system here was still on the American pattern, blocks of roads with a one-way system that could have you driving round for days just to get to back where you started. Walker hit the green lights and turned to the left again. He was coming up to the rear of the bank from the other side when he saw a small dead-end turning to the left which led to the staff entrance. He slowed the car to a halt at the end of it, and looked down the street with its rubbish bins and refuse and parked cars. At what he judged to be the rear of the bank he saw a metal trunk being loaded into the back of a blue Buick by two security guards, the woman thanking them and giving them something for their trouble, then climbing into the Buick and starting the engine to drive out of the street right in front of where Walker had stopped.

The blue Buick drove south at first, out onto the six-lane Avenida Abraham Lincoln, towards Bello Monte and El Rosal. Then the woman turned left and began to ascend the slopes of the Avila mountain that led to the Country Club. Walker watched her swing the car through automatic gates into a long, palm-fringed drive that led up to a house built like a moorish castle. The gates closed behind her and Walker switched off his engine, sank back in his seat and closed his eyes. It was just after ten in the morning. Now the waiting began again.

At midday, a different pick-up arrived, the gates swung open, and Walker watched it disappear up towards the battlemented front of the house before they shut again. The man, Franks, had been at the wheel, and there was a vast array of fancy lights and auto club memberships pasted along the front bumper. There hadn't been time to look at the registration number, but it was a different car and a different colour from the one Franks had driven off outside the bank. But apart from the arrival of Franks, confirmation at least that Walker had made the right decision, there was little activity in the Country Club that morning or through most of that afternoon. There were no tennis parties, wives shopping,

167

servants in white uniforms shaking out rugs in the front gardens: nearly everyone had gone. Further up the street, Walker heard a gardener mowing someone's lawn, but that was all. The place was silent, apart from the birds.

By the time the gates opened again, Walker was asleep. He'd parked well over a hundred yards away from the entrance to the house, and backed the car into someone else's drive to be inconspicuous, so it was lucky for him that the pick-up turned left out of the drive instead of right, otherwise he would never have heard it. Even so, he cursed himself for his carelessness. Suppose another car had left the house earlier and gone in the other direction? There weren't going to be many more opportunities to follow Franks and his money. Jimenez had told him that it had already dwindled from twenty-three to less than eight million since the account was first opened. Whatever operation it was that Franks controlled, it hadn't got much longer to run.

It was with a shock that Walker noticed the time was nearly four-thirty. He didn't know when he'd fallen asleep, but the heat inside the car, combined with his previous insomnia, had made it impossible to stay awake. He was just in time to get the car moving before he saw the Chevrolet disappear over the hump in the road and begin its descent towards the city. He would hang back until they left the Country Club, Walker decided. Once in the city he could move up closer to the Chevrolet, in the heavy traffic of the rush hour where he wouldn't be noticed. This time the person who drove the car ahead was neither the woman nor Franks. He looked younger than Franks and had black, shoulder-length hair – it was all Walker could make out as the car passed. There was a risk in following him, Walker knew, but the day was coming to an end. The curfew began in an hour and a half, and it was a fair guess that this would be the last trip they made out of their castle until the following day.

For more than twenty minutes Walker had no clue where the Chevrolet was going. It was easy to follow, the traffic was slow and jammed together: commerce still continued in the city even in times of civil disturbance. And after half an hour, he began to worry. He could follow the Chevrolet only so far if he wanted to have time to return to the hotel or the Correspondents' Club before the curfew was enforced. Already they were going through the suburbs of the city where the fighting was taking place. There were roadblocks on the big route to the sea, and though the army was waving most people through, they occasionally stopped someone for a real shake-down. Walker watched as the Chevrolet eased around the chicane of the roadblock and he prayed that he wouldn't be stopped either. He had almost reached the point of no return; if he didn't turn back in five minutes, he would have no time to get back to the city. Up on the sides of the hills, the lights of the barrios were beginning to come on, and ahead the road wound on, across the bridges over the valleys and though mountain tunnels. The decision must be made now. The curfew was only enforced in the capital and in the two industrial cities to the south, on the Orinoco. The army admitted it could not control the country as a whole: five miles outside the city limits was the decree. Walker decided he would not return, not that night. Whoever was in the Chevrolet must have had plans to stay clear of the city and the curfew, and whatever happened, Walker had to follow whoever it was in the car in front.

It was dark by the time the Chevrolet turned off the freeway that led to the sea, and Walker knew immediately there would be a problem. He had assumed that the car would continue down to the coast, to the airport perhaps, or one of the big towns that serviced the capital, but it turned off on a steep, narrow road that led away from the capital and away from the sea – to the west, high up in the mountains. There was a big moon that disappeared from time to time behind scudding clouds, and the wind that had started since they left the city suggested that there was rain on the way. Last time, he remembered reading somewhere, last time the country had descended into real civil war, the guerillas had always stopped the fighting when it rained. On public holidays and when it rained.

The problem for Walker was that as soon as the Chevrolet left the main road, it had left all of the traffic as well. He couldn't hide behind another car because there were none on this naked mountain road. He pulled over as soon as he saw the car ahead turn off, and watched the lights of the Chevrolet wind slowly back and forth in a zig-zag up the mountain, almost vertically it seemed in the dark. And then, when his eyes had adjusted to the light of the moon, Walker started his own car up the pot-holed road behind the car ahead – with no lights, no warning for the driver of the Chevrolet that he had company. It wasn't as hard as he'd thought it would be. The moon, when it was clear of a cloud, was very bright, too bright. If the driver of the car ahead looked back, he would see a car behind him, the roof glinting far below in the moonlight – but even then, Walker hoped, he would simply assume that, along with most other cars outside the city, its lights just didn't work. With luck, he wouldn't notice the Chevette at all. And with only the steady zig-zag progress of the Chevrolet to follow, high up and far ahead it was much easier for Walker than following a car in traffic.

The road passed low houses made of wood and mud, with donkeys tethered up outside them, and noisy dogs whose rabid bite would certainly be worse than their bark. The fields changed as the hill steepened. At first, there was pasture and some maize and sweetcorn: then the land changed to terraces that faced the morning sun, impossibly steep, well-tilled rows of earth cut into an almost vertical hillside. There were neatly-planted lines of coffee bushes, with banana trees every few paces to protect them from the worst of the sun. Then the cultivation petered out altogether, and there was just bush and scrub, thorny, tangled trees bleached white by the sun, where snakes and lizards slept through the dark hours.

Finally, the road emerged onto a flat plain. There were the lights of small villages dotted across it and, far ahead now, the Chevrolet seemed to be taking a right turn towards one of them. Still without lights, Walker crossed the plain and followed the track the other car had taken. They had been driving for three hours, but the winding mountain road had kept the pace slow, and they still weren't so very far from the city.

The village had a dusty earth street that ran through the centre of it. There were one or two pick-ups parked alongside low houses with ornate wooden doors, unpainted for decades, and a few thin donkeys and goats roamed here and there, grazing from refuse left lying in the front yards. As Walker had approached across the plain, there had been sudden flicker of light and then the whole village had been a plunged into darkness. Somewhere in the mountains, where the threatening storm had already started, there was a power cut. Streaks of silent lightning from far off lit up the town with a white light that neutralised the colours of the cars. There seemed to be no cafés or bars, and just one decrepit one-storey hotel called The Stella, but nevertheless the street was filled with people all travelling in the same direction – towards the far end of town. They walked like a procession, slowly, as if they were going reluctantly to a funeral. They were all men or boys. A few women stood in open doorways talking to each other, but whatever there was at the far end of the village, it was strictly for the men. They wore filthy slouched straw hats, and some were barefoot. Up here in the mountains, Walker noticed, it was a lot cooler at night than in the city.

He parked the Chevette at the beginning of the village and walked in the same direction as the procession. Somewhere up ahead the car he had followed had also parked. There was nowhere to go in this town, it seemed, except to wherever it was the men were walking. The young man with the black shoulder-length hair was sure to be going there too. They were mostly farmers and would rarely see a gringo up here, but they still took little notice of Walker. There was no curiosity, only a sullenness. The pick-ups in the street suggested a kind of prosperity, but the land that Walker had driven through was bare.

THIRTEEN

The Gallera

'*Turista, turista!*' the voice shouted in Walker's ear, and a short man with a thin black moustache ran alongside him and jostled his elbow. 'You want horses? I rent horses. You want hotel? I rent room. Very beautiful here. Riding in the mountains. Many, many tourists. I have best horses, best price. You like my price. Better than others. Don't go to others, they have bad horses. Starved. They not go fast. My horses are fastest!' The man paused and looked expectantly up at Walker as he ran along sideways. He had a twisted mouth, whether by nature or from the desperate hope of a sale, Walker couldn't tell. There was another, hawk-eyed man with him, younger and less eager, who walked evenly, looking straight ahead and smoking a hand-rolled cigarette. 'Gold? You want gold?' the little man said, clutching at Walker's sleeve. 'I have gold. You want diamonds? I have diamonds. Indian carvings? Very, very old. Very expensive. I have them. Be careful, don't go to the others. They will cheat you.'

'I want a drink,' Walker said. He could see the Chevrolet parked up ahead, the chromium reflecting the moonlight.

The answer seemed to fox the salesman for a moment, but he quickly rallied. 'We have best Venezuelan beer. You know Venezuelan beer? Polar. Best in the world! You like beer? I go find you a beer.' He began to run off but Walker grabbed his sleeve.

'Where's a bar?' he asked.

The younger man looked round for the first time. He had thin, almost slitty eyes, Walker noticed. He was a Colombian, a worker who'd come across the border in the good times, to harvest some of Venezuela's wealth.

'There is a bar,' the man said casually. 'Next to the *gallera*. Everyone is going there. You want to go to the *gallera*?'

Walker wondered what he was talking about. The young man raised his hands and made them into two cockerel's heads, like a shadow-play. Then he struck the 'beaks' together. 'This is the *gallera*,' the man said. So that was the reason for the steady flow along the street, Walker thought. Everyone was going to the cockfight.

They were walking past the Chevrolet pick-up now and he saw that the man with the shoulder-length hair was not inside. 'I'm here to see a man at the cockfight,' he said. Ahead of him he saw the man, the long dark hair lying over his shoulders like an Indian's. He, too, was spending his evening at the cockfight. 'Let's have beer,' Walker decided, and stopped to reach in his pocket for some money. The two men had stopped and the short man looked eager and held out his hand. 'We'll wait here,' Walker said, and gave the man some notes. He scampered off in the direction the flow of people was taking. Walker sat down on the wooden step outside a house and motioned for the young man to join him. He didn't sit, but moved over and leant on a pillar and chewed a matchstick thoughtfully. Walker didn't want the Chevrolet's driver to know he was there, but it was difficult; they were almost certainly the only two gringos in the town, and a gringo was conspicuous in a place like this. If the man saw Walker, he would surely know that something was wrong. He watched as the group the long-haired man was in turned off the street and disappeared from view towards the *gallera*.

'You may know the man,' Walker said. 'Tall, long black hair. A gringo.'

The Colombian shrugged. Maybe he knew him and maybe he didn't.

'That's his car,' Walker said, and pointed at the pick-up. The man took the match out of his mouth and turned his head with the minimum of effort to look down the street. He looked back at Walker and re-inserted the match. 'You know him?' he said through the match.

173

'We have a mutual friend.'

The man stared at Walker without replying. It was impossible to say whether he believed him or not. It looked as if he was weighing up both possibilities.

'I want to watch the fight.' Walker said. 'Are there seats which are separate from the rest? I don't want the man to see me until after the fight. How much will it take?' he asked, and carefully took a handful of bills from his pocket as if he'd had a completely different thought.

The short friend appeared with three beers and tore the tops off all three with his teeth. He didn't offer Walker any change, he just looked excited, whether at the prospect of the fight or simply the free beer, it was hard to say. The Colombian had taken the money from Walker's hand. He peeled away two of the bills and gave them to his partner with rapid instructions spoken in the sing-song Colombian accent. There were seats on a second level: you could sit above the gringo and behind him, it appeared. The man dashed off, spilling his beer on the ground in his haste.

When he was gone, the Colombian slowly rolled a cigarette and stuck it in his mouth, replacing the matchstick which he put carefully in his pocket. Walker lit the man's cigarette with his lighter, and the slit eyes watched it closely. '*Turista*?' he asked, without his friend's professional interest.

'No'.

He didn't speak for a moment. He was a man who drew things out of people by his silence. 'Why have you come here?' he said at last.

'I told you. To meet the gringo.'

'The city is full of gringos,' he replied, as if it were the answer to a question.

Walker didn't reply and the Colombian shrugged. 'It is a long way from the city,' he said at last.

Walker looked directly into the slit eyes and saw expressionless deceit. 'Can you help me?' he asked. 'Has the gringo been here before?'

'That depends.'

174

'Have there been others? I can pay,' Walker said. 'What's his name?'

The Colombian took a long draw on his cigarette and the red burned unevenly, far down the thinly-packed paper.

'I can pay for his name.'

'He doesn't have a name.'

'Who were the people he was walking with?' Walker tried. 'Locals? Friends? Are they from the city too?' He took a bill from his pocket and offered it to the Colombian for nothing, a gesture of goodwill. 'I can pay,' he repeated.

'He came last week to the *gallera*,' the Colombian replied carefully, and took the note without looking at it.

'Is that the only time?'

'And the week before,' he added.

'Always the *gallera*?'

The man nodded.

'What time does it start?'

The Colombian looked at his watch, a cheap, dirty digital with a cardboard strap. 'Sometime soon,' he said vaguely, and it could have meant five minutes or next spring.

'And he stays for the fight? The gringo?'

'He stays for two or three. Then he goes.'

'Who are the men he was talking to?' Walker asked. The Colombian looked at the bill in his hand and didn't answer. Walker sighed and dug another one from the pocket of his jacket, but didn't hand it straight over. He wasn't going to let him have it all his own way. 'You know them?' he said.

'They are the *camionistas*,' was the reply. 'Always the *camionistas*.'

'Why do they come here?' Walker asked, but the Colombian didn't speak, just looked back at him, weighing him up. What is he sizing me up for, Walker wondered, and hoped it was just for his money.

Why was the long-haired gringo meeting the truck drivers? Not just truck drivers, the man had said, *the* truck drivers. Why was Franks' associate driving three hours out of the city to meet a bunch of *camionistas*? It didn't make any

175

sense. Perhaps the money wasn't in the pick-up after all. Perhaps the whole thing was just a wild goose-chase.

The short, jumpy friend of the Colombian's returned and his eyes danced brightly with excitement. The Colombian looked at him without any particular interest, as if he wasn't quite sure who he was. The little man tugged on Walker's arm and gestured that they should go to the *gallera*. 'The first fight will be starting soon,' he said. 'Not a big fight, but you must see it. Quickly, quickly.'

'Is the gringo sitting in his seat?' Walker asked.

'Yes, yes. The *gallera* is full.'

Walker got to his feet and followed the two of them down the dusty street. He shivered in the cold but they took no notice. The Colombian walked slowly, with a sway in his gait as if he were a movie cowboy waiting to draw; the matchstick was back in its place, slowly being chewed over, like a thought. They turned left onto a grassy path between two houses and walked away from the main street. The power was still off and Walker could only see a crowd ahead, milling around the entrance to the *gallera*. Through cracks in the wood there was light, the warm flickering glow of hurricane lamps. Perhaps it was a good thing the storm had come in the mountains – it would make it more difficult for the long-haired gringo to see him. There was a thin mountain drizzle beginning to spray the grass so that it sparkled in the moonlight.

When they reached the *gallera*, Walker could see that the building was an old wooden barn which had been converted inside to form an enclosed ring with seating round it on two levels. The Colombian put his hand on Walker's shoulder and told him to wait outside. He disappeared into the shack next door, which had one wall open to the elements and was the bar he had mentioned earlier. The short man hopped beside Walker, from foot to foot, like a child. There was a childish enthusiasm in everything he did. 'Good beer,' he said, 'the best in the world.'

The Colombian returned with two large bottles in one

hand, held precariously by their necks. Inside them was a clear liquid and the Colombian opened one of them immediately. He offered it around to a group of people standing close by, and eventually it was passed to Walker. The liquid burned his throat and hit his chest so that he gasped. It was a local-brewed *aguardiente*, firewater that was better for disinfecting cuts than drinking. Leaving the bottle with the group, the Colombian led the way into the barn, still holding the second bottle.

'*Turista, turista*!' the little man shouted to anyone who could hear, until the Colombian turned round and told him savagely to shut up. The small man was proud to be the friend of the gringo. He never left Walker's side.

Inside, the barn was packed with people. The ring was on the other side of some high wooden doors, and Walker couldn't see it; the doors were firmly shut to all but ticket-holders, and without a ticket no one would get a view. Somehow the Colombian seemed to have tickets in his hand, but Walker hadn't seen his friend hand them over. There was a weighing scale where the two cockerels for the first fight were being placed one after the other in sacks. Around the walls hung other sacks with struggling birds inside them. There was pandemonium as bets were called and taken, odds reserved, then reinstated when the weights were called. The crows of the birds split the air, and the two for the first fight were now in their owners' hands, surrounded by onlookers watching for signs of strength, aggression and fearlessness. Two assistants on each side were holding the birds' legs and tying the vicious barbs onto their upper claws. They didn't fight with razors, they were too valuable, but with an inch-long thorn from a particularly tough bush that grew in the mountains. They were as sharp as a razor, and slightly hooked at the point to make them deadlier. They were fixed onto the claw with a metal ring that tightened to hold them firm. Already the birds were being deliberately shown to each other and there was no mistaking their threatening behaviour.

Walker looked at the braying mass of farmers and *campesinos*, and he couldn't see the gringo. The gringo must have gone inside already. It was nearly time for the first fight.

'You want to bet?' the Colombian asked. 'Which one?'

Walker looked at the two cocks and picked the smaller bird. The Colombian took his money and paid another man who gave Walker a crude betting slip, and they walked into the pit.

From the upper ring on the inside of the pit, Walker looked down on the long-haired gringo below. He was talking, leaning forward on his knees and gesturing to the four men who sat nearest to him. He was explaining something, and pausing once in a while as if to make sure they understood. It looked as if he was giving them instructions, but perhaps he was just telling them a joke.

The Colombian passed the *aguardiente* up and down the row until the bottle was empty and he sent for another. In the pit, the two owners of the cocks were standing facing each other on the raked sand. They held the birds so that their heads were a foot apart, and occasionally they thrust them at each other to work up their frenzy. The shouting had begun now. It was as if the fight had already started. Suddenly, at some signal, the birds' owners threw the birds on to the floor and jumped out of the ring. The birds strutted forward and then threw themselves into the attack. Their claws lashed wildly, they bumped each other and one fell, but it was just a matter of balance – no cut had been made. The noise in the pit was deafening. Men sitting at the edge were leaning over the rail and screaming, spit was flying, they were shaking their fists and hammering the wooden rail with bottles. One of the birds was less eager for the fight than the other. Men who had bet on it were shouting with equal rage at the bird and at its owner. It retreated, and its opponent flew at it, scraping along the sand with clipped wings. Suddenly the attacker looked vicious. Its beak was open in a silent scream and it lashed at the neck of its victim. The din was appalling. The noise and the feeling that it was gaining the advantage made the attacker more vicious still. With its wings opened in rage, it looked like a bird of prey. The faces of the men by the rail were almost in the sand. Fists punched the air and the screams of encouragement and aggression fought with each other above the birds.

Suddenly the losing bird fell on one wing and the attacker lashed at its head. It struggled, but it couldn't regain its feet, and the aggressor lashed at it again and again. The two owners jumped into the ring and picked up the birds to examine the damage. It was difficult to see from the seats how bad it was, the feathers were too thick to show any wounds. The owner of the fallen bird picked it up and stood it again and again until it kept its feet. It stared blankly. The eyes of birds have no expression. The victor was strutting and turning its head sharply as cockerels do, as if each movement were the result of an electric shock. When they had checked for damage, the owners released them again and the screaming blew up around the ring. The aggressor flew at the weaker bird, which hardly moved, and made no attempt to defend itself. It slashed its head and the bird fell, then struggled to its feet again under a rain of cuts from above. It even struck back once or twice, but it failed to make any contact. Finally, it fell again, and this time it stayed down as the attacker stood over it, occasionally swiping it with its hook until the owners jumped into the ring again to separate them. The owner of the fallen bird tried again to stand it up to fight, but it sagged more heavily than before. Walker saw the blood spattered on the sand. 'It's over,' the Colombian said. 'You have won.' But the owner was still trying to make the bird fight until the bets were called in and the fight declared over.

'It is dead,' the Colombian said.

Walker watched the owner shaking the bird, but its head had sagged sideways now over its neck. Hands came to wrestle the hook from its claw to use on another bird, and the victor, held high by its owner, looked jerkily around the edges of the pit as the pandemonuim reached its crescendo and arms reached out to touch the victor and to claim their bets. The fight had taken less than five minutes.

The long-haired gringo kept his seat, Walker noticed, when the audience spilled outside to the bar, and waited for the next fight. The Colombian passed Walker the third bottle of *aguardiente* and he took a drink from the neck. He had won the price of another bottle, the Colombian told him. The others nearest them had gone out too, and only he and the Colombian now drank the liquor. The bookmaker came round with the winnings and Walker bet blind on the next fight. He didn't relish another death-struggle in the ring, but he knew he couldn't leave until the gringo left. He had to see the gringo hand a case, a case of money, to the *camionistas*. And then he would have to find out why.

The second fight began in the same way. The noise and the raised arms and yelling heads of the audience swam around Walker. He saw the Colombian watching him, then turning away quickly, back to the fight. The second fight was longer, the two birds were stronger and more experienced. The victor won without killing his opponent, and Walker saw the gringo rise out of his seat in the tumult of the victory and begin to edge out of the pit before the rush began. He too stood up, and waited while the gringo and the four men with him walked past the stairs beneath him. Then he climbed down, the Colombian following. The childish friend of the Colombian's had vanished. Outside it was colder than before and Walker tugged his jacket around his neck. He felt separated from his body, as if he were watchng himself walking up the alley behind the gringo. His head had been perfectly clear inside, but now it pulled at him and he began to sway like the defeated bird. The *aguardiente* seemed to be affecting him more with every step he took, and he looked at the Colombian and all he saw were the wells of deception in his thin, black eyes.

'This way,' he heard the Colombian saying, but he dragged himself away from the arms that tried to guide him. They were on the street now, and Walker stopped, holding himself with one hand against the wooden wall of the building. He looked up from the ground and tried to focus on the other side of the street. He saw the gringo unlocking the passenger door of the pick-up and lifting out a large, bulging cardboard case. It was the money, Walker thought hazily, it had to be the case of money. He saw the gringo hand it to one of the men, and felt a pull from behind on his jacket. With effort, he shook off the Colombian's hand. His head felt unbearably heavy and he knew he couldn't hold himself up for long. He had to get to the car.

He heaved himself away from the wall, and a sharp, agonising blow caught him in his kidney. But he didn't fall. He felt other blows, and saw faces dancing around in front of his own. They laughed, and a fist came out and shattered his vision, and he tasted the blood pouring from his nose. His head was going to burst. From behind, he felt hands trying to put a noose around his neck, but it was wire, and with the last strength and thought in his body, he managed to slip his hands between the wire and his throat. His attacker tugged viciously, and the wire tightened and cut into the sides of his neck like a knife, but he prevented it from cutting his windpipe and felt the warm blood trickling through his fingers where the wire cut into them instead. He was being strangled. He was being strangled, but they weren't going to cut his throat with the wire, he wouldn't let them cut his throat. He felt the blood vessels in his eyes bulge and burst and a huge redness soak over him, the sound of popping blood vessels in his head as he opened his mouth and tried to scream. They hit him from the front and held him up by his neck behind.

'Fight, gringo! Fight, gringo!' they chanted, but Walker could no longer see anything at all. His fingers went slack on the wire, but they were still being pulled into his neck by his assailant, and his legs buckled under him, but still they held him up by the neck like a chicken. There was just red pain, and then black.

FOURTEEN

The Transcript

There was a bright orange bird in the tree above, and beyond that a clear blue sky with a single pillow of cloud. The sun had turned the land to dust.

There were no shadows here, but the body on the ground didn't sweat in the heat. There was no margin for such ordinary physical luxuries: every cell, every fibre, every heartbeat had struggled inside the inert form just to keep it functioning. Throughout the cold of the night and into the boiling dawn, the fight was waged invisibly for the intended corpse. The blood on the earth around Walker's head swarmed with ants. A buzzard flew high up in the sky, waiting to be sure, and the orange bird sang.

They had cut off his fingers, he thought. Brick-red stumps, discoloured at the end of his fist where his fingers had been. That was why he couldn't move them, he thought. He shut his eyes again to spare the effort of seeing, until he felt his fingers crackle away from the palms of his hands where they had stuck to the blood, and where the wire still protruded, clamped in his fingers like the jaws of a dog in rigor mortis. Only then did he flicker open an eye.

The field was empty and the mountain seemed closer in the daylight, though he could barely see through the cracked and broken vessels in his eyes. He lay for some time, counting his heartbeats as if he were cheering them on in a race. He felt almost relaxed for a time, until he tried to move. Then the pain rose from his kidneys and his crotch, it streamed over his chest and around his neck until it split his head. He groaned, and began to move each limb as if he were a new creature trying out its potential. When he moved his head sideways, he saw the village, not far away. It must have been an hour before he struggled to his feet, and the buzzard circled for a few times before it dipped it wings like a saluting plane and wafted away on an air current until it was a distant blot in the sky.

They had smashed the window of the car, but there was nothing for them to find inside. Walker struggled with his crooked fingers in his pockets until he found the key, and aimed it several times for the lock before it wedged itself in and he opened the door and slumped inside. There was no one in the street. He looked at where the sun must be and thought that it was afternoon. It was as if the night before had never existed, as if the village had been populated for one night only, like a fairground. It must have been half an hour more before he stirred himself to start the engine and painfully turn the car onto the dust road that led down from the mountains. They thought he was dead, that was all the satisfaction Walker was to have for twenty-four hours.

When he reached the city, it was dangerously close to curfew again. The shocking state of his appearance in the Hilton lobby raised the kind of service you only got when your laundry came back a different colour or there was glass in the salad. For twelve hours, doctors and sleep occupied his time, his eyes were frozen behind lint bags of ice and his throat and neck were bandaged white.

On the following day, around midday, his messages arrived. There was an urgent one, to telephone Slick, and one from Armando Higson from two days before. Walker dressed slowly and took a taxi up into the commercial district, forgetting to telephone London.

'To some people,' the document read, 'a billion dollars is a lot of money.'

The transcript lay on the table between them. It was opened so that from Higson's side of the table it was upside down, but Walker could read it easily. It was just after midday, and around them in the artificial darkness of the

Cowboy Bar on the Avenida Urdaneta, the tables were half-full. There was a long wooden bar to the left with western saddles instead of seats, and the wooden walls were lined with photographs of bucking broncos from the American West.

Walker, however, was not in the mood for reading the transcript or anything else. The whites of his eyes were still blood-red from broken blood vessels, and resembled a cheap special effect from a hounds-from-hell film. He was glad of the darkened interior of the bar. He also had a thudding headache from whatever it was they had put in the liquor thirty-six – or was it forty-eight? – hours before. He had a faint recollection only of what had happened after the cockfight – after the *camionistas* had taken the cardboard cases from the gringo. He remembered being punched and kicked, and he remembered the wire they had slipped around his neck to garrotte him, his eyes bursting as they tried to throttle him. They had left him his wallet and the money in his pockets; it wasn't his money they were after. He wondered what it was that had saved his life. His throat burned where the wire had cut into the flesh, and there was a dark-red and black bruise around his neck which he had attempted to cover with a bandana: he just hadn't felt up to putting on one of his sixties cravats.

Higson sat opposite him and watched him, but he had said nothing about Walker's bloody eyes nor about his odd, bedraggled appearance. He was waiting with ill-concealed excitement for Walker's reaction to the transcript. He sat hunched slightly forward, his gold teeth grinning through half-open lips and his dark eyes recessed into his face as if to conceal their expression or hide his real feelings.

'Of course, I have the tapes to back it up,' he said. 'You'll want to hear the tapes.'

'How did you obtain them?'

Walker didn't bother to look up when he spoke. Perhaps it was simply that he couldn't meet the other man's eyes with his own. He felt ill, and very conscious of his pupils swimming in their pools of blood. The faces of the taxi driver, the faces of the people in the street when he dodged as quickly as he could from the taxi into the bar, had told him how he looked. He knew he looked horrible.

But of course, Higson was right. He would want to hear the tapes; if they existed. The transcript was worthless without the tapes to back it up. And even then? Even with the tapes? He didn't know. He had every reason for not trusting the man on the far side of the table. 'How did they come into your possession?' he asked.

Higson shrugged and looked down out of the corner of his eyes. He didn't reply and Walker wasn't surprised. Higson was a journalist too; he would hardly reveal the source of his scoop, if that was what it proved to be. Not yet, anyway. Higson wanted to sell the transcript, he wanted contracts, legal documents, a water-tight profit. Only then, perhaps, would he say how the transcript came into his hands, and even then he might still be forced to protect his source. If it was an authentic document, the transcript was a phenomenon.

'The identities of two of the men in the document are falsified,' Higson said, to keep the ball rolling, to show Walker that he wasn't being deliberately unhelpful. 'But if you agree to a purchase, of course their real names will be part of the package. How I got the transcript? That is another matter. It is not necessary to know how. The third man who is speaking here is, alas, impossible to identify. At least, I have not been able to do so. If you buy it, you have the resources. You have all the back-up of a big paper. Perhaps you will be successful where I have not been.'

The third man? Was he the man who had taped the meeting, then? Walker wondered. Was Higson being genuine? Or was it 'impossible' to identify the third man because to do so would reveal the source? Perhaps the third man was a friend of Higson. Secretly taped? Impossible to identify? It all depended on how you looked at a document like this. There were too many twists, too many imponderables for a mind straightened out by piano-wire to contemplate. Chief amongst them, of course, was Higson's proven unreliability: the bodies-in-the-hospital story, which the other journalists in the Foreign Correspondents' Club had written up for front pages all over the world. But Higson, Walker knew, had lied about that – or else he had been the victim of another's story and passed on second-hand news. The question at the centre of Walker's thudding brain was, how much could Higson be trusted? Suppose Higson had simply made the whole transcript up? If he had, he must know that whoever purchased it would check its authenticity, otherwise the tapes could simply be three actors playing a part. But why would anyone go to such lengths? The facts, as Walker now saw them, were that Higson had been caught in some disinformation before, deliberate or not. Maybe now was the time to confront him with it. With Higson, it was a question not so much of how reliable the man was, but how unreliable.

'It's a selective document,' Walker said grumpily. 'Someone's edited the tapes. How do I know what the context of much of it is?'

Higson looked reasonable. 'I have cut out the comments that are distracting, irrelevant. Naturally, it would hardly make good reading in its entirety.' He shrugged again. 'Instructions to waiters, interruptions, side issues, they're all in the tapes if that is what you want. What we have here,' he tapped the transcript, 'are the main thrust of the conversation and the deal itself. You don't want to read what they all had for lunch?'

There was a tone of mockery that twisted at the end into hurt reproof. He conveyed that he was offended by Walker's suggestion; Walker was being unfair. In good faith, as one journalist to another, he had brought Walker the transcript and a story that could blow the President through the roof. He had documents, tapes, characters, all the paraphernalia to back up the story. It was a little *too* perfect, perhaps. That was what made him nervous, Walker thought.

'You are a good journalist,' Higson smiled the compliment away. 'What you can do with the transcript is far more than I can. You are a gringo, you can take this all the way to the top. To the President himself. You go to the President's press briefings.'

This was only half-true. The President had so many press briefings these days, it would have been impossible to attend them all. Some of the older journalists down at the Club joked that the President kept a permanent press briefing going in order to keep reporters off the streets.

'You can strike at the heart,' Higson said dramatically, and leant across the table, gold teeth flashing like a smile – but with Higson it was the leer of the salesman, a permanent freeze-frame of the features. 'There is nothing I can do with the transcript. For a Venezuelan paper to follow this up would be suicide. Literally, for me,' he said forcefully. 'The government would crush me and they would put the paper out of business for good. You know how it is. It is bad enough in normal times. Now? Now it would be the iron fist. These are dangerous times.' He leant over further, with a look of dreadful sincerity. 'It might not just be the paper that is closed down. You follow?'

He spoke in a low, nervous voice. Closed down. That, Walker knew, was one of the euphemisms the army was using. 'They can close you down for ever,' Higson continued, wide-eyed. 'Our lives are at stake. Me, my family, all of us have always been fearless in pursuit of the truth. You only have to look at our record to see that. My father was shot on the steps of the paper's headquarters thirty years ago because he criticised the dictator. We have never been afraid,' he said – illogically, Walker thought, in view of current circumstances. 'But I have to do the best thing, we have to act like journalists. The best thing, not just for me, but for the paper and for the sake of the truth. This,' he tapped the transcript again, 'this is more important than me, than you. That is why I am doing the next best thing to publishing it myself: giving it to a paper that can print it without fear, in full – a paper that can follow it up in a way I never can in the present circumstances. I have to involve you, you see.' Higson leant back in his chair and looked crafty. 'At least,' he said, 'I have to have someone who will publish the story.'

Involve the gringo journalists, Walker thought. It was perfectly logical. What was the point of Higson trying to publish his story if it never got off the presses? Let someone, anyone have it as long as it appeared in print – and foreign interest might be the only way a document like this could see the light of day.

He looked at the man across the table. Perhaps he was judging Higson too harshly. He was doing the right thing, after all. Perhaps he wasn't so unreliable. He had the chumminess of a man who accepted his predicament and was happy to give his story to the competition; an easy acceptance of his position – resignation, a hint of long-suffering – lay over his face like a warm blanket. He wasn't being slyly persuasive or bullying, he was simply offering a deal. The gold teeth flashed and the oiled-down hair shone in the dim light, and his manicured hands and his fine-cut suits gave him an air of impotent prosperity. Walker looked down at the transcript again.

'All right,' he said. 'When did the meeting take place?' He picked it up and tapped it thoughtfully as if he were weighing its value. 'How long ago was it?'

'Four weeks,' Higson answered. 'Just the three men here,' he nodded at the document in Walker's hand. 'They met at the Hilton Hotel, you know, the one down in . . .'

'I'm staying there.'

'Of course, of course.'

'But what were the results of the meeting? All the transcript tells us is what they say they are going to do. How do we know they did it? Did the money ever appear here? It seems from the conversation that a deal was struck, but what about the proof? At the moment, this is just conspiracy, it isn't action.' He threw the transcript casually onto the table as if its significance still had to be proved. 'Unless the money was actually raised and made its way to Venezuela, there's no story.'

'Once you have established for yourself the identities of the participants – once you have their names – then you would have to follow that up yourself. Of course, I am just offering a document. I cannot invest in it any further, I must get rid of it,' Higson said. 'There is nothing I can do.' He spread his arms wide to indicate his helplessness.

'My paper won't buy something like this,' Walker said. 'Not unless I have the chance to take it further beforehand.'

'There is nothing I can do,' Higson repeated with a hint of desperation. 'There are too many restrictions for us here, as I have said. Dangers. It is not for me to take it further.'

'My paper won't buy a lead, they don't do that. They buy stories. I have to check the authenticity of this before I can even ask them in London.'

He looked down at the front page of the transcript again and focused on the first line of Higson's selected editing. 'To some people, a billion dollars is a lot of money.' The main speaker, the speaker the transcript called simply V, came out through the written words and into Walker's imagination. What kind of a man made a remark like that? The supreme casualness of it. Was it arrogance, or was it simply bored familiarity with that kind of money? A billion dollars.

'Let us look again,' Higson said, and scraped his chair half round the table so that he could see the transcript at least sideways on. 'The key phrases are highlighted.' The bits that Higson considered particularly important were indeed coloured over with a marker that allowed the writing to come through. The colour was a sickly, metallic yellow. 'We want to bail out the government,' Higson read. 'Like Mauritius. You did it for them, now do it for us, the Venezuelans.'

Higson looked up at Walker from where he was stooped over the table so that his voice wouldn't travel. Or maybe, Walker thought, he was a man with short sight who was too vain to wear glasses. He looked at Higson's smooth-cut, almost effeminate appearance again. 'Why should a company like Continental want to help this government?' Higson asked easily. 'This or any government?'

Walker suddenly felt confused. He had been tracking Rausch and twenty-three million dollars: now the transcript in front of him talked of a billion, raised outside the open market by another multi-national, apparently on behalf of the government. You might not be able to do much in a country with twenty-three million dollars, but a billion . . . A billion dollars in a country like Venezuela . . . A billion dollars, raised from someone other than the big lenders – raised, according to the transcript, on behalf of the President himself – surely swamped in importance whatever Rausch's secret fund was doing here.

'Continental USA are a big company,' Higson was saying. 'They have big interests in the country. So what do they get in return for such a loan? It is obvious: they have a reciprocal deal with the government – some favourable trading status, perhaps. That is the obvious answer. That,' he leaned into Walker's ear, 'would be a story. What if Continental supplies the President with the money he needs to buy the loyalty of the army, for instance? A loyalty he needs in order to repress his own people.'

Walker thought of the looting and the riots. The army had stood firm behind the government. There might be anarchy, but it was anarchy from below; the army was holding the line and supporting an elected President. But did the President have to buy their loyalty the way Higson suggested? He thought of the barracks of the Regimiento di Guardia Honor, right opposite the Miraflores Palace where the President lived. It was easy to imagine the President's honour guards becoming the President's gaolers. They hadn't yet, but was that simply because they had been bribed? With Continental's money?

'Perhaps he's using it to pay interest on a foreign loan,' Walker said. 'Maybe he's going to buy out the oil companies, or invest it in the interior – mining, forestry, agriculture, roads. Maybe he's buying expensive jewellery for his wife.'

Higson ignored the sarcasm. 'Then he would go through the normal channels.'

'Perhaps he can't go through the banks.'

'For over twenty years,' Higson shrugged, 'all the countries in Latin America have borrowed from the banks.'

'And half the money has ended up in private Swiss bank acounts. But all this is speculation. We don't even know if the money ever arrived.'

'The banks will never stop lending,' Higson said, ignoring Walker's objections. 'Not to my country. Not for as long as we have gold and diamonds and oil. Not as long as we owe them thirty-three billion dollars. So, if the President doesn't choose to borrow from the banks it must be for some secret reason. To me that is clear.'

A doomed President borrows a billion dollars on the black market in a last-ditch attempt to hang on to power; a national army agrees to defend its government in return for a slice of the money. That was how Higson wanted it to be, and in South America it sounded only too plausible: a dirty campaign funded by Continental for the very reasons Higson suggested. Walker looked across at Higson and saw the sharp, shrewd face with its glint of gold through the permanently parted lips. That was why Higson had brought him the transcript, he was sure: not just because he thought it should be investigated, published and made known, but also because of what he believed. Higson believed his theory – or wanted to believe it, perhaps? Walker knew he felt a prejudice against the man who sat opposite to him, and he fought against it. But even if Higson had a hidden motive for wanting him to take the transcript, his theory about the bribe was very likely to be correct. The Venezuelan President wouldn't be the first Latin American head of state to make use of legitimate commercial interests in his own country in order to pursue a personal advantage. If the Venezuelan President was found to be involved in bribery, no one would care much, one way or the other. But it would be different for Continental. If Continental were involved in the way the transcript suggested, it could do them serious harm.

'I still can't pay you anything for this,' Walker said. 'Not without showing it to the paper. It's too much to pay on spec, even with what the transcript purports to say. Maybe it's something, maybe it isn't, but at this stage you're going to have to trust me, Señor Higson; to give me the tapes and transcript for a period of time so that I can follow them up. You will be protected, freed from the responsibility of handling them. Then, if the paper wants to use them, we can arrange a price.'

'I can't just give them away,' Higson said, shocked, and looked guiltily around and dropped his voice again. Two of the western saddles at the bar were occupied, and the two men who sat in them had their feet in the big leather stirrups as they sipped pale Mexican beer from bottles.

Suddenly the saloon doors at the entrance to the bar smashed open and a soldier walked in, his hand on his gun-barrel where it was slung over one shoulder. Higson paled, and drew in his lips as if he hoped to suck himself into a hole. Another soldier followed the first one, and they both stopped just inside the doors and looked around carefully. Whether or not they saw what they wanted to see it was impossible to tell; they walked across the bar, past where Walker was sitting, and looked down at him with heavy significance, as if by doing so they would draw a confession from him. But they passed on, and one snapped two fingers at the barman, who hurried along the long wooden counter and waited to be told what it was they wanted.

Higson had fallen completely silent, and was holding his hands tightly together as if to stop them shaking. Walker looked as incuriously as possible at the soldiers, but they had their backs to the table. There was an incomprehensible babble of Spanish and a lot of pointing at the beers the other men at the counter were drinking. The barman siezed two Mexican beers from the cold tray behind the bar and whipped off the tops as if he were entering a de-capping competition. The soldiers snatched them without paying and clumped back across the wooden floor, looking nastily once more at the table where Walker and Higson were sitting. Higson's face was averted and he was breathing nervously. The soldiers' expressions suggested that nothing was odd about such cowering, it was expected – you didn't have to have something to hide. In their book, it was the people who refused to cower who needed to be 'closed down'.

They left the bar with the same aggressive smashing of the swing doors that had announced their entry. Higson's arms were over the transcript like a schoolchild hiding an exam paper from cheats. 'I can't just give it away,' he complained again. But this time he sounded less sure than before. 'It isn't like any other document,' he complained. 'I have no rights over it. Of course, there are no rights over such a thing, unless the original owners of the voices can be said to have rights. I own it. Own it!' He looked at Walker appealingly. 'But there can be no copyright. Your paper can publish it and not give me a thing. There has to be a special deal.'

Higson's eyes and gold teeth flashed, and for a moment he looked angry. It was nervous anger, Walker thought; the soldiers had made him unhappy, they had made him realise how vulnerable he was with the transcript in his possession. But it wasn't just the soldiers who were worrying him, Walker thought. He was also flustered because he thought he had given away too much to Walker already. By showing him the transcript at all, he had taken a risk. The story was there in the reading, and Walker already knew too much.

Walker saw these thoughts as clearly as if Higson had spoken them aloud. What Higson had wanted to say, what had been on the tip of his tongue, was, 'You could sell the transcript, you could take it and profit from it and I would have nothing.' That was what Higson feared, because he judged people by his own standards. If their roles were reversed, Walker thought, Higson would do exactly what he feared that Walker would do now: steal the information and profit from it.

But then a light seemed to sweep across the Venezuelan's troubled face. He had remembered that he still had the names of the people in the transcript – and the tapes – and he became his old, reasonable self once again. 'Sure,' he said in the smooth American accent he adopted when he felt confident. 'Sure, Mister Walker, you cannot pay good money for the transcript like it is. I am an editor. I know!' He spoke as if Walker had been arguing the opposite and he was correcting him. This was a different Higson, a calm, reasonable Higson who was there to smooth out the troubles that were of Walker's own making. 'I have the names, think of that! The names, with the transcript, will make it a proper package. A nice property that a paper will buy. *Your* paper. When I saw you at the Club I knew you were the right person for this. Like me,' he tapped his head, 'you are a journalist. You think. I knew I was right to bring this to you. You can find the truth where we dare not. Alas,' he said, and his mouth turned down like a cartoon Mexican's.

'Was that what you were doing at the Club?'

'What, Mister Walker?'

'Deciding who to show it to.'

'Yes, yes. Of course.'

But Walker was thinking again of the hospital.

'It is not so much money that I am asking,' Higson said, like a mechanic weighing up the cost of a car repair. 'Money is nothing for a paper like yours. You can sell the story to the world! You will be on every front page. You, you personally, will make your name.'

'You have offered it to someone else?' Walker said.

'No, no, no.' Higson's palms came out to force that heretical door shut.

Why me? Walker thought. He doesn't know me.

'I will give it to you,' Higson said suddenly. 'Okay? To you exclusively. You have first refusal. As you know, I have to get rid of it, and if you don't want it I will take it to one of the Americans. But it is too important to haggle over. I will trust you because it is too important not to. You must take it. Please.' He held the transcript out in both his palms like a supplicant. It was an offering. An offering, Walker thought, that you couldn't refuse. He stopped wondering why the man across the table had picked him out, him of all the journalists at the Club. It didn't matter: the transcript was hot, and he and Higson both knew it. No journalist in the world would turn down an offer like this. Walker took the offering from the Venezuelan's hands and he saw the man's eyes smiling, the teeth still in their perpetual gold grin.

'Give it to me for two days,' he said. Higson's offer had caught him right off balance. 'Just two days, for nothing. Tell me the names, and what I can find out in two days will be reported to the paper on the basis that they pay for the transcript. If they don't want it, it's yours. Out on the open market again.'

The Venezuelan looked for the first time as if he might relax. The tight hunched shoulders came down, and his hands caressed rather than gripped each other. Black hairs sprang out from underneath a thick gold ring on his index finger, Walker noticed; for the editor of a small national paper he was a man of considerable means. Perhaps he didn't just edit the paper, perhaps he and his hero father before him owned it as well.

'Two days,' Higson mused, trying unsuccessfully to appear to weigh the suggestion in his mind. 'Two days, okay? You want more, perhaps? Why not a week? The time has come for trust, Mister Walker. As an editor I would not give any one of my staff just two days to investigate a thing like this. I trust you. Take it for a week. Keep in touch, sure. Let me know developments. Perhaps I can help. I know one of the voices in the tapes, for instance. I know V. He is here in Caracas now, presumably to supervise the loan. He has worked for the President before on other such ventures. He calls himself an economist when he is in South America.' The thought drew a laugh from the gold mouth. 'It is like a street-corner card-sharp calling himself an international bridge player.'

Walker picked up the transcript, watching the Venezuelan as he did so to see that he meant the offer seriously. He folded it carefully and put it into his inside jacket pocket. 'A week then,' he said. Higson's eyes followed the transcript into his pocket like a person who watches a departing train which contains a loved one, but he made no objection.

'And the tapes,' Walker said. 'I shall need the tapes. I shall need to be able to recognise the voices in them, for one thing. The voice of V.'

Higson carefully leaned across the table. 'His name is Jeremy Quince, Mister Walker. He has lived in Caracas for many years, on and off – I don't know, maybe he was born here. Some people say he came out here for the first time in the gold rush in the fifties, when the dictator opened up the interior to foreigners, after the prison at El Dorado was closed down. There is another story that he is the illegitimate son of an Irish worker who was here before the Second World War. His father left him here, and left his mother with money to keep him here.' Higson shrugged. 'If so, he is more gringo than Spanish. He wears old-fashioned English suits and he talks like an Englishman, like an old-fashioned Englishman. He wears a bow tie.' The eccentricity of this seemed to amuse him. 'Whatever he is,' he continued, 'there is no doubt that he made money from the gold rush, like many of those who managed to survive. Those were bad times, unforgiving times, Mister Walker. The prospectors who came out to the south to find gold also found diamonds, for the first time in this country, and many of them switched to diamond-prospecting. You know the way they used to find the diamonds? The way they still do? Two men would be in a boat on a river, way down in the jungles to the south, near the Brazilian border. The two men would feed out a line to a diver below. One of the old-fashioned things, you know – no tanks of oxygen, just a line for air to the surface, a globe helmet and a heavy suit. The diver walks along the bottom of the river bed, it is as simple as that; he walks down the river looking for the diamonds. When he finds some, he signals to the two above to drop anchor. When they do so, they also cut the airline to the diver below. He has done his job. They take the diamonds and split them two ways instead of three, and then they find another "partner" to act as a diver and to meet a similar fate. That is how Quince made his first fortune, Mister Walker. That is the man who is V, and who since then has progressed to raising billions of dollars for governments and to calling himself an economist. He is here now, as I say, in Caracas.'

Higson paused, to feel in the pocket of his jacket for the tapes. They were wrapped in cellophane and tied so profusely with Sellotape that it was impossible to see what was concealed beneath the wrapping. Higson looked once, nervously, around the bar, and when he was sure they were alone – apart from the two men still drinking Mexican beer at the bar, and the barman – he handed them casually to Walker, who slipped them into the pocket of his jacket. 'The other man I can identify in the tapes is M,' Higson said. 'He is the negotiator for Continental at the meeting, the senior man. The third man is less important, I believe.'

The third man is your contact, Walker thought; but as if reading his thoughts, Higson looked sharply across the table. 'The taping was done with a concealed microphone,' he said. 'Hidden in a part of the hotel room where they met.'

Walker met Higson's eyes and they held steady, but both men knew what the other knew. There was a lie, and it was known. To Walker, it suddenly seemed not to matter. If the third man was Higson's contact, nothing changed. The tapes and what they contained were all that concerned him. How Higson had come by them seemed unimportant now. He had the tapes, and the names.

'The third man is a Continental director in Caracas,' Higson said. 'He is not the chief executive here, but most people believe he has connections that are most important to the company – important enough for him to keep a low profile. Security connections in Washington, for instance. In South America, the big American companies and the CIA don't keep each other at arm's length, shall we say. He is a man called Nethercott.'

It was Higson's manner that was unfortunate, Walker thought. His earlier prejudice against the slick, oily manner, the rich, effeminate clothes and permanent gold smile that wasn't a smile, he now tried to overcome. It was dangerous to be put off by someone's manner, dangerous and foolish; you had to look beyond such things. Which was why he felt uneasy now. Because, try as he might, he did still feel a prejudice. Was it prejudice against the man's manner or was it something deeper, a doubt about something more important than his expert veneer? There was something wrong about Higson. Walker looked at him, and he saw a fraud. What was it that bothered him? For nearly two hours they had sat in the Cowboy Bar on Urdaneta with a drink apiece between them and discussed the transcript; they had haggled over its value, and Walker had said he could pay nothing at this stage. But now, suddenly in the space of a few minutes, Higson had capitulated. He had given him the transcript, extended the time limit, handed over the tapes, too, and the vital identities of the participants. That was what was worrying Walker. Had it all happened just a little too easily? And once more, Walker thought of the hospital.

'Why did you tell the story of the hospital?' he said. 'Of the hospital morgue? The five hundred dead?'

Higson blinked and his brows knitted into thick, black caterpillars on the move; his head tilted to one side and he frowned. It was the classic prelude to a pretended misunderstanding.

'At the Club,' Walker reminded him. 'You said that there were five hundred victims of the President's crack-down lying dead at the University morgue. Remember?'

'Yes, yes. Of course.' Higson remembered, and his expression cleared.

'I went down to the morgue,' Walker said slowly. 'Your story, you know it appeared on the front pages of just about every paper in Europe and America?'

Higson smiled, and the gold widened.

'But there weren't five hundred corpses there,' Walker persisted. 'There were twenty. Just twenty.'

Higson's brow was now completely calm and his recessed black eyes danced a little as he placed the event and its context. 'Ah. Why did I tell the story, Mister Walker? That is what you are asking? It was told to me. I was just repeating something that was told to me. There are not the five hundred corpses?' He shrugged. 'I wasn't there. I was told this, by a reliable source. I don't know, perhaps they were moved.' He shrugged again and his mouth turned down in its comic way. 'I don't know. I was told this,' he repeated. He looked levelly into Walker's eyes and their thoughts met briefly. 'The time has come for trust, Mister Walker.' And silence filled the room.

There was a smashing of splintered wood and a shout of command from the bar's entrance that snapped the silence. Walker looked round in shock. He had his back to the door. He had the tapes in his pocket and he had the transcript. There were two soldiers who had burst in, and one of them had smashed one of the swing doors from its hinges, aiming his army boot directly at the hinge. It was a gesture of pure destruction.

Walker looked at Higson, expecting to see a smile, a look of triumph on his face: Higson had set him up. With one hand Walker gripped the edge of the rough wood as he prepared to push himself up and run, but sense stopped him from doing that – there were soldiers already in the room. He wanted to throttle Higson. He wanted, before the soldiers came and took him – for that was what they were there for, he was sure of that – to grab at Higson's throat and strangle the lies out of him. A rage gripped him, and he cursed himself at the same time for falling for a trick like this. It had been Higson's choice, the Cowboy Bar, and Higson's timing. He hadn't trusted Higson, and yet he had walked straight into the trap that Higson had set. He would make a lunge at the Venezuelan and give him something to remember before the soldiers took him.

But when he saw Higson's face, something stopped him. The Venezuelan was looking towards the door – towards the thin, bright streak of sunlight that shone blindingly through it into the darkened interior – with the same scared look he felt on his own face. There was panic in it, in fact; Higson's recessed eyes had emerged from their sanctuary in sheer panic. It was not the look of a man who had set someone up and was sitting back and waiting for his pay-off. Walker turned again to the door, uncertain. There were six soldiers now: two by the doors to prevent escape, their automatic guns levelled at the bar as if they were facing a mass assault; four more approaching through the gloom, three of them with automatic weapons and the leader with a drawn pistol. The leader wore a smart officer's uniform with red loops under the epaulettes and a gold band around his cap. He had mirrored glasses on his face, and there was a moment of unpleasant farce as he was forced to remove them in order to make his way in the near-darkness. He shouted angrily at the man behind the bar and the room was suddenly filled with lights. The soldiers, adjusting their eyes after the bright sunlight in the street, now looked greedily at Walker and Higson.

The men drinking Mexican beer at the bar sat half-turned in their seats, as if frozen in the middle of a question. The officer barked an order, and two soldiers peeled off towards them and demanded their identification cards. They produced them swiftly and with a careless glance, the soldiers ordered them to get out of the bar, and they left without even picking up their hats.

The two soldiers turned and walked back to the table where the officer and the other two already stood looking down, thin-lipped, at Higson and Walker, in an exercise of power and intimidation.

'Identification!' the officer snapped. The soldiers held their guns within inches of Walker's ear. Suddenly Higson's delicate, effeminate clothes looked ridiculously out of place. He was a show poodle in an abattoir.

'*Periodista*,' Walker said, and tried to rise up out of his chair to face the officer. He felt his pocket bulging where the tapes were, and the thick, unflattened folded transcript pushing out the lapel of his jacket. He must face the officer on level terms, he thought. Nothing made the soldiers act more arrogantly than when they had you at their mercy; fear titillated their cruelty. But one of the soldiers roughly struck Walker with the barrel of his gun and the officer screamed at him to sit. Walker felt the blood trickle down onto his chin and begin to drip heavily onto the floor.

Higson took his Venezuelan papers from the pocket of his jacket, and the officer snatched them from the hand that couldn't hide its trembling. He flipped through them perfunctorily and checked once to ensure that the photograph was authentic. He then flicked back through them a second time. A sweat broke out on Higson's face. He's taking his time, Walker thought, the bastard's taking his time. That's what they like to do, make you sweat, make you literally sweat. Those that can understand how to read, that is. The others just go through your papers a half-dozen times because they want to pretend that they can read. The officer finished the book of papers and looked at Higson. Then he turned to Walker, but he kept hold of Higson's papers and tapped them on his other hand as if he were the percussionist waiting for the rest of the band to come in.

'Periodista,' Walker repeated, and pulled out his press card.

'Passaporte,' the officer demanded, and took the press card, glancing briefly at it and adding it to Higson's papers. Walker pulled out his passport. It was illegal to move around without a passport, even in normal times. The officer looked disappointed that he had it.

'Okay, okay,' he said, and nodded for one of the soldiers to stand behind Higson's chair. Higson shifted and ducked as if he expected to be struck from behind with the man's gun. Then the officer flicked through the pages, again perfunctorily, and brought out the press card from underneath. 'Periodista,' he said, half-question, half-statement. 'Periodista Britannico,' he said, and looked around the grouped soldiers with no expression. They grinned at Walker.

'What are you doing here?' the officer said suddenly, and his head snapped up.

'Reporting the crisis,' Walker replied. The officer put his head on one side questioningly. 'The riots, the President's briefings, the reactions of the politicians,' Walker said.

'And the army?'

'Sometimes the army. You cannot report the riots without including the army.'

Walker kept his voice steady and low. He didn't want to betray any weakness, to show he was scared. Higson was visibly trembling, the sweat rimmed his eyes. He's a Venezuelan, Walker thought, he doesn't even get the flimsy protection a foreign national can sometimes count on.

'And what are you doing here?' the officer said, stressing the final word and nodding at Higson.

'I'm talking to the editor of *La Prensa*,' said Walker. 'He's more experienced in your country's affairs than I am.'

'Experienced, yes,' the officer said vaguely, and smiled at Higson in a way that didn't suggest he wanted them to go and share a steam bath together. 'Why do you come to Caracas?' he said.

'I told you, to report the crisis,' Walker said.

'Perhaps you are a spy?' He didn't say it with much conviction. 'You should mind your own business. Spies are always journalists, isn't that right?' he said, returning to his original thought. He had perfectly white teeth that must have had the best attention Miami dentists could give, Walker thought.

'I'm just a journalist, I'm afraid. Accredited, registered at the embassy, known to the President's press staff and staying under my own name at the Hilton,' Walker said levelly.

'The Hilton is nice,' the officer said. Walker didn't reply. 'How do you want this man – Señor Higson – to help you?' the officer continued. 'What has he got to say that will help you in your work?'

'I want to know more about your country,' Walker said without a pause. 'Some facts about the economy, industry,

202

routine stuff that's published in every paper in the country. A local man saves a lot of time.'

The officer tapped the press card in his hand again and read it out loud. *'Periodista Britannico.* Why in Spanish, Señor Walker? Why write this in Spanish?'

Oh God, Walker thought. You try to ease the way, help them out, and all it does is antagonise them, make them suspicious. They were always going to be suspicious. 'In your country,' he said, 'Spanish is the language. That's the only reason.'

The officer paused and seemed to consider this. 'You come here to interfere, that is all,' he said at last, but it didn't seem threatening to Walker, it seemed like a lecture, a little homily you give some offender before you let him go. 'Why don't you stay in your own country? We are not a circus here. We are not a place for you to come and take your pictures and make your reports and then go. We are a civilised country. We are a democracy, we have an elected President. We have industry and agriculture that is the best in all the continent. We are rich, we are a First World country. We have roads and cities and a Metro, but you come here to make up your stories of the wars and the riots and the deaths. You come and pick the bad things we have, and show it to the world as if that were all there is.'

'If there are riots in my country, I report them too. I report whatever there is to report, wherever it is.'

'You only want the bad things,' the officer said. 'You only want the bad things in my country. That is all that matters.'

Walker couldn't tell if the man was being cynical, if his boasts of civilisation and democracy were a sham, but he thought not. The man was sincere. Walker didn't reply, the officer's last remark had not demanded an answer. Now the officer was tapping the press card thoughtfully on the back of his other hand. Finally he stopped, took the passport from his hand and added it to the press card, and gave them back to Walker. With Higson's papers still in his possession, he turned to the Venezuelan. The man's lips were bathed in sweat and his forehead ran. His suit was looking crumpled now, where before it had looked crisp like the man himself. He wore the look of supplication, begging for reprieve. He wasn't going to be a hero, like his father.

'You,' the officer said. 'You will come with me.' He nodded to the soldiers behind Higson's chair, who hauled him out of it by his arms.

A look of terror crossed Higson's already stricken face. 'I have done nothing wrong,' he said, his voice suddenly stronger than his fear. But the soldiers would not allow any quarter now. They had their orders and they looked as if they intended to execute them with the fullest enjoyment. They dragged him away from the chair before he was able to step around it. They forced him to bend double with one arm high and twisted behind his back. They pushed at him, preventing any normal movement, beginning an indignity that, later, they would no doubt carry far beyond this. He was not to be allowed to stand straight or speak. Under the pressure, his clothes ripped and his breath was suddenly rasping. A third soldier came over and grabbed the expensive scruff of Higson's neck and dragged him towards the remaining swing door.

Walker tried to jump out of his seat, but he was jabbed with the full blow of a gun-butt in his back. He sank down, the muscles in his shoulder in agony. 'What's he done? What's he done wrong?' he managed to say through the pain. 'Why are you arresting him? What charges? He's done nothing here. He's only given me ordinary information, information that I could read anywhere. He hasn't betrayed anything. Like you, he is a supporter of freedom and democracy.'

But the officer didn't reply. 'Go back to your country,' was all he said. 'Report the bad things in your own country.'

The soldier raised the butt of the gun to strike Walker again, but the officer sharply ordered him to lower it and he turned away from the table. From the corner of his eye, Walker saw Higson dragged through the door and bounce against the doorposts before disappearing into the street, into whatever van waited for him there. The officer and the remaining soldier swept through the entrance after them, and Walker thought he was alone in the bar. 'You,' a voice hissed at him. He looked round and saw the barman who had crept up behind them during the interrogation. 'Get out of here.' He spat in Walker's face. 'Get out and never come back.'

It was a sunny, bright day and Walker's bloody eyes were burnt by the brightness. He was glad of the chance to put on a pair of sunglasses. There was no sign of any military vehicle. Pedestrians hurried along the pavements in swarms with their heads down, but this was normal, not necessarily a reaction to some scene of violence they had just witnessed. Walker tried to stop one of them, a middle-aged man who looked like a civil servant, a man who wouldn't be scared by an approach. 'Where did they take him? Where?' he asked.

The man looked at him coolly for a few seconds before replying. 'Who?' he said, and lowered his head and walked on.

Walker hailed a taxi and climbed into the back, his shoulder throbbing and his head still pounding from the liquor, and asked to be taken to the Hilton. The shops were open, people were going about their business, the scene was normal. But a man had disappeared, taken away by the soldiers: Higson had been arrested. Walker felt in his pockets as the taxi tore through the streets to the Parque Central. He still had Higson's transcript and the tapes which he had edited it from. Thank God the man had given them to him. It hadn't been a set-up, it was Higson who had been arrested. As he calmed down, and as the breeze that flowed through the open window softened the thudding in his head, Walker's thoughts returned again to the scene before the soldiers came.

Higson had capitulated on a price for the transcript; it had been sudden, too sudden. Yet he couldn't have known that the soldiers were coming – so what had prompted the sudden change of heart? Just a natural fear? Or was it more than that? Had Higson wanted Walker to have the transcript all along? Was the rest a feint, a smokescreen?

The taxi drew up under the awning outside the Hilton. A uniformed flunkey opened the door – it could have been Park Lane. And although, across the boulevard, the theatre posters were beginning to flap with neglect and the lawns of the parque were untended, these small signs of decay were hardly noticeable. Caracas, in the square mile around the Hilton, the international banks and the government's and army's headquarters, was functioning normally. It was hard to believe that a mile up the road the editor of the country's main newspaper had been bundled into an unmarked van. Walker stepped across the lobby without pausing at the desk. Inside a phone booth, he tried to ring the information ministry, to speak to a contact there. He was kept waiting for five minutes before his question was fielded to another switchboard, and then another. The señor he had asked for was, alas, unavailable, but the message would be passed on. They were all most concerned to hear about Señor Armando Higson, a respected and respectable figure. The information minister himself was not available either, he was with the President – the reply came after some more time and some further lies and explanations. Walker tried once more, but there was no one who could help. The message would be passed on, it was the best he could do.

Walker replaced the receiver. He knew the information ministry, and he pictured for a moment the three gorgons who sat at the old thirties reception desk. It simply wasn't worth trying again. When he picked up the phone a second time, it was to call London. He got through to Reilly immediately. At least the switchboard in London still knew who their foreign editor was.

'Have you heard?' Reilly asked before Walker could say any more than his name. He spoke in the high-pitched, foxy voice he always used when he was on the phone. 'They've closed the airport. There are tanks right around it.'

Walker was stunned.

'What the hell are you doing there?' Reilly asked. 'You're not still chasing a bloody bank account?'

'They've arrested the *La Prensa* editor,' Walker said. He could hear Reilly at the other end puffing and panting as he took his shorthand notes. He still used shorthand, never a machine.

'It's all over Reuter's screens in London,' Reilly went on, apparently ignoring Walker's story, but Walker knew he was perfectly capable of speaking and take notes at the same time. 'Tanks circled the place at three this afternoon. Where the hell have you been?'

'Watching the editor of their national paper getting himself arrested,' Walker repeated. He didn't mention the transcripts or the cockfight. He didn't know what the story was himself.

He picked up his room key and two letters that had been delivered. He crossed the foyer again and called a lift and waited a few seconds for it to arrive. There was no one staying at the Hilton now who wasn't connected with the crisis. Most were journalists, some three hundred had now gathered in the city, and they wouldn't be going far now, not until the airport was reopened. Walker felt a faint stifling sensation. When they closed the airports, you were trapped. He couldn't be called home now, and he couldn't get out even if he wanted to.

He unlocked the door to his room and double-locked it behind him. The tapes he threw on the bed, the transcript he locked in the room's safe. It wasn't secure if they really wanted to get at it, but it would be secure, he hoped, for the remainder of the afternoon. He took off his jacket and opened the first letter, which was enclosed in one of the hotel's envelopes. There was no international mail, so anything that came for him would have come from inside the city or else have been faxed from elsewhere. It was a fax from Barnaby in London: instructions that if he intended to stay for ever in Caracas, he should make arrangements with a car-hire firm approved of by the paper, not some hick local firm whose bills and invoicing would only foul up the system. What he really meant, Walker knew, was that he should go through the proper channels so that Barnaby could check he wasn't cheating the system. He screwed up the sheet and threw it in the bin.

The other letter was in a plain white envelope, and when he opened it he saw it was typed on an old portable manual. Not a Spanish model, an American one probably. It was typed badly, the letters were sometimes a space apart in the same word and occasionally rose up out of the word as if they were taking off. Bits of red ribbon and the occasional red letter mottled the fading black. It was smudged, and the paper was crumpled and clumsily folded. The message itself, however, was less indirect. 'Walker,' the ugly letters said, 'your activities are known to us. You are known to us. We know where you go and we know who you see. You are no longer endurable. You will stop. You know what we do to people. Eventually, we close them down. You have twenty-four hours to leave or we will close you down.'

Walker looked at the last sentence separately. 'But first you will scream for us. Just like they all scream for us in the end.'

He inserted the first of the tapes into the machine and stood by the window for a long while, looking out over the twenty miles of riot-torn city and scrub mountain towards the airport, which was closed.

FIFTEEN

The Fishing Party

The men sat together in a corner of the room, drinking tea and smoking cigarettes. Three of them relaxed in wooden chairs with their legs stretched out lazily in front of them, the other two leant against the grey brick walls of the room with their legs crossed. Two of them were uniformed, the rest were wearing Wrangler jeans and football shirts which read 'Cleveland Oilers' and 'Denver Cowboys' and 'Miami Dolphins' on the front. They were taking a fifteen-minute break from interrogation.

The two in uniform were the youngest, and appeared to be contributing the most nervous laughter to the conversation as they hugged their mugs of tea to their chests and sipped at them with small, sudden movements like birds. The others, in their thirties or early middle-age, could have been office workers dressed for the weekend. Their faces were time-worn, their eyes held more experience than the youngsters'. They drank in even draughts, they smoked steadily but without chain-smoking. One of them stood with the flat of his palm against the wall, as if he were pushing it, and had his legs crossed casually two to three feet away. In his free hand he held his mug and his cigarette. The two in uniform looked to him and listened to him, but in other respects their eagerness to emulate the boss was unconvincing. They smoked as if they were trying to tug their last breath of air from an airless room. The conversation ranged across every kind of subject but the one in the room with them.

The three eldest, in the football shirts, were married, and they groused amongst themselves about their wives' expensive habits and the cost of keeping a home as the currency plunged, but when they talked about the local soccer teams or the previous weekend's racing at the great Rinconada track, the younger, uniformed men – boys really – joined in enthusiastically, eager to add their contribution, as if someone would try to prevent them unless they spoke a little too loud and a little too fast. They were like any small group of workmen anywhere. They could have been a bunch of building workers taking a break, or electricians perhaps – which in a perverse way was what they were. For though their conversation ranged extensively, it never touched on their work in the room. They didn't even look at the naked, inert figure that was strapped face-up to the slab at the far end of the room, the electrodes turned off for the time being, while they had their tea and smoke.

'Just one more day till the weekend,' the boss sighed, after a pause in the chat had left an opening for a change of subject. The boss was a shortish man, five feet five inches, perhaps, with a thick bushy-black moustache and a rotund, lived-in face. It could have been a kindly face, it had that sort of cosy plumpness. He had a little pot-belly that pushed the white football shirt out over the top of his jeans. He checked his watch, but ignored what he saw.

'It doesn't make much difference to us,' one of the young ones said, 'the weekend. They never give us a moment off, we're always on duty. As long as all this goes on,' he added, and buried his face in his mug, afraid he had said too much. The conscripts, it was true, were kept under tight supervision. That was the best thing for them. Professionals, now – professionals needed time off with their families if they were going to do a good job the rest of the time. When he realised that what the boy had to say didn't demand any reply, the boss, who had looked at the soldier while he spoke, turned to one of the others, closer in age to himself.

'Where are you going to be, Emmanuel?' he asked. 'Home or away?' They laughed.

'We play at home this weekend,' the man called Emmanuel said, smiling. 'The wife has a sick relation, an aunt who has to be looked after. I'll take the kids to the beach on Sunday. The youngest, Sophia, is learning to swim, and all she wants to do is get in the water, though it's mostly splash, splash, splash. She thinks that's it.'

The other two married men nodded at the memories this prompted of their own kids. 'Me,' the boss said with plump satisfaction, as if he'd just finished an excellent pastry. 'Me, I'm going to take my son fishing.'

'Your son?' one of the conscripts said, in order to say something.

'We go to the foothills outside Merida,' the boss announced, ignoring him. 'Just where the Andes start.'

'How old is he?'

'Eight. Just eight. He's been fishing since he was four years old,' the boss said proudly. 'He first fished on Christmas Eve with a rod I made myself over four years ago. Caught two snapper off Caracas port. That was at sea, of course. Now he knows how to catch trout. Anyone can put a line over the side of the boat and pull it in with a few snapper attached, but trout are a different thing entirely. You play them,' he explained sincerely to the conscripts, as if they were suddenly his own eight-year-olds. One of them was from the Merida department and his face took on a rapt look as soon as the boss mentioned it.

'Merida is beautiful,' he said. 'The most beautiful province in Venezuela.'

'But it's a long way,' the other conscript said. 'You can't get much further from the capital.'

'You fish?' the boss asked the Merida native.

'No, no. Hardly at all,' he said. 'We do not live in the hills.' He blushed.

But the boss was not going to attempt to make him any more ill-at-ease. He put his mug down on the small shelf that was screwed into the wall, and pulled out a cigarette and lit up. He checked his watch. The time was fine. The second conscript automatically filled the boss's mug and put in the sugar, six spoons heaped to overflowing, and the boss picked it up and stirred it himself.

'No, you're right,' he said. 'It is the most beautiful. The best climate. It's cool, there are fields of green crops in the spring. In winter it is cold high up, of course,' he said, like a geography teacher, 'But at the right height, in the right season' – he shrugged – 'you can't beat it. Even the streams in Chile are not as good. You should see the pictures. Have you seen the pictures?' he asked. The other two married men were not fishing enthusiasts and they shook their heads. 'It is like Switzerland there,' the boss said. 'The streams are clear and the mountains behind are capped with perfect white snow. It is perfect for trout, a perfect place to get away from it all. The peace and quiet.' He began to look at the far wall, as if he could see the picture he had painted somewhere in the distance. 'My son can catch a brown trout now almost as well as I can,' he said proudly. 'Just a little strength, but an awful lot of skill. They are the only trout worth the fishing,' he said to the conscripts 'Remember that.'

There was a groan from the far side of the room. The boss sighed and looked at his watch again.

'Time for another cigarette,' Emmanuel said.

'Yes. One more.' They all ignored the groan.

'Rainbow trout and brown trout,' the boss said dreamily through a cloud of exhaled smoke. 'With the others, you can drop a naked hook in the water and they'll catch onto it in a flash, just because it glints. They are very stupid fish. The brown trout, now he is the king. He will give you a game any day.'

'I have fished,' the conscript from Merida piped up, his past embarrassment overcome. 'Not up in the hills, but near them.'

'Trout?' the boss said.

'No,' he replied dejectedly when he saw the boss's lack of interest.

'That's what I like to do at weekends, and the weekend's nearly here,' the boss resumed. 'Tomas, my son, and I, we take a tent, some camping things, a small stove, and head up there for the hills. You are one with nature up there, you know. You can feel the presence of God. His fingerprints are on the mountain ranges, the valleys are his footsteps. You would not believe the beauty of it.'

From the other side of the room a louder groan rattled from the throat of the no-longer inert figure on the slab but still no one paid any attention. The boss sipped his tea thoughtfully and the others looked at the floor, or kicked little pieces of broken cement from between the stone flags, or drummed their fingers on the wall to wait for the lapse in conversation to be filled.

'You have to teach your children things. Useful, practical things. That's very important,' the boss lectured. 'That's what they get from their father. Especially the boys, of course. Their mothers will love them – in the conventional way, I mean. I love my son too, but I love him in the broader sense. I can see his whole life before him, whereas his mother just sees him as he is now.'

'I'm taking my eldest to carpentry lessons,' the third man said. 'That's an important thing to learn.'

'That's exactly what I mean,' the boss said above the increasing moans and crying from the corner. 'That's what I mean when I say that a mother's love is not enough. It's too enclosed, if you're not careful it will make a boy inward and shy. A father, a father can actually demonstrate his feelings by drawing the child out, by introducing him to the world through practical things.'

There was a ghastly, strangled choking from the slab. The boss at last took notice and glanced across the room. 'Better have a check, Emmanuel,' he said.

Emmanuel stubbed his cigarette out with the toe of his shoe on the stone floor, and exhaled the last of the smoke that he'd drawn in almost from his finger-ends, the butt had been so low. He stepped over to the slab and looked down at the prostrate figure. With his thumb and forefinger he eased open an eyelid and peered in. He was a doctor and he knew what to look for. The figure screamed at his touch, then subsided into whimpering when no immediate pain was inflicted.

'Okay now,' Emmanuel said, and walked back across the room to join the others. The boss sighed and stubbed his cigarette out on the floor. The others followed, and stood up from their chairs or gathered themselves away from the wall. Cups were put on a tray and packets of cigarettes tucked into back pockets. The boss yawned and stretched his arms so far up into the air that he had to stand on tiptoe.

'Roll on the weekend,' he said. 'All right. Back to work.'

They moved to the slab. Emmanuel took his place by Higson's head. One of the conscripts sprayed water from a hose over Higson's body. 'Mind where you're pointing that thing,' Emmanuel complained. He crouched down next to Higson's head, where he could offer heartless condolences to Higson when they switched the electricity on. *We don't want to hurt you, we want to help you.* The boss moved a couple of the electrodes away from a place where the skin had gone a bit black. The body groaned in anticipation.

'All right,' the boss said, a little wearily. It was late in the afternoon. 'Back for some more fishing. Ask him to tell us about Walker.'

SIXTEEN

Francesca Santos Calderon

Walker left the hotel in a hurry. A day had passed – half a day – since the threat; half a day since he'd heard and brooded over the Continental tapes, now locked up in the hotel's main safe, along with the transcript, as one package marked 'Doctor's Thesis'. The tapes were genuine, Walker was in no doubt of that whatever. Now he wanted to see Francesca Santos Calderon. She was the only person who could help him now, and perhaps, he was the only person who could help her. But time was running out. Half a day in the life of a man under a twenty-four-hour sentence could be half a lifetime. It was just before eight o'clock in the morning and the sun was growing hot and great over the city. Señora Santos Calderon would already have been at work for nearly two hours now, since six o'clock when the curfew was lifted.

Reilly's Reuter's reports from the day before had been premature, or if not premature, then they had drawn the wrong conclusions. The implication had been that, with tanks ringing the airport, there must have been a military coup. Tanks, as Walker had discovered, had indeed ringed the airport, but they were on direct orders from the President and certainly did not indicate that there had been a split between the government and the army. The army, as the government's enforcer, was now an accustomed presence in the city, and though fighting still took place in the suburbs at night, down in the poorer barrios, even former protesters against the government were now turning against those who fought on. Today, as on every other day during the past two weeks, there was a calm and businesslike atmosphere in the centre of the capital. People were trying to carry on with their

215

work. Burned-out buses still littered the streets, and gangs still came in at night, under cover of darkness, to sabotage the Metro and the telephone system – which had now been closed for nearly twenty-four hours. But there was a general suggestion that the worst was over. Which was why, in Walker's mind, the closing of the airport was so strange. Was the President now going to use the bought loyalty of the army – if that was indeed where the Continental money had gone – in order to settle old scores? Or perhaps it was a case of the army buying him? A president they could use, a president who would be a front for them. A new dictator. . . .

But what was bothering the population of Caracas more than the army was the lack of supplies. The truck driver's strike was beginning to bite, and in a country with hardly any railway the *camionistas* were the only means of supply. Little was coming up from the country now, and the shops and markets were almost empty. Soon, if the strike wasn't broken, there would be food riots to add to the rest of the country's problems. Every day there were stories of maverick food-trips up from the country which ended in the lorry being stopped and destroyed, the driver macheted to death. There was greater foment outside the capital than inside it.

Walker stepped across the boulevard in front of the hotel and walked below the flyover over some waste-ground. He looked behind him. He could see no one but if he didn't want to be followed it would be foolish to simply pick up a taxi outside the Hilton. He waited for more than five minutes behind a concrete stanchion, then looked again. There was a man in shabby trousers, and a shirt half-out of them, who was scrubbing about in a pile of refuse a hundred yards away. He was behind Walker and slightly to the right, in the part of the triangle that was made up of the Hilton, the national theatre and the pile of refuse. Walker looked at him as he stooped and picked, examined something, then threw it away and stooped again. Sometimes he found something he wanted, and it went into a hessian bag around his shoulders that looked in better shape than his clothes. The man was not an object of suspicion. Secret police in Caracas didn't disguise themselves as tramps; when they came for you, they came in big, shining cars you couldn't miss, with at least four men in each one.

We know where you go and who you see. Walker looked around in a wide arc, but there was no one else. There was no one behind him, no car with dark windows parked two hundred yards away, which started moving whenever he did. *We know where you go . . .* Such threats were rarely as well-informed as the makers of them would like you to believe. But he thought of Higson, thought how the soldiers had known where to find them both. Was it Higson they had watched, or was it him?

He stepped away from the concrete stanchion and ducked through an area of refuse and half-green, worn-away grass that marked the central reservation of the road beneath the flyover. There was the remains of a small, foot-high box hedge here, broken by the hordes of commuters who never used the subways, but charged across the boulevard in front of the hooting cars. On the far side of the carriageway was another path that followed the road, against the traffic, and wound upwards to meet another intersection a quarter of a mile away. It was lonely ground, bad ground to be caught on, but at least, Walker thought, a car would find it hard to follow him here.

The first taxi crawled around the bend in the road behind him at what seemed a snail's pace. Taxis do that, Walker thought, taxis always creep along the edges of the roads when they're looking for a fare. But this one was so slow. The tarmac beneath the wheels was melting in the tropical sun, and a shimmer of heat wrinkled its approach. He couldn't see the driver, the sun was against the screen, and there was a green sun-filter stripe across the top of it, with the driver's head hidden further by a visor on the inside. Walker looked once behind him and walked on. When he looked again, the taxi was still sliding around the long curve and it was still behind him, not far, but there. He found he was beginning to quicken his step, and deliberately slowed himself. It was no good. If they were in the taxi, they could pick him off anywhere along this stretch. He wouldn't look again – he would force himself to do that, at least. The taxi drew level and passed him with apparent reluctance. Walker was a gringo on a lonely stretch of road in the heart of the concrete city, out in the wasteland just out of reach: he saw the driver lean across the passenger seat, give the gringo every chance of hailing him. But Walker carried on. Two cars passed, and a bicycle with a pannier on the front of it. There were few vehicles out on Caracas' streets any more; the oil tankers were another victim of the truck drivers' strike, only the army was fed with oil now. Walker flagged down the second taxi that crawled around the bend nearly ten minutes later, and climbed into the hot plastic stench of the back seat.

An open sewer ran through the middle of the Los Chorros barrio. On either side of it were concrete paths, and every fifty yards or so a simple concrete arc made a bridge across the sewer. The barrio was mostly built on a steep slope, and the sewer had harnessed an old stream that ran down from the Avila mountain. There was another stream of fresh water that crossed the sewer, but even above the crossing it was too filthy to wash clothes in. The sewer itself flowed a milky grey past the low, single-roomed houses of clay and the more recent constructions made by the immigrants from flattened-out kerosene cans. The houses were pock-marked with bullet holes, and over the flimsy roofs the occupants had piled stones on wooden boards to deflect the pot shots the conscripts aimed down on their heads from the Country Club above.

Already lost, Walker picked his way behind the barefoot scrawny boy. He had had no trouble getting into the barrio: the slack cordon of soldiers at the entrance was hardly bothering to enforce any entry system at all. Some lazed under the banana trees, some slept in the back of open personnel carriers with their legs hanging over the back like dead men, and their guns drawn up across their chests even in sleep. Walker had easily found a way in behind the sheets of corrugated iron that were supposed to prevent anyone from edging along the wall of the sewer. They stuck out over the foul water, and had once had coiled barbed wire around the ends of them but that had long since been stripped off by the slum-dwellers, and it was a simple matter for Walker to bend back the edge of a piece of the corrugated iron, step out over the sewer and swing himself round to dry land on the other side.

Inside the barrier, three boys, no more than six years old, were playing with some old wooden hoops which they whipped along the dusty ground with sticks. They stopped and stared at Walker as if he were a creature they had never seen before, their hoops careering off into the crawling undergrowth of brambles or plopping into the grey water of the sewer. They watched him with a sullen, starved interest. When Walker spoke, at first they didn't reply. They neither acknowledged nor rejected the existence of Francesca Santos Calderon, they just stared.

Then another child appeared on a wall at a safe distance and began to chant, 'Gringo, gringo, gringo', and the others all laughed and shook their sticks, but only muttered 'Gringo' under their breaths because they were within Walker's reach. They still had perfect white teeth, Walker noticed, though the rest of them was withered and crooked: it was like seeing a brand new component in a rusty engine. One of them finally replied, simply, 'Senora Calderon', and Walker nodded and gave them all money and promised more if they would take him to her. The boy on the wall shouted at the others to stay, and then beckoned Walker to follow with his stick.

Since then it had been only ten minutes, but Walker was completely lost. The inside of the barrio, mostly open to the sky, was not claustrophobic – but it was a maze. They had crossed the sewer three times on the concrete arcs, and had wound their way up mud stairways and round corners, down again along other narrow passages, through tunnels and up more stairs, and had once even gone through the middle of one of the dust-floor homes where a mother suckled a baby in a corner and looked at Walker with a sullen disinterest. The boy walked always ten paces ahead. Walker did not know whether or not he was imagining it, but every time he tried to close the gap between them, the boy maintained an exact distance, as if it were a rule of the barrio, like a traffic law.

At last they came to what seemed like a dead end. There were some evil-looking men sitting against a wall drinking a home-grown potion of their own. Their eyes were glazed, but Walker felt in them a hint of latent violence, a watchfulness, as if they were weighing up a simple choice: kill the gringo or let him go. The heat was stifling in the narrow alley, and for a moment it was a struggle to breathe. The dryness was in the dust and the mud walls, in the cracked feet and faces of the men, and in the choking air that wrapped itself around Walker's mouth and throat like a tight scarf. The sewer bubbled its grey poison mockingly past him. But though they stopped, it was not because the boy had lost his way, nor was this a dead end. There was a low door – perhaps a door to let animals in and out – set into the bright white wall past the slumped men. The boy rapped with his stick several times before it swung open, and a crouched old crone with a scarf over her head and a toothless hole for a mouth peered unseeingly out. The shaft of sunlight that struck her face made no impression on her eyes whatever.

Walker could only make out the words 'Santos Calderon' and 'gringo' in the scratchy slang that followed. But eventually the woman pulled away from the door and it swung a little further open, and the boy told Walker to enter. The boy's part of the journey was now over, and Walker gave him money. Inside, it was pitch black, but there was a small light at some distance, towards which Walker felt rather than saw the woman lead him. The light got bigger, and finally lit the floor and walls of a dirt hut, and the glow of eyes – children's or dogs', Walker could not be certain. They reached the opening, and Walker once more found himself in the killing heat and the blinding sunlight. Here there were a few more drunks slumped on the ground and locked in sleep or oblivion. This was near the far edge of the barrio, Walker guessed – the walls here were constructed of kerosene cans and would have been built quite recently. The woman just pointed at one of the huts, and when Walker didn't immediately pick out the right one, flapped her hand impatiently. He walked across the open span of sun-white dust and peered through the doorless opening of the hut.

There was a man in a hammock inside, with a sick, grey face and one leg, heavily bandaged, hanging over the side. Around him were his family in various states of grief or resignation, all looking towards the man as if he were a saint about to cure them. But the saint was the woman who stood at the head of the hammock with a patch of yellowed, antiseptic cotton-wool in her hands, and mopped at an open wound that wouldn't stop seeping. She didn't look round when Walker entered, and he stood back, away from the sick man and his family. They were crouched on such low stools that their legs came up to their chins, but the stools were indications of status. Real squatting, on the ground, was for the bums and drunks and deadbeats outside the tin-can hut.

Finally Francesca Santos Calderon put her hand to the man's brow and looked away from him, at Walker. She dipped the cotton-wool in a bottle and slowly passed it to one of the women near the hammock, then wiped her hands on her apron. When she came over to where Walker was standing, he saw oblique lines of tiredness drawn down her cheeks. The heat in the hut had already drenched Walker with a sweat that penetrated right through his clothes and stained the canvas bag he carried on his shoulder. She stopped in front of him and looked at him. 'It's cooler in the sun,' she said, and moved past him without a word, the movement drawing him to follow her through the door and into the sun that hit him like a cymbal.

'It's stupidity, of course,' she said when they were outside. 'It's all a matter of status. It needn't be so hot in there, but they believe a corrugated-iron roof makes them better than their poorer neighbours. But their neighbours are the richer for using the old materials. The palm leaves soak up the sun and let the breezes in, while the corrugated iron turns the huts into baking-tins.'

She walked across the round space outside the hut, the diameter of a threshing floor, and sat down on the earth against a shaded wall. Walker sat down beside her.

'But when it rains,' he said. 'Isn't it better when it rains?'

'When it rains, the iron channels the water into streams that undermine the huts and cause landslides.' She paused and looked away, as if she thought the words were wasted. 'They once used the leaves of the moriche palm, it dries faster than anything. The man in there is lying on a nylon hammock, but once it would have been a moriche hammock. Outside the cities they use the old materials, but here they like the gringo goods,' she added. 'Only the gringo goods.'

Walker picked up a stick and poked the dust between his drawn-up knees. 'What happened to him?' he asked, and nodded at the hut.

'He got a bullet through the calf-muscle. But he left the wound, and now it's dangerous. Both his brothers and a son have been killed,' she said. 'His daughter has run off with a soldier.'

Walker poked a hole deeper into the dirt. She was completely calm, but he knew that behind the composure the question hung between them. She would never ask it, but he would have to answer. 'I don't know any more about your husband,' he said at last, and dared not look at her. She didn't move. The same serenity with which she bathed a fatal wound enabled her to measure now the emotions that were involved in the murder of her husband. There was nothing religious about her serenity, she was simply at ease with the world. She had no fear.

'So you never found the murderers,' she stated.

'It isn't finished.' He paused. 'I've not come here to tell you anything new about your husband, but because of something

222

else. It may be that the two things are connected. I don't know. Maybe, but I don't know,' he repeated.

The stick traced a melon-shaped head in the dust with a banana mouth in its centre.

'I need your help', Walker said. 'You said your husband had great loyalty from many of his men, and that you too were involved closely with the union's affairs. You knew many of the people he dealt with. Three nights ago I went to a village called San Martin. It's way out to the west, a hundred and fifty miles or thereabouts. I was following a gringo in a car with two suitcases filled with dollar bills. They come in two denominations, just fives and tens. I don't know exactly the amount but on two previous occasions there was seven million dollars drawn from the bank, and four million. I don't know whether that money went the same way, and I don't know who the gringos are – the one who draws the money, or the one I followed to San Martin. It's a tiny village, you don't know it?' Francesca Santos Calderon shook her head, but turned to Walker and looked at him to encourage him to go on. Her perfect calm unnerved him momentarily. 'Millions of dollars,' he continued. 'All going to a tiny village miles away from anywhere, and all in cash. The gringo I followed met a man, several men, at a cockfight in the town. It was Tuesday, the day they have them in the villages. I watched him for two or three fights, and then I left after him, and saw him hand the cases to the men at the fight.' He paused at the memory of the attack.

'Your eyes?' she said.

Still the livid red ruts of the veins obscured the whites of his eyes, but the brightness, the scarlet colour, had ebbed.

'I was drugged and then attacked. They tried to strangle me. I don't know why they didn't complete the job. They stole nothing, just cut a hole in my neck with wire and exploded my head with some drugged liquor. They must have left me for dead. Before the fight, I asked one of the people there who the gringo was meeting, and he said the gringo had been there before, and always met the same

223

bunch of men. When I asked him who they were, he said they were the "*camionistas*".'

He looked sideways at the woman, and squinted against the brightness of the far wall behind her. The stick trailed in his hand in the dust, and brushed the face away in a maze of lazy strokes. 'Do you know who they are? Who are the truck drivers who take the gringo's money?'

She looked from the shade into his squinting eyes, and this time there was something more behind the tranquillity. They held an expression of hope. But when she spoke, it wasn't as he expected. 'You're going to bring yourself a lot of trouble, Mister Walker.'

'I already have.'

'You don't know what trouble is.'

Walker dug into his jacket and pulled out the tatty piece of paper which now hung limply, soaked with sweat. She looked at it, and he put it on her drawn-up knees so she could read it without moving. Halfway through reading the death threat, she laughed.

'What?'

She laughed again and looked at him. The paper fell off her knees to the ground. From under her apron, from some deep pocket in her skirt, she withdrew an older and tattier piece of paper. Walker took it. It was typed on the same typewriter, and had the same mix of red and black smudges. The message was different, but that hardly mattered. The threat at the end was the same.

'It's a circular,' Walker said, and smiled. 'They're giving them to everyone.' For the first time since he'd arrived in Caracas, he was amused. He looked back, and she was grave. 'Are they serious?' he said.

'Oh yes. They can do what they like.'

It didn't strike Walker until afterwards that they had never questioned who 'they' were. 'They' were the enemy, the oppressors, the murderers of Señor Santos Calderon. You would know who 'they' were when you knew who had murdered Francesca's husband and who had stripped his face away. You would know 'them' when you saw them.

'But you ask me if I know who are the *camionistas*,' she said 'Do I know who are the *camionistas* who take the gringo's money? I know none that take his money.' Walker was struck with disappointment. This was the end of the road for the Rausch account. He needed only to know who the dark-faced men at the cockfight had been. He hadn't expected the woman to know their identities, just what type of union members they were. A group? A breakaway faction? Some cabal that were for or against her husband, perhaps.

'But I do know the men who *don't* take the gringo's money,' she added. 'They are here, in the barrios, in hiding. Not just in Los Chorros, but everywhere, all over Caracas, wherever they have family to hide them. There is a man here now. At the back.' She waved vaguely, as if he could be behind the wall or in Quebec. 'He is an old friend, an old friend of us both. He refused to take the gringo's money and now they want to find him. If they knew where he was they might send him a letter too.' She paused and looked somewhere into the middle distance. 'More likely they would come and take him without warning. It's the small people, who can cause them more trouble alive than dead. You and I are privileged, Mister Walker. We have someone, at least, to watch over us, even if they cannot help us in the end.'

'Can I see him?'

She drew her knees more tightly together, and wrapped her arms over the long skirt that came nearly to the ground. She thought directly, and she spoke as she thought. She was not afraid to be blunt, even to those who were her friends. Anyone can be hard with an enemy, Walker thought when she spoke at last, but it took more guts to be tough on the people who were there to help you.

'You cannot find my husband's murderers,' she said, and looked straight into his eyes. She had an unfair advantage, Walker thought, with the sunlight behind her. 'Why should I risk the life of someone for a newspaper story?'

'I wouldn't use his name,' Walker said automatically, and checked himself. The glib response wasn't worthy of the situation. She deserved more than a stock-in-trade answer, but did he have one any more? *Why should I risk the life of someone for a newspaper story?* Walker lost the present, for a moment, and the face of Luis Jimenez rose up in his mind. She didn't say anything, but when he shook the image from his thoughts he saw she was looking at him as if she knew his dilemma.

'The point is, I *needn't* use his name,' he said.

'How do you know?'

How did he know? How did you ever know when you didn't need a name? 'You're making it a matter of trust, then?'

She didn't reply, but put her hand on his arm and looked at him with trust.

'I won't reveal his name. I don't *know* his name, for God's sake, but I won't identify him. I won't say where I met him or how. I won't say on what day, or what he was wearing, or how old he is, or any of these things. I promise. But what he says to me, and what I know, together may close the gap and enable me to find the people who killed your husband. I don't know. It may.' He was angry with himself for saying that. It sounded like a parent saying, we might go to the beach but *I'm not promising*. 'I promise you that even if I need to use information about him, I won't.'

It felt more like a deal than a pledge. He saw the face of Luis Jimenez again and he thought, I'll keep my promise if you rid me of the face of Luis Jimenez.

'I believe you,' she said, and took away her hand.

She stood up from the dust and crossed the yard to the hut. He watched her go inside while he stood uncertain about whether she wanted him to follow her there or not. There was a deadly silence in the high heat. It was almost midday and the occupants of the barrio, those who thought they emulated the gringos, were cooking inside their tin homes. Even with the thin breeze on his cheek, the heat was intolerable to Walker. He felt it cake his face like a second skin, it sucked the sap from plants and animals alike and shimmered in the air like an evil presence. She finally emerged. 'There is someone fetching him,' she said. 'But he is not coming here. Follow me, we must meet him in one of the hovels.' It surprised him that she called them hovels, and then he remembered that she, like her husband, had been educated in America and, unlike the foreigners who saw the barrios and were polite about them, as if they happened to be the small, dirty, but quaint local custom, she saw them simply as what they were.

They walked out of the threshing-floor yard and into a passage Walker hadn't seen before, disguised by a wall that was built out in front of it. But she didn't go far before she ducked to the left through a dirty bamboo curtain and into the heat of a tin-can hut, where a man squatted in the semi-darkness as if he were waiting for something. That was the feeling there was in the barrio at Los Chorros, that nothing was ever going to happen. People here lived their lives in reaction. They simply waited to be moved or goaded or taken away to die. Francesca Santos Calderon spoke a few words to the man, and he rose to his feet and left.

'You will write about my husband?' she said as his eyes adjusted to the dark.

'I already have.'

He waited, but she didn't ask him more. 'I wrote about his murder,' he said, 'and I wrote about his work for the union and the likelihood that it was because of his work that he was killed. I wrote that he had died because of his beliefs.'

It sounded trite, and he was glad of the darkness.

They waited for ten minutes without exchanging a word. Then a man dipped at the entrance and threw the bamboo aside. Francesca Santos Calderon moved across the hut, and they kissed each other's cheeks. The man turned and watched Walker, but made no gesture of greeting.

'*Periodista*?' he said.

'Yes.'

'*Americano*?'

'*Ingles*.'

The man nodded like someone who knows the answers to his questions but nevertheless has to hear them to be sure. They sat down on low stools like the ones Walker had seen

227

before. It was quite uncomfortable enough; he didn't know how they squatted for hours just on their haunches.

'What is it you don't know?' was the way the truck driver put it.

He was a short man, stocky without being fat, like most men in his profession. He had a rough face with a broken eyebrow, and dark skin flecked with grey bristles. There was a mottled brown section of skin on his left cheek, some form of cancer, and Walker guessed he must be about sixty. His head was covered with a baseball cap and he wore old, oily brown trucker's boots. Between the cap and the boots were once-blue overalls, darkened with years of oil and dust and filth. One eye was completely white.

Walker told the man the story of San Martin as he had told it to Francesca Santos Calderon. The man didn't move his cramped position on the stool and hardly blinked, while Walker shifted and stretched for comfort. When he had finished, the man looked somewere across the semi-darkness to Francesca, as if for agreement, and then back at Walker.

'You know this gringo?' the man asked.

'I know where I can find him,' Walker said. 'Where I can find him today,' he added. 'Tomorrow he might be in another house in another street in another country, for all I know.'

The man sucked his teeth as if uncertain how to begin. He looked neither pleased to see Walker nor happy with the situation in general. For a moment it crossed Walker's mind that maybe he was beginning to regret his loyalty to Santos Calderon. Maybe he was beginning to regret rejecting the gringo's money. Now, instead of dollars in his pocket, he had a price on his head. He looked unhappy, like a person who has made a bad decision. There was worry on his forehead and in his eyes.

'Tell Mister Walker how it began, Nieve,' she said. *Nieve*. Snow. Mister Snow. It was probably a nickname, Walker thought. 'Start from when you were first approached. Mister Walker has my trust.'

'Ten weeks ago,' Nieve began, 'just under ten weeks ago,

there was a meeting at the local branch of the union in Maiquetia, where I belong. It was just after the death of Señor Santos Calderon.' He crossed himself. 'The officials were calling for a strike. All out, they said. This time we're going to get a living wage, they said. We have the power, we have the government by the balls, we'll strike until we get what we want. We'll strike for our families, that was how they put it.' He made an attempt at mocking the heavy-handed rhetoric and waved one fist in the air. 'They told us that the devaluation of the currency would starve us and starve our children,' he continued. 'There is only one way, they said. Fight. This time, they said, we fight for our lives.' He lowered his voice at the memory. 'There was a lot of passion at the meeting. Many of the drivers wanted to strike but the majority didn't want it. The majority believed that if we went on strike, our jobs would be in danger. Better to have a tenth of our money than to go for all and lose all. That was the mood of the meeting. But there was ugliness. The officials were unanimous, all they needed was us, their members. They put conveners into selected parts of the crowd and they tried various methods of persuasion. They encouraged us at first, then they heckled anyone who spoke against the strike, then they began the threats. It was frightening.'

He paused and rubbed the back of his hand. 'Nevertheless,' he continued, 'when the time came to vote, the vote was against the strike. The leaders were furious. They had thought that at least if they couldn't persuade us to vote with them, they could fix the vote at the end, but under the new laws they couldn't get control of the counting and the count went in our favour. After that, there were many more threats. The strike wasn't just for us, we were told, it was for everyone; we were being selfish. But we were still in the majority, still a bigger group than they were, so their intimidation had to be selective. At first it was simple stuff. Some of us were spat at, sometimes a driver would get beaten up, but not so badly. Or the ones who wanted to strike would only help you on the road if you signed a form saying that you backed a strike. Then,' he continued with a sigh, 'they began to pay visits to our homes. To frighten our wives and even our children. It was not so terrible really, you understand, but it was frightening to them. And our families began to put pressure on their husbands and fathers.'

Nieve paused, and looked towards the bamboo curtain as if there might be someone there, but then he turned back. The temperature had cranked up a few more degrees in the hut and Walker felt his head swimming from the heat. 'They got a few to join them,' Nieve shrugged, 'but nowhere near enough to win a strike vote. Their tactics weren't working. If anything, they were strengthening resolve in the opposite direction. Then, suddenly, it all stopped. There was no more intimidation, our families were left alone, they even began to behave pleasantly to us in private. There was a nastiness underneath which they couldn't really conceal, but on the surface everything was as it had been before the meeting. Ten weeks ago. Just under ten weeks.' He said it dreamily as if he didn't quite believe it had ever happened. Then he looked back from his reverie and saw Walker again, and Francesca encouraging him with a pat on the arm. 'All was quiet for a while until the rumour.'

'What was the rumour?' Walker asked.

Nieve looked up as if he was surprised at the question. 'The rumour,' he said, as if it were obvious to everyone. 'There was a rumour that we were all to receive a sum of money. Gratis, for nothing. There was a benefactor for the truck drivers. They wanted to help us, it seemed, whoever they were; they knew these were hard times for us, they knew we were vital to the economy, that we kept the whole trade moving throughout the country. I didn't believe the rumour.'

'Why not?'

'Because if there was a benefactor, there were plenty of people in the country who needed him more than we did, that's why. We had jobs, we had wages. Our wages had suffered, sure, they had dropped by ninety per cent, but we had something. A real benefactor would have found someone who needed help more than we did without having to look very far.'

'And was the rumour true?'

'Four weeks ago, six weeks after the original meeting, I and several other drivers were approached individually. Always individually. We were made an offer. The way it was put was that there had been a widespread misunderstanding about the strike. What we had failed to realise, they said, was that we wouldn't be risking our jobs and we wouldn't be losing any money if we went on strike. In fact, the opposite was true: by striking we would make more money than we would if we continued working. The offer they made was that they would help us financially while the strike went on, for as long as necessary. They even said they would pay us in dollars. That's what swung the majority. The currency was dipping even further, and anyone who had dollars was privileged. Anyone who had dollars could weather the storm and more. They offered to help us over the financial problems caused by the strike.'

'Or they offered you money to strike in the first place,' Walker interrupted.

'That was how I figured it,' Nieve said. 'Someone wanted us to go on strike. It was a fraud to say they were helping us, because we never wanted to strike in the first place. They were offering a straight bribe.'

'And who were "they"?' Walker said. It always boiled down to 'they'.

'I don't know. I don't know. The people who approached us, one by one, they were all local conveners. They were drivers themselves, or officials. It wasn't their money, that's for sure.'

'The *camionistas*,' Walker said to himself.

'And the gringo you say you followed,' Francesca said. 'Where did he get the money?'

Walker looked at her for a long time without replying.

'Where?' she said again.

'He got it from the Brunner Bank in Caracas,' Walker said at last. 'From the Brunner Bank,' he repeated.

There was another silence. The driver didn't react to what Walker had said. He seemed to Walker to be immersed in his own thoughts, stirred up by the recollections of recent history. Walker could see the indecision in his face. He had wanted to be loyal to the union, he had been ready to support the widow and the memory of Santos Calderon, but he hadn't reckoned on a situation where his life was at stake.

But Walker saw that Francesca Santos Calderon clearly did know the Brunner Bank. Her reaction had been immediate. Her clasped hands had pulled apart at his mention of the name and she had looked sharply in his direction. He watched her. 'You know Brunner?' he said.

She didn't say anything for a moment. 'Brunner is no friend to the government,' she said. 'He has caused a great run of money from the country.' She paused. 'They say he killed his wife,' she added. 'In a yachting accident in Curaçao. His wife fell overboard, though they say he killed her. I don't believe the story. What I think is that Brunner is so hated, no story is too grotesque to invent.'

Walker looked back to the truck driver. Nieve sat with his hands clasped in front of him, looking down at the floor like a man praying.

'This money,' Walker said. 'How was it distributed? Did you ever see how it was done?'

'I saw it once,' Nieve said heavily. 'The first time I was curious and I went along. We were told to go to a small fishing village about an hour west from Caracas. There we were told to meet in a stinking refrigeration building – they have one in all the villages on the coast, no matter how pokey they are. They keep the fish in there until it's full and then a lorry picks it up. I don't know, but I expect they're all owned by our union. We met, and a man I've never seen came in a pick-up with a case full of money like you described, which he distributed inside this building. He gave us all a week's wages plus twenty-five per cent. Bonus for striking, he called it. The money was all in ten- and five-dollar bills, I remember that. And when he had distributed what was due to us, the case was still practically full. He clearly had plenty more calls to make.'

Even the cicadas had been silenced by the heat. Occasionally one made a feeble attempt at a sound, but gave up immediately, as if a foot had landed on it. The children ate the cicadas when they were hungry enough, but they couldn't find them in the middle of the day because at midday they made no noise. Walker remembered, as they walked back through the barrio, that you were supposed to be able to tell the air temperature from the regularity of the cicada's chirrup. So many times a minute, and then you added thirty-five. They walked against the heat like a tide.

The same drunks and drifters hobbled and crouched in the stinking alleys like damaged, fur-less cats. Instinctively, Walker put his arm through Francesca's, as if they were walking through the New York subway at night. Four hours earlier, Walker had been scared for his life. Now he was scared for hers. They could pick her off at will, like an insect, if she bothered them. They. They had sent her a death threat. They had killed her husband. They were casual enough to remove anyone they chose without even an excuse. They could close you down. Walker stopped by the low animal door and faced her.

'It's dangerous for you to stay,' he said. 'Why didn't you go to America with your children? When you had the chance.'

Walker thought of his own children. They were fatherless too, it crossed his mind. He had abandoned them and returned, like her, to his own personal mission. Unlike her, however, he had possessed no secrets, until now, that could warrant his murder. She had lived under the shadow of death for a month or more.

'If they know you know why your husband was killed, they will kill you too,' he said. 'They have to.'

She paused, and looked around the barrio as if it were a battlefield at the end of the battle. Perhaps she was trying to decide whether now it really was time to leave. But then she looked back at Walker.

233

'If you find who killed my husband,' she said softly, 'then I'll go.'

It didn't seem to matter to Walker that, with the airport closed, going was just about as impossible as it could be. He wanted her to get out. He wanted her to live, a corner of goodness in the wreckage that surrounded them. He would find out who killed her husband, if only to get her out of the pit before it closed over her head. The shifting logic of his mind made it clear to him that in helping Francesca Calderon and her children he would be giving the help he had denied his own family.

'If you find out who killed my husband,' she said, 'I will be here for the next two days. It is too dangerous to stay for longer anywhere. Then I will be in another barrio, to the west of the city. It doesn't have a name except to the people who live there. They call it La Futura.' She laughed ironically. 'It is the last of the barrios before the road to the coast. On the left of the highway.'

They looked at each other for a moment, and Walker wondered if he would see her again.

'I'll find you,' he said, and ducked through the low animal door and down the winding passages to the road.

A boy stood ankle-deep in the grey sewer. He watched as Walker picked his way through the animal faeces and the cracked concrete along the sewer's edge, and he kept watching as he crossed the last concrete arc over the sewer. Then he bent down; he was looking for something in the water, it seemed to Walker. The boy scrabbled with both hands below the surface as he crouched, completely absorbed now, the stinking grey water washing around his thighs. When at last he found what he was looking for, he held it up to Walker with a cry of delight and waved it at him enthusiastically. From where he stood on the bridge, Walker made out a split shell from a tear-gas gun. The boy jumped out of the gurgling excrement and ran excitedly away, out of sight behind the huts, to find his friends.

Walker watched him go, then turned. The enigma was

234

unravelled. Rausch were not doing anything as crude as buying guns to combat the bullets and the gas of the President's army. They were dissolving the very foundations of the Venezuelan economy.

SEVENTEEN

Untying the Knot

Walker waited just inside the entrance to the Tamanaco Hotel. The President's strong-arm men were everywhere, and the limousines were banking up outside, under the gold and aquamarine portal, because their occupants were too slow to disgorge. Uniformed doormen waited, semi-inclined, with white-gloved hands on the doorhandles and expressions of total blankness on their faces. The ambassadors and their spouses were unpotted from back seats while the lesser guests, mainly from the press, arrived in taxis which had to park a hundred yards away in the hotel's car park. It was five-thirty, half an hour before the diplomatic circuit's cocktail hour, a time chosen by the President for his latest press conference, in defiance of his own curfew. The dignitaries would receive personal escorts home, provided by the army, and the press and others had been issued with special passes for the evening.

It was generally considered to be an attempt by the President to show that things were returning to normal. Most of Walker's colleagues in the Foreign Correspondents' Club, however, thought the attempt desperate and ill-judged. The night before, after Walker had returned from Los Chorros, there had been what could only be described as a pitched battle, followed by a massacre, within a mile of the President's palace at Miraflores. The presidential Guardia Honor had even been called out. But by then it had been too late to cancel the evening's announcements, so that this, the latest of the President's attempts to shore up belief in the continuation of his government, would take place as planned.

Walker had arrived early, hard on the heels of the extra hired staff, in fact. There was hardly any food now in the capital, and army trucks were supplying the needs of the elite. For this evening, special crates of hors d'oeuvres had been flown in on army planes from Miami and unloaded at the trade entrance – all spice to the meat of Walker's story. The strikes had spread right through the country, from Merida in the west, which normally sent cheap Colombian produce to the capital, to the ports of Maracaibo, and Cumana in the east. The road to Brazil in the south was virtually unused – there was no more petrol. The truck drivers had succeeded in their purpose. It was an odd time for the President to be celebrating his conduct of the crisis, Walker thought. Would he have anything new to say tonight, or would he once more try to pull the wool over increasingly cynical eyes?

And tonight, too, there was the usual diplomatic contingent who would turn out for a party whatever the occasion, just as long as the champagne flowed and the band played. The ambassadors of Senegal and Sweden, Gabon and North Yemen, had already arrived. Walker was fairly sure Mauretania would not be far behind, the Israelis rarely let go, and there would be a dozen others, including Australia, a few from Eastern Europe, and the President's remaining supporters in Central and South America. The Americans were sending an ambassadorial envoy, which could mean anything, depending on who you were and how you wanted to understand the title. The Germans, the French and the British were all supplying first secretaries. It was hardly an overwhelming expression of support for the President; nations were prepared, and perhaps preparing, for a change.

As the VIPs and their wives descended the circular, red-carpeted staircase to the ballroom, Walker stood by the revolving doors and watched for the man he wanted. He had a description, he had even seen a photograph – from which it was clear that the man would be hard to miss. The arrival rate increased, the limousines backed up still further, and the journalists, and the photographers with their camera bags, sidled in, brown-shoed, to stand next to the impeccably dark-suited Country Club brigade. Pinstripe, pinstripe, jellabah, three pin-stripes, a turban, a shambling, creased-jacketed member of the press corps, more pinstripes. And interspersed among them, the embassy women, looking around anxiously to see if they had worn the right thing. The strong-arm men were doing their stuff, handling anyone who looked expensive with respect, falling just short of roughing up anyone, especially the press corps, who didn't. Walker waited.

There was a sudden flood of last-minute arrivals, and in the rush Walker feared that he would lose the man he was waiting for. In his worst moments, he thought Jeremy Quince would not turn up at all. When the flood had ebbed to a trickle and Walker was craning his head desperately between the plants to see out through the glass to the car park, he saw two figures. One was rotund and pink-cheeked and wearing a bright bow tie; the other, who looked like a small circus strong-man with black hair and swarthy skin, was walking doggedly behind him and scowling a perpetual scowl. When they entered, it was uncertain for a split second whether the presidential guard would frisk Quince's bodyguard, or vice versa. Walker turned and followed them down the red sweep of stairs to the ballroom below.

There was the usual rush for the food tables, and the Miami buffet disappeared in a cloud of paper doilies. Puffy-eyed waiters and waitresses dispensed continuous champagne, and Walker hung back behind the round figure of Quince, who stood near the centre of the vast room and seemed to have everything brought to him – not just champagne, but food, and even people for introductions. And always behind him was the squat figure of his shadow. He was a curious travelling companion, it struck Walker. Not the type you would expect to complement the flamboyance of Jeremy Quince. They never talked; he was not so much a companion, Walker realised, more a leech. His little Levantine eyes bored continually into Quince's back as if he were looking for specks of dust on his velvet jacket. Walker feared the man would never leave, and he knew he could not approach Quince until he was completely alone.

The President had moved slowly onto the dais, passing through well-wishers and earnest diplomats, his statesman-like passage across the ballroom punctuated by laughter, suggesting an ease he could not possibly feel. And all the while his bulging-shouldered protectors parted the crowd ahead of him with the finesse of a snow plough. Now, standing on the dais and flanked by officials from the government, with the national flag unfurled huge behind him, the President waited between the table and the micro-phone for his cue to step forward and begin the difficult task of convincing his audience. When he did so at last, every face was turned towards him, and the semi-circle of photographers below him let off a barrage of flashlights and jostled each other for the best picture of his waistline or for a soaring shot of him towering above them against the flag. Just at the moment when the applause had died and he began to speak the opening words of welcome, Quince's squat detective edged away from behind the green velvet jacket and pushed himself rudely through the crowd – Walker almost missed it. He stepped into the space the man had left, and pushed aside an Indian woman who was standing next to Quince, and squared himself next to the man's bulk as the crowd closed in around them. Quince stood, a tumbler of rum held between a thumb and forefinger, apparently oblivious as the President's words unfolded in a mass of half-truths and appeals, gravity and encouragement, quips and dire warnings.

'Quince,' Walker said quietly, 'I know who you are, you're Jeremy Quince.'

The corpulent figure next to him didn't blink. Walker took his elbow this time, so there could be no doubt. 'I have to talk to you,' he said. 'A man has died.'

Quince didn't move, except to sip from his glass of rum. He

239

didn't turn his head or step away, his whole attention was apparently reserved for the President on stage. But then he spoke.

'It's all right,' he said. 'I heard the first time.'

'We must talk alone,' Walker said, and immediately felt the absurdity of the request in a room full of a thousand people. 'We must leave while your friend's away,' he added.

'Oh, *he's* gone, has he?' Quince replied loudly. 'Probably gone for a piss. He's like a bloody dog, you could lock him in the back of a car for three days and he'd hold it in until you let him free. I expect he thought I couldn't get away in the crush.'

He still hadn't turned his head to acknowledge Walker, or even to check, out of curiosity, who it was who had accosted him. One or two people had turned when Quince spoke, there were looks of disapproval. Walker was temporarily confused by the man's reaction. It was as if he knew exactly who he was talking to and had been expecting the approach.

'I have a record of your meeting with Continental,' Walker said quietly. He had to shake the man's composure. The President's speech whirred on in the background like a recording in Walker's mind, he was concentrating so hard on communicating with the man next to him. 'Your meeting was taped,' he said, next to Quince's face. 'You and a man named Nethercott were identified. I have those tapes.'

'Who are you?' Quince said.

'You married Continental to the man up there.' Walker pointed towards the dais. 'I have the tapes,' he repeated. 'But we must talk now, or they get passed on.'

Quince didn't reply, but when he sipped again at his glass it seemed to Walker to be a gesture of anxiety. From the dais, the President's words spead smoothly over the room, fooling no one. 'Everything is now under control. Soon things will be returning to normal. The flight of capital has stopped.' It had stopped because there was precious little left to go, and the President, of course, did not say that he personally had frozen foreign transfers anway.

'My man could break your neck,' Quince said.

There was a smattering of applause at something the President said. 'If we don't talk now, it's your neck,' Walker said. 'We leave now, go upstairs and talk.'

Walker watched Quince drain his glass to the bottom and put it into the velvet side-pocket of his jacket. 'This way,' Walker said. 'If you're coming.' He turned and began to press his way through the crowd in the opposite direction to Quince's minder, going back towards the stairs. He didn't look behind him, just prayed that Quince was following. He had no doubt that Quince was right, the squat muscleman could easily break his neck; it looked as if that was exactly what God had created him for.

Walker didn't stop until he'd reached the edge of the diplomatic mass. There were angry grunts and resistance as he pushed his way through, and when he stopped at the rim of the crowd, he was dishevelled and hot, his tie hanging loose halfway down his shirt. He tugged it up to the neck and looked back. Quince was already by his side and looked as if he'd been sitting quietly in an armchair for an hour, reading a book. He was completely composed, the glass now out in his hand again and being proffered to one of the ring of waitresses who stood waiting by the wall for the President to finish, when glasses would be charged for a loyal toast.

'Not here,' Quince said when he saw Walker put his foot on the bottom stair. 'We can be seen all over the bloody room if we go up here.'

He turned along the free stretch of floor between the waitresses and the audience, and Walker followed. At the end of the ballroom, thirty yards perhaps, there was a service entrance. Quince walked straight through it and beckoned to Walker. There was a maître d'hôtel standing there, arms crossed in front of him, wearing a grubby evening suit.

'*Buena sera*, Señor Queence,' he said, and Quince nodded in return – the staff in the plush Tamanaco were all imported Italians. There was a concrete passage with metal trolleys parked in it, like a school canteen, and ahead of them a noise from an open door indicated the kitchens. The walls were painted cream and were flayed from heat and neglect; the luxury had stopped as soon as they stepped over the threshold. At the far end of the passage Quince turned up a metal spiral staircase that led away to a service area on the ground floor above. He puffed ahead of Walker, drinking the tumbler of champagne in draughts and occasionally spilling it through the open metalwork of the stairs. He was in a hurry. It occurred to Walker for the first time that Quince was afraid of his own thug – as afraid as he, Walker, was. They came up through the floor into another concrete corridor with two swing doors at the end, and a carpet-stop just visible beneath. Quince headed for the doors and pushed through them into a cocktail lounge. Walker followed him and stopped at the bar. 'You have a room?' Quince asked him.

'No.'

'We can't use mine.'

Another manager in an evening suit, much smarter this time, came into the bar. He also knew Quince as an old and favoured guest, it seemed.

'I need a room, Giorgio,' Quince said in English. 'Just a small private room. What have you got? Projector room, broom cupboard, something like that.'

'Of course, sir. Come with me.'

They followed the Italian out of the bar and into the foyer. He snapped at a receptionist to give him keys and caught them in one hand, and Walker followed Quince down another, carpeted passage, past a number of conference suits to a room at the end, next to a fire door marked Staff Only.

'Very good, Giorgio,' Quince said, and parted with a twenty-dollar bill. The door was unlocked and Quince was given the key. They both entered, and Quince locked the door behind them. He snapped on all the switches and light flooded the room. For the first time Quince looked at Walker, and belched.

'If he finds us, he'll enjoy breaking your neck,' Quince said. 'And so will I.' He walked to a table in the centre of the room – it was the sort of room that was used, perhaps, for staff meetings, Walker thought – and sat down. His tumbler of champagne was a quarter full; he sipped at it, and for the first time since Walker had mentioned Continental, looked as if he was drinking for pleasure rather than out of need. 'What do you want?' he said. 'If it's money, forget it. You can't bleed me. I don't blackmail.'

Walker sat down in a chair out of Quince's reach. 'I'm a journalist,' he said.

'Good God!' This time the tumbler remained at Quince's lips for a longer time. 'Then I might just make an exception,' he said with heavy sarcasm. But he looked worried and his voice turned serious. 'What is it you want?'

Walker pulled a copy of the transcript from his pocket and threw it across the table so that it skidded to a halt under Quince's nose. 'If Continental pays you and Continental funds the government, what does Continental get in return?' he said.

Quince glanced briefly at the transcript but didn't bother to give it anything but the most cursory attention. He seemed convinced, Walker thought; he didn't look as if he was going to waste time on pretence. 'What does the government want with a billion dollars?' Walker pursued. 'That's my question. Or should I say, what does the President want with a billion dollars? If it's to fund the army, that might not be such a popular revelation out there.' He nodded vaguely at the window. 'Your thug might be worth respect, but there are a lot of people out there who would be fascinated to know who's buying the bullets.'

Quince laughed. 'I am an economist,' he said, and smiled openly at his own joke.

'I don't think they'd see it that way.'

Quince looked for a moment at the telephone. 'There are other copies of the transcript, of course,' Walker lied. 'In other hands. There's no point in trying to get rid of me now.'

Quince looked cornered. 'What makes you think I ever succeeded in raising that money?'

'Because you're here.'

'Here?'

'In Caracas,' Walker said. 'And here at the Tamanaco. You're in the President's entourage, you're on the inside. One of the favoured.'

Quince reached into the top pocket of his jacket and pulled out a dark leather case in which five cigars were fitted in their individual compartments like torpedos. He selected one, and clipped the end and filled his mouth with it. As a demonstration of rich comfort it befitted a man in the President's circle, but as a gesture, Walker thought, it looked like someone in the water looking for a float. When Quince had lit the end of the cigar with a huge flame, he steadied his gaze in Walker's direction through plumes of grey smoke.

'I don't believe you understand the complexity of a deal like this,' he said after some thought. 'What do you expect Continental to get out of it? Ninety per cent interest? Freedom to strip the country? A seat in the cabinet?'

Walker thought of Higson. 'Trading concessions, maybe,' he said. 'Certain privileges to buy Venezuelan goods. Who knows? Maybe they lent the money against something they were going to take out of the ground, gold or diamonds, oil – I don't know. Why don't you tell me, Mister Quince? The President has fifteen minutes left to speak.'

But Quince wasn't going to be hurried. 'Who have you been talking to?' he said.

Walker didn't answer.

'Because there are people who are spreading rumours in this city. It's a city ripe for rumours. There are people, like you perhaps, who are prepared to believe whatever they're told. There are factions, splits, cabals in the government itself, let alone outside it. And we haven't even touched on the army,' he added with a flamboyant wave of a hand, cigar smoke circling in the air. 'Will the army be the *deus ex machina*?' he suggested, as if he were giving a lecture.

And here was somebody who was about to spin one more story, Walker thought. 'If the army are taking the President's shilling, then they're unlikely to interfere with him, are they?' he said.

'You have been listening to the wrong people.'

'Then perhaps I should listen to you,' Walker said sarcastically.

Quince laughed. 'I thought that was why we were here.' His shoulders slowed their rocking. When he laughed it was like turning an oil tanker – the process took a long time to complete. 'You've been talking to Armando Higson, haven't you?' he said, and he suddenly leaned across the table that separated them and looked at Walker with ice-cold eyes from which all joviality had vanished.

'I've seen Higson,' Walker said, and was irritated at his own defensiveness. Quince, far from being nervous about the tapes, had chosen to attack.

'You won't see much more of him,' Quince said.

'I was there when he was arrested,' Walker said. 'Why?'

Quince pulled on his cigar in a leisurely way. He looked at Walker as if to assess how much he knew. 'Higson wasn't very clever with the President,' he said. 'He chose the other side. The wrong side? Who knows? We have yet to see the final act. But whoever wins, it won't be much good to Higson now. He was arrested because the President couldn't put up any longer with him spreading the kind of tales he no doubt told you. The situation is too fragile to allow the Higsons of this world free reign. We are in a war, you understand, and tactics develop accordingly. Higson was the editor of a national newspaper, as you know. He should have reported the news as a national editor is required to do. Instead, what did he do? You talk about the President's shilling, but Higson is the one who was on a payroll. Higson was financed to run the news in a certain way. If you look at *La Prensa*, you will see that Higson has been running a campaign against the government for two months. Nothing wrong with that, unless there is someone who is paying him to do it, unless he is selling his position to the highest bidder. It is *La Prensa* which has stirred up this truckers' strike from the start. Read the back numbers. In whose interests is a truckers' strike? The country's? No. And certainly not the government's. It is the truckers' strike that will destroy the government unless it can win first. That is what the President is talking about downstairs. Meanwhile Higson is locked up, perhaps dead. Is that so bad?' Quince leaned back.

'Where's the evidence?'

'He was observed, receiving money. No doubt they want to know who is paying him. But you have listened only to Higson's story, and Higson's story is that the government receives money, am I right? Higson says that it is the government who is corrupt.'

'Never mind Higson,' Walker said. 'I have evidence of your involvement in Continental's financing scheme. Where is the money? What was it for? Why raise money like that? Illegally, under the counter? Black money for a secret purpose. That's here on paper. Let's stick to what we know, and what we know is that you raised one billion dollars for the President outside all normal banking channels.'

But with the back of his mind Walker was thinking about what Quince had said. It was almost irresistibly plausible. Rausch, he now knew, were paying the truck drivers to go on strike, in order to destabilize the economy; wasn't it more than likely that they were paying other people, too, to do exactly the same? Of course, Higson *might* have been attacking the government and recommending a strike entirely off his own bat. Might have been . . . He thought about Rausch, its huge power, its awesome efficiency. If they set out to do a job like destabilizing a country's economy, Rausch would do it properly.

And Walker thought again about what had troubled him in his meeting with Higson: the insistence that he should pay for the tapes and the transcript – and then the sudden climbdown. Suddenly, it had all been fine to take the lot scot-free. It had bothered Walker at the time and it bothered him now. 'Yes, I raised the money,' Quince said, and looked at Walker with a cool arrogance. 'But why should I know what it was for?'

'You must know what it's for, because otherwise I'm going

to walk out of this room and have this published in every paper you've ever read,' Walker said. 'How you raised money on behalf of Continental to prop up a government which fires live bullets at its own citizens in its own capital. How are Continental going to react to that?'

'Dimly, I should imagine,' Quince said. 'But you are like Higson. You would rather print a lie than the truth.'

It was the response of a man with little left to say, Walker thought. 'Then why don't you tell me the truth?' he said. He saw that a light sweat had broken out on Quince's forehead. He was holding his tumbler in one fat hand and swilling the contents around as if, by looking in the glass, he would discover a way of escape.

'Unattributably?' Quince asked.

'If you want.'

'The man you saw downstairs, he doesn't just have a strong bladder. You saw him. You know what kind of man he is.' The sweat had broken out in drops on Quince's face now. He was in a corner. 'This is bloody extortion!' he breathed, and sagged slightly at the shoulders. 'You know what I'm saying?' he said at last.

Walker removed his wallet from his jacket, and pulled out his press card and threw it across the table so that it slid against Quince's forearm which was resting on the wooden surface. Quince didn't move, and the cigar smoke oiled around his neck like a noose, but finally he adjusted the card with his cigar hand and puffed again as he looked at it the right way up. 'Walker', he said. 'Harry Walker. *Periodista*.' And he read the paper's name over to himself several times. 'Well, Harry Walker', he said. 'Either you file your story with my name in it, and set my watchdog on me and screw up the facts to kingdom come, or I tell you about Continental and you write your bloody piece and leave me out of it. Is that about it?'

'That's about it,' Walker said.

'Because you know what will happen to me otherwise?'

'I can guess.'

Quince leaned across the table to make his point unmistakable. 'We are dealing with some very serious people,' he said. 'Very serious money, and very serious people to go with it. A billion dollars is just the stake, what goes in the pot. Whoever wins the pots gets much, much more than that. A billion dollars is place money. What we're playing for here are the revenues of a nation, Mr Walker. A rich nation. Venezuela is a very rich nation if only it has the right people to look after its wealth. It can't, you see, do it on its own. It needs the banks, it needs the skills, and most of all it needs the corporate strength. It needs the multi-national companies.'

He leaned back and puffed. Now that he had made the decision to speak out, he seemed more at ease than before. 'You ask me why the billion dollars was raised without the banks,' he went on. 'I'll tell you. It was raised in that way for the simple reason that the banks wouldn't lend the money themselves.'

'The banks will always lend money to this country,' Walker said, quoting Higson. 'As you say, they have the resources.'

'They lend according to conditions, Mr Walker. Six months ago, this President decided to introduce certain reforms – social reforms – and he planned to do it by restricting the profits of the big companies here – companies that were given a free hand by the last president. You know these companies, Mr Walker. Renault and Volkswagen, for example, who were both here until a few weeks ago, when they realised they weren't going to be able to sell a car here for the foreseeable future; Unilever, IBM, Rio Tinto – you know all the names. But by far the biggest single corporations in the country are the Continental and Rausch groups. Huge, they're like countries in themselves. They're in agriculture, mining, oil, manufactured goods, everything, and they've been here since Venezuela began.

'Now, what the President was proposing didn't suit these companies at all. In particular, it didn't suit Rausch. Would you believe, Mr. Walker, that one of the reforms the President wanted to institute was the provision of free milk to children under eleven?' Quince laughed. 'Not an earth-shattering proposal, you might think. Not something that would lead to revolution.' Quince paused. His cigar had gone out while he was talking, and he knocked the inch-long ash from the end and relit it, laboriously pulling at the end until the wetness seeped up the tobacco to his fingers and a brown stain was left on his lips.

'But he had two problems,' he resumed. 'You might say three, if you count the bloody naivety that made him believe he could get away with the plan in the first place. The first thing he had to do was raise the money for this admirable social gesture,' Quince said, rolling the 'r' to show he was not fooled by admirable social gestures. 'Who controls all the milk in the country? Not the government, that's for sure, or he could tax the rich and give his milk sops to the poor. No, Rausch. Rausch supplies every carton, every tin of powder. Rausch controls the milk supply from the cradle to the grave. So what did the President do? He tried to make an agreement with Rausch: a special concession on the price of some of their milk in return for various concessions in the government's trading agreements with them. And Rausch refused. They kicked up a row that made itself heard in the corridors of the IMF and the World Bank – let alone the ordinary commercial lending banks. "This government is trying to stop the progress we've made," they said. "They're trying to turn the clock back, just when the country is at last prospering as it should. They want to undermine our good work." It was a powerful argument, Mr Walker, and it had particular weight for the banks who have recently lent money here.'

Quince stubbed out the fatted, frayed end of the cigar in the ashtray at last. He screwed up his face at the bitter end-taste and picked some bits of tobacco from his teeth where he had chewed too violently. He was a messy man; he drank carelessly, there was nothing delicate about him. He told the story as if he were unnecessarily revealing the brutal details of a murder to a relative of the victim. Everything he said was a challenge to Walker to protest, an invitation to object. He pronounced each word as if it were a weapon to bludgeon the listener with.

'And then the President made his second mistake,' Quince said. 'He tried to screw Rausch. No one has ever done that here, no one has ever felt the need to. Rausch have always looked after the presidents of this country, if you know what I mean; they have always made sure they have an extremely good relationship with whoever's in charge. But this President threatened Rausch. He tried to tell them that if they didn't offer the milk concessions he had asked for, he would get them by legislative means. He would force Rausch to drop its prices.'

Quince picked his teeth with his tongue. 'You don't use a word like "force" when you're dealing with Rausch, Mr Walker.'

He clambered clumsily out of his seat and walked to the end of the room, his tumbler, empty now, gripped in one fist. He looked as if he were searching for something. Walker followed him with his eyes. Quince was tense. He looked like a man with a streak of intense recklessness all of a sudden, like someone who could turn violent – who could smash a glass on the edge of a table and jam it into another man's face. Perhaps, briefly, that was what was going through Quince's mind. He looked trapped, as if he wanted an escape. But if his violence had ever been directed against Walker, even in his mind, he now vented his feelings on a wooden cabinet at the far end of the room. With great force, he kicked the door, in the process shattering a glass lampshade that stood apparently unassailable on the top of the cupboard. Although Walker already had misgivings about Quince, the gesture shook him. It was a gesture that ill became this big, ungainly man who called himself an economist and carried himself with the hauteur of a successful pimp. That was what he was: a pimp. He would raise money for anyone, it didn't matter who, it didn't matter why. As long as he got his cut and he got away scot-free, that was all that mattered to Quince. Or so Walker thought.

'I need a bloody drink,' Quince snarled.

He wrenched at the door of the cupboard, but it was locked. He bent down and shook it, and the sound of heavy glass bottles banging against each other disturbed the earlier quiet. Walker realised that he had been completely absorbed by what Quince was saying; now that he had stopped talking, the sound-proofed silence of the room buzzed in his ears. The cupboard door didn't open and Quince rattled it again with a violent tug of his hand. This time the wood splintered. He pulled again, and the cabinet nearly fell, but instead the lock tore away and the door opened to reveal a set of bottles, one of which had fallen in the fracas. Quince reached inside. He was sweating again, Walker saw, and he looked faintly absurd, crouched on the floor in his dapper clothes and his impeccable bow tie, with a broken door in his hand. He pulled out a bottle of ginger-coloured rum, the Ron Anjero the Venezuelans loved.

'Best in the bloody world,' Quince said.

He poured a shot that nearly reached the rim of the tumbler and put the bottle down, then had second thoughts and carried it back with him to the table. He slumped down, the beads of sweat coursing along the lines of his face until they ran out of a place to go and fell onto the table.

'You don't use a world like "force" with Rausch,' Walker prompted softly, like a doctor with a dying patient. Quince was cracking up, that's what it looked like.

'Yes,' Quince said vaguely.

They sat in silence, and the smell of decay might have been just airlessness – or the rotten smell of deceit that Quince sweated out with his story.

'We have only minutes,' Walker said at last.

Quince nodded vaguely and sipped thoughtfully at the rum. 'So what does the President do?' he said at last, half to himself. 'He goes to the banks to borrow for his social reforms, and they tell him to get lost. They tell him to get his house in order and then they can all get together to think about free milk another day. They're beginning to dislike his way of doing things. He threatens them too, says that loan repayments will stop. They tell him he's playing a very dangerous game indeed. Very, very dangerous.' Quince looked up at Walker as if he had been addressing someone else and for the first time realised Walker was there.

'Of course,' he said, 'we all know Rausch had been there before him. To the banks, I mean. And Rausch carries a lot of clout, Rausch has no trouble at all in demonstrating to the banks that the President's policies are going to jeopardise their repayments. To the banks, it is people like Rausch who *are* the country; without people like Rausch the whole thing falls apart.' He pulled at the neat rum.

'So,' he said, his eyes ice-cold and concentrated again. He was a man who drifted in and out of concentration, Walker noticed. He could lose himself in a pit of thought, and then be on top again in a second. 'The President has no money and the economy takes a knock from the banks. Instead of handing out social programmes like bread, the President suddenly finds he has to put prices up, for Christ's sake! Suddenly he's forced to do exactly the opposite of what he's always wanted. And he's desperate for money, not to flannel the voters with free milk any longer, but just to stay alive. And he can only sweet-talk the banks into lending him some by agreeing to their terms and paying back their loans on cue, which will make him even more unpopular. There are riots. The currency collapses. The whole thing has been very badly handled by everyone.' He blinked at Walker. 'Or is it everyone?' he said.

Quince looked over Walker's shoulder at some unidentified speck on the wall which was to provide a focus for what he had to say next. 'So Continental arrives on the scene. Rivals of Rausch, you understand. They make an offer, they try to help, they put me on their payroll because I've done this before.' Quince said it as if the whole thing seemed faintly unreal to him all of a sudden. 'They offer to raise a billion dollars for the President. Meanwhile, his own supporters are getting out of hand; they think he's let them down. There are riots. And where there is anarchy, all sorts of things can happen, all sorts of changes can take place. Anyone who is organised can take control. You asked me what Continental were to get in return – will get in return – if the President succeeds. It's so simple. Things are turning very nasty now,' he said, as if someone had suddenly introduced another topic. He slurped the rum and it ran down his chin. One finger dug into his right ear and scraped. He was suddenly a man adrift. His clothes and his voice and his whole demeanour were falling apart. When he talked now, there were traces of an Irish accent. His face had mottled. It was like watching someone die from slow poison.

'If Continental could get him the money,' Quince said, 'the President would take measures against Rausch. He would effectively take half of Rausch's business in the country from them and give it to their big rivals, Continental. The roles reversed at a stroke, you see. Rausch, now the dominant multi-national here, would slip to second place. Their business would quite simply be appropriated.

'That's what I mean by force, Mr Walker. And that's what I mean when I say you don't use words like force when you're dealing with Rausch. They aren't going to let that happen, you can be sure of that. So what do they do?'

Quince tried to reach inside his velvet jacket, but couldn't get his hand the proper side of the flap at first. When he did succeed, he took hold of something in the inside pocket and began to pull it out. It was a piece of paper folded in half, and he'd got one half of it in his fingers. It came out sideways and crumpled, caught in the pocket as he tugged at it, increasingly irritated by the resistance. At last it was free and he opened it up, turned it the right way round and blinked at it, apparently not sure whether it was what he thought it was.

'Yesterday's paper,' he said. 'Hot off the presses.' He belched. 'Of course, they've planned it for months – weeks, anyway. They'll fight any way they can to hang on to what they've got, and they have a very good chance of succeeding, I should have thought.' He threw the sheet of paper across the table at Walker, but it caught the air and flew up, then collapsed. Walker picked it up.

It was a page from the *Wall Street Journal*. He glanced at the two names in the opening paragraph, and stopped. *They've planned it for months.* He read it through twice before he looked back up at Quince, who was leaning on his drink like a man in a pub who doesn't ever want to go home. There was no expression on Quince's face. 'Yesterday's,' he repeated absently.

Walker looked for a third time at the paper in his hands. 'An announcement was made on Friday in Lyons,' Walker read, 'that the Rausch Corporation have launched a bid to take over one of their chief rivals in Central and South America, Continental USA.' Three lines, a snippet at the side of a page; the paper obviously had no further information when it went to print. It was a last-minute announcement, precisely timed, Walker guessed, to make the late news – the extra column at the side – but not to allow opportunity for any analysis of the situation before the next day. He remembered Peter Clive's vague rumour of a bid three weeks before, in Slick's office.

Quince had got out of his chair again and wandered around the table. He was looking anxiously at his watch. The President was due to stop speaking at any moment, but it was certain that he would go on for longer than planned. Walker watched Quince closely. Clearly Quince didn't know of the money Rausch was paying to the truck drivers – paying them to strike. Who would benefit? Where there is anarchy, Quince had said, anyone who is organised can take control. Rausch financed a strike that brought the country to its knees, then announced a takeover bid for their main rival: an offensive on two fronts. If they could get rid of the President, well and good. And the way to get rid of the President was to plunge the country into a crisis he couldn't control. A coup would follow, with Rausch wooing the army away from the President. If what Quince said was true, Continental's money was never intended for the army. But how much longer would they go on fighting the President's battles when they probably didn't even agree with the policies behind them? Walker looked up wearily. He saw the plan at last from Quince's point of view. The Continental defence could head off the strike, raise wages, perhaps, give the truck drivers what they wanted. And yet they had no knowledge of the secret fund, the connection between Imronal and Rausch. When Walker sat down in his room and wrote his piece, the story of a lifetime, Rausch would be discredited and the President could take whatever action against the company was necessary, with the world's approval.

'It's a difficult story to swallow,' he said.

Quince didn't look round. He was standing, cradling the rum in one hand and rocking slightly from side to side. He was thinking what he had thought in Paris, weeks before. This was the last time. He was getting out, he couldn't go on living the extremes any longer. He was old, too old for it. He had lost the stomach for it. This time, after this one, he would draw the curtain, call it a day, retire. Retire with a lot of money and a little brooding satisfaction, and drink himself to death.

'No one,' he said, still without facing Walker, 'no one could make all that up.' He laughed to himself, and the rum spilled slowly onto his freckled hands and dripped onto the carpet like an open wound. From the sharp, aesthetic figure of half an hour before, Quince had dwindled to a shambling shadow. It was as if his private knowledge had puffed him out and preened the green velvet of his jacket, and made him debonair – and in giving up his story, he had given up his strength. There was nothing to him any longer. 'It's time to go,' he said. 'If you've finished with me,' he added, with a touch of his former spark.

Walker stood up and pushed back the chair, and looked once more at the press cutting. Who had a copy of yesterday's *Wall Street Journal* when the airport was closed? he wondered. The American embassy, they were the only people who could procure that, from their base in the west. So what? If Quince knew the top-to-bottom staff of the Tamanaco Hotel, he should know someone at the American embassy. It wasn't important. No doubt the President's staff still had their papers delivered somehow, too.

Quince walked to the door and put his hand on the door handle. He turned briefly, glass still clutched in his other hand, and stared at Walker.

'I won't shake hands, if you don't mind,' he said.

He unlocked the door and opened it to the corridor outside. He was halfway through it before he stopped, apparently baffled. Facing him from the other side of the corridor was his hired brute. Walker saw him over Quince's shoulder and felt Quince's shock. The Israeli was staring, unblinking, at the fat, drunk figure before him. He looked like a terracotta soldier – except that there was nothing brittle about him, and you wouldn't put him in a museum unless it was to scare the children. He stood totally still. He looked as if he had no blood in his veins.

'You!' he snapped, and his eyes moved, still without blinking, over Quince's shoulder and bored into Walker's. 'You fat bastard!' he said, and his eyes swivelled back to Quince.

Quince turned back to Walker. 'If they get me,' he said, 'it's all part of the service. Remember that.'

Then he shuffled away, up the corridor towards reception. The brute looked at Walker and flicked a finger up at him like a knife. His right eye travelled down his finger as if it were a gunsight, and his face was empty of everything but pure malice. Suddenly, he clicked sideways like a soldier on parade and disappeared down the corridor after Quince.

EIGHTEEN

The Forty Committee

Nethercott looked round the table and thought again that fourteen was too many for a meeting. Fourteen didn't promote discussion, it only created noise and, ultimately, misunderstanding. It also meant that the meeting would go on ten times longer than it would with only four, say. Nothing, in Nethercott's opinion, could be achieved in five hours of talk that couldn't be achieved in thirty minutes; you just had time to talk around the issue in a dozen different ways, but the end result would be exactly the same.

Looking around again, it was a strange mixture of disciplines Nethercott saw at the table. A number were obviously Company or ex-Company: the committee had been CIA-inspired in the first place, so that was not surprising. He and his opposite number, Stratstone, in fact, had both been signed up by Special Forces for off-the-record duties after Vietnam. They had never actually worked together as far as Nethercott remembered, but they had certainly been on the same side. Now, however, they were diametrically opposed, both ideologically – if you could call loyalty to a multi-national company ideological – and geographically, at the table. Stratstone sat opposite him with his hands clasped and an unnaturally relaxed expression on his face.

It was typical of the Company, really. They trained up so many people over the years that there was never enough for them to do at the end, and though the Company gave them the best training in the world, they could never pay commercial rates. So that was where companies like Continental and Rausch came in. Agents drifted off, as he and Stratstone had done, and found their work elsewhere, bringing to it a number of skills you couldn't learn in college. In a company like Continental, they didn't call them spies, though that's what they were. They called them special operatives, or consultants, or just advisors. That was how the Company's trained agents were sent out into the world, to scrape their living as best they could. And inevitably, where professional armies were concerned, they often found their old Company colleagues looking at them down the wrong end of a gun barrel.

This was called the Forty Committee because there were, theoretically, forty of them altogether, though, thank God, not all of them ever turned up at once. Nethercott had been a member before his special assignment to Continental; Stratstone was here as a special guest, because he was Rausch's advisor on the situation – though the chairman of Rausch was present too, as well as the chairman of Continental. Nethercott was Stratstone's opposite number on the Continental side, though no one present, including the chairman of Continental, knew he was also still working for the Company – apart from the CIA director himself, of course. In fact it was Nethercott, with his recording of the meeting with Quince in Caracas about funding Continental's government support operation, who had originally tipped off the Company. The Forty Committee was an intriguing mix of U.S. business and U.S. foreign policy interests.

Next to Stratstone was an ex-Secretary of State, Lineham, who had bags under his eyes like open suitcases. He now had a consultancy business in Washington, where the Committee always met in one of the low-ceilinged, grey-walled rooms the Company lent them, at the end of two miles of corridor. If you added together all the corridor space in Washington's warren of committee rooms and 'silent discussion bases', you would have a large enough area to build the White House in five times over. Just the corridors. Whatever happened to meetings in corridors? Nethercott wondered. You could double committee output at a stroke.

Next to Lineham sat Schwammburger; they had been colleagues when the Democrats were last in power, and were now united in Lineham's PR consultancy. Next to Schammmburger was Oates, the CIA director, the most important man here and probably the most important man anywhere on the whole Forty Committee. He was the only one who had a reasonable chance of knowing half of what was going on half of the time. Then there was the Republican, Manse, from Defense, and two men Nethercott had never met before and whose names he had forgotten, though they'd been introduced to him. Then the Swiss, Hofer, who was here to represent Rausch, which was fair enough as he was the chairman; then Senator George Dupont; Averill, the head of IBM; and the chairmen of United Fruit, Merill Lynch and Venzoil, the joint U.S. and Venezuelan oil company. After them was Stratstone, Rausch's man on the ground – Nethercott didn't have any idea what his official title might be. And finally there was himself.

The problem, according to the shreddable minutes, was the Rausch takeover bid for Continental – although in fact conversation had revolved around everything else but that. This, however, Nethercott thought, was the way it should be, because it wasn't the takeover bid per se that concerned the committee, it was the effect all of this was having on one of America's surer-footed allies on the Southern Rim. And the effect on Venezuela was damaging both America's foreign policy interests in the area and those of international business. Hence the resort to the Forty Committee, which dealt in areas of mutual interest. Stability was always good for business and, sometimes, good for foreign policy. And where instability was recommended for political reasons, it was often recommended by business interests too. The Company and the multi-nationals tended to agree on what form of government suited them both best, wherever their activities overlapped.

So why couldn't the minutes have read 'Stability in Venezuela'? Nethercott grumbled to himself. Then perhaps there wouldn't have been all this beating about the bush. 'Rausch bid for Continental' only told part of the story. What everyone round the table wanted to achieve in the country was a return to normality, a return to profit on one side of the argument, and a return to a reliable political alliance on the other.

'Let's just return to base,' the chairman, Lineham, was saying. 'What's the net take-away here?'

Some of the others leaned back in their chairs and waited for Lineham's lead. The room was getting hot and stuffy; there were no windows in this maze of committee rooms, and prickly heat was visibly beginning to irritate one or two. Anyone who suffered from claustrophobia would not have felt at home in the room, either. There comes a time when a person turns round and says, 'Let's open a window', and if there is no window to open, the outreach, as Lineham would have said, shrinks dangerously.

'The request to you, Herr Hofer, is that Rausch drop their takeover ambitions for Continental USA. In return you want certain guarantees that Rausch's interests will cease to be threatened in Venezuela in the way they have been in the past few months. Your specific demand, therefore, in return for dropping the bid, is that Continental sever its dealings with the present government. That entails, as we all know, the abandonment of the loan raised by their agent, Quince, at their behest, on behalf of the present Venezuelan government.'

Everyone around the table, Nethercott noticed, had now taken up Oates', the CIA director's, cue and began talking of the 'present' Venezuelan government and the 'current' president of Venezuela, as if there was a common understanding that these might be short-lived. Oates sat with one arm around the back of his chair, his jacket stretched right back to reveal a super-white shirt, and the other arm in front of him on the table, holding a pencil with which he seemed to be doodling with total absorption. His head was bent right down, and he looked as if he was sitting in the sort of position very fit people sit in in order to show how fit they are. 'Herr Hofer has agreed to drop the bid,' he reminded everyone without looking up. 'Now it's up to Continental to agree to sever relations with the President and his government.' He looked up at the chairman of Continental. 'Isn't that about right?' he said. He wasn't exactly asking him the melting point of titanium, Nethercott noted.

'I think we can come to some arrangements about that,' the chairman said, and looked round to Nethercott. 'What is our situation at the moment? Where does the money stand?'

'It's all offshore,' Nethercott answered. 'A Cayman holding company has the bulk of it, and the rest is arriving in the next few days, if the Arabs keep to their promise. Then it's to be transferred to a special government account in Caracas.'

'But surely it's now beyond your control?' Oates protested. 'If the Arabs want to lend it and the Venezuelan government want to borrow it, how can Continental interfere now?' Oates suddenly looked quite upset. The point of the pencil dug into the messed-up paper on the table until the lead broke.

'Even if both the parties still wanted to – as I'm sure they do – ' Nethercott said, 'they can't go ahead without Continental's guarantee. It would be a completely different deal. I say "can't", but I mean won't. The Arabs won't go ahead without a guarantee of some sort, and that's what the government can't provide. If Continental withdraw their support, that's it.'

Oates appeared somewhat mollified.

The chairman of Rausch had looked completely calm throughout this. It was as if he was letting Oates, director of the CIA, fight all his battles for him. It hadn't been difficult to stop Rausch from going ahead with their bid. In the first place, the bid had only been a tactic to bring things to just the point where the Forty Committee would want to step in. Rausch were sitting pretty. If the Forty Committee could agree on this, everything would return to the *status quo ante*. Rausch would have their interests intact in the country in spite of a hostile president – and that too could be dealt with.

'And what about the operation there?' Oates chivvied Nethercott. 'How quickly can that be wound up? This man – Quince, is it? – what sort of a position is he in? We don't want him getting in the machinery. What are you going to do about that?'

Nethercott still spoke for the Continental chairman, who had no idea of his dual role. By leaking the tapes of the meeting in Caracas, Nethercott had jeopardised the whole Continental operation, yet here he was, their spokesman. That was the way the Company worked. Sometimes they needed an overview on a commercial situation, and this time, in the Company's plans, Rausch were to reap the rewards and Continental were going to have to back off. 'He's running on an account and a bonus,' he said. 'He's watched, so he can't go out of sight for long. We can cancel his account this afternoon and throw him out on the street, or we can pay him off with a fat golden handshake. Whatever we do, he's out as of today. Out of the game and out, preferably, of the country.'

Oates looked at Nethercott as if expecting a secret signal. They both knew that Quince was not a problem. Quince was nothing. Why else employ the Israeli? If they wanted to get rid of Quince there was an easy way to do it, but it was better –in present company – not to voice it openly.

There was silence for a moment as Oates looked at the chairman of Continental for agreement, but he got a stony-faced lack of response.

'And let the situation unravel there normally,' Lineham said with democratic optimism. 'Let events take their natural course.'

Nethercott looked at him with contempt. If Lineham thought things were going to run their natural course in Venezuela, he really couldn't tell his arse from a hole in the ground. 'Yes, that's right,' he said. 'Leave them to sort it out for themselves.'

There was an almost tangible air of suppressed disbelief at this, but no one rocked the boat. The Forty Committee was a committee which existed to agree. Lineham looked sideways from his chair to the Rausch camp. There, expressions were of a benevolent, accommodating nature. The Forty Committee had reconciled another situation, Lineham was relieved to see. Business was happy, American foreign policy was happy. Manse, in Defense, hadn't even felt the need to speak as yet. He just monitored the tos and fros of the argument and, apparently, was completely satisfied. Two hours of talking, Nethercott thought with disgust, and what's happened amounts to Rausch dropping its bid and Continental pulling out of its financing deal. It could have been done in a quarter of the time. But everyone had to look at everything ten times over.

'And Rausch will be able to resume its business without loss of revenue?' Lineham asked.

Stratstone looked across at Hofer, who nodded slightly to indicate that Stratstone had the floor. 'Let me give you the missionary position on this one,' he said. 'As long as this President stays in power, there's going to be trouble. He doesn't like us, doesn't like the work we're doing. It doesn't seem to have got through his thick skull yet that Rausch has been making the country work for over a hundred years. Maybe what's happened will make him change his mind. I hope so.' If Stratstone had put his hands together in prayer, it would not have been out of place.

When the meeting broke up, Lineham and Schwammburger left together, with the chairman of United Fruit. Rausch and Continental stayed together in their separate camps. The others drifted off in twos and threes except for Oates. He gave a curt goodbye to a few of them, Nethercott included, and to Hofer especially, and left for urgent duties elsewhere. He went at some speed, unaccompanied.

The others didn't know how successful the meeting had been, both for himself and for Rausch, Oates thought as he wound his way through the warren of corridors like the White Rabbit. It was the victory he had been looking for. Stratstone was one of the his best men, and no one even knew he still worked for the Company. Raush knew, but even Nethercott – who sat looking so smug at him, in the knowledge that he was on the books and it was a secret between the two of them – even Nethercott had no idea that Stratstone had never left the Company in the first place. The Forty Committee, steered by himself, had just negotiated a 'fair deal' for both Rausch and Continental. But no one – himself, Stratstone and Rausch apart – knew of the secret payments to the truck drivers. Whatever happened now, the country would soon be on its knees, and when the country was on its knees and there was no alternative, the army would have to step in – provide the country with some form of government as present authority collapsed. Then, only then, could they settle the score. Rausch had taken very good care, as their relations with the President had slipped beyond recovery, to cultivate a very good relationship indeed with the generals.

Oates turned at last into a brightly-lit office that was the same as a hundred others he had passed. There were loose ends still to be tied down, of course, one of which was Quince. Perhaps the time for simply watching Quince was now over.

NINETEEN

Dance with the Devil

The bed was stripped to the mattress and an eighteen-inch bayonet stuck out of the middle of it. The carpet was torn away from the four corners of the room. Drawers, lamps, fixtures – the paintings on the walls – lay scattered around, smashed and kicked. The ugly shapes of twisted and shattered hotel-room comforts testified to the kind of madness that had been let loose here. Walker stopped at the door, streaming with sweat, his shirt soaked through and his hair matted from the climb. It was eleven floors from the basement – they were watching the lifts. He thought he had been clever, but they had been here already and his time had run out.

There was nothing in the room for him. Everything they hadn't smashed, they had taken; his shaving things even, the can of foam and the travelling razor that screwed together in three sections. He wondered what that had meant to them. To them, it would be a weapon. There were plenty of people in the army, undoubtedly, who believed James Bond existed and was English. He heard a step outside in the corridor, and jumped back behind the door and watched the orange carpet of the hall through the gap between the hinges. But it was nothing. A new sweat began to crawl across his chest and he felt cold. Just a hotel noise. The building lived, and its digestive system growled from time to time like a human's.

He moved round the door and looked both ways down the hall. There was nothing for him here. He couldn't get to the hotel safe now, he was sure his presence in reception would elicit the very opposite of deference. For the last eight hours the hotel, like everywhere else in Caracas, had been in the hands of the army.

265

He checked to the left again, stepped out into the corridor and hurried in the direction he had come, towards the service stairs that led to the basement. There was a cut-out halfway between the ground floor and the garage below, a door used by electricians that led out onto the artificially green lawns at the rear of the hotel, where there was a power house designed to look like a garden shed. Creepers covered it, and it had white-painted, slatted doors reminiscent of a beehive. If he could descend the way he had come, without a challenge from the soldiers, he could reach the gardens and get out, get back to his car and go. Go? He had nowhere to go any more. Guards were posted at the doors of the Foreign Correspondents' Club and the airport was tight shut. If the fight the President had waged against the rioters had been brutal, it was nothing, everyone knew, to what the army would do now that they had taken power into their own hands. They would keep the country's doors bolted until their cleaning-up operation was over, and there would be no one to count the dead.

He reached the top of the service stairs. They were carpeted for the first flight so that guests wouldn't be alarmed by the sight of concrete, but as he turned the corner, out of sight of the guest part of the hotel, the carpet ceased and his shoes made the slap of an unsoftened echo, like footsteps on the stairs of a multi-storey car park. He leapt down two at a time, and paused at every flight to listen for any sound below, to peer down the narrow gap between the metal handrails in case he could spot the barrel of a gun or a booted foot casually resting on a rail. But there was no sign or sound. They had given him twenty-four hours to get out two days ago, but they had given him nowhere to go.

Even while the President was making his speech the night before, the army had been preparing for this. Perhaps they had taken the opportunity the President had given them. Always before, his press briefings has been held at the Miraflores Palace, opposite the barracks; was it a sign of confidence that he had gone to the Tamanaco Hotel? Walker didn't know. For him, the events of the night before could have taken place in another country, at another time. They didn't have any connection with leaping two steps at a time down the concrete service stairs of the Hilton for fear of . . . For fear of what? Assassins, death squads? He thought of Higson again.

He covered five floors and then stopped. Going down didn't seem to be appreciably easier than climbing up had been, it just hurt in a different way. Car keys, did he still have the car keys? He felt frantically in his pocket for a moment, scared that the jumping down had bounced them from his pocket. But they were there, underneath envelopes and notes, and wrappings of chewing gum and cigarette packets and matches, the flotsam of a day on the hoof. Earlier he'd watched the tanks rolling in to the city centre, their guns pointing a different way now: the ring they had made at the city's outer edges to keep the barbarian out had turned inwards. They could deal with the scum of the shanty towns at any time now, in any way they liked – now that they didn't have even the vaguely restraining hand of the President to stop them. The first thing they had to do was consolidate their power in the capital.

Walker felt in the pocket inside his jacket. The transcript was still there, its copy in the hotel safe where the soldiers might or might not have looked. The wrecking of his room had not just been mad anger. They knew, or suspected, that he had the transcript – but what would the transcript mean to them? What had Higson said? It seemed to Walker now that Quince had been right: Higson had been engaged in disinformation. He had been arrested by the troops loyal to the President, the same troops who had put up a fight outside the Palace in the past eight hours, until they'd been overrun. Higson had brought him the transcript in order to plant another story – just like the hospital story that had found its way onto the world's front pages. It was a masterpiece of disinformation when you thought about it: a real meeting, a real deal to raise the government a billion dollars, real Islamic bankers who bartered through the services of a man like Jeremy Quince. Higson had given him all that. And when Walker had been convinced in his own mind of the story's authenticity, when there was no room for doubt, Higson had slipped in a reason for the billion dollars as if it were all part of the package. The money was to bribe the army. And then Quince – Quince, for all his slyness, all his untrustworthiness – had been the one to show Walker what it was *really* for. To keep the country on its feet when Rausch had squeezed the situation to breaking point.

Walker swung himself to a stop at the corner of a flight of stairs, holding a handrail as he did so to slow his momentum. He had heard a noise, somewhere below. He was nearly down to the ground floor now, the noise must have come up from the basement. And then he saw and heard at the same time: the tramp of heavy army boots, the flash of a gun barrel and a streak of camouflage trouser, two, three flights below through the painted metal rails. The clank of the door was the door to the basement car park. He remembered that the air lock that closed the door gently had broken, so that the heavy door crashed back into its metal frame with a noise that reverberated like the door to a prison cell.

The metal rail was surprisingly cold, or perhaps it was his own heat which made it seem so. There were two soldiers, he saw. They had ascended the half-flight from the basement to the ground and stopped to talk. Walker, suspended three floors above them, could do nothing. If they came on, he must retreat. Back to the room? There was nowhere above he could hide. It would be like running to the top of a burning building. But perhaps they weren't under orders to comb the building from the ground floor up. Perhaps they had been placed at the foot of the service stairs, a few feet from the electricians' door, to stop anyone from slipping in and out as Walker had done. Even now, there might be other soldiers ascending in the lifts, and they would drive him down like an animal in a shoot – a sweep from top to bottom which must snare him. His only hope was that they didn't know he was here.

The muffled sounds of conversation drifted up through the stairwell, and the scrape of boots and tin laughter hung echoing from the walls. Walker never took his eyes away from the glint of the gun barrel, the pale flash of an arm on the rail. He slid off his shoes and tied them by their laces round his neck. He couldn't move further down, and at any moment he might have to run, back up to where he had come from. He would hug the walls, stick to the walls – but if he could see them down the well, they would see him if it came to running. He kept his hands off the rail, just his eyes boring down to where they stood. They must have stayed where they were for ten minutes, perhaps more; changing positions, leaning on the rails, one foot up behind, then an elbow or a yellow-brown hand against the khaki of their uniforms. Hollow, tinny laughter. They were relaxed. There would be no more fighting for them, just slaughter.

Just when Walker was starting to think they were there for good, he heard a movement and a scrape of boots, and a tone of voice that suggested they had stayed where they were as long as they dared and had better get back to where they should be. He caught a smell of cigarette smoke, filtered by the air three floors above. With a sigh of relief, he heard the rhythmic scraping of a boot, side to side, side to side, that crushed a cigarette butt underneath it. They had come in here, like him, to hide, to snatch a moment. To smoke out of sight of their commander.

They moved away from the rails and Walker lost them for a moment. Then he saw there were three of them, and they were all heading to the door that led to the hotel foyer, a heavy wooden fire-door that, when opened, admitted the soft, distant sound of foyer music. The Hilton still played its canned music, and the reassuring melodies clashed harshly with the sound of the soldiers' slung guns hitting the door as each passed through it. The door hung on its closing mechanism for a second and then began its long, painful progress back, the music fading as it closed on its hermetic anti-fire seal. Walker stood back. His head felt faint, as if he were hanging upside down. He covered the remaining three floors to the electricians' door in less than half a minute, the shoes banging around his neck and his heart leaping with his stride.

The fumes were what he noticed first. Waves and waves of grey exhaust that banked across the green lawns, enveloped the palm trees and settled in a low, massed cloud around the hotel. The tanks and personnel carriers were rumbling past him, a hundred yards away, the low grumble ascending to a high-pitched scream as they spun round the corner or ground up over the pavement and crushed the stone beneath them. The great new civic projects were being ground beneath caterpillar tracks and solid wheels: Walker had no idea the army was so heavily equipped. The noise was deafening, the electricians' door had muffled it. This was an army on the move. To where? That morning Walker had watched as the battle raged around the barracks of the Regimiento di Guardia Honor, but even the President's own guard had turned out not to be completely loyal. The army had won its battle swiftly, and now they were turning their sights elsewhere.

Walker looked down the narrow street, the private road the Hilton used for its guests' cars, and saw the Chevette. Would they know he had the car? Would they have it watched? And all the time he thought about the death note. The death note had been sent by the same people who had half-strangled him at San Martin; the people who knew he knew about Rausch, the people who had snatched power in the past eight hours. It wasn't the transcript they were after, it was the papers that showed the transfers from Zurich to Liechtenstein to Panama, that ended with Imronal at the Brunner Bank in Caracas. He could give them up if he was caught. But what they also wanted, he couldn't give up so easily: his witnessing of the transfer from Brunner to a small village in the mountains, to the *camionistas*. He couldn't give that up without giving up his eyes. If they found him, they would never let him get away. They would close him down as they had closed down Francesca's husband, and a hundred others.

Walker pulled his tie back up to the collar of his shirt and tucked the shirt in. He unknotted the laces of his shoes and put them on, and ran a hand through his hair. In a war zone it paid to look smart; when you looked unruffled, they ignored you. If you ran, if you panicked, if you looked as if you'd been dragged backwards through a cactus, they noticed. He straightened up and walked the long walk across the stiff, tropical grass of the hotel lawn towards the Chevette. The tanks were ice-cream vans, the soldiers, passers-by. The army was in control. That was good, good, he told himself again and again. Order restored. Be calm, be normal, smile. You are on their side and they are on yours. The gringo; the army always supported the gringo.

The key in Walker's shaking hand went into the driver's door first time, and the door opened without a flash and a bang and a meet-your-maker. He sat inside and automatically reached with his right hand for the ignition, and guided in the key and waited to catch a breath before he turned it, without thinking, without giving himself the time. The Chevette responded normally. A shake of the bodywork, a shudder in the engine, a tearing wrench of the screaming starter, and a crump when it knew it couldn't manage. Walker could have cried with relief. The second time, it started.

The road to the Tamanaco Hotel was lined with the refuse of war. A collapsed wall, a flaming house the fire had torn apart in a wild rage of gasoline and heavy artillery, dozens and dozens of empty cartridge boxes strewn in heaps in the gutters, tyres, once aflame, that now just smoked evilly, pumping black, stinking poison onto the streets. There were rocks and stones in the road, gouges made by a heavy bombardment earlier in the day, a torched drive-in restaurant and fragments of human life. An arm, a head, occasionally almost a complete human form, stuck out of piles of crushed

271

masonry or littered the streets for dogs to gnaw. A plume of smoke, several blocks away, rose over the telephone exchange near Bolivar Square, the centre of democracy – the Liberator himself now ready to be hijacked by one more regime. *There could never be a revolution in a city with a modern Metro*, Walker remembered that from the Club. A few days ago, was that all it was?'

At some point he turned on the radio, he didn't know when or where. The road to the Tamanaco was direct, and he was driving blind, the images of destruction everywhere to dull the senses. He drove through the gouts of black smoke that drifted over the road, around rocks and rubble. A patrol with a makeshift barrier waved him through without a question, but the tightening in his chest didn't leave him. The radio scratched and whined. He fumbled to tune it, and realised that most of the stations were now under army control, or just blacked. At last he found the sombre tones of the messenger who brings bad news: keep calm, keep calm – that was what they always told you when the bullets flew. 'The situation will soon be under control, the rebuilding of our country . . . traitors . . . foreign interference.' There was nothing like the invocation of foreign interference to get the people behind you. Never mind that the army was responsible for it, that they had invited it. And all they had needed was the anarchy engineered by Rausch.

The car park at the Tamanaco was almost empty. A few old rusty cars, taxis probably, sat mouldering round the edges, and there was a jeep parked squarely in front of the hotel entrance, its wheels up over the pavement, but that was all. They were looking for him at the Hilton, Walker thought. In a war zone, there isn't time for detail. They might want him desperately, but they couldn't put the whole army on alert.

He parked the Chevette a distance from the jeep, and walked slowly towards the swing doors into the hotel. His sweat had dried on the drive here, but his scalp prickled. Through the doors and into reception, no challenge, no curt '*Attende! Attende!*' from some mirror-spectacled officer with more time spent on the grooming of his moustache than on his manners. He was through, and at the check-in desk, and a clerk was standing in front of him, as bored as if Walker were one of a package of gringo tourists who'd come for the Angel Falls.

'I want a room,' he said.

'Identification.'

'Do you have one?' He didn't want a room, not in the normal way. The clerk shrugged. Maybe he had one, maybe he hadn't. Come back next year.

'Is there a Mr Quince staying?'

A frown, a shake of the head.

'Quince. *Quince*.'

'Ah! Queeeence,' the clerk said, as if Walker should see a speech therapist. 'Why you want him? Friend?'

'What room is he in? I want a room next door.'

Walker reached for a pen to fill in the hotel form, and pulled a bunch of dollars the size of an encyclopaedia from his wallet. 'Next door,' he reminded the clerk.

The clerk flipped his eyes down like a light-switch and combed the book for answers. 'I was told Mister Queence left this morning,' he said without raising his eyes from the register. 'For two, maybe three days.'

'Then where's his key?'

The clerk shrugged.

'Then I'll take the room next door,' Walker said. 'I can't wait.'

'Two hundred feefty-eight,' the clerk said. 'You wan' two hundred feefty-nine?'

'That's right.'

The clerk turned for the key but didn't part with it. Instead he hung on to it like a monkey with a stolen handbag. 'Identification.'

It was the English word he had honed to perfection, Walker thought – the only one. He held out a hundred-dollar bill to the clerk and with his other hand beckoned for the key. 'Abe Lincoln,' he said, and flapped the picture on the bill.

The clerk laughed through broken teeth. 'Mr Lincoln,' he said with a gleeful mock bow, eyes shut tight with amusement, and plucked the bill from Walker's hand at the same time as he dropped the key onto the counter. The Tamanaco, Walker thought with relief, was down to the very last of its skeleton staff.

He stepped across the carpet onto the marble floor in the centre of the foyer, and walked to the lifts. Two soldiers, presumably from the jeep, lounged inattentive and smoking in voluminous leather armchairs. They didn't take any notice of Walker – not that he would have known, for he had no intention of catching an eye now. The lift took him to the second floor, and his eyes took a moment to adjust to the dullness of the lighting after the glare of the lift. Eventually he turned to the left, following the signs to the high two fiftys, then left again, and right into a dead-end corridor. The key slotted into two five nine, and he opened the door and shut it behind him immediately. He took off his jacket and threw it on the bed. Quince's key had not been on its hook downstairs, so how could he be away? All that mattered now was that he didn't bump into Quince's hired brute.

He opened the sash window with its net curtain and looked out on the ledge he had seen the night before, the ledge that ran right round the inside of the hotel. The Tamanaco was built in a sqaure, with a square hole in the middle that looked down over a dirty obscured-glass roof covering the hotel's breakfast room. The hotel had been built by a French company, Walker seemed to remember, and was modelled on one of a dozen Parisian hotels from the thirties. He slipped over the sill and onto the ledge.

The first surprise he had was that it was far narrower than he had imagined. It was the width of half a shoe, and it looked in places as if it wouldn't stand the weight of a small bird. For three feet along the wall there was nothing to hold on to. Whether he faced the wall or kept his back to it, he would have to edge along the ledge with no hand holds, take such small steps that three feet grew to nearer thirty. He turned his back to the wall. Below him, two floors down to the glass roof, was a long drop. If he fell here, he would arrive more or less in the stand-up ashtray one of the soldiers was using as a spitoon. He wondered if what he hoped to find in Quince's room was so important after all.

His fingers felt their way along the rough stone behind him, and each foot moved a fraction at a time. Anyone watching would have said he was standing still. He didn't look down after the first time. He remembered what someone had once told him: when a person is at a precarious height he shouldn't look down and he shouldn't look up, either is unbalancing. He must pick a spot to watch that is close to the level he is on, that is safest. Somewhere on the far side of the square, for example; another window on the second floor.

His heels scraped along the back wall, one foot sideways on the ledge, the other straight out over the drop. Some fragments of stone-dust slipped away and scattered, floating to the glass below. There was no one else in the hotel, it seemed, just the two soldiers, a few staff and himself. He stretched his left arm out sideways to feel for the gap where Quince's window should be. The tiny movement shifted his shoulder blade, which pushed him fractionally away from the wall, and he felt himself suspended for a second, his heels the only contact with solid ground. He hung there without breathing. Slowly, the upper half of his body tipped, leaned backwards an inch to the wall, and he exhaled his frozen breath. The pressure of his whole weight on his heels had made his knees weak. He was afraid they would shake. Any movement now seemed certain to tip him forwards, but his left hand grabbed the curved stone window-opening. It wouldn't save him if he fell, but it was a psychological handle, and he moved the two steps to the left, eased back onto the windowsill, and gasped for air he hadn't dared to breathe.

The window was unlocked, as the one in his own room had been, and he eased it up behind him, regretting now that he was facing away from the room. He had an unpleasant feeling that there was someone inside. It would take only a small push to send him through the glass below. The window opened, and he gripped it and edged around, just the toes of his shoes on the ledge now, and lifted the sash completely and pulled himself over the sill into the room. He was completely exhausted. The effort and the concentration and the fear had all taken their toll. He didn't even bother to look at the room, but sank down the wall by the window to the floor, his knees drawn up in front of him and his eyes closed. He was almost finished.

When he opened his eyes again, there was no thick-set, evil-looking face staring into his and no killer's hand at his throat. The room was quiet . . . He remembered his arrival in his own room two hours before. The paintings were on the wall, the bed was made, but slightly rumpled as if someone had lain down on it and read a book, and the waste-paper basket was upright. Walker's eyes travelled around the walls a second time. There were marks on the wall nearest to the bathroom at about head height. They were black scrapes, they looked like tar or treacle. Walker got to his feet. The wall also bore signs of damage. Part of it had split, he noticed, a dent about the size of a man's head had been concaved into it. As he walked towards it, it looked as if someone had hit it with a heavy object, a wooden mallet perhaps; then there were other marks, gentler and more rounded. The blackish scrapes along the surface looked less dark when he approached. He touched one of them with his hand and it was hard on the outside, but he felt a softness underneath. He picked the skin away like a scab and it revealed, inside, a reddish glow like an old fire in a dying hearth. The outside, dried with time, concealed the blood. When Walker stood back, he saw that the whole section of the wall in this part of the room had the black scrapes, the dents and gouges he had seen before. Someone had been battered against the wall, thrown against it until their skin split. The force must have been tremendous.

The Lebanese cut their enemies' throats, was the thought

that came illogically into Walker's mind. If you slept with the wife of a Lebanese, they cut your throat and ran you round and round the room until the walls were red in lines of blood, and then they dropped you out of a window to shatter on the ground below. But this was only a small section of wall, a section big enough to fling a man against, repeatedly.

Walker's foot touched something on the floor and he looked down. It was an empty wine bottle which rolled away from his foot as he stooped, and he saw another sticking out from under the edge of the bed. His eyes turned to the telephone. It hadn't been beside the bed where you would expect it to be but he hadn't noticed that particularly. Now, he saw that it lay on its side on the floor. It was an old-fashioned, heavy telephone, and the casing was split away in a jagged line across the front and the flex had been ripped from the wall. The receiver was nowhere to be seen. The metal of the dial was slightly bent, and Walker saw the black blood-marks over the casing and over the numbers on the dial.

He looked through the open door into the dark bathroom. Without walking into the room itself, Walker put his hand round the door frame and felt for the string light-switch. His hand hit it once and lost it, then found it again as it swung back, and he pulled it and light flooded the room. It was all mirror, and the mirror was smudged black and red, and one corner of it over the bath was cracked. On the other side, some sort of implement had torn a hole right into the wall to reveal the plastic casing which concealed the electric wiring for the room. The copper wires were sticking out at all angles and had been cut and pulled out through the wall by some immensely strong hand. On the floor was the swollen, misshapen corpse of Quince. Walker hardly recognised it.

There was blood leading to the corpse, across the carpet from the bedroom where Quince had obviously been dragged. His body, naked except for underpants, was wrapped like a joint of beef with the copper wire that had been torn from the walls. The wire was plastic-coated in parts, and Walker saw that it was part of an alarm system in the room. Whoever had done this had done it very methodically. The alarm was literally ripped from the walls, through plaster and hardboard, but the killer hadn't wasted it, he had spun it round the torso like a sausage and the knots were tied like any good butcher's. Looking at the destruction, Walker couldn't believe that only one person had been involved. The fat corpse of Quince looked like a vast, inhuman cut of meat. The floor was a mess of blood. Toilet fixtures had been ripped out of the walls and they, as well as the bottles and the telephones, had been used selectively to beat Quince to death. The marks on the walls in the bedroom, Walker realised – with horror at the sheer power of it – were where Quince, for all his sixteen/seventeen stone had been picked up and hurled against it again and again. He had been bludgeoned with the bottles and the telephone in the bedroom then dragged in here semi-conscious, where his attackers had continued the job after trussing him with the wire that was now cutting into his flesh and disappearing altogether into its folds. The beating was brutal, insane. Ordinary objects had been used, but Walker guessed they had been used by professionals. On some parts of the body, the beatings didn't seem frenzied at all but deliberately selective, designed to cause the maximum agony. Whoever had beaten Quince to death had done so after beating him for information. The murder looked senselessly brutal, but actually he had been methodically tortured first, then killed.

Walker turned from the bathroom with eyes half-closed against the horror, and returned to the bedroom.

He opened the cupboards and saw Quince's suitcase at the bottom, and some clothes hanging from the rail. There was the green jacket from the night before, and half a dozen bow ties. He pulled out the case and opened it, and rummaged through the bits of paper; there were flight details, some financial brochures, a letter addressed but unstamped. He closed it again. It wouldn't be in there. Quince would have a briefcase or a wallet – but Walker couldn't see the clothes that had been stripped from him before his death. He looked under the bed and on top of the cupboard. He didn't want to have to go back into the bathroom, he really didn't want to have to do that. He knelt down and checked the bed properly, feeling it through the covers, but there was nothing that felt like documents. His eyes turned to the bathroom again, and he rose to his feet and pulled open the drawers in the cabinet next to the bed. There was nothing in them but a laundry list and some signs to hang on the door. Please Make Up This Room was duplicated. There was only one Please Do Not Disturb, the other, Walker guessed, would be hanging on the door. In anger and frustration he pulled back the bedclothes right down to the mattress, but there was nothing.

He walked again into the bathroom. The mirrored cabinet was closed. He opened it and looked inside, his hand rummaging through the things that Quince took with him on his travels, the aftershaves and the scent, the various toothcleaners, the brush and comb, the special sponges, nail clippers, some kind of breath freshener, deodorant, lip salve – it was a chemist's shop. But there was nothing here that he wanted. He looked at the corpse again, it's features contorted in agony. Where would Quince have hidden it? *If they get me, it's all part of the service.*

He turned away and went back to the bedroom. The laundry lists were lying where he'd set them down. On the shelf behind the bed was the plastic folder in which the hotel advertised its services and telephone numbers. Walker picked it up and opened it. It looked untouched. There were two sheets behind see-through plastic, one on either side of the folder. They gave numbers for room service, laundry, restaurant, gym – the list was some twenty or thirty different items. The two sheets of paper were captured behind their plastic protection and pinned at all four corners. Walker pulled one sheet out and there was nothing but the blue inside of the folder. He pulled out the sheet on the other side and there was nothing there either. He put the folder down and turned over the list of hotel services, and on the back was a small, type-written print-out. Quince had typed it onto the back of the hotel's service sheet.

Walker sat down on the bed to read it. From the bathroom came the dull hum of the extractor fan. 'Soren. Yossi,' the document was titled. The name was underlined twice and then written in the English way as Yossi Soren, the first name first.

Age forty-eight to fifty. Born in St. Louis 1940–42. Father a leading figure in the Humane Society of America, mother unknown. First appears in London in 1965, owning a promotions firm in Bolton Gardens, Kensington. Has a small business in quartermaster's supplies. Soren takes Israeli nationality. Buys small-time military magazine on the decline and revives it to an impressive-selling centrepiece for his new business. Arms, 1970, Israel. Probable Israeli Defence Forces. 1974, insurance salesman in Jerusalem. Printing business in Jerusalem, 1976–78. Main core of printing business, the Israeli Air Force equipment and spares sales index, a readily available catalogue that lists surplus equipment the Air Force is willing to sell. Most of this equipment is American. 1980–83, no record. Probable Mossad training camp in Jordanian desert. Re-emerges Jerusalem 1984. Managing director of company named Nomad. Offices in Paris and London. Company employing ex-Mossad and military specialists, bodyguards, hit-men, military trainers and advisors. Nomad licensed to deal directly in arms with the U.S. Partner in Nomad dies in London aged forty-two of 'a stroke complicated by acute alcohol abuse'. 1988, employed by Continental USA as consultant. Specific duties uncertain until April 1990. Assigned to protect Continental interests in raising a sum of money for the Venezuelan government.

At the bottom of the information Quince had obtained from whatever source he'd used, was a handwritten list of names. The handwriting was Quince's, Walker assumed. The list started with Quince's name, Patrick Jeremy Quince. The name that came next was Walker's own, with, in brackets after it, the title of his paper. Five names followed, all Spanish, the last of which was Francesca Santos Calderon. Each of the four names Walker didn't recognise had a neat pencil line through it, but his own name, Quince's and Francesca Santos Calderon's had none. In his mind, Walker put a line through Quince's name. This was Yossi Soren's killing list.

The road to Los Chorros took him under the mountain where the jacaranda grew. The shanty town spread out below it, a mess of tin and corrugated iron through the green, and he turned down the slopes of the Avila mountain until he saw to his right the narrow stream that entered the barrio a hundred yards further on and immediately turned to grey. Walker parked in a street off the main road, next to a row of cars that were covered with dust and had obviously been abandoned by the owners of the villas on the mountain. There was an unaccustomed quiet.

He was at the opposite entrance to the one he had come in by two days before, but since on that occasion he had had to walk right through the shanty town to find Francesca Santos Calderon, he reckoned this was about right. The high breeze-block walls here would give better protection than the corrugated iron on the other side; the soldiers, when they came, would have to crash through from lower down and give whoever they were looking for an opportunity to escape in the maze of the barrio. Walker approached the pile of broken-down fridges and rocks that blocked the entrance. The face of yet another child looked at him, and disappeared when he asked for the Señora. Walker waited. She might have left already. He felt exposed, standing here against the walls. If anyone drove down the hill they would see a gringo at the entrance to a shanty town, and he would certainly be checked, perhaps arrested. How many of them knew they were after him?

He began to climb the tumble of rock and metal that flimsily blocked the entrance. A tank could roll it over without even checking its speed, but it was awkward for a man to climb, full of holes and jagged edges. The top of the wall was lined with broken glass six inches long, and the drop on the far side was higher than a man. It was a fortification built for children; only they could crawl through the holes between the barricade, and consequently they acted as the shanty's lookouts. Walker rolled a few of the rocks away and made a hole just big enough to squeeze through, then he pulled himself under the ledge of broken glass, face flat to the pile of junk, and dropped onto the other side, his shirt and jacket ripping as he fell. He picked himself up and started to turn as a rattle of automatic fire shredded the air somewhere further to the south. A thin, panting dog stood, head down, as if waiting to be sentenced, and two men stood behind it in the dust. They gripped cudgels in their fists, with three-foot handles smoothed and curved and ending in a ball of polished wood like bone the size of a cricket ball. The men were boys, half-crouched against a shaded white wall above some narrow steps that led down to the sewer and then lost themselves in the puzzle of the shanties. One of them swung his weighted bludgeon in a perfect arc, and the dog's head exploded like a watermelon.

Walker faced the sun and looked blinking behind them to the steps. '*Estoy un amigo.*'

They didn't reply. In the glare he dimly saw that the dog had disintegrated; it looked as if it had never been a living thing at all. '*Estoy un amigo di Santos Calderon,*' he said.

There was a movement on the steps behind them, and the face he had seen through the rocks appeared at the top. Another burst of gunfire broke the baked silence, and this time it was followed by the thud of a gas canister. Walker saw it high in the air, trailing its ignition smoke behind it and already gushing tear gas as it dive-bombed to the barrios below.

'*Soldados*! *Soldados*!' the small boy cried.

Another canister followed, and another. Suddenly the silence was broken by shouts from deep inside the barrio, and Walker saw the look of uncertainty cross the boys' faces. Bursts of automatic fire ripped over the roofs of the shanties and thudded into the walls of the houses on the slope above their heads. It was at least two hundred metres across the barrio from here, Walker thought, two hundred metres of twisting narrow tunnel and passageway. The soldiers were going to douse the area with gas before they came. The boys tugged scarves from their trouser pockets and wrapped them with one hand around their faces, not taking their eyes away from Walker.

'You bring bad luck,' one said before he covered his mouth. The other hesitated, then pulled another strip of cloth from his clothes and threw it to Walker. He tied it across his face. The first fumes of gas had reached them from the far entrance, and even though it had dispersed in the air, it stung Walker's eyes. 'Francesca Santos Calderon,' he shouted at the pair of eyes opposite him, but the child didn't answer. Behind him, Walker saw her climbing up the steps with a bag in one hand.

'*Soldados*! *Soldados*!' the little boy cried again.

A plume of smoke shot above their heads, and the pump action thud . . . thud . . . thud of a heavy machine-gun raked the shanties further down, and shattered some door or obstacle that had been put in the soldiers' way. 'They're coming in!' she said. 'This time they're really coming in.'

'They're coming for you,' Walker said.

He grabbed her arm and shouted for the way out. She looked confused. Her head turned towards the piled up rocks and rusty fridges, and she shouted the same request to the two armed boys. The noise around them was continuous now. Walker had no idea how long it would take the soldiers to smash their way through the shanties, or what the resistance would be. Normally the dwellers in the barrios melted away in the face of an attack, they were no match for gas and bullets.

The boys with the cudgels suddenly began to squabble. The best way out was the subject, as far as Walker could tell. Francesca dropped her bag and ran to them. 'Quick quick, they will kill us all,' she shouted. Walker picked up her bag as the boys beckoned to him to follow. 'They want us both,' he shouted at her.

They ran back down the steps from where she had come, and turned to the right down a shaded passage between two high walls that cut out the sun. It was dark after the glare; there were other people running, but in different directions. An old man was dragging a lame leg after him like a stick, and there was a wounded man on a stretcher, carried by two girls. The passage ended in a solid wall. One of the boys pulled a brick from it and climbed easily, using the side walls to press his hands against and the hole where the brick had been as his only foothold. It looked impossible for anyone else, Walker thought, but Francesca half-climbed and was half-pulled to the top as Walker threw the bag over. It must have been seven feet to the top. The second boy crouched and beckoned Walker to tread on his back and haul himself over.

From the top of the wall, he saw the full extent of the military operation. Troop carriers were drawn up almost in a circle around the barrio, and there must have been hundreds of soldiers. Before he was pulled down the other side, Walker saw a short, heavy man a hundred yards away beyond the far wall of the barrio. He stood, one hand on hip, the other gesticulating a complex set of instructions to the commander of the raid, who stood beside him with a pistol in his hand. He wore the same suit, the hard, gun-grey suit of the night before.

On the far side of the wall was a refuse tip, the waste and junk the shanty-dwellers couldn't throw in the sewer. The stink of the steaming, living mass of filth was worse than the tear gas, it choked the air. The two boys already stood and beckoned, shouting beside an invisible hole in a mass of tangled wire and concrete blocks. The noise of the machine-guns was continuous, and Walker hardly heard what the boys were saying. A helicopter was hovering on the far side of the barrio, swinging its tail angrily over the shanties and sending up clouds of dust with its rotor blades. The sound ricocheted off the metal roofs and fought with itself over the flimsy buildings. A half-track tank ploughed through a wall and took two houses with it, dragging behind it the plastic sacks that had been spread beneath the flattened kerosene cans of the roofs, and grinding one wall inside its catepillar tracks. Bullets peppered the wall that they had all just climbed, and buried great holes in the thin breeze-blocks of a house behind them.

Beyond the invisible hole as he crawled through it, snagging and losing part of his jacket, Walker saw a small avalanche of rocks that fell through overgrown creepers and plants, down a gorge to the stream below. There was no road or even a path. This was the side of the barrio that backed against the mountain, and it was built precariously, high up on a small cliff that fell almost vertically to the water. The soldiers were driving the inhabitants of the shanties into what they thought was a trap – but the two boys had found a way. It was concealed beneath the long grass and traversed the cliff, doubling back on itself like a donkey path. It took them to the bottom, and back upstream. Then it climbed away from the barrio towards the mountain and the clean air. When he looked back, Walker saw the dim outlines of the shanties through a fog of gas, and columns of soldiers in masks rushing the narrow passages.

It was dark. Walker sat smoking in the driving seat of the Chevette with Francesca Santos Calderon beside him. He had told her hours before who had killed her husband: the short, thick-set Israeli brute they had glimpsed a second time as the attackers became infuriated by their lack of success. It was now an hour before dawn, an hour before the curfew lifted.

The smell of tear gas had drifted up the mountain all night and choked the air. But there was death below.

They had held hands in the darkness, but now, with the fingers of light reaching from behind the mountain, she withdrew her hand. She had not commented on her husband's death. She had not even made a gesture or a movement to show what she felt. Walker lit another cigarette and looked across at her. In a few minutes it would be safe for them to go. Safe? It was twelve hours drive to the Colombian border, even if they weren't stopped long before that. Walker looked back at the torn city. Fires smoked from the night's fighting, but the army was in control now. He saw a huge, two-storey hole punched in the side of the Miraflores Palace by a tank shell. There were pockets of resistance still, but the main fighting was over. The mopping-up would begin now, an operation like the one that had tried to dig out subversives from Los Chorros four hours before – an operation that had just missed him, and the woman he had returned to save.

When the light broke, he switched on the engine and it made the inevitable torn shriek of complaint. They drove to the west, across the top of the city on the road that rings the mountain. And before they reached the big freeway that drops to the ocean, they turned off onto what was little more than a track, taking them beneath the huge pillars that supported the freeway over the valleys. There were patrols and checkpoints above them somewhere, but the track dropped through the valley, the car crashing on its suspension as it descended from the mountain fortress of Caracas. It was seven o'clock by the time they reached the sea and headed west again, along the coast road the led to the Gulf of Maracaibo and the border at Maicao.

There were the normal checkpoints every hundred kilometres or so, lazy affairs that consisted of a hump in the road and a hut at the side, and sometimes oil barrels, painted a faded red and white, that bent the road into a chicane and almost halted the car. The checks were cursory, there might not have been a revolution going on in the country at all.

Perhaps these soldiers had not heard the news of the coup, Walker thought. But later he found out that he was wrong.

They were in the province of Falcon and it was around midday. There was a truck stop, with the usual open fires with fish and meat cooking, and a crowd of *campesinos* and Indians standing there with things to sell. Plainly they still trusted the road for their living, though hardly anyone would have come along it since the truck drivers' strike. The road at the truck stop widened out into a huge circle where trucks pulled off and parked, and the road had become indistinguishable from the land around it.

The crowd of *campesinos* here was unusually large, and Walker saw why when they drew up to the checkpoint. They and the soldiers were nervous. The Chevette doors were forced open, and Francesca was dragged out and thrown against the car, the shouting of the soldiers incessant – instructions to their captives came in a constant stream of abuse and invective. The soldiers were panicking, Walker had seen it before, and when they panicked, they were dangerous. After he too had been pulled from the car and spread-eagled against it, he saw the reason. Beyond a row of empty trucks was a wall, and against it stood a line of men with their hands behind their heads. More than a hundred soldiers, Walker guessed, patrolled behind them, gun on their hips, cocked for firing. and every five minutes or so a crash of bullets sent the latest line of men to the ground, any who still struggled being despatched with a single bullet in the neck. Beyond the soldier who was frisking him, Walker saw that the victims were tied with hobbles on their feet, some even dragging rocks behind them to the wall where they were executed.

An officer came over to the car with an expression on his face that said they were unwelcome gate-crashers at his party. 'Papers,' he shouted.

Walker took a passport from his pocket, not the one he normally used. It was out-of-date, but the Venzuelan visa was still valid and that was all they ever looked at.

'Businessman? What kind of businessman?' the officer snapped.

'I have a farm in the south,' Walker said.

The officer took Francesca's identity papers. She didn't show her passport. They had agreed it was unnecessary to arouse suspicion by implying that she was leaving the country.

'Why are you travelling together?' the officer demanded. Behind him another salvo dropped another line of men against the wall. It seemed to embarrass the officer.

'She has relatives in the south,' Walker said.

The officer nodded and walked round the car. He made a careful note of the number and make of the car in a small notebook. 'Where are you going?'

'San Cristobal,' Walker lied.

'It is not a good time to travel.'

'No,' Walker replied, and his eyes travelled over to the wall and came back to fix on the man opposite him. The officer lowered his eyes. 'Go, go, go!' he shouted, and gave the passport and papers back without meeting their gaze. He turned away without a word, and they climbed back into the car and pulled back out of the dust and away onto the ill-marked road west. The smoke from the fires swept across the road like fog. In his mirror Walker watched the officer stop and go into a wooden hut. When he reappeared, he held a phone in his hand and was standing facing down the road, looking after the car. And then Walker lost sight of him in gusts of smoke and the lengthening distance.

'Who were they?' he asked, after a few miles. She didn't reply at first, and looked sideways out of her window across the scrub plains like someone who was too pained to talk. When she looked back, her eyes were shiny as they had never been for her husband. 'They are the *camionistas*,' she said.

Walker looked across at her. 'The ones who refused to strike?' he said.

'No. The ones who went on strike.'

'But . . .' He looked at her again, uncomprehending. 'They helped the army to power,' he said.

288

'They were paid to strike, yes,' she said. 'And when they achieved the purpose of the strike, they were ordered back to work. The army doesn't want a strike any more than the President. But when they've shot a few, they'll break the strike in a way the President never could.'

Walker sat in silence for a long time after that. He thought of the men in Europe and of the electric accuracy of everything they did – until his mind returned to the executions, and the officer on the phone as he watched the car receding into the smoke.

Maicao was the last border crossing anyone would choose to leave Venezuela, and the last place anyone chose to enter Colombia. The road gave out in a dust track long before they arrived, and the scrub vegetation was as barren as anywhere in the north. In the old days it was a crossing, used by drug smugglers, who now preferred more sophisticated routes, but the outlaw feeling remained. As they drove into the main street, Walker saw that the few shops there were closed – everything closed at three-thirty in the afternoon in the dusty strip of Maicao's main street, and after three-thirty it was dangerous to walk the streets. Gringos had been robbed and even killed travelling through Maicao. The immigration office was a wooden box the size of a bus stop at the edge of town, and there was a single soldier half-asleep inside. Walker was relieved. They had made the right decision after all. Either you got all the trouble at the smallest border posts, or you got none. The army was stretched, and Maicao had been left to rot.

He stopped the car as close to the hut as he could get, and they both stepped out. They walked to the sliding window, and Walker held the two passports for the soldier to see, but out of his reach. At the back he heard the sound of another person, and then a woman's head poked round the door at the rear of the hut. He could see Colombia four hundred yards away across the dust.

'Immigration?' he said.

'What do you want?' the woman rasped, and Walker looked back at her. But she was snapping at the soldier, not at him. 'Fish or meat?' she said.

'Chicken,' the soldier replied. 'Give me chicken.'

'There's only fish,' the woman said with finality, and disappeared into the back.

'What time is it?' the soldier said to Walker.

'Five o'clock. Just after five o'clock.'

The soldier rubbed his eyes and saw the car for the first time, and seemed to wake up. 'You take the car?'

'No, it stays here. The company will pick it up.'

'You have documents?'

'Of course. But it's not going to cross the border, it stays in Venezuela.'

'Let's see the documents.'

Walker returned to the car and opened the flap in front of the passenger seat and retrieved a folder full of papers. He walked to the window and placed them carefully on the worn wooden ledge. Francesca spoke rapidly at the soldier, and for the first time he gave a suggestive smile that woke as slowly as he had. He handed her two forms, and continued to hold them when she took them in her hands.

'Why you want to leave us?' he said, in what was a parody of Latin lustfulness. But she just pulled the papers from his flabby hand. They filled in the immigration forms and handed them back. 'You must take them to the office in Avenida Bolivar,' he said. 'They will give you a stamp there. Passports!'

He took the two passports. 'You get them back when your form is stamped.'

Walker looked at Francesca, but she shrugged.

It was twenty minutes before they returned to the hut at the border. The drive had taken them back into town, and when Walker explained to the official at the second office that the border guard was holding their passports, he told them it was impossible for him to stamp the forms. Walker argued, and then paid. They were given more forms, similar to the first, which had to be filled out before they could get the original ones stamped.

When the official had at last checked and double-checked, Walker saw him put the original forms in a broken filing cabinet with a heap of other papers that would never see the light of day either. It was getting cold, and Walker gave Francesca his jacket. In the far distance, over the Caribbean, a storm was gathering that would hit land in half an hour or so. When they reached the border hut again, the soldier was eating a plateful of fish with a mound of yams. Further up the dust track, between them and the border, Walker noticed another soldier. He was standing with his gun, unstrapped, and held, not cradled, in his hands. A distant rumble of thunder rolled in from the sea.

'Keys. Give me the keys.' The soldier rudely flapped his fingers and Walker dropped them on to the ledge. The soldier snatched them up and, resuming his eating, spoke without looking up. 'Tomorrow,' he said. 'You must cross tomorrow.'

'We want to cross now,' Walker said angrily. 'Why send us across the town to sign more forms if we can't cross tonight?'

'The border is closed.'

Walker fought down the urge to reach through the window and push the man's face into his plate of food. It was something the soldier was managing to do perfectly well on his own, anyway; drips coursed down his unshaven chin, and whenever he tried to fill his mouth he invariably overestimated its size and spilled quantities of half-chewed fish and vegetable on to the counter. From time to time he stopped and carefully pulled a long fish bone from the glutinous mass in his mouth.

'The border closes at five-thirty,' he said.

The woman came through from the back and removed an empty bottle of Colombian beer, replacing it with a full one whose contents spilled down over the side. The soldier slammed the sliding window to the street shut.

At first it was just a black speck in the south where the sky was still blue, but turning slowly to orange over the llanos. Walker saw it above the one-storey wooden roofs of Maicao, the sky now divided, the pitch black, rolling in from the Caribbean and pushing back the sunset, and Maicao lying at the centre of the divide. Squalls were greying the scrub to the north of the town, but to the south the black speck held perfect definition in an untroubled sky. Five, ten miles away, it grew as it approached, an urgent black message to a long-forgotten outpost.

They were standing in the only place open in the dead town, a seedy bar-brothel where the only other customers were three nasty-looking cowboys half-blinded with alcohol. When Walker saw the speck in the sky, his first reaction was to search his pockets frantically for the car keys. The car. They should have never taken the car as far as this, not to the border. They should have dumped the car fifty miles back – more – and they should have paid a taxi to bring them here. But the car that had led them into this was not going to get them out. Walker remembered that the last duty the guard had performed was to take the keys.

He grabbed Francesca's hand and pulled her with him out of the bar and into the street. The first spoons of rain had started to kick up the dust, and the black speck had grown and taken on a low noise in the fading light. They ran down the length of the street, past the immigration office, to where the line that marked Venezuela was drawn in rubber across the dust. Beyond were cement-filled oil drums in red and white, and beyond those, the four-hundred-metre walk to Colombia. Both soldiers were now lolling by the drums, the second one, in his food-stained uniform, with a wide-awake expression on his face. He looked freshed-eyed with the brutal excitement of anticipated violence.

The rat-at-at of rotor blades emerged as a distinct sound out of the anonymous din, and the speck took form and grew and could not be dislodged from Walker's consciousness. He turned and pulled Francesca with him, and felt the wind of the approaching storm as it clattered a piece of broken cardboard across the street and slammed it into the immigration office wall with a crack like a bullet. The rain struck the dry ground like a person beating a garment clean. The force of it seemed to rock the buildings, and the wind of the storm was whipped to a fury as the helicopter hovered twenty yards behind them. The rain coated it in a skin and brought it down, one tread banging into the street and bouncing it away, then the other, as it slewed around to face the wind that tried to smash it sideways. It gained some height again, then stabilised and sank to earth intact. The door flapped back open, and four soldiers leapt down onto the ground and stood across the street, unsure who they had come for and shying at the gaps in the buildings. Walker and Francesca Santos Calderon caused them neither fear nor animosity. Behind them, cordite-grey, was Yossi Soren.

He snapped his fingers at the officer behind him and issued an order. Walker didn't even hear the sound of his voice through the rain, let alone the words themselves. The officer came through the line of soldiers and indicated that Walker and the woman should follow him. He led the way, without checking whether they followed, across the street to the immigration office and banged open the door with a fist. Walker held on to her arm and they went in out of the rain. In the distance, Colombia disappeared behind a sheet of water. Soren entered the hut behind them and didn't bother to sit at the only chair. He might have just dropped into an office next to his own to issue some swift instruction, his cold efficiency was so natural.

'Congratulations on getting your article through to London,' he said. 'I'm sorry you didn't have the full story.'

Walker didn't reply.

'I was, of course, hired by Continental to watch that fool Quince,' Soren continued. 'But neither he – nor you, Mr Walker – had any notion at all that I was working for Rausch from the start. You see? They hired me months ago. Continental never had a chance.'

He put his hand into the pocket of his jacket and Walker

tensed, but it was a sheet of paper he brought out. 'You failed to receive this at the Hilton,' he said.

It came from the opposite side of his jacket to his gun, Walker noticed. It was a single fax sheet, addressed to himself and sent by the paper in London. It was a reply to the six thousand words he had despatched thirty-six hours before: the story of Rausch in its totality, the full story, from the bar in a cobbled Geneva street to the bruised and swollen corpse in a Caracas hotel.

'You intended to cross the border, I assume,' Soren said.

Walker took the sheet without replying and read the lines O'Reilly had composed in a self-pitying, half-sycophantic, half-apologetic style that blew Walker's mind.

> Excellent. Really, really excellent. Everyone is very
> pleased indeed. I'm not the only one who envies you
> this one, as I'm sure you'll guess, and it's welcome
> back on the books for good as soon as you return. But
> I have to warn you that we do have some problems.
> We've already heard from up above that it's a non-
> starter. Bloody lawyers, of course. We need more
> corroboration. I know, more, more, more, I feel a shit
> about it, Harry, but we need affidavits from the
> woman, Santos Calderon's widow, and from Quince.
> We can't go with it otherwise. These are orders, I'm
> told. I hope you can get the affidavits. I'm sure you
> can.

It was signed with just his initials, as if he couldn't bear to put his actual name.

When Walker looked up, he saw that Soren was stamping his passport with his own hand, giving him an overland exit visa stamp. Was this a cruel joke or did they really intend to let him go? They knew in London that you couldn't get signed affidavits in the middle of a bloody war. And no one had ever got a signed affidavit from a dead man. Up above. What kind of pressure was the paper getting from 'up above'?

Walker looked at Soren's expressionless face and knew that if they were going to let him go, then Rausch had one more card to play. A card in a newspaper office in London.

'You can go,' Soren said.

With a bullet in the back? Walker thought. For illegally crossing a customs post and avoiding arrest? Who would know or care? Maicao was a million miles from anywhere. Soren stared, unblinking.

'I'm not going without her,' Walker said.

And Soren shrugged. 'She is a Venezuelan citizen. You are British.'

And you, Walker thought with fury, are Israeli. 'I'm not going without her,' he repeated.

Soren seemed to think for a moment. 'Fine,' he snapped. 'Come with me.'

He beckoned to Francesca Santos Calderon, but she didn't move. The officer roughly took her arm and pulled her away from Walker, but he pushed after her, shouting at Soren until a gun butt caught him in the side of the face. His hand went up as he fell to the floor, and his eye flooded with blood. He dimly saw Francesca being forced through the door and into the rain, and the door slamming and bouncing on its lintel. Back and forth the wind shook the door, until it steadied in its place.

'No, no, no, no, no,' Walker shouted. A soldier kicked him in the side and he rolled over. Beyond the door, a pistol shot rang out. Walker climbed to his knees but got no further. The door crashed open and Soren, soaked from head to foot in streaming rain, stood in the opening against a darkened sky. His face was pure Evil.

'You can go now,' he said through the water that gushed from the roof above. 'Your responsibilities to the woman have been discharged.'

Two of the soldiers picked Walker up by his arms and dragged him from the room. They held him up to Soren.

'You're free,' he said.

When he didn't reply, they dragged him past the bleeding

ground where Francesca's blood was already washing into the earth. He saw half her dead face before another blow to the back of his head shut his eyes in agony.

They carried his body over the white line that was Venezuela and dumped it a few feet from Colombia's side, where it lay motionless as the dust turned to mud and the mud turned to water.

In the morning, the sky was blue. Walker looked ahead, to another customs post, and beyond, across the fresh green scrub, towards Riohacha.